October 6, 2003

It was a beautiful early fall night in Chelsea, and the man in the black trenchcoat wasn't looking forward to another disaster. He stood on the edge of an ancient wooden pier, looking downward into a dark river. A crisp but gentle breeze passed through his slightly graying hair, and he sighed, hoping fervently for a quick resolution. So far, it didn't seem likely, and he had a five-alarm headache that seemed immune to aspirin.

Thirty feet away, a looming metal monstrosity, barely recognizable as the ship that it once was, jutted from beneath the calm waters. Behind him, a small army had descended on the pier, ready for anything from a catastrophic accident to a terrorist attack. Already, a small rowboat was on its way back from the wreckage, manned by two Massachusetts State Troopers. They tossed up a line to a few of their colleagues, then carefully handed them what looked like a sheet of metal. The man in black approached them, making sure his ID was visible on the cord around his neck. He located the highest ranking cop within the group and got his attention.

"Trooper, I'm Major Devonai of the Central Intelligence Agency. I hear you're missing a boat or two."

The man, who wore the rank of sergeant, looked at him with barely concealed surprise. "The CIA? What's your interest in this?"

"We have a field office quite near here. We're authorized to respond to unusual incidents."

"How come I haven't heard of it before?" asked the sergeant, scrutinizing Devonai's ID card.

Devonai cocked his head slightly. "Very unusual incidents."

"Well, whatever," he replied. "If you're local then you should already know what this was. The USS Portland, a Navy support ship, decommissioned earlier this year and left here in mothballs. There was little of value, so they only had one night watchman. He was asleep when it happened."

"What do you think happened?"

"I don't know. We got a report of an extremely loud crash by nearby residents. When local law enforcement arrived, this was all that was left."

The trooper handed Devonai the piece of metal. It was far too light for normal steel. Devonai tried to bend the sheet and it broke into several pieces.

"What the hell? It feels like a tortilla shell."

"We're planning on putting some divers into the water for a closer look," the trooper said, pointing to a van parked nearby. "I don't know about you but this looks like the practical joke of the century."

"You think somebody made off with the ship and left this stuff behind as a joke? You don't just turn a key and drive off a fourteen thousand ton ship, you know."

"I know that," said the sergeant, annoyed.

"Well, go ahead and put your divers into the water. Be careful. Meanwhile, I need to meet with your field commander."

"That's Lieutenant Bradley, over there."

"Thank you."

Devonai walked a few yards to where the austere lieutenant was standing. He displayed his ID to the tall, thin-faced man.

"Lieutenant, I'm Major Devonai with the CIA. I've been asked by the DIA to start up a preliminary investigation into the disappearance of the Portland."

"News travels fast, I see. I'm Lieutenant Bradley. I just got briefed on your new field office last week. Welcome to the neighborhood."

"Actually, we've been here for a few years now. Anyway, I'd like to set up a command post." Devonai pointed at a nearby building. "Let's see if we can gain access to that structure. We'll work out of the first floor. Until then, my Humvee will be the CP. I also need you to make sure that the local police department understands the sensitivity of this situation. Everyone here is being exposed to information that will without a doubt be classified."

Bradley nodded. "I understand."

"Nobody leaves this pier without being debriefed by a member of my staff. My guys are wearing woodland camo. I need to know how many officers are involved and I need a list of their names."

"Got it."

"Good. Now then, are they any witnesses to what happened?"

"Not that we know of. The security guard was asleep. There aren't any residences within the line of sight from the pier. Anybody who saw what happened would have had to have been on the river or on the pier. According to the responding officers, the pier was deserted, other than our narcoleptic caretaker."

"Okay. Send your guys over to the gate now, I don't want anybody slipping by and leaking information to the press. I want every person and every vehicle accounted for. So far we have what, the Chelsea Police Department and the State Police here?"

"Yeah. There's also some scientists that showed up just before you did."

Devonai looked surprised. "Scientists? From where?"

"SETI, I think. They're over there in that Bronco."

"What the hell is SETI doing here?"

Bradley shrugged. "I don't know. Why not ask them?"

"I'll do that. Are my instructions clear, Lieutenant?"

"Yes."

Devonai nodded. He walked briskly over to the Bronco. There were two occupants, a bearded male and a demure female with light brown hair. They looked anxious at his approach. Devonai walked up to the driver.

"I'm Major Kyrie Devonai. Who are you guys?"

The man spoke, attempting to sound casual. "Hi. I'm Levi Marks, and this is Dana Andrews. We're with the American Space Transmissions Research Association."

"ASTRA? I've never heard of it."

The woman chimed in. "It's like SETI, but without the money."

Devonai felt like miners were tap-dancing on his head with lead shoes. "What are you doing here?"

"What exactly is going on here, Major?" asked Marks.

"I'll ask the questions for now, if you don't mind."

"Okay. We've been tracking a signal of interest. We haven't been able to identify it, and it's been moving all over the place over the past couple of days. We finally got a strong hit on these coordinates."

"What do you mean, a strong hit? What kind of signal are we talking about?"

"A repeating waveform with distinctive patterns," said Andrews. "The kind of thing ASTRA is looking for all the time. This one originated in lower orbit and ended up here."

"Are you sure?" asked Devonai.

"Quite sure," said Marks. "We've been crunching the numbers from three different locations. Almost all of our staff is working on this one."

Devonai put his hands on his hips. "Well, there's been a major incident here. I'm afraid I'm going to have to ask you to leave. You'll have to do your scientific readings somewhere else."

Marks smiled. "You're sure you can't give us a hint of what's going on?"

Devonai smiled back wanly. "I'm quite sure."

"All right. Sorry to bother you. I guess we'll hear about it on the morning news."

"Probably." Devonai keyed his radio. "Richter, this is Devonai. Please inform the gate that we have one vehicle, a Ford Bronco, with permission to exit the cordon. It's heading out now, over."

"Roger out," said the radio.

"Have a nice day," said Devonai.

Levi turned on the Bronco, put it in gear, and pulled away. Devonai headed back over to the CP. Richter, the picture of a professional soldier, was waiting for him. The younger man was wearing a camo field jacket devoid of any name tapes or patches, and a black watch cap.

"Divers are in the water, sir," he said.

"Good."

Richter gestured toward the gate. "Who were those guys?"

Devonai put his head in his hand and took a deep breath. "Just scientists out for an evening drive. They don't know anything."

Ten minutes later, Devonai let loose a string of expletives so vile that he surprised even Richter. The corporal stood up from examining a metal fragment and looked at his boss.

"What the hell, sir?" Richter said, astonished.

"Those scientists! Damn it, they knew something about this! They were tracking a signal and they said it led them here."

Richter looked at his supervisor in astonishment. "And you let them leave? Have you lost your mind?"

Devonai shook his head. "I'm distracted, damn it. This whole mess is really bad timing for me."

"With all due respect, sir, you'd better get your head out of your ass. Whatever destroyed that ship is probably going to be a serious problem for us."

"I know," said Devonai. "We have to track those two down. I got their names, and I'm assuming you got their license plate number."

"I'm not the one making amateurish mistakes tonight, sir," said Richter, smirking. "I'll call Brockway."

"Please do. She'll be tickled pink on this one, Richter."

"No doubt. Can I have your office after you're gone?"

1. September 25, 2003

Eleven Days Earlier

John Scherer pulled up on the parking brake, and turned off the engine. He had arrived, at long last, home. Working late was tolerable, but working long past sunset on a perfectly good fall evening was not. Wrestling with bad traffic that seemed to mock his efforts, and the fact that the traffic was entirely unusual for the time of day, had left him drained. He paused before exiting the car, as if to try and recapture the peaceful place the vehicle usually was on his drive home.

John walked up the path to his house. His girlfriend Rachel was sitting on the front steps. She was dressed in a sweat shirt and scrub pants, and her brown hair was tied back into a ponytail. She looked exhausted.

"Hey, honey," he said, "It's good to see you."

"I'm here to break up with you, John," she replied without a hint of sadness.

John sighed. "I thought we were going to talk about this."

"I think we've talked about it enough. As long as you're going to continue to be unresponsive to my needs, and let your career languish..."

"I already told you," interrupted John, "I'm looking for something better. You just need to be patient."

"And yet you won't even consider going back into the Air Force."

"Do you have any idea how boring avionics was to me? I need to do drafting, and it's only a matter of time before I can find an aircraft company that will hire me."

"You think your current job is boring, too."

"Yes, but it's a means to an end. Frankly, Rachel, I'm surprised that my career path is so important to you. It's not like I'm pulling in chump change right now, and my earnings will only increase."

John's cat, named Friday after a Heinlein novel, leaped onto the nearest window sill and yelled at her human through the glass.

"None of that is my point," said Rachel, standing. "It's your unwillingness to take risks. I don't understand how you can spend so much time playing flight simulators but have no desire to become a pilot."

"Flying for real is far more challenging, and besides, I'm too old for that kind of career path."

"Oh, bullshit, John. Are you going to have a mid-life crisis at twenty-seven? See, this is exactly what I'm talking about. If you really wanted it bad enough, you'd do it, no matter the risk."

"And that's a deal-breaker for you? What if I applied the same logic to your career? I've never had a problem with your place at the hospital."

"That's the other thing. You don't invest yourself in my life. It's like I'm just Girlfriend Mark Two and you expect me to be the same, all the time."

"That is not fair."

"Last Saturday when I met you here, you never asked me about my day, but you were more than pleased to tell me all about the Focke-Wulf 190 variant that you'd supposedly mastered on your stupid computer."

"I didn't think you were paying attention," said John detachedly.

Rachel began walking down the driveway. "I was. You weren't. I already got my stuff out of there. The key is in an envelope in your mailbox. Say goodbye to Friday again for me."

Stunned, John watched Rachel walk down to the street. She turned a corner and jumped in her car, which he hadn't noticed on his way in.

Friday greeted John at the door, showing her typical enthusiasm. Immediately, John lost a small percentage of his frustration. Shedding his belongings haphazardly, he left a trail of debris in the hallway as it led to the kitchen. Friday's bowl was empty, but John had another priority. After a sufficient amount of bourbon had been poured, John turned his attention to Friday's needs.

John looked in the refrigerator, almost out of habit rather than hunger. He cooled his shins for a few seconds, then grabbed a beer and headed into his living room. He flopped into a recliner and thought about what had just happened. His relationship with Rachel had never been particularly serious, but he wasn't expecting it to end so abruptly. While he believed she was being too hard on him as far as his career, he couldn't argue that he had been neglecting her as a girlfriend. As he considered the last few weeks, he realized that he'd been treating her more like a drinking buddy than a lover. Still, he hoped that something might be worked out in the future, maybe as soon as next week.

It was in this confused haze that John finished his beer and bourbon. He had relinquished his lap to Friday, and was falling asleep when the phone rang. He unceremoniously ejected Friday and crossed to the phone. He slipped slightly on the hardwood floor, grabbing the receiver in a gesture to keep himself upright. The floor was always a little slippery when wearing only socks, as John was, due to it (and the rest of the house) being cleaned regularly. It was a simple two-story ranch, but it was his, and unlike the apartments that had come before, John actually cared about keeping it neat.

"Hello?"

"Hey John! It's Ray."

"Ray! Hello! God, how long has it been? A year?"

John already knew that it had been a year. July fourth was a hard date to forget, and for this particular college friend, it had been far too long ago.

"Yeah. God, I guess so. I didn't mean for so much time to pass before I called you."

"Well, it's not like I couldn't have tried to track you down. The last I heard you were still at the academy."

"Yup. I got finished six months ago."

"Where are you living now?"

"Manchester."

"Is that the same town that hired you?"

"Yes."

"Isn't that the one you wanted?"

"Actually I wanted a smaller town, but coming from Massachusetts, Manchester is small enough to suit my tastes."

"Oh, good. How is the job itself going?"

"Okay. I've only been out on my own for a month. My supervisors thought I needed more time for training, so before that I was still on probation."

"On probation?"

"In this context it means that I was still considered a rookie, riding along with another officer."

"Oh."

"Then, just when I think I'll be on my own, the department decides that certain beats require two-man teams. I have kind of a rough neighborhood, but in comparison it's really quite all right. No high speed chases, shoot-outs, or anything."

"That's in the other part of town."

Ray laughed. "Right. The other side of the tracks."

"Hey chief, we got another portal to hell opening up."

"You want us to send Bailey? Nah, he's still on that domestic disturbance."

John and Ray laughed. They'd quickly fallen back into their usual banter, which often involved fantastical scenarios and ridiculous dialog. It was so familiar that John almost forgot about Rachel.

"So, what prompted you to call on this particular night?" John asked.

"I read about your promotion in the alumni magazine."

"Promotion?" asked John, scratching his head. "To what? I didn't get promoted. Or do you mean in the Air Guard?"

"In the magazine, it says, 'John Scherer '99, living in Woburn, Mass, was recently promoted to project manager at Breakbeat Design Corporation.' At least that was the gist of it."

"Oh. You know what happened? I got assigned to a new project and I happened to be the primary engineer on it. I told my parents about it and they must have sent in the blurb to the alum magazine. It sounds like they either took some liberties with the actual significance of what happened, or they misunderstood it. Either way what happened is unremarkable."

"Well, congratulations anyway. I didn't even know you were out of the Air Guard."

"Yeah, I felt like my military career was going nowhere, so I decided to switch to the civilian side of things. Thanks, by the way."

John, unfettered by the cordless phone, walked into the kitchen to obtain another drink. This time, he chose a hard cider.

"So anyway, we should get together. This once-a-year crap ain't cutting it."

"Definitely," Ray said. "Perhaps there's a nice halfway point where we can meet."

"How about the 99 in Lowell? You can scoot down 93 to 495 and I can scoot up."

"Okay. How's Sunday look for you?"

"Fine. I was going to start mastering the Ta-152, but I think I can squeeze you in."

"Still playing those flight sims, eh?"

"You know if World War Two breaks out again and they need pilots, I'm going to get the call, right?"

"Right. Sorry, I forgot. How is one o'clock?"

"Perfect. See you then."

"Cool. Bye."

John plopped back down in his chair. So Ray Bailey had at last become a cop. With some effort, John could see Ray as a police officer. He had the commanding presence for it. Last time they'd seen each other, Ray weighed 240 pounds and was 6'2" tall. He might weigh less now, or more, but his height would forever guarantee him a certain impression. Ray was always good to have around for a night on the town. They never had trouble of any sort.

John was eager to see him. As much as he liked his friends at work, he could never relate to them on a wide scale. Parts of his life that he had shared with his college friends remained locked inside him at work, first at the Guard and then at Breakbeat, for they would neither understand nor care about it. He needed different friends for that, and the relationships that he had built up during college had been adroitly scattered to the four winds by graduation. Ray wasn't the furthest one, but still a one hour drive away. Arianna Ferro was closer by, having taken a job in Boston, last John knew.

Ari had been growing apart from their circle of friends towards the end, but John still thought of her as a close companion, and often wondered about tracking her down. With a get-together with Ray on the board, he would have the perfect segue-way for a message to her. She was an attractive woman with Algerian and Japanese heritage, and with the best features of both. When John had first met her, he believed she was just wasting time with John, and a year later, Ray. It wasn't until they knew each other for two years that he finally realized her friendship was sincere. That was good, because Ari was rarely sincere about anything else. She was a skilled manipulator, and managed some amazing feats with the three or four boyfriends she kept during school. Neither John nor Ray ever gained that status, at first by a put-upon lack of interest (at least for John) and then later by their own education. When they really got to know Ari, friendship was as far as they wanted to go. Ari, wary of her inability to lead her two companions around by their reproductive organs, had accepted them and dropped any ulterior motives she almost certainly had. During the last year, however, he began to wish he'd taken advantage of the opportunity when it was presented.

This thought caused a flash of adrenaline as he again considered Rachel's words. Despite the complete disconnect with reality that the fantasy involved, John imagined himself with his arm around Ari as the two of them ran into Rachel somewhere. He instantly felt stupid for having that desire; how immature that not thirty minutes after they broke up, John wanted to make Rachel feel jealous. It was pointless to indulge in such fantasies, although Ray's phone call had made them much more palpable. Every time his logical side rejected the feasibility of a physical relationship with Ari, his emotional side asked, "What if?"

John passed out while thinking of Ari's smile. He wouldn't move from the chair for another three hours, sleeping through several of his favorite television shows. Friday was pleased.

Arianna Ferro awoke, and became aware of a throbbing in her head. A filmy tankard lay on its side next to her arm, which was dangling off of her futon. She drew her hand away when it touched the cool glass. Ari wearily moved to identify the source of her surprise, succeeded, and rolled over onto her back. It had been a Bass Ale, the consumption of which was gone from her memory. She did remember the purpose of the shot glass which remained upright on the other side of the room. Ari resolved herself to a shower, which was unpleasant only in that it required her to stand.

Ari managed about three minutes under the cascading water. Then she crumpled to the bottom of the tub, her head at last spinning out of her control.

Thirty minutes later, Ari leaned forward and turned off the shower. She found a towel, dried off, and attempted to wrap it around her. It was too small to cover everything. Less concerned with her upper body, she tied it around her waist. Alone in her living room, Ari dialed work.

"Ari here. I left my lights on last night. Yeah. No, my neighbor is giving me a jump. I guess... forty-five minutes. Okay."

Hanging up the phone, Ari wandered into the utilitarian, tile-lined kitchen. Three aspirin were chased down her throat by a swig of flat cola, a familiar aftertaste informing her of a previously pleasant addition. More of her evening became available to her. The bottle of rum had been rinsed and placed in the recycling bin. She didn't remember that. A chill washed over her, and she padded into the bedroom to get dressed.

"I brought in the mail."

One each of a pair of jeans, a t-shirt, and a pair of socks later, Ari returned to the kitchen. A stack of mail lay neatly arranged on the table, sorted by priority. There was only one letter on the right side, which was the important pile.

"Boston Police Department?" Ari said aloud.

It could be but one thing. Her firearms permit. Ari brazenly assumed this, as it could also be a rejection letter. She held the envelope up to the light. A square object occupied slightly more than half the interior. Ari tore the empty space open. A laminated card fell into her open hand. Ari was filled with pride, as if she had actually earned the right to possess it. Her priorities changed, and she picked up the phone.

"Ari here. There wasn't enough charge in the battery to jump it. Yeah, I'm going to. I should be in at noon. Thanks."

2. September 26, 2003

Professor Christie Tolliver sprinted up two flights of stairs, late for her two o'clock class. She glanced down at her watch as the hallway blurred around her. She had two minutes to spare before her students could give up and leave, the rule allowing her fifteen. It was the first time this semester that she was so horridly tardy, so perhaps the new round of kids would give her some temporal latitude. At least her only burden was one textbook, pages stuffed with loose note paper. It wasn't slowing her down as much as her half a pack a day cigarette habit. Pausing just outside the auditorium, she attempted to calm her breathing. It wasn't going to work, and Christie had no choice but to enter the room winded.

"Sorry, folks. Time dilation applies to a really good cup of coffee, too."

If anybody got the joke, they didn't show it. Most of them should have, anyway. It was going to be on the next exam. The comment would go unexplained for today's session, however. The subject would instead revolve around something more enjoyable to Christie, and usually, more interesting to her student constituency as well.

"When we left off on Tuesday, I told you we'd be discussing the possibility of life on other planets. Even if we'd all be dead and buried by the time any of our spacecraft encountered anybody, they may have other means of propulsion that would negate any effects of time dilation."

Christie decided to mention time dilation again, if only to remind the class that it was important for some reason.

"Now most of us are familiar with science fiction's best approximations of faster than light travel. We have warp drive, which supposedly folds space back upon itself, decreasing the distance between two points. We have hyperspace, which brings us into another dimension where distance is either diminished or negated. Modern astrophysics hasn't brought us anywhere near any way to actually achieve either of these forms. Regardless, if we could travel to other solar systems, or if they could get here, one has to wonder what they'd look like."

Christie was about to take a detour away from basic astronomy, but so far nobody had ever noticed. In fact, Christie's free-flowing form of teaching was never criticized, at least to her face. Her easy-going manner and open mindedness to student input could at times diminish the overall course content, but the way she saw it, it never diminished from learning. Her astronomy course therefore remained popular, forever repeating a pattern. Fall semester she could barely attract enough students to fill the first two rows, by the spring, she was turning people away. Since hers was a freshman-level course, those who were turned away after the class was full rarely got a spot, since it meant another student would have to drop out. This year, a young man by the name of Byron had enrolled for another semester after his senior year, making him a "super-senior" in the local vernacular. He'd left his name on a waiting list just long enough for someone to change their mind and quit. Byron was very intelligent, sat in the third row, and more often than not Christie found herself talking directly to him.

"The fauna here on Earth has shown us that life can take many forms. I apologize in advance for anyone who doesn't believe in evolution... it's the easiest way to understand the issue. If we evolved from apes, then it's reasonable to see how any of the large mammals might have grasped the knowledge of tools as well, were circumstances different."

"You mean, if they had opposable thumbs," Byron said.

"That's the advantage that apes apparently had, in their ability to manipulate their environment. But if any of you have ever owned cats, you might notice that some of them can work pretty well with their paws. If they ever learned how to walk upright, they could certainly carry things and create tools. Anyway, the point is that alien life is probably carbon based, breathes oxygen, and looks something like one of the mammalian species here on earth. Certain science fiction shows have focused on felines, both seriously and as an avenue for comedy."

There was an uncomfortable pause. Usually by now, Christie had managed to engage several students in the discussion. Byron was a given, but why wasn't anyone else raising their hands? Christie was young for a college professor, at twenty-nine, and occasionally she intimidated some of the guys who enrolled in her courses. If that was going on this time, she didn't feel like encouraging anyone. She was tired from her run from the cafeteria, and seemed content to talk to Byron.

"Science fiction represents the vast majority of alien species as humanoid," began Byron. "Rarely do we see a race that was obviously descended from something other than monkeys. But I think that's due to production costs and the fact that most actors are human to begin with. Perhaps as computer-generated graphics become more advanced, we'll see more things like talking cats, dogs, and super-intelligent shades of blue."

Now they were really off the subject, and there was still sixty-five minutes to go. Christie made an attempt to steer the discussion back toward a more legitimate astronomical subject.

"There's a formula that was created to estimate the number of solar systems that could support life in the universe, given a reasonable estimate of the number of what we can actually see out there. It's called the Drake equation. Basically, you assign a percentage of likelihood to a number of attributes, each essential to life. What percentage of solar systems have a planet the appropriate distance from the sun? What percentage of those planets then have the correct condition for life to form? What percentage of those planets will at this time be at the point in their development, assuming a millions-of-years cycle, to have intelligent life forms there residing? The chances are, well, astronomical, but the estimate is still in the tens of thousands. Carl Sagan thought it could even be in the hundreds of thousands. And since we still don't know the limits of the universe, if any, the number could be more. If we or another civilization develops faster than light travel, then it's quite possible we could have an intergalactic community similar to what we've seen on television."

Byron said, "I'd like to think that there are communities out there like that already, Miss Tolliver. We're just too far away to be part of them."

An hour later, Christie and Byron stepped out onto the street and took a left turn. The class had continued in vibrant conversation between the two of them, with an audacious number of students falling asleep in the wings of the auditorium. It was a little too loud and a little too cold for them to continue talking while they traveled, so they concentrated on making it to the Derne Street Deli first. Christie had also managed to consume a cigarette on the way, stopping outside the eatery to pinch off the burning remains and dispose of the filter in a trash bin. Once inside and with food on the way, Byron picked up the subject.

"What I'd want would be a room that you could view space from in a three hundred and sixty degree field. Through holographic imaging, one would see space all around them. You could even make it a variable gravity room. What a great way to relax."

"That would be something. I think I'd definitely spend a lot of time staring out the windows. I've often thought that it must be very distracting to astronauts to have such a great view. It's the view that I'm most jealous of."

"Do you think we'll have space tours before too long? We've got the technology."

"Sure, but I'd give it another fifteen years. Let the companies who want to do it get a bit richer first. Then, I'm sure we can take a ultra-high altitude tour. Once there, though, I'd never want to leave."

"You know, it's great to meet someone who really loves their job. I mean, you're really interested in this stuff, Miss Tolliver."

"Evidently. And I think you can call me Christie, Byron."

Byron smiled, slightly embarrassed by the comment.
"Do you mind if I ask you something?"
"I don't know what it is, so I guess not."
"How old are you?"
"How old are *you*?"
"I'm twenty-two."
"Well, if you must know, I'm twenty-nine. I've been Suffolk's assistant astronomy professor for three years. Before

that, I worked at the Hayden Planetarium at the Museum of Science. Before that, I was a student at Suffolk myself."

"So you've been in the neighborhood for what, ten years?"

"Eleven. I moved to Boston to go to college. I'm from New Hampshire originally. Way, way up north."

Christie felt a twinge of adrenaline. She searched her mind for a reason for the feeling. She didn't want to know Byron that well, and she realized that she didn't want him to know her that well, either. It was still a friendly conversation, but Christie felt the need to steer it away from her personal life.

"So I've always had an interest in the subject. What about you? What's your major?"

"Political Science, actually. I can't honestly say that I'm going to be doing anything important with your course. But I can say that you're convincing me to take up astronomy as a serious hobby."

"There must have been some interest in residence before. You enrolled in the course, after all."

"Honestly, I was just filling up my curriculum. I'm sure glad I chose astronomy, though. I'm having a great time."

It was a sobering thought, but Christie began to suspect that Byron wasn't as wonderful as she'd grown to believe.

"Ah, you're just a kid. You can afford to explore different areas. Once you graduate, you have to stick with the money-makers."

Byron was very obviously insulted by Christie's comment, but he didn't say anything. The food arrived, allowing the pair an excuse to stop talking.

When they'd finished, Byron politely took his leave. Christie began to feel guilty, because she'd allowed her personal feelings to get in the way of an otherwise perfectly appropriate student-teacher relationship. The guilt kept her in her chair long after other patrons had come and gone, eventually earning her a query from the proprietor.

Cast out of the deli, Christie headed for the subway. She felt like she needed to apologize to Byron, but she couldn't figure out how. She resolved herself to remain friendly, and avoid any more belittling of the younger man.

Jupiter was visible even before the sun left the sky, and Christie stared it for a few minutes before heading down into the claustrophobic depths of the underground.

3. September 28, 2003

The 99 Restaurant was very busy that Sunday night. John had arrived fifteen minutes before the agreed-upon hour, and entertained himself with a glass of ale while he waited. His waiter seemed to doubt that John had another person on the way, as if the space he was taking up was too precious to be wasted on the expectation of another patron. It would be another fifteen minutes after one o'clock before Ray arrived. John was tempted to stand up to greet him, but couldn't muster the strength.

"Ray, you look great."

"Thanks. The police academy pretty much eliminated any chance of me gaining weight."

Ray sat down, and perused the menu.

"Sure, but that was six months ago, right? You're not being forced to work out anymore."

"No, but my job keeps me busy. Anyway, what's going on? How's the job?"

"Real fun, Ray. How about you? How's the police business?"

"Let's talk about you, first. How is your job going?"

"Work is really boring, Ray. I go because I have to. I'm happy putting in my eight hours and heading home. My real interest lies in my free time and my flight simulators. God, that sounded pathetic."

"Have you considered going back into the Air Guard?"

"Not seriously, no."

Ray corralled the waiter and ordered a margarita.

"This makes me think," John began, "that we should get a hold of Ari. It would be good for all three of us to get together again."

"I take it you're not dating anyone these days?"

John shrugged. "What does that have to do with Ari?"

"You always had a thing for her, right?"

"No, I'm not crazy, Ray. You never cared for her much yourself."

Ray smiled briefly. "That's because my brain and my unit never had equal votes like yours."

"I've known Ari for a year longer than you. Before you really knew her, she was a real sweetheart."

"I can hardly believe that. And are you saying I corrupted her somehow..."

"No," John interjected, "I mean that she started to change the year before we all started to hang out together. It was her relationship with her boyfriend at the time."

"Which you never appreciated too much."

"At the time, no. I've since come to realize what a disaster we would have been, so I'm glad I never got the chance."

"And after everything that happened, you still want to try and maintain a friendship with her?"

"You can't act like we were never friends, Ray. You and I both considered her a friend, for all her faults. We knew there was a good person beneath all the posturing and attitude."

"Deeper than the Marinaras Trench."

John smiled. "Sometimes, Ray. Sometimes."

Thirty minutes later, John and Ray had finished their meal. Their conversation during that time had consisted mostly of meaningless banter and slightly more meaningful reminiscing. John was reminded of the friend he had in Ray, which only made him feel worse about being apart for so long. Ray had kept changing the subject when he asked him about work, though. He was definitely holding something back. John considered the other man as he picked at the remnants of his food.

"You know what we should do?" John asked. "We should all go up to your parent's cabin again, like we used to."

"That's not a horrible idea, but for a first visit in over a year, don't you think it's too much?"

"Maybe. Well, maybe if we get together a few times first, we can go up later. I just loved going up there for the weekend."

"Me, too. Come to think of it, I haven't been up there since graduation. My parents made some improvements to the building and I haven't even seen it yet. They added a whole new bedroom."

"Nice. Here's what I think we should do. I'll call Ari, or e-mail her. I'll invite her for something casual and I'll meet with her. If she's interested in hanging out as a group, we can plan for something casual for all three of us. Strictly speaking, we should go to the cabin whether or not Ari wants to go. She's hardly the lynch pin."

"Of course."

"Then it's settled."

It took John about twenty minutes get home after dinner. During this time, John realized he was worried about contacting Ari. In fact, he was downright scared. Once home, he decided what to do. Off of his kitchen was an area referred to as the "breakfast nook" by the real estate agent. John had never used it for this function, instead placing a comfortable loveseat there. Devoid of the distraction of a television set, and offering a view of his comely back yard, John would often sit there to smoke and reflect on things. At this moment, John was using it to achieve a sound buzz before picking up the phone. He was drinking some mid-priced rum of the Dominican variety, as not to waste money on such a capricious task. The number he had for Ari was obtained during a brief e-mail some fourteen months ago, so he didn't entirely expect it to be valid. Once he was happy with his level of artificial courage, he dialed the phone.

"Hello?"

"Ari? Hello, it's John Scherer."

"Oh, hi, John. What's up?"

Ari's tone of voice was as if they'd spoken yesterday.

"How are things going?"

"Fine."

"It's been a long time. Over a year. I thought we should get caught up."

"I suppose."

"Yeah. Ray Bailey and I were thinking about doing something next weekend. Maybe taking a trip up to New Hampshire."

"Ray Bailey? I thought he disappeared for good."

"No, he's just been busy. He's a Manchester cop now."

"Uh huh."

"So, I was thinking maybe we could have a poker night, up at Ray's cabin. It worked pretty well last time."

"Last time being over four years ago."

"Yeah. Like I said, it's been too long."

"My only problem with that last trip was Ray's chickie drooling all over him."

"You mean Kate? They broke up a while ago. It would just be the three of us this time. And Ray and I will abstain from going shooting for hours and leaving you alone with nothing to do."

"What makes you think I wouldn't want to go shooting with you?"

"You weren't interested last time, that's all."

"You stuck me with a complete stranger for four hours. I would have gladly put up with your noise compared to hers."

"Even still, catching up with each other would be the point of the trip, not punching holes in paper."

"Actually, we should go shooting. I just bought a brand new Glock 17 and I haven't had the chance to fire it yet."

"Since when are you into firearms?" asked John, genuinely surprised.

"I'm not 'into' firearms, John. They're a necessary evil in today's world. I realized that I couldn't defend myself with martial arts in the face of all possible threats."

"That does sound like the Ari I remember. I have to disagree with your use of the word evil in this case, but if you want to get some practice in with us you're more than welcome. I guess that means that you'll come this weekend?"

"Sure. Maybe I can swing by Logan and see if my Glock will get by the metal detectors."

"You do realize that's complete bullshit, don't you? Glocks are forty percent steel."

"I know, I'm kidding. You know, if I remember correctly you were never into guns much either, besides owning one or two."

"As you probably know, Massachusetts recently enacted a bunch of Draconian bans. That's when I started paying more attention to the laws and my own rights. Firearms are hardly evil as you said, and if we don't fight for our rights we'll lose them. That's all."

"I could care less about the politics, John. I like all the restrictions here in Mass. I had to go through a lot of red tape to get my permit. But that's good; it prevents just anybody from getting a gun."

John was tempted to call Ari elitist, but that was so self-evident as to be redundant.

"Well, if you're going to be carrying that thing around with you, you'd better be able to shoot straight. It's a lot more difficult to accomplish despite what Hollywood might have you believe."

"Whatever. I did okay in the required course. I'm sure I'll do fine."

There was an uncomfortable silence.

"Anyway," began Ari, "we should get together before then. I've taken a liking to fine restaurants, but I so rarely have anyone to go with me."

"I find that hard to believe," John replied lowly.

"You do realize that I find maintaining a relationship a rather ponderous undertaking, right?"

"No shit. Don't tell me you've lost your fondness for the four month, self destructive tryst?"

"Actually, yes."

John chuckled. "There may be hope for you yet."

Sometimes, Christie regretted owning a dog, if only for the fact that her small Somerville apartment allowed little room for Tycho to roam. Here at Bradley Palmer State Park, however, there was nothing to prevent him from bounding about. Tycho was a fourth generation domesticated wolf-dog, perhaps borderline away from feral to be safe around humans. Christie was aware that leaving Tycho alone with small children probably wasn't a great idea, but having no contact with children on a regular basis, it was an infrequent concern. Christie also thought it prudent to have the most prominent collar possible on Tycho, to prevent him from being mistaken for a wolf. Tycho hadn't been Christie's first choice. She had her eye on a Rhodesian Ridgeback, a powerful breed originally used for hunting dangerous game in Africa. Upon querying a breeder, she discovered that purchasing such a dog was much more expensive than your average German Shepherd. The breeder also balked when Christie mentioned where she lived, insisting that such a dog needed "at least a hundred acres to be happy." When Christie settled on Tycho, she didn't mention where she lived.

Tycho was obviously pleased to have the chance to run around at the park. Christie figured that all dogs loved this kind of thing. Tycho appeared to be ecstatic. The only problem that ever arose at the park was when they encountered a horse and rider. There were several well-used equestrian trails through Bradley Palmer, and Tycho had a singular reaction when meeting such an animal. He would go into stalking mode, hiding in the woods or tall grass and sniffing the air. He would never follow through with an attack, and Christie guessed that this was due to her presence and little else. On his own, Christie might end up with an expensive lawsuit or worse. One of the main horse trails had become overgrown from disuse, a fact that brought Christie a bit of relief. Perhaps the park was falling out of favor with equines. All the better for canines.

The sun was shining that afternoon, bringing back a modicum of the warmth that Christie had so enjoyed during the summer months. As much as she appreciated the changes of all seasons, her body had yet to accept the colder nights and brusque breezes. Despite the warmth, Christie suspected that removing her jacket would become problematic quickly. She unzipped the front halfway and lessened her pace.

Christie was on a diet. She looked good to a casual observer, but not to herself in her mirror at home. She was also tired of wearing the same three outfits to class each week. The remainder of her clothes, favorite or not, were purchased after a whirlwind two week tour of Europe, during which time she chose lodging over food more often than not. On her frame this weight looked almost emaciated. It may not have been her body's natural weight, but nevertheless most of her clothes were closer to it than her current status. Christie didn't need to drop back down to that weight. A nice spot at the median point would suffice.

Budgeting her time for exercise was easy enough. Christie spent exactly zero time preparing for her classes, and almost as little grading papers. Christie was a certifiable genius when it came to astronomy and physics, a fact that was only in suspect by her and unknown to anyone else, save for her own professor. His insistence that she was brilliant was taken with a grain of doubt, but to anyone who had actually read her bachelor's thesis it was practically irrefutable. If she had chosen to, she could have been admitted to MIT, Berkeley, or any other academic organization offering a master's level degree in astrophysics. Instead, in a move her parents classified as "haughty," Christie applied directly to NASA after graduating. They found her thesis was as brilliant as she herself was under-qualified, which coming from NASA was a huge compliment. They encouraged Christie to go back to school for at least another four years. By then, however, she had obtained a job working for the Hayden Planetarium at the Boston Museum of Science. She presented both the introductory and the advanced exhibits, and had become one with the Zeiss projector. One reason why she was so enamored with this job was because she could come in after hours and use the facility. This was frowned upon, so Christie had used her feminine ways to manipulate her supervisor. It was the first and last time she would use this tactic for anything, including speeding tickets. For the use of the Zeiss projector, even three lousy dates with a terrible kisser was worth it.

Tycho took off after a bird. Christie called him back. It usually took three or four attempts to get the dog back to her side. Christie wasn't in a hurry at the moment. In fact, she wasn't in a hurry about any part of her life. Applying for the position of assistant professor of astronomy at her alma mater was as much self-improvement as she'd demonstrated in the past three years, not including her current weight loss efforts. Most of her desire to obtain the position had to do with pride. Somewhat less of it had to do with the way she missed college life. This sentiment went away quickly, however, as Christie realized that she had simply grown up too much during her five years at the planetarium. It was remembering this fact that led Christie to think about her thesis.

Christie's thesis had to do with subatomic particles and their application to astronomical measurements. Christie was convinced that photons, the basic element that makes up light, could travel faster than light itself. Her theory was that since light exhibits attributes of both a wave and a particle, then perhaps the particle was the temporal aspect of it. If an element was energized to a certain point, then the light it gave off might have enough energy to accelerate it past the known maximum of 186,000 miles per hour. The photon could accomplish this by leaving space-time itself and appearing again elsewhere in the universe. If she could prove that this phenomenon was occurring, and where, then she surmised that she could more accurately predict the age of the universe. Or at the very least, the age of a single star. Since current methods were considered accurate enough, and the mannerisms of the photons that she described were completely improvable, her theory was at a dead end. It did contain enough sound mathematics and original thinking to get her an "A+," and the laudatory but empty praise from NASA. Exhausted from the work of synthesizing her theory, Christie had all but given up any efforts to refine it. On this crisp September afternoon, she had a flash of new insight.

Byron had been telling her last week about his own theory on faster-than-light travel. He was of the opinion that there was a region of reality above our own, what he called "superspace." He preferred this term to the more popular "subspace" due to the fact that his region consisted of hyper-energized particles. He theorized that dark matter, the yet-unproved matter that might make up the majority of mass in the universe, was in fact the by-product of superspace. Byron thought that if one could discover the process by which the hyper-energized particles are converted into dark matter, then we could suspend a spacecraft in a force field, reverse the process, and send the craft into superspace. Once there, the operators could travel faster than the speed of light by riding the currents of the particles, which conveniently enough operated like trade winds between planetary systems.

It was a nice theory, but had none of the requisite research to be taken seriously by anybody but an assistant professor of astronomy. It did give Christie a possible solution to a significant problem on her own theory, and for this she realized Byron deserved a free drink.

4. September 30, 2003

Black and White was a trendy bistro on the northern end of Beacon Street, on the other side of the block from Suffolk University. It was trendy enough to have a dress code, so when Christie proposed to Byron that they go there after class, Byron had to run back to his dorm to get a tie. Byron had been absent from class on Monday. Christie had been so excited about her new idea that she had almost called Byron's room. She had rapidly come to her senses. On Tuesday, Christie ran into Byron on the street. He admitted he had blown off class on Monday to sleep off a hangover. This made Christie's intention to buy him an alcoholic drink awkward, so she'd proposed coffee instead. Waiting alone at the restaurant that Wednesday afternoon, Christie found herself with a serious craving for a Martini, so she was a bit buzzed by the time Byron returned, resplendent in a green paisley tie. Despite his horror story, Byron ordered a whiskey and joined Christie at her table.

"This damn smoking ban," Byron said. "This place used to be so cool."

"I can take it either way. I can wait until I leave to smoke."

"So you wanted to talk about my theory?"

"Yeah! I realized that it helps me deal with a problem with my own theory."

"You mean your theory from Suffolk?"

"Yeah. Did you read it?"

"Well, the e-mail you sent me didn't get formatted properly. There were a bunch of weird symbols instead of equations. Other than that, I think I was able to get a sense of it."

"Did the symbols look like this?"

Christie withdrew a pencil from her pocket and scribbled on a cocktail napkin. Byron looked sheepish when he saw it.

"Yeah."

"I'm sorry, I should have mentioned that the document included physics symbology. They're Greek letters."

"Oh."

"I didn't expect you to understand them."

"Ohhh."

"By the time you get to a four-hundred level astronomy course, you'll know what they mean, for the most part. It doesn't help that most of them have several different meanings, of course."

"I would imagine not."

"So, what did you think of my theory?"

"It's interesting, but to be honest I found it a bit stuffy. It's not like you're unraveling the mysteries of God."

Christie was insulted, but kept it to herself. Byron had described exactly what she thought she was doing all along.

"Perhaps not, but it took a lot of research nonetheless."

"How does my theory help yours?"

"Well, it's like this. Your theory on superspace is that it's essentially a dimension of highly energized particles, right?"

"Yeah."

"You see, my theory involves photons leaving our space and entering another dimension. I could never come up with a really good explanation of exactly where they went while they were gone. In fact, I didn't address the issue at all. Professor Caraviello, who was my professor when I went here, mentioned this problem in his critique of the theory. Your idea of superspace fits nicely with where the photons go when they exceed the speed of light."

"Cool."

"That's why I wanted to buy you a drink. I think this new idea is going to give me the incentive to start working on the theory again. This time, maybe I can get it published in one of the academic journals, if I can refine it enough."

"Then you and I do have a reason to celebrate."

Byron raised his glass and Christie met it with hers.

"We should have dinner, you and I," Byron said.

"Okay, let's get some menus."

"No I mean dinner. At dinnertime. Just the two of us."

"But we're already in a restaurant."

Christie realized what Byron meant. Her happiness melted away and she let a long sigh out of her lungs.

"You mean a date?"

"Naturally."

"Byron, I can't date you. It would be inappropriate. You're my student. Maybe if you weren't in my class, but even still you're a student at Suffolk and I'm a professor."

"This is my last semester. I'm just tying up some loose ends in with my requirements. I've already finished my major. Come December, I'm out of here."

"It's not December. I can't date you no matter how much time you've got left. I have to be able to objectively grade you on your performance."

"Well, we're both adults, aren't we? I think you're perfectly capable of keeping your personal feelings separate from your class. I won't be insulted if you grade me based on my performance, even if it's a mediocre grade."

"That's beside the point. It would be too easy for others to find out about it."

"Is that really your only objection?"

"Byron, you're a nice guy..."

"Don't give me that nice guy crap. You don't have to try and spare my feelings. If you don't want to go out with me, then you don't want to go out with me. Like I said, we're both adults."

"Fine, I don't want to go out with you. And *that* won't effect your grade, either."

"Okay. I guess inviting a guy to a nice restaurant for a drink doesn't mean what it used to any more."

"You know why I invited you here."

"You didn't have to invite me here to tell me what you did. It would have taken you five seconds after class to do the same thing. What am I supposed to think about this? I'm sorry if I got confused."

Christie unintentionally raised her voice. "I invited you here because it's a long tradition among scientists. I was trying to treat you as an equal. I was just being polite. I'm sorry if *you* got confused!"

Byron stood. "I see what's going on here. That's fine. If you say it won't effect my grade, all right. We'll let time prove it."

Byron left the restaurant without paying for the whiskey.

John was never one to pretend he didn't see what was going on around him. The conversation between the woman and the man in the restaurant was no exception. It was convenient enough to have a seat where neither one of them would notice his audience. John hadn't heard anything but the last few sentences of their conversation, but it sounded like the man wasn't being fair to the woman. All John knew is that she didn't look like any scientist he'd ever seen before.

The woman teased the rim of her empty glass for a few minutes. When she arose to leave, John noticed her binder had the name Suffolk University on it. John wondered if he actually knew who she was and had forgotten. They looked like they were the same age. The woman opened the front door, allowed Ari to enter, and was gone. Ari thanked the woman for holding the door, then stood and scanned the room for John. He waved her over. Ari stopped at the bar to order something before joining John.

"Good evening," she said.

"Hi."

John stood while Ari took her seat. She was wearing jeans and a leather jacket, the latter item being of the sport bike variety.

"This place is nicer than I remember it," she said.

"Yeah? I was never a huge fan of it. Although it used to have a different name and a different style, if I remember correctly."

"You do. I come here every so often, though, so I think I've seen it several times since they changed the name."

"What did you get yourself?"

"Barbancourt."

"Good choice."

"Thank you. You're the one who got me into this brand, remember?"

"Um... I don't."

"Remember that party at Beth's? That huge one where we hardly knew anybody else?"

"I don't remember much about that party. I learned never to mix red wine with any other alcohol. By itself, or not at all. Otherwise it's evil."

"You brought Barbancourt. You talked me into having some despite the fact that I insisted I wouldn't like it. I was wrong, but I didn't admit it."

"Even with something so inconsequential, you can't admit being wrong."

"I don't know if that's an apt comparison."

"Maybe not."

Ari smiled at John. She was no worse for wear over the past year. When she smiled, John noticed crow's feet lines appearing by her eyes. She was, like the rest of them, getting older. There was no denying it for any of them. The impossible age of thirty was approaching. John looked on the bright side. He thought his wrinkles, still subtle at this point, gave him a distinguished and wise appearance. His opinion of Ari's face was that it had improved over time. While beautiful before, she now looked less like a spoiled brat and more like a lady. John wondered if her inner beauty had grown as well.

"So I got myself a Glock," Ari announced proudly.

"So you mentioned."

"Do you think it strange that I bought a pistol?"

"Not entirely. You were always aware of your personal safety. You committed yourself to years of martial arts training; this is simply a continuation of that training. I didn't expect you to think that you needed a pistol, that's all."

"Why not?"

"Because you're so good at Aikido, that's why."

"Aikido can't help me much when somebody's shooting at me."

"Agreed. It seems to me that your chances of needing Aikido are much higher than your chance of needing a firearm. Am I wrong?"

"No. I'm just not prepared to risk not needing either. I'd rather have it and not need it than need it and not have it. I don't need to tell you this, John, you own guns."

"I do."

"You have an unrestricted license, right?"

"Yeah."

"Are you carrying a weapon right now?"

"No. Are you?"

"Naturally."

"How can you use the term 'naturally' if you just got your permit?"

"I think it's an appropriate use of the word. Natural and new are not mutually exclusive."

"I suppose not."

"How come you don't carry a weapon?"

"I don't consider the possibility of needing it to be that high. This isn't Los Angeles or D.C., after all. I stay out of the bad neighborhoods when I come to Boston. If I felt like I needed to carry, I would. I do. When we went up to New Hampshire I always carried. We were alone and isolated miles from nowhere. It seemed prudent."

"I think the city presents much more of a threat than New Hampshire, but I understand your position."

"If it makes you feel any better, I feel safer knowing you have a weapon."

John was lying. He had no reason to trust Ari with a firearm as of yet. The required safety course in Massachusetts couldn't teach good judgment. In this equation, John wished that he was the one with the firearm, not Ari. He wanted to trust her, but his gut feeling on the matter was negative. He really wanted to grill her on firearms law and the rules of engagement. There would be a better time for that than now.

"You'll get the chance to show me what you can do this weekend," he said.

"You bet."

Ari picked up the menu for the first time and began to scan it.

"So, how's your social life these days?"

"I enjoy being alone."

"By that you mean stagnant?" John asked, smiling.

"By that I mean I enjoy being alone."

"Okay."

"I have plenty of friends; I don't need to waste time making new ones."

"You mean Ray and I? I guess that's plenty. I guess we're glad you wasted your time on us back in college."

"You know that's not what I mean."

"I hope not."

"The truth be told, I haven't been on a date in over two years. Last time I saw you was… just about the anniversary of my last breakup. I haven't had the energy to try again."

"Like I said over the phone, perhaps you wild days are over?"

"Maybe. Maybe this new Glock is a sign that I'm looking for a whole new kind of wild."

"Fun comes after safety."

"You know, you were always a bit of a killjoy."

"Such praise."

Thirty minutes later, John and Ari were walking down Beacon Street. The meal had passed without much more conversation, and so far their walk promised to echo that silence. It wasn't until they reached Charles Street before John tried again.

"Do you think you'll try dating again any time soon?"

"Why do you keep asking me about my love life?"

"Well, I guess because it was something we always talked about before. Really we had little to talk about other than philosophy, computers, and relationships."

"There's nothing to talk about right now. I'll get back to you after a few good lays."

Ari's tone was that of annoyance. John knew that despite Ari's past alleged promiscuity she was never one to speak lightly of it.

John and Ari stopped at the intersection. Boston was bright in the cold air. John realized how much he missed the city, forgetting for a moment all the traffic, parking tickets, and weirdoes. He looked at Ari, and felt a twinge of adrenaline. It surprised him.

"I still live on Marlborough Street."

"Oh, yeah?"

"It's only five minutes from here."

"I know."

"Do you want to walk me home?"

John gestured. "Isn't that what I'm doing?"

"I wasn't sure you wanted the evening to end quite yet. It's only nine o'clock."

"No, we should call it a night. We both have work in the morning. I mean, I assume you do..."

"I do."

"Okay. Then we walk."

The light changed in their favor and they crossed the street. John heard a match light and smelled a cigarette. Ari inhaled deeply next to him. He was reminded that he hadn't brought his pipe.

"Cloves?" John asked.

"Yep."

"How's work going?"

"Ask me later."

John was sure of it now. He was attracted to Ari. Not just in terms of physical appearance, that was nothing new. He found himself attracted to her personality, which as far as he could tell hadn't changed all that much from college. Therefore, either his taste in women had changed, Ari had become a better person; or most likely, John had recently gone insane.

5. October 3, 2003

The sun had long set by the time John and Ari arrived at Ray's place. Ari had met John at his place, and they'd left her car behind. It hadn't been established whose car would be left at Ray's, and John hoped it wouldn't be his. Ray's Expedition was bound to be better suited to the task, even if there was only a mile of dirt road to overcome. John wasn't a big fan of driving long distances either.

John and Ari hadn't said much during the thirty minute drive to Ray's. John was worried about maintaining his normal personality so much that he refrained from making conversation almost completely, in itself a failure of the effort. Ari seemed happy enough staring at the starry sky. John was glad to get off the highway, since it gave him a chance to concentrate on finding Ray's apartment.

With the Expedition parked outside, this wasn't too difficult. Ray appeared almost immediately after John parked. He had a rifle case in one hand and a backpack in the other. John and Ari got out. John waved to Ray.

"'Sup, yo!" John said.

Ari smiled at Ray as she crossed the street.

"It's been a long time, stranger," said Ari.

Ray offered his hand. "That's for sure."

John had apparently decided to force the vehicle issue, and was unloading his gear from his car. He had a rifle case of his own, as well as a backpack. He also grabbed Ari's pack and shuffled across the street.

"We're taking my truck?" Ray asked.

"Is that all right?"

"Sure, that's fine. I'm having trouble justifying it as a commuter vehicle, you know. Now I can say I use it for off-roading."

"Right, the once a year you do it."

"This gigantic beast is yours?" Ari said, grinning. "Cool."

Ray hit a button on his key chain and the rear gate opened.

"It'll be a lot cooler when I get it paid off. At least I'm getting zero percent interest."

John and Ray loaded up the truck. Ari helped herself into the front passenger seat and began poking around.

"Ready to take off?" John said.

"You bet."

John and Ray climbed into the cab.

"Hey," John said to Ari, "I don't remember hearing you call shotgun."

"Shotgun."

"You know, Ray and I actually have shotguns. You shouldn't be so flippant being the only one without."

"You both brought shotguns?"

"Yeah. It's going to be Monkey Night, didn't you know?"

"Right, I must have missed that on the news."

"It's only an hour from here," began Ray, "so if you have to pee halfway there I'm not stopping."

"For this we paid first class?" said Ari.

"No," said John, "first class is an outhouse with a roof."

A roof it had, but the outhouse was still thirty yards from the cabin. Ari was reminded of this fact an hour or so later when the trio arrived. The cabin was in a small town called Orfordville near the Vermont border. It lay at the end of a dirt road, about a mile off the paved road. It was, relatively speaking, not very isolated. When the sun went down, however, that dirt road had a way of looking a lot longer than five thousand feet and change. Plus, the surrounding forest was known to expand for several miles in the other directions. Ray pulled the Expedition as close to the front door as was practical and turned off the ignition.

"Here we are. Now we get to see how well my folks have been maintaining it."

Ray said this because his parents, once frequent visitors to the cabin, were only getting up there once or twice a year. Ari had an unpleasant flash of images involving insects and rodents.

Upon stepping out of the truck, a change in temperature became obvious. Whereas back in Manchester it was around fifty degrees, here it had to be fifteen degrees lower. John was immediately glad he'd brought his favorite military jacket. Ari began to doubt the wisdom of the trip.

"Ah, fantastic," Ray said. "I love this air."

Ray proceeded to struggle with the lock on the front door while John and Ari unloaded their gear. Hidden by the formidable truck frame, John spoke his mind.

"Ray seems preoccupied with something tonight."

"Does he?" Ari replied.

"Yeah. Usually when something is bothering him he'll bring it up. At least our company never stopped him before."

"If he wants to talk about it, he'll talk about it. Maybe he just had a hard day. I don't know."

"I'm sure you're right."

Ray grunted and there was a bang as the door gave way. John was sure Ray said something crude about somebody's mother.

"Grab the stuff!" Ray added with more volume.

John and Ari shouldered bags and grabbed supplies. Ari grabbed more than she could handle but shrugged off John's attempt to aid her. John allowed her to lead the way and she hobbled inside.

The interior of the cabin was much as John remembered it. It was also clean, to their collective relief. Turning on the gas lights would soon reveal more.

"Isn't this place bigger than last time?" Ari asked.

"Yeah," said Ray, "my folks added another bedroom."

Ray walked into the area in question and said, "Ooh, big new room."

"Great, maybe we can actually see it?"

Ray returned. "Sure, hold on."

"Heat would also be a good thing," added John.

Ray leaned over a lever near the floor next to the sink. As he moved it, a faint hissing could be heard. Ray grabbed a box of matches and began lighting the lamps.

"You got a woodstove, too."

John pointed at another new addition. Before, they relied on the gas heater.

"Yes. Why don't you make yourself useful and build a fire in it?"

"Ugh. Me make fire."

Ari began a self-guided tour while John fiddled with the woodstove. The cabin had a single layer of insulation in the walls. Ari remembered being distinctly unhappy with the insulation's efficacy. The furniture was simple, and ran the gamut from rustic to retro. Ray had said he'd been going here for over twenty years, and some of the furniture proved it.

"How old is this place?" Ari asked.

"Twenty-five years old, I think." Ray said.

"You know, I think they invented electricity in the last twenty-five years."

"Do you have any idea how expensive it is to run electrical line? My folks figured it out once. It's like ten thousand dollars every hundred meters. And it's over two kilometers to the road."

"Two hundred grand? That doesn't sound right."

"That's what I remember them saying. Or maybe it was a thousand dollars for every hundred. Either way it's not very convenient."

John spoke, his head halfway inside the woodstove.

"Electricity would kind of defeat the purpose of this place, in my most humble opinion."

"Not in my book," Ari said.

"City girl. Now, watch the master at work."

John took a step back from the stove and posed with a match. He lit the match and tossed it inside.

"No way that's going to work, John," said Ray.

"Shit. I was hoping for a long distance light. Then you'd think I was all cool and stuff."

Ari smiled. "Yes, John, we've been waiting all these years for proof of your match throwing prowess."

John lit the fire the conventional way, and wiped his hands together.

"Now, it's time for the ATF."

"ATF?" asked Ari.

"Yes," said Ray, "the traditional after trip f..."

"Shut up, Ray. The traditional laying out of all the goodies we brought. In this case, alcohol, tobacco, and firearms."

John and Ray opened up backpacks, unzipped cases and rummaged through grocery bags. Ari shrugged and removed her Glock from her hip. John and Ray froze in horror.

"What?" asked Ari.

"You were carrying your pistol on you?" John said.

"Yeah, I told you I would be."

"Please tell me you sent away for your New Hampshire permit," said Ray.

"No," said Ari, "I didn't. I was told a lawful person doesn't need a permit to carry in New Hampshire."

"Holy shit, Ari," began John, "that's Vermont, not New Hampshire. You need a non-resident permit for New Hampshire."

John withdrew his wallet and showed his permit to Ari.

Ray shook his head. "Do you realize what would have happened if you were discovered? I mean, for God's sake I'm a New Hampshire cop. I've had nightmares that were more pleasant than what would happen to us."

Ari was ashen. "You're not going to say anything, are you?"

"No, but you are not to carry that pistol concealed outside of this cabin again. Are we clear?"

"Crystal."

"Good."

"Shit, guys, I'm sorry. I screwed up. I'm new to all this. Vermont, New Hampshire, I mean come on, it's all hick country. No offense."

"Forget it," said John, "it's okay."

Ray said, "Now that it's been cleared up, you *can* carry in the open without a permit. Just make sure your weapon is plainly visible and we can avoid any legal snags."

"Wait, I need a permit to carry concealed but not in the open?" asked Ari. "What sense does that make?"

"I don't make the laws, Ari. Just please do as I say."

"Fine."

There was a long pause. Ari was genuinely embarrassed, which was the first time ever as far as John knew.

Ray gestured towards the table. "Now clear and lock that thing so we can get this tradition going."

The three arranged the items on the table by classification. When they were done, an impressive spread lay before them. There was a bottle of Elijah Craig bourbon, a bottle of Genevir from Holland, and four bottles of extra-high proof French ale. On the other side of the table lay Ari's clove cigarettes, John and Ray's pipes, and two kinds of pipe tobacco. On the side closest to John there lay a Glock 17, a Remington 870 twelve-gauge shotgun, a H&R twelve-gauge shotgun, a M1 Garand rifle, and a Beretta M92 pistol. The last three belonged to John.

"God bless America," Ari said.

"I see you bought that H&R you'd been drooling over," said Ray. "I wondered which shotgun you'd meant over the phone."

"Why did you buy a single-shot shotgun?" Ari asked.

"Because it's fun," John replied.

"Isn't it practically useless for combat?"

"You want to stand in front of it?"

"That's not what I meant. It just seems way too slow to reload."

"Ari, listen, and I'll use small words so that you can understand. *Because it's fun.*"

"Right, right. Fine."

John noticed something he'd been looking forward to was missing.

"Ray, where's your Smith and Wesson?"

By the time Ray had finished answering this question, a third of the bourbon was gone and John and Ari were more uncomfortable than they'd been in years. Ray had just lost his partner, Pete, in a shootout with two bank robbers. Ray had just barely survived himself, and had been forced to kill both suspects. His favorite Smith and Wesson revolver had been taken for the duration of the investigation.

John already knew what needed to be said, and it wasn't much, but Ari was stricken to near panic with the dilemma. She had no idea how to respond. Fortunately for her John decided to go first.

"Jesus, Ray. I'm sorry. I'm sure Pete was a good guy. I mean, what cop deserves that? We'll be here for you, we're not going anywhere. But we're obviously quite happy that you're still alive."

"Yeah," said Ari.

Ray sighed. "It's just, part of me can hardly believe what I did. I guess I had this doubt deep down inside that if the time came, I wouldn't be able to act."

"Nobody knows for sure how they'll react, Ray," began John. "That's what training tries to conquer. The fight or flight reflex is mostly flight. The training you got was meant to make sure that you knew when to fight."

"Pete didn't freeze up either, but he's still dead."

"Sometimes you can do everything right and still end up dead. Training helps you beat the odds, but the odds are still there."

"I really wish I could stop feeling guilty about it all. I know it's not my fault. I mean, maybe I'd feel a little better if I'd been wounded. Somehow it doesn't seem fair that I walked away without a scratch."

"Your friends and family would hardly think it fair if you were dead."

"Yeah. I know."

"Let's have a toast," said Ari. "A toast to Pete."

"Yes, let's," said Ray.

The three raised their glasses. A solitary tear escaped Ray's eye. For the first time, he felt sadness.

6. October 4, 2003

Byron was thinking. He sat on a bench in the commons, overlooking the Frog Pond. On this particular Saturday morning, a day on which the first few leaves of fall freed themselves from their homes, he had reached a conclusion. The conclusion was very simple. He was infatuated with Professor Tolliver.

He wasn't so immature as to use the term love. He knew he couldn't love her based on what he knew of her. The person she presented to the class was bound to be different than the person she really was. How different, Byron suspected, could be discovered if he could just spend more time with her. So far, he hadn't noticed any difference during the times that they'd spent outside of class, but those encounters were so casual as to be almost meaningless. Except, of course, the last time they got together. And except, of course, that Byron had blown it by asking her out too early.

And so, Byron thought. He thought about scenarios that might result in her forgiveness for Wednesday's gaffe. He thought about whether or not Christie had a boyfriend (likely, it seemed). He thought about ways he could impress her.

The most obvious thing was to study astronomy. If he could get ahead of the curriculum, he could remain authoritative during class. If he could get ahold of some of the textbooks for subsequent courses, he could even best Christie at her own game. He'd just have to find a way to do it that was flattering and not arrogant. Byron had no idea how he might accomplish this.

Byron figured that the more he knew about her personal life, the more he'd be able to impress her. If he knew what she liked to do in her spare time, he could pretend to share those interests. If he could get Christie to become apologetic about Wednesday night, it might give him enough credit to start over. Maybe by the time the semester was over and he graduated, he could have enough of her faith to ask her out again.

Besides studying his astronomy book, then, there seemed little Byron could do. Then again, there was passive research.

Byron reached into his pocket and pulled out a cell phone. He dialed three numbers and waited.

"Hello. I'm sorry, I don't know exactly. Boston area. Yeah, address and phone number. The name is Christie Tolliver."

A few minutes later Byron had boarded a train at the Park Street Station. The red line went to Somerville. Byron had gone there before with friends, so he knew it would take about fifteen minutes to get to his desired stop. The train wasn't crowded, so Byron put his feet up.

The friends that lived in Somerville were gone. All of Byron's friends were, in fact, gone. His need for a ninth semester at Suffolk had left him behind while his friends had graduated. To his dismay, none of them chose to remain in the Boston area. For the record, four had gotten married, one had joined the Army, and one had moved to Europe. The last summer had been a lonely one, and Byron was quite glad to have classes start up. He could have tried to make new friends, but it seemed pointless with so little time left for him. Byron had also come to regard the students he interacted with as plebeians, since all of his classes were introductory level courses that he put off until now. Freshmen and a few sophomores were all he ever saw. Christie was much closer to his own maturity level, he thought. He thought it quite unfair that she didn't differentiate him from the other students.

Byron knew he'd have a hard time finding Christie's apartment. If he'd bothered to go home first, he could have looked up the address on the internet. He knew where the police station was, so he thought he could go there as a last resort. He wasn't sure what kind of useful information could be gained by scouting out the apartment. Perhaps he could note some landmarks and become familiar with them. In the future, knowing the area might come in handy. He could say he had a friend from high school who lived in Somerville. It might backfire, however, if it turned out that Christie didn't like Somerville. Seeing what kind of neighborhood she lived in would certainly help establish that.

For some reason, Byron found himself thinking of a song by The Police.

Ari had never been to the gravel pit that the guys used for a range. It was immediately obvious why it was a good choice. The dimensions had to be something like 250 yards long and 75 yards wide, and the walls, or "berms," as Ray called them, were ten yards high. Ray said they could shoot in three directions at once as long as there was nobody else around. That was true today.

There was certainly enough evidence that this place was used as a range. Brass cases littered the ground, and various targets flapped in the gentle breeze. John and Ray wasted no time in complaining about the state of the pit, indicating the possibility that the town might shut it down if things got worse. In fact, before they got any shooting done John and Ray picked up all the trash they could find and consolidated it near the access road. The only thing they left behind was the brass. That completed, Ray began to set up some targets while John loaded the magazine of his Beretta. Ari watched him, a cigarette hanging out of her mouth.

"That wouldn't have been much help last night," she said.

"Excuse me?"

"I mean, if something happened."

John patted himself on the hip. "I have another magazine filled with hollow points. It was in the pistol last night."

"Oh."

"Besides, Ray had his Remington loaded. As long as one of us is ready we'll do fine."

"Right."

It was overcast and cold. Ari picked up John's Garand and examined it.

"Be careful you don't stick your finger into the magazine. You'll trip the bolt."

"It's not loaded, right?"

"No, but the bolt could break your finger."

The fact that a firearm could hurt you without actually being fired was a strange idea to Ari. Why this was the case with the Garand seemed to point to bad engineering.

"With all the technology we have, they can't avoid it doing that?"

John smiled. "First of all, this rifle is over sixty years old. That's misleading, though. The rifle is working exactly as it's supposed to. When Ray gets back to the line I'll show you why."

Ari nodded, and brought the rifle up to her shoulder. It seemed impossibly heavy. She pointed the front sight at Ray and tried to imagine what it was like to fire.

"What the hell!" Ray said, returning to the others.

"Ari, it's really bad form to point a weapon at someone. Even if you know it's unloaded."

Ari lowered the rifle. "I know. Ray trusts me, though."

"I trust you," Ray began, "not to shoot me on purpose. This is how accidents happen."

"Sorry."

John held out his hand to Ari. "May I?"

Ari gave him the Garand. John picked up a clip from the tailgate.

"The reason why the bolt will release like that is because it automatically loads the first round in the clip. You take the clip with your right hand, hold back the charging handle with your pinkie finger and press the clip in with your thumb. Then you release the handle and the bolt will close."

John demonstrated this. The bolt snapped into place.

"Now the rifle is loaded and a round is chambered. You can remove the safety and begin firing. Ears?"

Ray and Ari both placed foam plugs into their ears and nodded.

"Going hot!" John said.

Using the sling as a brace, John tucked the rifle into his shoulder and fired. Ari jumped and smiled sheepishly. John continued firing until the clip was ejected.

"Piece of cake," he said.

Ninety minutes later, the trio began packing the weapons back into the truck. Ari was pissed beyond words, something that worried John and Ray. They'd never seen her this mad. John would joke later to Ray that he was keeping his crotch guarded at the time, although the source of Ari's rage was not the two men.

Ari had just discovered that she was a terrible shot. The only thing she was any good with was the scatterguns, and John had initially referred to this as "so easy a blind, alcoholic Panda" could do it. It was the wrong time for some friendly ribbing. Ari had already come to see that with the boomsticks that only fired one projectile at a time, she was out of her league. Ray had heaped more direct encouragement on her. It was of no use. As they got into the Ford, John tried again.

"There are so many aspects of shooting well, Ari. Nobody is going to get them all down their first time out. Stance, sight alignment, trigger control, follow-through... this sort of thing requires lots of patience and commitment. I sucked when I first started. It was with Duncan's Beretta. I couldn't hit a pie plate at seven yards."

"You'll do better next time, Ari."

Ari remained silent. John knew why she was so mad. As far as he knew, Ari never failed at anything, except relationships. And to hear her tell it, it was always the boyfriend's fault, not hers. The results of the late morning shooting session were undeniable, and the blame lay squarely on Ari's shoulders. That it mattered so much was something John could understand, even if he didn't agree.

Ray pulled the truck onto the road. "You'll have plenty of chance to work out your frustration when we go hiking."

Ari folded her arms, and said, "Hrumph."

There was silence in the Ford. John decided to let the issue rest for now. Ari would probably snap out of it once they started heading up the mountain. The fact that you had four hours of hiking ahead of you tended to grab your attention once you got out of breath, which for the three of them was bound to be pretty quick. On the way up John had asked Ari about her exercise schedule simply as something to make conversation. Ari said she hadn't been doing any exercise lately. Ray probably had the best chance of all of them. The police academy, however, hardly focused on medium-paced steady-incline hiking, to use his own words. John began to think about the task of cleaning the firearms which awaited them that night.

"Whadya think of my H&R, Ray?" John asked.

"Well, that was certainly fun. It was quite instructive to see the difference between it and my Remington using the same loads. Men must have been of tougher stuff back in the forties."

"That thing," said Ari, "is a torture device. The Marquis de Sade would have loved it."

John grinned. "It wasn't meant for combat use, like I said. It was a hunting weapon. You don't normally fire fifty shots in a row through it."

"I liked it," said Ray. "It makes such a satisfying sound when you eject the shell."

"It doesn't take a lot to make you two happy, does it?" said Ari.

John smiled. In fact it did not.

Thirty minutes later, Ari was well into working out her frustrations. She was also well ahead of John and Ray, as she was all but sprinting up the side of the mountain. The two men were happy to keep a slower pace. The sun had come out, and filtered through the colorful foliage.

"I underestimated Ari," John was saying.

"She's got a bit of a problem with handling her anger, don't you think?"

"That's always been so."

"True."

"You know, it always bugs me when I have to carry my pistol after I fired it, if I haven't had the chance to clean it yet."

John wasn't trying to change the subject. He had a way of coming back to old conversations that were often considered long finished by others. Ray was used to it and never objected.

"I bet Ari's really pro-gun now that she's got one, huh?"

John furrowed his brow. "Actually, the only thing she said to me was quite elitist. Ask her yourself, if you want. I think time will bring her over to our way of thinking."

"That doesn't surprise me, really. Nothing makes you feel elite more than the first time you strap on a pistol. Reality comes creeping in soon enough."

"Aye."

Talking while hiking made a difficult affair even harder, and the men stopped to catch their breath.

"I should stoke up my pipe," John said, "this is getting too easy."

"So you never finished telling me how work was going."

"I never intended to."

"Oh, come on."

The two continued up the trail.

"What can I say? Work is boring. I wanted to design aircraft, Ray. Now my greatest accomplishment is an industrial integrated HVAC unit that we're helping develop for Hamilton Sundstrand. I am not pleased."

"That sounds pretty high tech. Why are you allowing yourself to languish in your current job?"

"I just don't care about it anymore, Ray. I'm happy enough coming home at the end of the day and kicking back. The only thing I feel like I'm missing is spending more time with my friends."

"You think you'll be happy with this pattern indefinitely?"

"Probably not. But I'm happy with it for now."

"You know, it was the thought of turning thirty without accomplishing anything that made me become a police officer."

"Yeah?"

"And, I think at some point you're going to realize that you can't waste your life away doing something that doesn't matter."

"Do you think it actually matters whether or not I design aircraft?"

"I meant it matters to you."

"Oh. What about you? Are you going to jump right back in the saddle after your leave is lifted?"

"I have no idea, John. I haven't been thinking much about it, honestly. I'm awfully wrapped up in the recent past. I simply hold onto the fact that the job will be waiting for me when I'm ready to go back, and that's enough to keep it out of my mind."

"Okay."

There was a pause. John and Ray huffed and puffed.

John looked up the trail. "I certainly hope Ari's waiting for us at the top, or we'll never find her out here. If she got lost, her bad aim is going to be the least of her problems."

"Too bad it's not the least of ours."

Some hours later, the trio was in various stages of refreshing themselves from the hike. Ari was indeed waiting for them at the summit, announcing their performance as akin to geriatrics and saying little else. John and Ray would have been happy to stay up there longer, but the fact was that the sun would set before they returned if they lingered. Despite Ari's mechanical pace up the mountain, she idled back down the trail without enthusiasm. John guessed that her emotional stress and physical exhaustion had finally caught up with her. He sincerely hoped that a stiff belt of gin would help restore her more amicable side.

After they'd each in turn dunked their heads in the nearby stream and changed out of their sweaty clothes, John broke out the Genevir.

"Don't you think we ought to eat something first?" Ray asked.

"It's never too soon to start drinking," said John.

"Roger that," added Ari.

"Well, I don't feel like cooking," said Ray. "So if anybody wants anything other than bologna sandwiches, step right up."

"Bologna sandwiches," John and Ari said together.

Ray rolled his eyes and opened the cooler. He began to assemble the sandwiches. John retrieved his Beretta and unloaded it.

"Annie, get your Glock," he said. "I'm going to show you how to clean a pistol."

"Ooh, exciting," Ari said, reaching over to her backpack and withdrawing her weapon. She unloaded it and placed it on the table.

"Do you have any idea how to take that thing apart?"

"No."

"Allow the master to do his thing."

Ray smiled. He always appreciated John's sense of humor. He finished his simple task and grabbed one of his creations.

"Sandwiches are on the counter."

As John walked Ari through the steps of cleaning, Ray allowed himself a moment to be alone. He munched on his sandwich in no particular hurry, staring at the faint lines of the dying sunset through the window. He was glad he came, but the tragedy of Thursday afternoon was inescapable. He had been doing a mighty job of keeping it from consuming him, and indeed he wondered if John and Ari thought him to be too quickly recovered. Still, he didn't know how else to address the issue with them.

Ray never wanted this. Even if Pete had survived, the experience was powerful enough to change Ray's mind about combat forever. When Ray first got involved in firearms after college, he longed for the day he might get to test his skills in combat. Ray got into the habit of going for long walks at night, mostly for the fresh air and time alone but also to stroke his secret desire to get into some trouble.

Due to the massive amount of time he spent doing this, he did find trouble on occasion. Nothing bad ever came of it, and the police were never needed. However, these incidents made Ray realize that carrying a firearm didn't give him more freedom to deal with troublemakers, it gave him less. Fully aware of the seriousness of involving a firearm in a situation, Ray found that he couldn't respond as forcefully as he wanted. When confronted by a lone antagonist, for example, Ray couldn't stand up to him. With a pistol under his jacket, he had to turn around and all but run away. The consequences for allowing such a situation to escalate were far to dire to allow anything else. These realizations tempered Ray's attitudes about firearms, but also galvanized his desire to do the right thing in all situations. This was responsible in part for bringing back his motivation to become a cop, which was his goal after college but had become muddled with four years of odd jobs, little money, and the end of what had been a good relationship with Kate. The fact that Kate had left him over the guns he was buying was an uncomfortable detail that Ray tried to avoid remembering. "Choose me or the guns," she had said. Ray knew this was a flawed argument, and thought he could have talked her into a compromise, but his ego got in the way. He never came right out and said which he preferred. Kate knew by his lack of action and the gun safe which didn't disappear.

John, his roommate at the time, was sympathetic. Having no girlfriend he had no reason to compromise on his firearm (he only had the Garand back then), and he was only helpful to a degree. Then again John was never as militant about the entire situation as Ray. Ray wondered what Kate was up to these days. He was surprised to think that it had been two years since he'd seen her.

"Hey Ray, are you going to stare out that window all night?"

John's voice sounded distant. Ray turned around and sat at the table. He didn't see the bologna sandwiches any more so he had to assume they'd been consumed. John and Ari were hard at work cleaning their pistols. Ray grasped the glass of gin that had apparently been poured for him. John looked at him.

"Aren't you going to start cleaning your Remington?" he asked.

"I don't know. I'm in no hurry. It's a very forgiving machine."

"Am I supposed to clean the magazine?" Ari queried.

"Wipe it down," said John, "it doesn't need much else for now."

"Is this supposed to take this long?"

"Sure, if you want to do a good job. You can maximize your efficiency if you're pressed for time, though. That's why we started with the barrel, recoil spring and recoil rod. If you're in a hurry, you can concentrate on those first. Then, clean the slide the best you can. The frame is the last priority. If you're interrupted during the process, hopefully you've done as much as you can to keep the weapon running reliably. Of course, we only put a hundred rounds through each pistol today. Ideally you could fire five times that much without cleaning them."

"Wow. If this is the result of a hundred rounds I'd hate to see five hundred."

"Yeah, things get messy."

"Well, I need a smoke break."

"You can smoke in here, you know."

"I want some fresh air, too."

"Okay, I'll join you. Ray?"

"No thanks," said Ray, holding up his glass, "I've got some catching up to do."

John and Ari stood up, grabbing their jackets from the backs of their chairs. Ari retrieved a cigarette and lit it. John opened the door for her and they exited. The cold air was an instant relief to Ari, who was a bit displeased with the gun cleaning solvent. John shut the heavy front door, cloaking the pair in darkness.

"Do you want to walk up the hill?" Ari asked.

"Sure."

The cabin was at the bottom of a small hill, the slope of which constituted the only open ground besides the road. It was too small to afford a view above the trees, but there was nowhere else to go. John followed the dancing ember of Ari's cigarette as they walked. At the top of the hill, Ari unceremoniously flopped down and sat cross-legged. John joined her.

Ari sighed and directed her gaze upward. The stars were astonishingly clear that night, and the Milky Way cut an impressive swath across the lower portion of the sky. John knew some of the larger constellations, the rest were a mystery.

"I'm sorry I was such a bitch this afternoon," Ari said.

"It's all right. Ray and I know when to let you work out your anger."

"It was so frustrating. To hear you guys talk about it, shooting is the easiest thing in the world. I mean, Bruce Willis jumps around corners, rolls on the ground, and flies through the air and bad guys fall like dominoes."

"Now you know how much bullshit all that Hollywood action really is."

"I'm so disappointed."

John loved the smell of clove cigarettes, but not so much so that he ever had the inclination to buy a pack. They fit her perfectly, being expensive, hard to find, and hazardous to your health.

"John, remember that time I came on to you?"

"How could I forget?"

"I think I owe you an apology."

"What for?"

"Because you were right. The reasons you gave me for not getting together were absolutely correct. I don't know why I thought that it was a good idea. We were obviously wrong for each other."

John noticed that Ari said "were" and not "are." He blushed at the implication and then dismissed it.

"You did put me in a difficult position. Not the least of which was that you were dating Silas at the time."

"You and Silas were never friends, right?"

"Not really, we liked each other fine, but he could have easily stomped my ass, given enough of a reason."

"You could have taken Silas in a fair fight."

"I don't think about things like that."

Ari laughed. "You just contradicted yourself. How do you know he could have stomped on you if you hadn't thought about fighting him?"

John rolled his eyes despite the darkness. "I meant that he could have tried. I make no predictions about who would have won. My philosophy is that if you are forced to fight, you have already lost. Stopping the attack while avoiding serious injury is a hollow victory."

"I'm not sure I understand."

"I'm coming from the perspective that winning is an inherently positive thing. The idea is that fighting is an inherently negative thing, so to win a fight is a hollow victory. You have still suffered from the antagonism of another man."

"So what, you should feel bad about winning a fight? With all due respect, John, that's really stupid."

"Feeling bad about harming another human being, and regretting the use of force are different things. I regret not the use of force but the harm done."

"If you ask me, that's splitting hairs."

"Perhaps."

"Anyway, I'm sorry I came on to you. It was inappropriate in the least and potentially harmful to our friendship at the most. I'm just glad you were so egalitarian about it."

"You didn't make it easy for me."

"I know. I mean, I... wait, what do you mean?"

"Come on, Ari, I have eyes. It's not like I wasn't interested. At least in the physical aspect of things."

"Really? I always thought that you were the Zen master of impulse control."

"Maybe so, but... that star is really bright. I forget which one it is."

John looked up at the starfield. Ari nudged him on the shoulder.

"Sometimes I wonder how much we've changed since then. I wonder how that scenario would play out now."

"Is that Altair? Is that even Aquila?"

"John, I'm asking you a question."

"What?"

Ari slipped her arm around John's. John snapped out of his stargazing and looked at Ari with surprise.

"I said, what if I was to ask you now?"

John sat in stunned silence. Out of the corner of his eye, he saw that star again.

"Ari, that star is moving."

"Damn it, John, I'm asking you for a straight answer! This isn't easy for me, you know."

John stood up, allowing Ari's arm to fall away from his. He stared up at the sky, his jaw hanging open.

"Jesus Christ, what the hell is that?"

Ari looked up. A bright blue star was moving down towards the horizon. It was the brightest thing in the sky.

"Maybe the space shuttle is passing overhead," said Ari.

"I've seen that happen before, that doesn't look like..."

John interrupted himself and grabbed Ari's arm. Ari was about to swear at him when she looked up again. The star was getting bigger.

"What the..."

The light, which was blue, grew in intensity. Subtle shadows began to appear around them. The object seemed to grow closer. Ari grabbed John's arm, and they stood watching, transfixed in horror. The object began to pulse. John had no idea how far away it was until the light reached the top of the trees a hundred yards out. It moved into the woods, lowering itself with maddening slowness. The blue light cast an ever-changing dance of shadows off the trees. John wanted to call out to Ray, but the words wouldn't come. The object came to a stop somewhere in the woods. The pulsing light continued.

"What's going on, John?" Ari whispered.

"I... I don't know."

John's voice was equally hushed. He was terrified beyond rational thought, and struggled to regain control. He finally had a coherent idea.

"Let's get back to the cabin," he said.

This sounded like a terrible idea, since they had to walk toward the object to get back there. Slowly they began to move, a force of will that was akin to walking a tightrope. After what seemed like an hour, they arrived at the front door. John turned the doorknob slowly, and opened the door a crack.

"Ray!" he whispered hoarsely.

There was no reply.

"Ray!" he said again, this time so loud he made himself jump.

Ray came to the door. "What the hell are you two playing at out here?"

"Shh!" John and Ari said together.

"Get out here, damn it!" John whispered.

Ray came out onto the steps, shrugging his shoulders.

"Yes, your majesty?"

John pointed and Ray followed his arm.

"Is somebody coming up the... what the *hell*?"

Ray fell silent. The trio stared at the light for a moment. John said something that he could hardly believe.

"We've got to go check it out."

"Are you insane?" said Ari.

"What else can we do? We're all alone out here."

"What if it's dangerous?"

John and Ray looked at each other. They rushed into the cabin, with Ari quickly following.

"What do you have left?" asked John.

John began to reassemble his Beretta with lightning speed while Ray retrieved his Remington. Their swift motion belied their near panic.

"Five rounds of buckshot," Ray replied. "And you?"

"I'm out of ought-six. I have sixteen rounds of nine mil."

"Shit."

Ari stood in the corner, aghast. "You blew off all your ammo? We're screwed!"

John loaded his Beretta. "We don't even know what we're dealing with. If you're coming, get your Glock back together."

"I'm sure as hell not staying here."

Ari fumbled with her piecemeal pistol. Ray stepped in and put it together for her.

"This is pretty much insane," she said, loading it.

"Are you going to top off the mag?" John said.

"What do you mean?"

"Never mind. Okay, single file, even spacing. Ray, you go first. Ari, you watch our six."

Ari shook her head. "Can't we just get in the Expedition and get the hell out of here?"

"The road goes past that point," Ray began, "if it's harmful we should deal with it on foot first. Otherwise we may not make it by vehicle."

This made absolutely zero sense to Ari, but John and Ray had obviously made up their minds.

"Let's go,' said John.

Carefully, the three made their way through the door. Ari pointed her pistol at the ground like John was doing. Ray led the way.

They soon entered the tree line. They couldn't yet see the object, only the pale blue light it was emanating. The unknown pattern of pulses made everything seem distant and uncertain. Ray held up his fist. John stopped, and Ari almost bumped into him. Ray gestured to his right, and John moved that way. Ari did the same. As the trio drew abreast of each other, they were all able to see the object.

Before them was a sphere. It was about the size of a basketball, and was suspended about five feet off the ground. It was incandescent with blue light, making it difficult to see its actual dimensions. It was stunningly beautiful and thoroughly eerie.

John took a step closer. The orb did not give off any heat, nor did it make a sound. In fact, the night was completely silent save for the breathing of the three humans. The pattern of light resembled the effect of an underwater electric lamp. John moved closer.

"Wait," whispered Ari.

John looked mesmerized. As he continued to draw near, he held up his hand to shield his face from the light. Almost as soon as he did this, there was a change in the orb. The light began to fade and the surface became darker. John stepped back. The orb remained almost completely dark. The surface looked metallic. John took a step forward, and a shape appeared on the surface. It was an outline of a human hand.

John, Ray and Ari stared at the orb. Nothing else happened.

"What should we do?" Ari said.

"I think I'm supposed to touch it," John said, holding his left hand up as if to do so.

"I don't think that's a great idea," said Ray.

"What else can we do?"

"Fine, go ahead. It's your ass."

John crept forward until he was close enough to touch the orb. He flipped on the safety on his Beretta and tucked it into his belt. Drawing a deep breath, he reached forward and placed his palm against the orb.

It was cold. No, it was warm. It was both. John had no idea what he was actually feeling. It reminded him of the feel of mentholated rub. The surface was as smooth as glass. There was a slight vibration coming off of it. After a few seconds, nothing changed.

"Nothing's happening," John announced.

As he said this, two more shapes appeared on the opposite sides of the sphere. John turned to look. There were two more handprints.

"I think it wants all of us to touch it."

"No way in hell," said Ari.

Ray moved forward. "If it was going to hurt us," he said, "I think it would have done so by now."

Ray leaned his Remington against a tree and moved up to the orb. He placed his hand on one of the prints.

Ari shook her head. "I can't believe you two are so cavalier about touching something which is obviously from another planet."

"I'm scared shitless," said John, "but we have no choice."

Again, this made little sense to Ari. She sighed.

"Oh well, we might as well all die together."

Ari moved forward and pressed her hand on the orb.

"Are you happy? Now what?"

7.

Before John, there was nothing. Behind him, there was nothing. John assumed that behind him there was nothing, since he couldn't tell where was before or behind. He couldn't even be sure he still had a body. When he tried to grasp himself, he found he couldn't feel his arms. John realized that it was quiet, but then it struck him how quiet. Even in the most silent place, he could still hear the low hum of his blood rushing through his body and the steady pace of his heart beating. Here, there was silence that was terminal and complete. A fresh wave of ecstatic fear washed over him. At least his emotions were still working.

"John!"

It was Ari's voice. John didn't hear it, though. It was simply there. He though about replying, and he heard his own voice.

"Ari?"

"John?"

This time, Ray's voice made itself present.

"I'm here," John thought.

"Where is here?"

"I don't know. I think we're inside the..."

John stopped thinking about talking. A person had appeared before him. That person was John. He was looking at a mirror image of himself, as if he was standing in front of a full-length mirror naked. For some reason, John did not feel embarrassed.

"Are you two seeing this?" Ari's voice said.

"Yes," said Ray's voice. "Not very flattering, is it?"

"What do you see?" thought John.

"I see myself," said Ari's voice, "naked."

"Me, too," Ray's voice said.

The image began to change. The first thing that happened was that the phantom John's hair began to shrink. It grew shorter until the phantom became bald. Then, the phantom's shape began to change. It was a slow process, but John realized that the phantom was losing weight. The lumpy features of John's midsection that he had gained over the past few years disappeared. The phantom became skinnier and less muscular, until John recognized what looked like his high school age body. Then the phantom's backward progress stopped.

"That's my sophomore year body," Ray's voice said.

"How can you be sure?" John thought.

"Because I gained a bunch of weight my sophomore year. This image I see got really chunky before it stopped. There was only one time I ever looked like that."

"I suppose this could be my sophomore year self," said Ari's voice.

"I'd like to get a look at what Ari's seeing," said Ray's voice.

"How can you joke at a time like this?"

"Why did it stop here?" John thought.

The phantom disappeared. Again, John lost all reference points to reality.

"That was strange," Ari's voice said.

"That's as far back as the three of us go," said Ray's voice.

The statement was correct, but John wasn't so sure. Suddenly another figure appeared. It was a human, at first glance. John stared at it in confusion. It was neither male nor female; in fact it was quite androgynous. John couldn't be sure since it was wearing clothing. It had black, ear-length hair, and green eyes. It was staring unwaveringly at John, or at least where John presumed himself to be. The clothes it had on were quite curious. It was wearing a jacket that resembled John's own, but was different. It looked leathery, and was greenish-brown as opposed to the olive green of his jacket. It was also a bit shorter around the waist. It was wearing jeans, which were dark blue. They were about halfway between the light blue shade of John's jeans and the black of Ray's. John had a flash of insight.

The phantom was a combination of all three of them. The jacket looked like a morphed version of John's military jacket and Ari's leather bomber. The t-shirt it had on was the t-shirt that Ray was wearing. The shoes didn't reveal any more clues since all three of them were wearing very similar brown hiking boots.

"Are you two seeing this?" said Ray.

"It's all of us together," John said. "It's all of us made into one human."

"Very damn strange," said Ari.

The phantom stared at John. Time passed immeasurably.

"Okay, now what?" said John.

"Okay, now what?" said The Phantom.

"Great," began Ari, "we found an intergalactic parrot."

"Hello," said The Phantom.

John smiled. At least, he would have smiled if he knew where he put his mouth.

"Hello," John said. "I'm John."

"I know," said The Phantom.

"Who are you?"

"I am."

"You are... what?"

"I am."

"Fantastic, it has a god complex," Ari said.

"What do we call you?" asked Ray.

"I am whom to which you speak."

"How'bout we call you Seth," said John.

"Seth?" exclaimed Ari. "Where do you get Seth from?"

"I don't know. It's the first thing that came to mind."

"I am Seth," said Seth.

"Yeah," began Ray, "but Adam and Eve didn't have a third person sticking their genes into the mix."

"You want to choose another name?" John said.

"I am Seth," said Seth.

"Fine, that's fine," Ari said.

"Where are you from, Seth?" asked John.

"A place."

"Can you be more specific?"

"A place. A place that is not this place."

"No shit," said Ari.

"Do you mind?" growled John. "I'm trying to communicate with this thing."

"I am Seth."

"Seth, where is the place you are from?"

"Not here."

"Are you intentionally avoiding the question or do you really not know?" said Ray.

"I am from the place that is not here. It is another place."

"Let's try something else," said John. "Seth, why did you come here?"

"To find you."

"To find us? Ray, Ari and I?"

"Yes."

"Or do you mean to find humans?" said Ray.

"Yes."

"We're humans, Ray," John said. "Seth why did you come to find humans?"

"To bring you back."

"Back where?"

"To a place."

"Damn it, are you an idiot or what?" yelled Ari.

"Take it easy, Ari," said John, "it has probably never communicated with humans before. Seth, why do you want to bring us back with you?"

Seth stared at John. It blinked.

"Hello?" said Ray.

"Hello," said Seth.

"Get me out of here," said Ari. "ET was smarter than this stupid mannequin."

In a flash, the three of them found themselves back in the forest. The orb pulsed slightly.

"Thank God, we're still here," said Ray.

Ari, who had lowered her hand, turned to face John. "What the hell is going on here?" she asked. "This thing comes all the way to Earth from who knows where, and all it can do is stand there and act like a dullard?"

John shrugged. "I think we need to give it more time to assimilate our language. It may be fundamentally different from the way it's used to communicating. It may not be used to using verbal language at all."

"I agree," said Ray.

"I'm starting to think that we should get out of here and leave this thing to the professionals," Ari said.

"Are you kidding," said John, "we'd never get anywhere near it again! And who do you think is the professional authority on this? NASA? They don't know any more than we do."

"Besides," said Ray, "what if we go running off and bring back the authorities and this thing is gone? We may have already gone crazy but that'll prove it to everyone else."

"You guys can do what you want, but I'm through with it," Ari said. "This is way too far off my weird-shit-o-meter."

John looked at the orb. The three handprints were still there.

"We need you, Ari. Without you we can't access it."

"Please, Ari," said Ray. "Like John said, if it wanted to hurt us it would have done so by now."

Ari tapped her foot. "This is so nuts. All right, fine. But if this thing can't get past shitting its britches I give up."

Ari placed her hand on the orb, and the men did the same.

Again, they were in the inky blackness, disembodied in silence. Seth appeared, looking quizzical. John noticed that this time he could hear himself breathing.

"Hello," said Seth.

"Hello," replied John. "How are you, Seth?"

"I am."

"Do you know where you are?"

"I am here."

"Here is a planet called Earth. Humans are from Earth. It is our home."

"I am on Earth."

"Where is your home, Seth?"

"A planet."

"Does your planet have a name?"

"Umber."

"Umber? Your planet's name is Umber?"

"Yes."

"You're here to take us back to Umber?"

"Yes."

"Why?"

"Because."

John felt his patience slipping. "Why do you want humans to go to Umber?"

"Because humans are to go to Umber."

"What is the reason you want humans to go with you?"

Seth appeared to think for a moment. "What is a reason?"

"A goal, a purpose, a point."

"This is going nowhere," said Ari.

"It's still learning from us," said John. "We need to keep talking to it. If it can learn our language then it can learn more complicated concepts."

"Like walking and chewing gum at the same time?"

"Yeah. Seth, your reason to come to Earth was to get humans. What is the reason for bringing humans to Umber?"

"This thing needs more help," said Ray.

"Help," said Seth.

John intended to raise an eyebrow. "What?"

"Save us."

"Is that why you want humans to go with you, Seth?" John asked. "You need our help?"

"Yes."

"Why do you need our help?"

"The reason."

"What is the reason?"

"The goal, the purpose, the point."

"What do you want us to accomplish?"

"To go with me."

"That's the first time he called himself 'me'," said Ray.

"I'm hitting the wall," said John. "I can't figure out how to get by his circular logic."

"I am way too buzzed for this right now," said Ari.

"Yeah," said John, "I wish I'd laid off the booze, too. We didn't know this would happen."

"Now you know why I don't like to drink too much," Ray said.

The black void changed. A much more palpable scene replaced it. John, Ray and Ari found themselves standing in a pub of classic English design. A long bar of mahogany stretched from the door to where they stood. Behind them, shadowy booths offered a privacy separate from the rest of the space. They were alone, save for Seth who manned the bar. All three of them instantly recognized where they were.

"It's the Publick House," said John.

"Yeah," said Ari, "and would you look at us!"

John and Ray looked at each other. John's hair was down past his ears. Ray was sporting a shaggy goatee. They turned and looked at Ari. She was wearing this semi-see-through skirt thing with a similar top that bared her midriff. Ray smiled.

"I remember that little number," he said.

"This is a memory," said John. "We're inside a memory. This is how we all looked senior year."

Ari nodded. "It must be. The Publick House was sold and renamed. It doesn't look a thing like this anymore."

"Hello," said Seth.

"Well, you're a crappy bartender. You haven't even asked us what we want."

"At least we're not disembodied anymore," said Ray.

"Seth," began John, "why are we here?"

Seth stared at them. Without looking down, he picked up a glass and started wiping it with a cloth.

"You three again," he said. "You're my best customers, you know that?"

"He's playing a role," said John.

Ray furrowed his brow. "With such a charmer as you, Seth, how can we resist?"

"You are learning," said Seth.

"High praise coming from him," Ari said.

"This is where you learned."

"Learned what?" asked John.

"About us."

"Look at it outside," said Ray. "It's raining."

John shrugged. "It's not doing anything, Ray, none of this actually exists."

"I think I know why we're here."

"Oh?"

"This is early senior year. This is the year we were all in Astronomy together. Today was the day that we'd all just purchased our textbooks. Remember? We came in here and it was empty. The bartender was the only one here."

Ari smiled. "That's right. We sat in the back and read the first chapter together. We were so studious."

John laughed. "Right."

"So by saying that we learned 'about us,'" began Ray, "Seth is talking about when we learned about astronomy. Since he's from the stars, that makes sense."

"How is it that we learned about Umber from the very first chapter?" asked John. "The first chapter was nothing but introductory."

"Yeah, but it summarized a little bit of what we were about to study. Maybe Umber was mentioned."

"I've never heard of Umber before," said Ari, "and if it was in that book I would have remembered it."

It was an arrogant statement, but John and Ray had no reason to doubt her.

John looked out into the rain. "Maybe it was called something else. If we had the textbooks we could look. Too bad we're a three hour drive from the nearest one."

"No we're not," said Ray, pointing.

In one of the rear booths lay three backpacks. The three approached it. John reached into his pack and removed a book. It read "Astronomy, Fourth Edition, by..." The author's name was missing, as was the publisher's. John turned over the book and there was an illustration on the back. The picture was out of focus and looking at it hurt John's eyes. John flipped open the book and found the same for the words inside.

"Shit," he said.

"We can't read it because we can't remember it," said Ray.

"Back to square one," said Ari.

"You are learning," said Seth.

"Yeah, we're learning that you're great at creating useless illusions."

"It is time for you to learn."

"We're all ears," said John.

"Good," said Seth, and smiled. It was the creepiest expression any of them had ever seen.

Time passed.

"Well, what's the lesson?" asked Ari, exasperated.

"Find me."

Like a slide being changed, the world switched around them. It was so disorientating that all three humans fell over. Back in the woods, they picked themselves up. The orb shimmered and was dark.

"Find him?" asked Ray. "What the hell?"

"The sphere hasn't moved," Ari said.

John rubbed his arm. "I think he means find Umber."

"Great, we'll just call up William Shatner and have him give us a lift."

"I think we need to find Umber in the textbook," said Ray. "Find out what we supposedly already know about it."

"What would be the point of that? It's not like he needs us to tell him where his home is."

"It's a test," said John quietly.

"A test?"

"I think so. Seth doesn't want just anybody. I think we have to prove ourselves."

Ari smirked. "If that's the case, I hope there aren't any follow up questions or we're boned."

John looked at the orb. The three hand prints were gone.

"We can't do anything else here right now. We need to get our hands on that textbook."

"I don't have mine any more."

"Neither do I," added Ray.

"I do," said John. "It'll take us six hours round trip just to get it, though. And there's no guarantee that this thing will still be here when we get back."

"You go," said Ray. "I'll stay behind. Hopefully it'll realize that we're still interested and it won't go anywhere."

"You've got brass balls, buddy," said Ari.

"There is no way I can drive right now," began John, "I say we try and get some sleep and leave first thing in the morning. We could be back by noon tomorrow with the book."

Ray nodded. "I agree."

Ari laughed. "Sleep? I'm going to need more gin."

8. October 5, 2003

The night passed fitfully for John and Ari. John was worn out enough as it was, but Ari's rest was chemically induced. Ray did not sleep as well, however. He worried that they were taking too many risks with the orb. He was also not so secretly terrified of being left alone with it, even in the bright daylight.

John had dragged Ari out of bed at 0600 sharp, his energy renewed. Ari objected heartily until John suggested that she stay behind. They quickly cleaned up, and were out the door. John had left Ray his Beretta and had talked Ari into letting him carry her Glock. Ray had no idea what he might do with any weaponry but had accepted the additional firepower without objection. According to John, there was always a chance that Seth might get pissed and become hostile to Ray. Again, Ray had no idea what any weaponry might do in that case.

Before leaving, John and Ari had checked on the orb. It was still there, but almost impossible to see in the daylight. Ray was neutral about checking up on it every once and awhile, as suggested by John. For some reason Ray was sure that it would wait for them whether he approached it or not.

Now that he was alone in the cabin, Ray began to make himself some breakfast. He stoked up the gas stove and set to work on some scrambled eggs. The scene was eerily similar to the time that Kate was with him at the cabin. Ray wondered what her reaction to the orb would have been. Kate was never the adventurous type. She would probably encourage them much more than Ari did to go to the authorities. As a representative of such, Ray knew what kind of reception they'd get. They'd have to make up some sort of story just to get a raised eyebrow out of a cop around these parts. Ray figured saying that they found a meteor would work. That would get the astronomers running.

John was still adamant about leaving the professionals out of it. Ray had his own doubts, but he kept them to himself. Sure, it was an amazing find, but what if they screwed it up? If they flunked the test, maybe it would leave Earth. Then they'd all go slowly mad and have to be institutionalized. Ray imagined himself sitting at a dusty computer hooked up to SETI's system, praying that Seth would pull a Christ and return some day. If NASA took over at least they'd go down in the history books.

Ray transferred the eggs to a plate and sat down at the table. They'd forgotten to bring condiments of any kind, and Ray was reminded of this as he ate. Eggs without salt was a venal sin.

Ray allowed his mind to go blank as he finished the eggs. He snapped himself out of this by remembering his shotgun. It still needed to be cleaned. Ray moved his plate to the sink and procured a glass of cola. He sat down at the table, this time with his Remington. He methodically unloaded it and began to take it down. It occurred to him to go get John's Beretta, now that he was no longer within arms reach of a loaded weapon. He did not, however, move. He just didn't care any more.

John was absolutely thrilled to see his house again, as if he'd expected it to be gone upon his return. Ari had slept most of the way, and expressed her pleasure at reaching their destination with a groggy groan. John unlocked the front door and allowed Ari inside. Friday met them and demanded attention.

"You got a cat," Ari croaked.

"The cat got me. Make yourself at home, I'm going to go get the textbook."

"I would love to use your shower."

"Go for it. Spare towels are in the hall closet."

John pointed in the direction of the bathroom as he walked away. Ari scratched Friday behind the ears for a moment and headed over. She could feel a hangover creeping up on her as she procured a towel. Ari closed the bathroom door. Normally she would have loved to look inside the medicine cabinet (nothing personal, just curiosity), but her priorities were unusually ordered that morning. She stepped into a hot shower and sighed with relief. Her head was still threatening a full-bore headache. Ari felt as if she was part of an inescapable cycle of morning-after showers. Still, some night-befores were more fun than others.

Ari buried her face in her towel after the shower. She was rue to step into the clothes she was wearing before but had no choice. She was just moving onto drying her neck when she heard John swearing. Ari cracked open the door and yelled past the swirling steam.

"What's the matter?"

"I can't find the damn book," was the livid response.

Ari closed the door and finished drying. John was still stomping around when she emerged fully dressed. He was walking past her towards the kitchen.

"Son of a bitch," he said.

"No luck?" Ari asked.

"Not yet."

There was a nice miniature living room off of the kitchen. John entered and threw open a cabinet. He began removing books and throwing them onto a loveseat.

"It's not the end of the world, right? We can still go into Boston and buy another copy from the campus bookstore."

"Maybe," muttered John, "but the bookstore isn't open today. We can't leave Ray up there for another twenty-four hours without returning. He'd have to walk five miles just to get to a phone."

John flopped down on the loveseat, crushing several books beneath him, and shrugged.

"Damn," said Ari.

"I just don't know. It's not in the basement, I know that."

"What about the attic?"

"There's nothing up there. I don't really have that much stuff."

"Did you sell it?"

"No, I would have remembered that. You always get jack squat for used textbooks, that's why I kept most of..."

John trailed off.

"What?" Ari asked.

"You know what? I... damn it, I gave it to Bryan!"

"Bryan Aylward?"

"Yeah! He wanted to look at it."

"Where is he now?"

"Fucking Egypt."

"Oh."

"We're screwed. Unless we can find another source of the same information."

"It *has* to be this book, Ari. The information we need is in the first chapter. Even if we find a different edition it might not be the same. They might be on the next edition by now. You know how they do it, they come out with new editions just to make sure students buy new instead of used."

"Why don't we just wander down to Suffolk and poke around the science department? Last I knew those buildings were never locked."

"I don't know what else to do. I doubt we'll find anything, but we might run across a student who has one. Otherwise, we'll have to drive back to the cabin, tell Ray what happened, and then come all the way back to Boston on Monday. And by then we'll have to go back to work."

"Just call in sick. I do it all the time."

The thought hadn't occurred to John, though it made perfect sense. John had never taken a sick day in his life.

"Okay. We'll go to Suffolk and look around. I'm going to go get cleaned up, do me a favor and make some breakfast for us."

"That I can do."

Forty minutes later, John and Ari were walking down Derne Street towards Suffolk's science building. It was a crisp morning and John was shivering. He was deeply worried that

Ray might be in trouble up at the cabin. He noticed that Ari was grinning from ear to ear.

"What's so funny?"

"I just realized how cool this is. We're like, secret agents working for the government or something."

"I really wish you hadn't said that. The last thing we need is the government finding out about the orb."

"Don't worry, I won't tell."

"You were the first one to suggest we go crying to NASA."

"I've had some time to think about it. I'm ready to face this thing."

"I'm so relieved."

The pair entered the appropriate building. It appeared deserted. John headed for the astronomy department with practiced ease. Certain things never left his memory and the layout of the university was one of them.

"The professor's office is likely to be locked," said Ari.

"I have my ways around that," said John with complete confidence.

Ari smiled. "I guess at this point you're not going to let a simple lock stop you. I like that."

"Well, I'd rather not get arrested, either. Let's keep this above board as long as we can."

John and Ari turned down a hallway towards the main lecture hall. A student was standing near the entrance and turned to walk away when he saw them. John and Ari entered the hall.

There was a woman inside, writing on the chalkboard. She was dressed in sweats and had her chestnut brown hair tied up in a hurried fashion. John recognized her as the woman he saw leaving the restaurant last week. He also recognized her as...

"Excuse me," John said.

The woman turned around. John's brain did calisthenics as he tried to recognize her name.

"Oh, hello," she said, "it's John, isn't it? Class of '98?"

"Yeah, John Scherer, and Ari Ferro, class of '98. And you're, uh..."

"Christie Tolliver. It's all right, it's been awhile."

"Yeah, you were in our astronomy class senior year. Weren't you the teacher's assistant?"

"That's right. Now I'm the assistant professor. Big surprise, huh?"

"Nice to see you again," said Ari.

"You too. I hardly recognize you with so much clothing on."

John thought he might see Ari blush for the first time, but she simply smiled.

"Indeed."

"So what brings you by? Reminiscing?"

"Not exactly," said John, approaching the board. "We're looking for a fourth edition copy of our textbook for that class. It's called *Astronomy, Fourth Edition*, but I can't remember the author. The cover was blue."

"That's an odd request. Did you find an buyer on E-Bay or something?"

"Uh..."

"We have a bet going," said Ari. "John thinks that the first chapter talks about the Umberian system, and I don't. We were heading into town anyway today, so we thought we'd settle it."

John jabbed Ari in the ribs.

"Ow, what's your problem?" she said.

Christie looked up in thought. "The Umberian system? I don't remember that one. Are you sure that's the name?"

"Yes," said John.

"Because an 'umbra' is the shadow cast during an eclipse. It's also the darkest part of a sunspot."

"Maybe that's what we're thinking of. I might have mistaken it for the name of a star system."

"A bet's a bet," Ari said.

"Yeah, do you have a copy we can look at? We'd appreciate it."

"I think so. Let's take a look in my office. I'm currently using the sixth edition but I might have an older copy kicking around."

Christie led the way out of the lecture hall and down the corridor.

"Looks like you lost your audience," Ari said.

"Excuse me?" said Christie.

"There was somebody watching you before."

"Oh. Yes, I admit, my blackboard inscriptions are quite popular viewing. So what are you two up to these days? You're not, er..."

"No," said John. "Still friends. I'm a CAD engineer and Ari is a computer programmer."

"That's cool. I sometimes regret not going where the big money is."

"Yeah, but you're doing something you're interested in."

"True enough."

Christie arrived at her office and unlocked the door. She waived the other two inside. There was an appearance of ordered chaos. A dead houseplant sat in one corner, desiccated by neglect.

"Sorry about the mess. I don't know what to do with all this crap."

"If you don't need the book," began John, stepping over a pile of papers, "we'll take it off your hands."

"Well, I don't know... here it is."

John and Ari shared a victorious glance as Christie removed the book from a tall shelf. She handed it to John.

"I suppose you can borrow it but I don't really have the authority to give it to you."

"We only need to check the first chapter," said Ari. "We can do that in a matter of minutes."

"Yes," said John, "but we might need it again later. I regret giving Bryan my only copy."

"Bryan Aylward?" asked Christie.

"The very same."

"What is he up to these days?"

"Fucking Egypt," said Ari.

John had the book open to the first chapter. He was running his index finger down the text. The women watched in silence. John turned pages and time seemed to slow. Ari and Christie looked at each other.

"So, still living in Boston?"
"Somerville."
"Ah. Nice."

John grunted and began reviewing the chapter from the beginning.

"Do you want some help there, chief?" asked Ari.

"No, I just need to... wait..."

John fell silent again. Ari smiled at Christie.

"So, how do you like teaching?"

"It's fine. Sometimes I feel like I'm at a disadvantage because of my youth. New students still mistake me for a student."

"I'd think that's a good thing."

"Oh, I agree."

John closed the book with a thump. "I don't know, Ari, it's not in here."

"You mind if I look?"

"Go for it. But the only thing I could find is a brief mention of the Large Magellanic Cloud and how there might be Earth-like planets there."

"Maybe that's it," said Ari, leafing through the book. "If it's the only mention of extrasolar planetary systems."

"What are you two talking about?" asked Christie.

"Maybe that's the answer," said Ari. "The Large Magellanic Cloud."

John turned to Christie. "What can you tell us about the Magellanic Cloud?"

"I can tell you there's no Umberian system in it. The only things that even have a name versus an NGC number are the Tarantula Nebula and the Reticulum Globular Cluster."

"How far away is it?"

"What does that have to do with your bet?"

"I'm just curious. I think I already lost our bet."

"It's about one hundred and seventy-nine thousand light years."

Ari was still browsing the textbook. "John?"

"Yeah?"

"I'm really starting to think this is not the toughest question we'll have to answer."

"So we'll take the book with us."

"Maybe it would be better if we had a more knowledgeable source than just this book. Perhaps someone who could better interpret what's inside."

Christie was becoming impatient. "Are you two working on some sort of project?"

John nodded. "You could say that."

"Then why all this bullshit about a bet? I would have gladly offered you the textbook no matter what the reason."

"Can you excuse us for a moment? Ari, may I see you outside?"

"Sure."

John and Ari stepped out into the corridor. John escorted Ari down the hall until they were sufficiently away from the door.

"Great excuse, Ari. A bet? Yeah, I bet on obscure pieces of astronomical trivia all the time!"

"I didn't hear you coming up with anything better!"

"Maybe not, but at least I'm not blabbing everything in front of her."

"Bullshit, you're the one who started blabbing about the Greater Magic Mystery Cloud!"

"Okay, okay. I'm sorry. Why don't we just take the book and get out of here?"

"John, I think we can use Tolliver. I think we should try to talk her into coming with us."

John paused and thought about this.

"No, she'll never believe us."

"We don't have to tell her exactly what's going on. We just have to get her up there. If she's as insane as you and Ray she'll want to check it out."

"Okay, fine... I might have a good cover story."

"Yeah, what?"

"Trust me, it's a good one."

"Okay, John," said Ari, drawing out the first word. "I guess it's your turn to offer a terrible excuse."

"It's a good one, don't worry."

John and Ari walked back into Christie's office.

"Professor Tolliver, we owe you an apology. Ari and I were trying to protect a potential discovery and we're wary about losing credit for it."

Christie smirked. "That's the most believable thing you've said so far."

"Since we're really bad at lying, here's the truth. Ari and I believe we've found a meteorite up in New Hampshire."

"Interesting. What does that have to do with the Magellanic Cloud and the first chapter of that book?"

"Ari and I both owned that book when we took Astronomy 101 senior year. When we discovered the meteorite this weekend, we remembered that there was a comet that passed by the Earth recently. The comet was supposed to have originated in a certain region of space. We couldn't remember the name of the comet nor the region of space it was supposed to have come from. I thought it was the Umberian system, but I guess that was a red herring. What I did remember is that the name of the region was in the first chapter of this book. For some reason this fact stuck in my mind. I'd done searches on the Internet, but without any names I was getting nowhere It was really driving me crazy. I figured the astronomy staff at our *alma mater* could help, or at least get us a copy of the book."

"We're kinda hoping to sell the meteorite," said Ari. "So we didn't want to risk somebody else getting the credit for it."

"Okay," said Christie. "There's only one problem. Any meteorite large enough for you to find would have produced a crater at least several hundred feet wide and vaporized everything inside. If that had happened recently you can bet we'd know about it."

"What we have is definitely a meteorite, I know that much. I did research on the geological characteristics and I'm quite sure that's what we found. Maybe it landed a lot longer ago than I estimated. I guess what we need now is an expert to identify it for us and date it."

"Nudge, nudge," said Ari.

"I'm hardly an expert on meteorites," began Christie, "but I could at least confirm your suspicions. You'd also have better luck attracting the right people with me sticking up for you."

"Name your terms."

"I don't care about fame. Fortune is another thing. I'll help you out if you make me an equal partner, but you can get all the credit on the official paper. Don't expect a million bucks and a Nobel prize, meteorites are nothing special really. You might get a larger university or a research organization to give you several thousand dollars for it if it is particularly rare. All I'd ask for is my fair share of that money."

"When can you come take a look?"

"How far north is it?"

"Three hours by car."

"How about next Saturday?"

"How about now?" asked Ari.

"Now? I can't go now. I have a lesson plan for tomorrow to finish. I have to feed my dog. What's wrong with next weekend?"

"We have our friend Ray up there right now guarding the meteorite. We can't risk somebody else finding it before we can claim it, since it's on land owned by the state and anybody can stake a claim on it. It's either you come with us now and help us determine what we've got, or we have to take turns missing work for an entire week guarding it."

"What are the odds that somebody else will come across it?"

"Slim, but we already dug it up. That will be difficult to conceal and more obvious to somebody walking by. We can try moving it but we want to preserve the specimen, right?"

"We'd really appreciate your help," said Ari. "If we're wrong we'll make it up to you. Your dog can come with us, that's not a problem. Maybe, give him some wide open space to run around him that's a bit safer than Somerville."

Christie sat behind her desk. She regarded John and Ari with an expression that was not reassuring.

"All right. You have a deal. Suffolk isn't exactly making me rich on this salary."

Byron leaned against the outside of the science building, bracing himself against the wind that had risen up. So Christie met up with two old friends. He might be able to use that to his advantage later. How he might do this escaped him, but any information was good information at this stage.

Byron's trip to Somerville was a complete waste of time. He couldn't find Christie's street to save his life, and ended up with good pair of blisters from all the wandering around. He would have to use a more direct approach. Byron figured with enough people on the street and in the subway that he could follow Christie undetected. Hence the hooded sweatshirt and sunglasses he had.

The front door of the science building opened, and three people stepped out. Byron turned his head just enough to confirm that it was Christie and her two friends. They took a left on Derne Street.

"I'm parked on Cambridge," said the man.

Byron waited until the three had made another left, this time onto Temple Street. He then headed after them. He turned onto Temple and found himself about twenty yards behind them. He matched their pace.

Christie wasn't speaking to the other two. Byron found that odd considering they'd just become reacquainted after years apart. The other two people flanked Christie, walking just behind her. If Byron didn't know better he'd think Christie was being escorted somewhere.

Byron slowed down a bit when they hit Cambridge Street. When he rounded the corner, he saw Christie being led into a black Ford Expedition. The weirdest thing was that the man looked both ways down the street before getting in. He didn't seem to see Byron. The engine roared to life, and Byron struggled to remember the license plate before the Ford rolled down the street and out of sight.

9.

Ari pressed down on the gas pedal and was pleased with the results. Ray's Ford was a nice piece of gear, and it kicked the crap out of her minivan. John sat next to her in the passenger seat, flirting with sleep. After they'd picked up Tycho, John had asked Ari to take a turn at the wheel. Ari was glad she did.

While Christie was inside her apartment, Ari and John took turns calling in sick to work. Ari had no idea how this would effect John, but in her case it would doubtless piss off more than a few people. Considering the circumstances, Ari would have been just as happy to quit entirely.

Christie was silent in the back seat, save for the occasional reassuring comment to Tycho, who didn't seem to need them. Ari didn't care for dogs, but this one seemed well-mannered enough. Christie must bathe the thing pretty regularly since Ari couldn't remember ever smelling a dog that didn't remind her of an outhouse. Perhaps living in a small apartment was a greater reason for keeping up on canine grooming.

The plan was to have Christie back in Somerville by ten that night. John and Ari expected Christie to cancel her class tomorrow as soon as she found out about the orb; for now they were content to let her believe she'd be back the same day. The only things Christie brought were a book on meteorites, a can of dog food, and a plastic bag for other sundry uses. Ari figured they had enough food to sustain the four of them for at least one more day. If things got really interesting they could always go to the store in Fairlee for more supplies.

"Ari," said Christie.

"Yeah?"

"You know how you said you thought that the meteorite could have come from a comet from the Magellanic Cloud?"

"Uh huh."

"Are you sure you weren't thinking of the Oort Cloud?"

"I don't know. From what John said, we were looking for a system or a galaxy or something."

"The Oort Cloud is thought to be the source of comets in our solar system."

"I see. Maybe that's what we were really looking for. John seems to be asleep but you can ask him later."

"Right."

Ari raised an eyebrow. That was a lucky coincidence, both things being called clouds. Ari had been ready to get Christie into the truck by threat of force, their original plan having failed so miserably. John would never go that far, of course. Ari looked at him. He hadn't shaved in a couple of days, and was starting to look a bit like Indiana Jones. Ari thought it was kind of neat. Then John started to drool.

"John, wake up," she said.

"Huh? What?"

"We're getting close to Ray's exit. Wouldn't it make more sense to have two vehicles at this point?"

"I guess so. That wouldn't leave anyone tied to the cabin should the Ford be needed elsewhere. Sure, head over to Ray's. I'll pick up my car and follow you two up."

"I thought you said you lived in Woburn," said Christie.

"I do, but my car was left at Ray's place in Manchester when we left for the cabin on Friday."

"Oh."

Ari hit the turn signal and began to exit the highway. So far, she liked Christie. She seemed to be strong willed and smart, which was good for figuring out the orb but bad for manipulating her. Their story about being duplicitous out of greed had worked, so Ari was trying to relax. It was unknown how Christie would react to their lies. Hopefully the revelation of their "meteorite" would provide sufficient reason for forgiveness. If not, what then? Would Christie go running to the authorities? They could kidnap her, but John and Ray would never stand for it. Ari began to regret her enthusiasm for bringing Christie along. She could really screw things up. Ari decided to test the waters.

"Hey Christie," she said.

"Yeah?"

"This whole meteorite business has got me thinking. What do you think about life on other planets?"

"I hope it's true."

"Me, too, but how do you think we'll find out about it? I mean, what's the most likely way that we'll establish contact?"

"I think the most likely way that we'll find out about intelligent aliens won't be contact, strictly. I think that if we receive any transmission from outer space, they'll be so old that whoever sent them will be long dead. It's just not possible for a transmission to cross such a vast distance in a short enough amount of time."

"Why not? Can't there theoretically be some sort of transmission that approaches the speed of light?"

"Well, the best transmission medium would be light itself. You could modulate a laser beam in such a way as to transmit binary code, for instance. But you'd still be limited by the speed of light itself, which is 186,000 miles per second. Proxima Centauri is the closest star, and that's still four light years away. It would take eight years just to have a two sentence conversation with someone there. The Alpha Centauri system is, by the way, a likely candidate for life, even though we haven't yet found any planets there."

"Okay, what about being visited by actual aliens?"

"The problem again is how to cross such vast distances. Conventional methods create time dilation, part of Einstein's special theory of relativity. As an object's speed increases, so does it's mass. The faster it goes, the more energy is required to keep it moving. It also creates time dilation, so time passes more slowly for the object than the rest of the universe relative to it. If a ship leaves Earth, achieves say three-quarters light speed, then comes back, hundreds of years could have passed on Earth. The trip did, in fact, take hundreds of years, only the crew is lucky enough to survive it. I forget the exact measurements."

"That's okay."

"To actually travel in space with any usefulness, you'd have to circumvent normal space entirely. You'd have to beat the system, so to speak, so that time dilation didn't effect you. I have my own theories on how that might be possible, but we're still probably decades if not centuries away from finding a method that actually works. Science fiction television and movies have provided their own theories of faster-than-light travel. All of them would require massive amounts of energy to work."

"We've been beaming out transmissions for years," said John. "Wouldn't we have heard back from Alpha Centauri by now if there was an industrialized civilization there?"

"One would hope so. If there is one, they're either ignoring us or responding in a way that we can't interpret yet. They might be jumping up and down in a television studio shouting 'look over here,' but we're not tuned to the right channel. That's what SETI is doing, they're looking for intelligent patterns of radio signals received here on Earth."

"What if," began Ari, "aliens sent some sort of object to Earth at sub-light speed? It may not get here for hundreds of years but at least we'd know they exist."

"I suppose that's possible, as long as their only goal was to let themselves be known. It might be meant as a way of kicking humanity in the ass about developing better space technology."

"If that object ended up in the United States, what would happen?"

"What do you mean?"

John began glaring at Ari. She caught the expression out of the corner of her eye, and ignored the intended message.

"I mean who would study it?"

"Well, NASA probably. The CIA or some other agency might want to keep it a secret, to prevent panic or to avoid it being stolen or sabotaged. There are a lot of people who think this has already happened. Look at the Roswell story."

"Do you believe that story?"

"Not really. It seems to me that given fifty-five or so years since it happened there would be something else to look at, or another event or point of contact. I can hardly believe the government could do that good of a job covering up something of that significance."

"Ari, are you sure you know how to get there?" asked John abruptly.

"I think so."

"You'd better pay attention. There are a couple of blind corners we have to take."

"As you wish."

Ten minutes later, John was following the Ford back on Route 93. He was able to pull Ari aside for a moment when they stopped, and tell her to stop her line of questioning with Christie. It may have seemed like idle banter, but they couldn't risk Christie suspecting any more until they arrived. Ari had rolled her eyes and agreed to change the subject. John was starting to wonder if bringing Christie along was such a good idea. What if she freaked out and ran away? They could hardly kidnap her over this.

John threw a CD into the stereo and tried to concentrate on driving. He had catnapped in the Ford but it seemed to do little for him. John really wished he could further mitigate Ari's conversation topics, finding himself short on faith that she would avoid anything too revealing.

John concentrated on the test presented by Seth. He suspected that Umber was located in the Large Magellanic Cloud, and that was the answer to the riddle. He was hoping that if a more precise answer was required that Christie could provide it. She seemed familiar with it, at least enough to name two of it's features. John wondered how to present this information to Seth. Could they simply show him the book? Did they have to point it out on a chart? Did they have to provide the stellar coordinates?

John began to accept the fact that the orb might be a job for NASA after all. Who were they to jeopardize something this important to humanity?

The truly terrifying thing was the prospect of being taken back to Seth's homeworld. John didn't find the prospect of being transported across thousands of light years particularly appealing. Besides, what he knew about the Heisenberg principle made that impossible. Then again, there was the orb, sitting in the New Hampshire woods. Even if the orb could find willing volunteers, what good could humans, with their current level of technology, do for the Umberians?

John realized that he'd left his pipe at the cabin, and what he really needed was a good smoke. It always helped him think, and nicotine was handy for staying awake. If it had occurred to him, he would have asked Ari for one of her clove cigarettes.

It was going to be a long two hours.

The time approached one in the afternoon, and Ray was starting to think about lunch. He was sitting on the front steps of the cabin, smoking his pipe. This habit he shared with John, but much less frequently than his friend. Ray preferred aromatic tobaccos, which smelled wonderful. It also tasted like recycled crap, a fact that caused Ray to prefer his pipe with an alcoholic beverage of some type. At this moment, though, he felt like alcohol would be too much of a crutch for dealing with what was going on. Ray had chosen cola instead.

It had been about an hour since the last time Ray had checked on the orb. Nothing had changed. As John and Ari had said, it was barely visible in the daylight. Ray wondered if they could access it at all during the day. Somehow working with it at night seemed more appropriate, if more daunting.

Ray was worried about their conversations with the thing known as Seth. The last few times it spoke it sounded more authoritarian. If it was learning their language, then eventually it would be able to make demands. If they lost control over it, that would be a whole new ball game. The thought was not comforting.

An approaching sound made Ray's heart leap into his throat. An instant later he realized it was a vehicle. He was tempted to go get a weapon. If it was a stranger, however, that might give the wrong impression. Then again, nobody but John and Ari had any reason to come up their road.

The Ford appeared while Ray was still debating his choices. He was relieved to see them; the last few hours had not been very much fun. Ray was not surprised to see John's car as well, that was a move that made sense. What surprised Ray was the additional woman and a wolf that jumped out of the truck. He stood up straight, almost dropping his pipe.

"Hello, Ray," said Ari.

"What's all this?" asked Ray, unabashedly confused.

"This is Christie Tolliver. She's the assistant professor of astronomy at Suffolk University."

"I remember you," said Christie. "You were in the same class as the rest of us, senior year. I was the teacher's assistant for Astronomy 101."

"You'll forgive me if I don't remember you," said Ray.

John closed his car door and headed over. "Professor Tolliver is here to take a look at the meteorite, Ray."

"The meteor... oh... oh! Right, the meteorite."

Ari placed her hand on her forehead, out of view of Christie.

"Call me Christie. Don't worry about your cut of the profit, by the way. The others and I have already come to an agreement."

"What do you mean, my cut of the profit?" Ray said, grinning around his pipe. "I'm getting a cut?"

"So, where is this thing?"

"Why don't you tie Tycho to the cabin?" said John. "He can run around later."

"Okay."

Christie tied Tycho's leash to one of the cabin's supports. John motioned towards the woods.

"Right this way. Are you coming, Ray?"

"Sure."

"I'll be right there," said Ari, and went inside the cabin.

"Don't be long!" John said.

John led the group into the woods. Tycho barked at them. Ari came running over before they arrived at the orb. The woods were filled with the sound of birds, a welcome addition over last night's eerie silence. They filed into the clearing. John stopped.

"Well, what are we looking for?" asked Christie.

"You're looking at it," said Ari.

"What?"

Christie looked around. She shrugged in annoyed frustration and was about to say something when she caught a glimpse of the orb out of the corner of her eye. Christie squinted.

"Did you guys see some..."

The orb became fully visible. Christie cleared about six vertical inches, inhaling sharply.

"Oh my God!" she screamed.

Ari smiled. "Welcome to the fold."

10.

Birds fled into the air in search of a quieter place. Christie stumbled backwards until her arms found a tree. She pressed herself up against the bark.

"What the hell is this?" she said breathlessly. "What's going on?"

"It's okay," said John.

"This is what we wanted you to see," said Ray.

Their manner was far too calm for Christie's liking. She was hardly reassured.

"That is not a meteorite," she said.

"You figured that, huh?" Ari said.

"What is it?"

"We don't know for sure," began John, "but it came down from space last night. We discovered how to interact with it and we've been learning from each other."

"What do you mean, came down from space? How have you been talking to it.?"

Handprints appeared on the surface of the orb. John approached it. There were four prints instead of three.

"It would be easier if we could show you," John said. "Guys, it wants all four of us to touch it this time."

"This is crazy," said Christie. "I'm not getting near that thing."

"It's perfectly safe," Ray said. "We've been interacting with it and we're fine."

Ray walked over and put his hand on the orb.

"See?" said John. "It's okay. We need to place our hands on it in order to talk to it."

"This is why you wanted me up here? I can see why you lied to me. I don't think I want to be part of this, whatever the hell is going on here."

"Christie," began Ray, "there's something going on here of great importance. We don't understand what it is yet, but we need your help. There are questions being asked that we can't answer. Only you can help us."

"I don't think so," Christie said. "You can find someone else to sucker. I'm getting the hell out of here."

Christie made a step back towards the cabin.

"Put your hand on the orb," said Ari, producing John's Beretta from her waistband.

"Jesus, Ari, what the hell?" shouted John.

"Lower the weapon, Ari!" Ray yelled.

"You people are crazy," said Christie. "This whole thing is crazy. What are you trying to do with me?"

"Call it positive reinforcement," said Ari, "now do as I say."

"Nobody is forcing anyone to do anything," said John.

"For God's sake, Ari," said Ray, "is this the impression we want to make on visitors from another planet?"

"Seth doesn't know his ass from his elbow," Ari said. "He only understands what happens inside there. I, for one, am sick of playing this game with the esteemed professor here. Do us all a favor, quit giving us this bullshit, and put your hand on the orb."

John stormed over to Ari. "I won't have this kind of behavior, Ari! You cannot point a weapon at an innocent woman! If you do this we'll never be able to trust you with a weapon again."

Ari smirked. "Isn't it a bit late now?"

John lowered his voice a bit. "No, it's not. I want Christie's help just as much as you. But this has to be her decision. We can't force her to do anything against her will. That's a crime and it's not right."

Ari sighed. She gestured in capitulation, and allowed John to take the Beretta. John handed off the pistol to Ray and turned to Christie.

"I'm sorry about this, Christie. We're all a little strung out over this. I hope you can understand why we had to lie to you to get you up here. The lies stop here. This orb is some sort of intelligence from beyond our knowledge. It says it needs our help. And we need yours."

"I think you'll understand that I'm having a hard time trusting you people," Christie said.

"Yes. First of all, no more intimidation." John drew the Glock. "Ray, take the pistols inside and come back, please."

"Christ, everybody's got a gun."

Ray headed back through the trees.

"That's got nothing to do with this," said John. "Look, this orb contains an entity. Last night we interacted with it and began to learn from each other. It appears to be learning our language and how we operate. It asked us a question and we can't provide the answer."

"Where is Umber," said Ari. "It wants us to locate its home."

Christie took a step closer. "That's what you were looking for in the textbook. What made you think that's where the answer was?"

"It's hard to explain," said John, "but the orb showed us where the answer was, or that we already had the answer and that we needed to look in the book to remember it."

"And the answer is the Large Magellanic Cloud?"

"That's what we're hoping."

John looked at the orb. There were still four handprints on it.

"If the answer is more complicated than that, then we might need you to help answer it," said Ari.

"How do I know that you're not still lying to me?" asked Christie.

"I don't know," said John, "I guess you'll just have to take a chance."

Ray returned from the cabin.

"Weapons have been stowed," he said.

John gestured towards Ray. "Christie, Ray is a police officer. He didn't know that we were bringing you and he didn't know that we lied to you. Don't hold him responsible for our actions."

"That's true," said Ray. "I was quite surprised to see you get out of my truck."

"Listen," began John, "if you want to leave, okay. Ray will drive you home. You can even file a report with the police against us if you choose. We won't stop you. Just please help us first. Take a look at what's going on here and then make up your mind."

Christie put her hands on her hips. "All right. I'll try it. But only because I suspect the three of you will bury me if I don't."

"Thank you. Guys, let's do it."

John and Ari put their hands on the orb. Ray joined them.

"Come on, it's peer pressure," said Ari, joining the others, "you can't resist."

"This is insane," Christie said, and planted her palm on the sphere.

There was darkness. Christie thought that someone had thrown a bag over her head. She grasped at her face, and found it unimpeded. She took a step forward and her foot banged into something.

"Ow, crap," she heard herself say.

"Christie, are you here?"

It was John's voice. Christie turned her head around. Something was becoming visible.

"Where are we this time?" said Ari.

Christie realized that her eyes were adjusting to the dark. A large oblong shape loomed before her. She stepped back, then recognized it. It was a Zeiss projector.

"We're... in a planetarium," she said.

"Oh, yeah," said Ray.

"You're right," said John. "When did we all go to the planetarium?"

"We didn't," said Ari.

"Not together, anyway," said Ray. "Did you ever go, Ari?"

"Yeah, with Silas."

"So we've all been here, at some point," John said.

"How did we get here?" asked Christie. She could see the others in the slowly dissolving shadows.

"It's an illusion," began John, "a memory. This is what happened before, only we were in a pub we all used to like."

"Hello," said someone. The voice was loud and seemed to come from everywhere at once.

"Hello Seth," said John and Ray.

"What's that?" asked Christie.

"That's the entity," said John. "We've been calling it Seth for lack of a better name."

Christie's heart leaped as she caught sight of Seth. He was standing behind the Zeiss projector control panel. He had been speaking into the microphone for the public address system.

"Hello, Seth," Christie said.

"You are new," said Seth.

"Yes, I'm Christie. How are you?"

"I am Seth."

"He's a little slow on the uptake," said Ari.

Christie walked towards Seth. As she approached him, Seth smiled.

"He's so... strange," Christie said.

"We think it's a representation of the three of us," said John, "sort of morphed together into one form."

"It's more than that. He's too perfect. I think he's more than just a visual combination."

"Why?"

"John has green eyes," Christie began, "Ari has black hair, and Ray has connected earlobes. Seth has them all."

"You think he's an actual representation of our... our, um, child?"

"Sort of."

"So is he really a he?" Ari asked, smiling.

"Are you male or female, Seth?" asked Christie.

"I am Seth."

"You wanna get him to strip down?" asked Ari.

Seth pressed some keys on the control panel. The Zeiss projector lit up and began to move. A starfield of the night sky appeared on the overhead dome. As soon as this happened, the dome seemed to melt away. Christie could clearly see the Milky Way.

"I guess he doesn't care to discuss it," said Ray.

"Look at this," Christie said, stunned. "This is far more than the Zeiss projector is capable of."

"Find me," said Seth.

"You're in the Large Magellanic Cloud," John said.

"Where?"

It was a truly odd thing for Seth to say, since he'd said the word with much more emotion in it than usual.

"Right ascension five hours, twenty-three point six minutes," said Christie. "Declination negative sixty-nine degrees, forty-five minutes."

"Damn, you're good," said Ray.

"I looked it up in the car."

The Zeiss projector whirred and spun around. The sky moved in a rather disorientating way. Christie was enraptured.

"Quite impressive," said John.

"We should be seeing the southern hemisphere. There it is."

Christie pointed straight up. In the center of the sky was a faint blur. The sky began to move again and started to get closer to the cloud. The feeling of movement was inescapable this time and all four of them were forced to sit down. The movement stopped when the cloud filled the entire hemisphere. The upper right hand corner of the cloud was particularly spectacular.

"It's beautiful," said Ari.

"How close are we?" asked Ray.

"I don't know," replied Christie. "This looks like at least a hundred magnification. But it's not magnified. It's as if we were actually that close, maybe ten or twenty thousand light years."

"Home," said Seth.

"Nice place you got here," said Ray.

"One more test."

The dome went black, and then everything disappeared. A shape materialized. It looked like a racquetball with a toothpick sticking out of it. At the end of the toothpick was what looked like a smaller ball of Styrofoam.

"What the hell is this?" Ari's voice said.

Christie laughed. "This is my ninth grade science fair project. It's supposed to represent a hydrogen atom. One proton and one electron."

The image changed. This time, there were two Styrofoam balls sticking out.

"I never did this one," said Christie, "but it's obviously helium."

The image changed to three balls.

"I don't know about you guys, but if this keeps going like this we're going to be shit out of luck before too long."

"Good thing I'm here," said John's voice. "I got an A-plus in high school chemistry. That's got to be lithium."

The pictures showing continued to grow in complexity. John rattled off the names of the elements, singing a familiar tune as he did so.

"Beryllium, boron, carbon, nitrogen, oxygen, fluorine, neon, sodium, magnesium, aluminum, silicon, phosphorus... uh, sulfur, chlorine, argon, potassium..."

The image did not change.

"I think you got that one wrong," said Ray's voice.

"Bullshit, I memorized up to zinc for my science project. That's why I'm singing, 'Row, row your boat.' That's how I remembered it. Potassium is after argon."

"Count the electrons," said Christie. "There are twenty of them."

"Ha! Seth, you bastard, you skipped a couple. Argon, potassium... calcium!"

The image changed.

"Nice one," Ray said.

John began the song again. "Scandium, titanium, vanadium... chromium,"

"Gently down the stream," said Ari.

"Do you mind? Um, manganese, iron, cobalt, nickel, copper, zinc, merrily, merrily, life is but a dream."

The darkness melted away, and they were back in the woods.

Ari blinked in the brightness of the sun. Everything looked exactly as it had before. Apparently, once again no time had passed inside the orb. Ari looked over at Ray.

"Was that it?" she asked.

"I don't know," Ray replied. "Christie?"

Christie rubbed her eyes. "I guess so. I wonder why we stopped at zinc."

"Maybe those are all the elements that Seth needs for... John!"

The others looked down. John was lying on the ground, his eyes closed.

"John!" Ray said, kneeling down beside him.

"Is he okay?"

Ari took John's hand. "John, are you all right?"

"He's still breathing," said Ray. "Maybe he..."

John sat upright so fast his head almost collided with Ray's. His eyes were wide open and he looked shocked.

"John?" said Ray. "Are you okay?"

"I am Seth," he said.

Dana Andrews yawned. It was way too beautiful of a Sunday to be trapped inside, but it was an imprisonment of her own choosing. She was intent to review audio file number 315, which was recorded on Friday, but she had to wait. It was a rather unremarkable file other than it came from her favorite part of the sky, among the constellation Cygnus. It also appeared to have a repeating pattern. This by itself was also not remarkable. There was something about this one, however, that caught her attention. She couldn't stay on Friday because she was taking her mother to the movies. It was something with cowboys, she remembered, and it had Kevin Costner in it.

Saturday was a washout, literally. Dana had laundry to do and her bathroom was in desperate need of cleaning. After that she didn't have the energy to drive to the lab, and crashed in front of the television for the rest of the day.

Sunday morning she had awoken with renewed vigor, and had rushed off to work after a quick shower and teeth brushing. She was also able to wear casual clothing, which was a huge bonus. Of course, it was unlikely that there would be anyone else there on a Sunday morning. Except for Levi.

Levi Marks was a colleague of Dana's. He shared her zeal for work, and often devoted his personal time to the research. Dana would hesitate to call him a friend, but they were affable enough to each other. The only time Dana tried to open up to him, he'd wandered away quietly while Dana informed her computer monitor about some of her mother's more annoying attributes.

Dana and Levi worked for a local chapter of the American Space Transmission Research Association, which drew it's funds from the equally local Lehigh University. This meant loads of college kids visiting and participating on a regular basis. It didn't bother Dana in the least, but it left Levi wishing for more privacy.

When Dana arrived that morning, therefore, she was surprised that Levi wasn't there. She expected he would arrive shortly. As the afternoon wore on, Dana had forgotten Levi and was engrossed in studying file 315. She had converted the wave patterns into a more useful visual format, and listened to the actual audio over and over again while she examined the pictures. There was a definite pattern to it, but it wasn't anything she could identify herself.

That meant a much more time consuming process of turning the data into a form usable by an algorithm program. That program would search for more recognizable patterns much more quickly than a human ever could, since it was programmed to search for binary information. Levi was better at using it and Dana began to hope that he'd make an appearance soon.

Dana's computer beeped. She had an incoming e-mail. Dana saved her work and opened the message. It was from a very small chapter of ASTRA operating outside of Atlanta, Georgia. It was addressed to all other ASTRA members and was had an audio file attached. The audio file was labeled "interesting.mp3."

"Hello, Dana," said Levi.

Dana swiveled around in her chair to face the man. Levi was about forty years old, and bore a full beard. He always reminded Dana of a cartoon character, in a good way.

"Good afternoon, Levi. What have you been up to?"

"This and that. You?"

"I've just been reviewing one of the audio files we collected Friday. It's gripping my mind."

"Nice."

Levi, in typical fashion, walked away without any ceremony. Dana turned back to her computer and opened the e-mail.

> To: usergroupall@astra.com
> From: shermansucks@astra.com
>
> Here is an audio file that I recorded on Friday night. We can confirm that it originated in the area of Ursa Minor. It has a pattern to it that is interesting, to say the least.

Dana opened the attachment and sent the file to her mp3 player. She clicked on play, and a very familiar sound met her ears. Dana stood up rapidly, knocking her chair across the room. Levi leaned over from his desk and caught it before it rolled into a network server.

"Are you planning on a repeat of last year's Christmas party?" he said.

"Listen to this, Levi! This is the exact same signal that we recorded on Friday."

"So it would seem."

"Yeah, but this one came from the Atlanta stations."

"Good. That means that they weren't asleep at the switch."

Dana crossed the room to Levi.

"Yeah, but they recorded a *different* origin point!"

"That is interesting."

Levi stood up and walked over to Dana's computer.

"Do you know what this means?"

"Yes," said Levi. "It means that the origin point was not Cygnus."

"Exactly. They recorded it as coming from Ursa Minor."

"That means that what we have is, in fact, a two point match on a new set of coordinates."

Dana sat down at her desk and procured a piece of paper. She began drawing a diagram.

"Okay," she said, "if we're here in Bethlehem, and they're down there in Atlanta... we know that when we made our recording, Deneb was directly overhead, at ninety degrees. Where was Ursa Minor for them at the same time?"

"I'm going to have to look that up," said Levi. He returned to his desk and began working on his computer. It didn't take him long to find the answer.

"Twenty-five degrees above horizon."

Dana scribbled. "Okay, then we draw a line from there to here to get the long side of the triangle. That'll be c, the sine of the curve of the Earth will be a, and the direct distance between us and Atlanta will be b."

Dana's tone had become much less enthusiastic. She had realized that this meant the most likely source of the transmission was an ordinary artificial satellite.

"Do you know the distance between us and Atlanta?"

"No, but I can look it up."

Leaning back in her chair, Dana sighed. She had become excited over nothing. Levi typed at his keyboard behind her. He soon returned to her side.

"That's about seven hundred and sixty miles."

"I need my calculator," Dana said, opening a desk drawer. "Okay, now we know can draw a straight line between A and B, and that changes our number slightly. The reverse angle is sixty-five, the sine of sixty-five is point-nine-three-nine, so the hypotenuse becomes eight hundred thirty and change. Then we use the Pythagorean Theorem..."

Dana worked silently for a few moments. She punched a few keys on her calculator and bit the end of her pen.

"You're cheating," said Levi, smirking.

"Don't distract me, Levi."

"I'm serious. Your method is fine for a rough estimate, but considering your background, you should be processing the proper orbital elements with either the perifocal coordinate system or the topocentric-horizon coordinate system. How else can you create a data set appropriate for coordinate transformations?"

Levi held up a worn, dog-eared copy of a book entitled *Fundamentals of Astrodynamics* to make his point. Dana grimaced at him.

"If this turns out to be something," she replied, "I'll do the proper grunt work. You know how much I hate longhand. Anyway, according to the data from Atlanta, the source of the transmission was three hundred and fifty-one miles above us."

"That puts it well above the ionosphere. That's well within the confines of low Earth orbit and common for satellites."

"Yeah, I figured we were probably dealing with a satellite when I heard you say twenty-five degrees above horizon. It's still an odd transmission type for a satellite. It doesn't fit into any of the commonly used wavelengths. Plus the fact that it was a burst transmission of only three seconds."

"It's possible that a satellite's radio transmitter blew out. That could cause a sudden spike in wavelength. What we might be hearing are some poor radio's death throes."

"I guess it's possible. I'll start crawling around the 'net and see if I can find out if any satellites shit the bed on Friday."

Dana saved the Atlanta file as 315-B and closed the audio program. Hiding beneath it was the receiver data program. Dana was stunned by what she saw.

"Levi, look at this. Another signal was recorded not ten minutes ago. It's the same waveform as the last one."

"Really? Where was it this time?"

"Let's see... Atlanta, zero degrees above horizon, bearing zero one five. Bethlehem, zero degrees above horizon, bearing zero four zero. Levi, the source of this transmission is on the surface of the Earth."

"I'll get a map," Levi said.

Dana converted the receiver data into an audio file in the usual fashion. She played the file, and same sound she'd become used to echoed through the room.

"This is very confusing," she said.

Levi brought over a map of the northeast United States. He began plotting the directions from the two receivers. The two directions converged on one point.

"Northern New Hampshire," he said.

"I don't get it. How does a transmission source get from three hundred and fifty miles above the Earth to the ground in New Hampshire in less than forty-two hours?"

"It can't. Only a very select kind of spacecraft are capable of re-entering the Earth's atmosphere without being destroyed. If the origin of this signal is man-made, it would have had to hitch a ride with the space shuttle or the Russians. The US doesn't have anybody up there right now and the Russians don't have any craft due to return this weekend."

"So what the hell is it?"

11.

"Christie, get the door! Ari, get his legs up over the stairs."

Ray struggled to hold up John's partially limp body as he, Ari and Christie tried to get him inside the cabin. Tycho, who hadn't uttered a peep at John before, was now growling at him. Christie held open the door while Ray and Ari all but shoved John inside. Ray dragged him to a sofa chair and dumped him down. John continued to stare ahead like a drugged maniac.

"John," said Ray, "can you hear me?"

"Yes," said John.

"Are you all right?"

"Yes."

"What's going on?"

"I can see now."

John straightened himself up somewhat. His eyes wandered until he saw Ray.

"Hi, Ray."

"You had us worried there, John," said Ari.

"No reason to worry. Seth is with me."

"What?" said Ray. "What do you mean?"

"Seth is with me. Inside myself."

"Seth... is inside your head?"

"Yes."

"What's he doing there, John?" asked Christie.

"He's showing me things."

"What things?" Ray said.

John looked confused. "I... I can't say. You have to ask me."

"Why is Seth inside your mind, John?"

"To show us the way."

"This is too creepy," Ari said.

Ray swallowed. "John, Seth said that he wanted us to come back to Umber with him. What does he want us to do for Umber?"

"To help us."

103

"We already know that. How does he want us to help Umber?"

"By coming back with us."

"Not again," said Ari.

John held up his hand. "Wait. I'm sorry. I don't think Seth knows why. We keep coming up with the same endless answers."

"How could Seth not know the reason for his mission?" said Christie.

"He could be misleading us," said Ari. "He may not want us to know the reason. It might be too horrible for any of us to accept."

"I don't sense any deception," John said. "We simply do not know the reason why."

"That's great. Why in the world would anybody put their lives in his hands?"

"I sense a massive amount of confidence from Seth. We don't seem to be capable of lying. We're so sure of the mission. We're also supremely confident that you guys are going to say yes."

"Not without a lot more information," said Ray.

"How are we going to get to Umber, exactly?" asked Christie.

"You go with Seth," said John.

"You're just going to 'beam' us there?" Ari said, laughing.

"No. There will be a ship."

"A ship?" asked Ray. "A ship will be coming?"

"No."

"Then where do we get the ship?"

"If you build it, they will come."

"What?"

"I'm sorry, I couldn't resist that one. Seth is telling me that you, I mean we, have to build the ship."

"Are you shitting me?" Ari said. "Perhaps Seth is unaware of the fact that the culmination of trillions of dollars and the efforts of the best astrophysical engineers in the world can only put unmanned robots on our nearest neighbors? How does he expect us to travel to another galaxy?"

"Hold on," John said, "We're having a hard time interpreting what Seth is trying to communicate."

"That made no sense."

John furrowed his brow. "A shell, an outer shell. A hull! We can make the hull and the... 'go-box?' No, that's not right. The driver. The engine. That's it. Seth can make the outer hull and the engine. You have to provide everything else."

"We are truly out of our league now," said Ray.

"We're not..."

John stood up, grabbing his head.

"John?"

"No, don't. I can't... Seth!"

John stumbled forward, and before Ray could grab him John sprinted out the front door. Ray and the others took off after him. John was headed back towards the orb.

"John!" yelled Ray, slowly gaining, "John, what's wrong?"

John ran up to the orb, which reappeared just before John smacked his palm against it. Almost immediately, he collapsed on the ground. Ray knelt beside him as Ari and Christie caught up.

"John, talk to me," Ray said.

John shook his head. "That," he said, "was not cool."

"What happened?"

"Seth tried to probe deeper into my head. He knew I knew how to design aircraft. He tried to help me use that knowledge. But it all came too quickly. I couldn't handle it. It was like all my avionics training, every memory of CAD, aircraft design, and playing flight sims was flashing in my head simultaneously. It was all I could do to run back here. Seth must have realized he was hurting me because he went back into the orb right away."

"Hopefully he won't try that again."

"I don't want to give him the chance. That entire experience was horrible. You try sharing a space meant for one mind."

"Well, maybe we can take turns," said Ari, "or insist on communicating with Seth only while inside the orb."

"Is that an option?" asked Ray.

"I don't know," said John. "All I know is that Seth was very happy to be part of my consciousness. It felt like... a childhood home. At least that's what I sensed he was feeling."

John stood up, fighting for balance.

"Easy there."

"I have to try again. We've got to find a way to make this work."

"Not right now. You need a break."

"Okay."

Ray took John's arm and led him to the cabin. Christie watched as the orb faded into its shadow state.

"We could indeed take turns," said Christie, "not that I want to experience what happened to John, but he can't bear the entire effort."

"So, now you're part of the team?" said Ari.

"I don't know yet. You don't seem to be the best at working together that I can see. I understand why you lied to me, but you shouldn't have threatened me to get your way."

"Well, it worked, didn't it?"

Ari picked up speed and arrived at the cabin first. She held the door for John and Ray. Tycho whimpered at them. Inside, John resumed his place in the sofa chair.

"God, I'm suddenly so tired," he said.

"So take a nap," Ray said. "We have a few things to discuss with Miss Tolliver here that you don't need to be awake for."

John nodded, and began to zone out. Ray offered a seat at the table to Christie. She and Ari sat down. Ray pulled his chair out and turned it around, sitting with his arms folded across the back.

"Christie, I hope that what you've seen will convince you to help us, despite our lack of, er, grace in getting you to participate."

"I can see how you're all a little stressed out," Christie said. "The last couple of days can't have been easy for you."

"Not exactly my best week, actually."

"I'll stick around for now. I'm way too curious to give up on things yet. I'd at least like to find out how Seth expects us to design and outfit our own interstellar spacecraft."

"I think that it's possible," said Ari, "that between the four of us we have what we need. John, you always wanted to design airplanes, right?"

John was asleep.

"That's right," said Ray, "not only was he an avionics technician in the Air Guard, but he also had a love for World War Two aircraft, to the point of studying schematics of some of them just for the hell of it. He also used to create elaborate blueprints for experimental designs. For all that talent, though, he could never get the attention of the right people, and it turned into nothing but a highly educated hobby."

Ari nodded. "Right. He might be able to provide the internal workings of the ship. We could research how they designed the space shuttle and learn how to keep the ship airtight, pressurized and oxygenated. Since Seth is apparently nothing more than a glorified stardrive, we don't have to worry about propulsion. I can't believe I'm even talking like this, this is totally frigging crazy."

"It's just talk," said Ray. "It can't hurt. I keep thinking that we should turn this project over to NASA, too. But another part of me is greedy and doesn't want to share. Like we said before, they'd probably lock us up somewhere so we wouldn't blab the secret to the evening news. They'd probably turn John into a Guinea pig, come to think of it."

"We're either totally in, or totally out," said Christie. "There's no in between."

"We need to consider how we're going to plan this. I'm on administrative leave indefinitely, so I don't have to worry about my job. I can work on the ship from here for the next few weeks if need be. Ari and John took the day off tomorrow, but somehow I think that this project is going to take a lot longer than forty-eight hours to finish. Christie, I presume you have to go back to work tomorrow."

"Yes."

"Then we're all going to have to decide how we want to handle our lives. Do either of you have any vacation time coming up?"

"I have two weeks," said Ari.

"I'm a college professor," said Christie, "and it's the middle of the semester. My vacation is summer."

"It will be a tough call for you, then," Ray said. "You could participate on the weekends, I suppose."

"Maybe. I don't know. As far as tomorrow is concerned, it won't matter if I don't show up for one class. I'll have to answer for not calling in but that's no big deal."

"We can take a drive over to Fairlee if you want to use a phone. Call in sick."

"Okay, fine. I will."

"There's something we're not considering in all this," Ari said.

"What's that?" asked Ray.

"If we're going to build this ship on our own, and provide everything we need from the shell up, where the hell are we going to get all the materials?"

"This is a wild goose chase, Dana."

Levi moved out of the way as Dana reached for a micro-recorder on the desk behind him. She threw the device into a backpack and walked back over to her computer.

"It's my time to waste, Levi. And I really think it's worth checking out."

"What if we made some sort of miscalculation? What if Atlanta got something wrong? Never mind the fact that you'll be acting as a member of ASTRA. What about the reputation of the organization?"

Dana walked up to Levi, plucked a pen from his shirt, and placed it in her pack.

"I'll be acting independently. Don't worry about the precious organization."

"Do you have any idea how long it's going to take you to get up to those coordinates? That's at least seven hours. You won't even get there until ten o'clock at night."

"So what?"

"So, are you going to spend the night up there? If so, where? Are you going to sleep in your car?"

Dana stopped collecting things and turned around. "Why are you giving me such a hard time about this?"

"I don't want to see you put yourself through a lot of trouble for nothing, that's why."

"Fine, if I come back empty-handed, you can say 'I told you so.'"

"Is there nothing I can do to change your mind?"

"Doesn't seem like it, does it?"

"Then I'm coming with you."

Dana smiled wistfully, and said, "Suddenly you think this expedition has merit?"

"I'm not going to let a young girl wander around in the woods by herself."

"I can handle myself."

"With what? Your car keys? Your cell phone? Sorry, Dana, they won't do you much good out there."

"I can hardly see you in the role of Grizzly Adams, Levi."

"I know more about that sort of thing than you do, that's a safe bet."

"Is that why you spend most of your time locked away in this lab?"

"I've got what, fifteen years on you? I didn't always work with ASTRA, you know."

"No, Levi, I don't know. You never talk to me about yourself and you don't seem interested in hearing about me, either."

"I didn't think it was appropriate."

"Grabbing my ass is inappropriate. Asking about my life is just polite."

"We're going to have plenty of time in the car together to make up for that."

"I don't want you coming along, Levi."

Levi looked genuinely hurt. "I didn't realize you disliked me that much."

"I like you just fine. I just don't see the point in both of us going up there. If we don't get back early enough tomorrow morning there won't be anyone around to open the lab."

"So, the lab can open late for once. Big deal. I want to come."

"Yeah, you only want to be there when I find out I'm wrong."

Dana couldn't help but smile. Levi looked relieved.

"That's right."

"Okay, fine. Your car or mine?"

12.

The sun was setting, and Ray was getting tired of waiting. John had been sleeping for more than four hours. Ari had followed his lead and snored gently in the other room. Christie was playing with Tycho out on the hill.

Ray may have been bored, but he wasn't about to wake up John before he was ready. The orb hadn't been interested in talking to the rest of them, as evident by the lack of any palm prints when approached. Ray was worried that the orb had chosen John as its only source of binding. Ray was happy to let John be the conduit. It hardly seemed fair, however, to force it upon him.

Ray had driven Christie to Fairlee a couple of hours before, where she made a phone call to Suffolk University. That being taken care of, Ray had busied himself setting up the last spare bed. Christie would have to sleep out in the common room, which was hardly a great inconvenience as that's where the woodstove was. Ray was impressed that even after everything that had happened to her, Christie was still able to run around, rough-house, and laugh with Tycho.

"Man, I feel like shit," said John, appearing in the doorway.

"You're finally up," said Ray.

"What time is it?"

"Almost six o'clock."

"Damn. I've been up for a little while, actually. I was busy."

"What, busy fapping it? I didn't hear anything."

"I had some weird dreams..."

"I'll bet."

"I dreamed I was talking with Shadrach, Meshach, and Abednigo. The three friends who were thrown into the fiery furnace by Nebudcanezzar in the book of Daniel."

"I remember the story."

"I was standing with them in the fire. They were telling me to build a ship."

John held up a piece of paper. There were diagrams drawn in pencil on it.

"Oh, that's what you were doing."

John handed Ray the paper. On it was a diagram of three floors of a ship, as well as front, side, and rear views of the exterior. Above it John had written *Reckless Faith*.

"Reckless Faith?" said Ray.

"Throwing yourself into the fire with no regard for the apparent consequences."

Ray looked over the drawings. "I like it. I notice you have six crew's quarters here on deck one."

"Room to grow, I guess."

"You've also got an armory here as part of deck three."

"The crew should be armed, right?"

"Oh, absolutely. Unless Seth informs us otherwise, the crew should be ready for anything."

"What about external weaponry?"

"Seth said all he was supplying was the hull and engine."

Ari appeared from the other room.

"Coffee," she said.

"Filters are above the stove," said Ray. "Coffee is in the cabinet. Use the basket filter and a small pot."

Ari busied herself with this task. Christie came inside, her cheeks red from the cold.

"I see everyone's finally awake," she said.

"Have a seat," said Ray, "John has come up with a preliminary design for the ship."

"So then," began John, "any external weapons would have to be of Earth design. And I don't know about you guys, but anything worth having is way outside our price range and ability to obtain. The best thing we could do is get a semi-automatic fifty caliber BMG, and then what? Roll down the window to fire it?"

"Okay, so external weapons may be out of the question. Maybe we could simply outrun trouble."

"We don't even know what trouble is waiting for the crew of this ship," said Ari.

"I agree," said Christie. "Until Seth tells us more about the mission we should focus on the basics."

Ray asked, "Why is everyone talking about 'the crew?' Aren't we planning on manning this ship?"

There was silence. After a few seconds, John spoke.

"I don't know about anybody else, but I'm not going to make up my mind just yet. The unknowns are still too great. We don't know how far we're going, how long it's going to take, and if we're even going to be able to come home."

"I'd take that chance," said Ray. "I'm in. I don't have anything left on this planet that I care about not counting those present."

Christie raised an eyebrow. She hadn't expected Ray to say that.

"I agree with Ray," said Ari. "I happen to be in a position to drop everything myself."

John asked, "How about you, Christie?"

Christie put her chin in her hand, and replied, "I'm going to help build this thing, for a while anyway. I may decide this mission is way beyond my ability to handle and bow out. As far as leaving Earth, I'm not too keen on the idea."

"Whomever ends up going may want to recruit help later," said John.

"That sounds like a good idea," Ray said, "But where are you going to get volunteers? Hover the ship over Times Square?"

"I don't know."

"Why don't we present the design to Seth," Ari said, "and see what he thinks?"

"I don't know if I'm ready for another session playing host to Seth," said John.

"We don't have any other choice," said Ray.

"We tried to access it," Christie said, "it seems to want you."

John sighed. "Fine, I'll try it. This design, however, isn't to scale. I need to draft an actual blueprint. And, by the way, if we're supplying all the internals to this thing, how are we going to build the floors? What about the walls? I learned a little bit about aircraft structural repair but that's about the extent of my construction knowledge."

"Maybe Seth can do the hull and the layout of the rooms," said Ari.

"All right, let's go ask him."

John led the way out of the cabin. The others followed him through the fading light into the woods. As John approached the orb, it became fully visible. A single handprint appeared on the orb.

"No," said John. "All of us."

There was a pause, and three more palms appeared. John motioned for the others to take their places. Together they put their hands into place.

It was apparent right away that they were back in the planetarium. The Zeiss projector beamed light like a supine Christmas tree. There was a new image on the dome of a colorful nebula with snaking and looping wisps of smoky light. Seth was at his place behind the Zeiss controls. John tiptoed around the chairs in the dim room and walked over to Seth.

"It's the Tarantula Nebula," said Christie. "It's one of the features of the Large Magellanic Cloud."

"Home," said Seth.

"Seth," began John, "I don't want you going through my head like you did before. It was very unpleasant. If you need to share my mind that's fine, but I call the shots while you're in there. Understood?"

Seth blinked.

"Clearly he does not," said Ray.

"You do not want to be one with me?" Seth said blankly.

"If it's the only way of communicating effectively with you outside this place, then I agree to it," said John. "I would simply like to maintain control of my thoughts and memories at all times."

"We also want to take turns, so that John gets a break," said Ray.

Seth looked at them. "John is better."

"I knew that already," said John, grinning.

"Tycho is best."

John, Ari, Ray and Christie expressed various forms of surprise.

"You mean the dog Tycho?" said John.

"The one named Tycho," said Seth. "John has... room for me. Tycho has more room."

"We can use the dog as a host?" said Ari. "That's fantastic!"

"Wait a minute," began Christie, "how the hell is Tycho supposed to talk to us? Dogs don't have nearly as sophisticated vocal chords as humans, not to mention the lack of lips."

"You will hear him," said Seth.

"What do you mean, like telepathy?" asked Ray.

Seth thought about this for several moments.

"Yes. In your mind."

"So why don't we go get Tycho and deal with Seth that way?"

"Wait a minute," said Christie, "how do we know that this is safe for Tycho?"

"How do we know it's safe for any of us?" John said.

"Fair enough," said Ray. "What we do know is that interacting in this illusion world isn't physically or mentally demanding, not like what we saw John go through."

"You got that right," said John.

"So why don't we continue working with Seth right here? We can start using our brains like canteens when we need to take Seth places.

"I cannot be taken places," said Seth. "I am bound to the ship. I can go only... two hundred thirty seven point three five feet from the ship."

"So then we put the orb in the truck," said John. "How much can it possibly weigh?"

Ari snickered. "Since when does weight matter? It's floating in midair, remember?"

"Right. Anyway, Seth, we have a proposal for the ship's hull. It's on a piece of paper in my hand outside in the world."

"Then it is here," said Seth.

John looked down. The paper was in his hand.

"That was easy."

John showed the drawing to Seth. Almost immediately the drawing appeared on the overhead dome. Slowly the yellow paper faded away and the pencil drawings became solid. Around them, the planetarium faded to black.

The four found themselves standing in front of a ship. The exterior was a flat gray, and some parts were out of focus and difficult to regard. A large ramp led up into the underside of the ship.

"This is all pretty much what I was imagining earlier," said John.

"It's huge," said Ari.

"It's only ten meters tall by thirty meters long; it's not that big really."

Giant letters appeared in John's handwriting on the ramp.

"Cargo Ramp," Ray read aloud.

"It looks like it's time for the virtual tour," John said. "Care to join me?"

The others nodded and followed John up the ramp. At the top of the ramp, more letters appeared. This time the words read, "Fore Cargo Bay." As they looked around, the floor, walls, and ceiling became better defined. A staircase materialized in front of them, and led up to a doorway that was equally as new. A word appeared on the door.

"Armory," read John. "Right where it should be."

Ten minutes later, or so it seemed, the humans were standing on what was to be the bridge. Each part of the ship that they visited was empty, and the details that they could see were far exceeded by the vagueness of everything else. Most starkly missing were windows of any kind, and when John mentioned this aloud, small portholes appeared along the walls. They looked monumentally stupid.

The bridge was a bit better off in this regard. Large, sloping windows ahead of them gave the impression of a windshield. There was nothing but a black void outside, but it was sufficient to comprehend the opening. Seth, who had been absent from the ship so far, appeared before them.

"This is a good first draft," said Ray.

"What I need is my CAD program," said John, shaking his head. "If I could do this up right, the finished product would all be in my memory to give to Seth."

"This is acceptable," said Seth.

"It's not finished yet. We need more time to design the interior."

"The exterior, as well," said Ray. "Right now it looks like a big gray suppository."

"When you have finished," Seth said, "I will create the hull. These approximate dimensions will require at least the following items: Two hundred tons of iron. One hundred tons of aluminum. Fifty tons of silicon..."

"Wait a minute!" shouted John. "I thought you said you would supply the hull for us!"

"I did. There are insufficient resources present to do so."

"For God's sake," said Ari, "we can't possibly bring you that much stuff."

"Then we will go to it," said Seth.

"Where are we going to find that much raw material?"

"There is approximately zero point zero zero one percent of the needed materials proximate to this location. Carbonic iron and aluminum are present only in small amounts."

"Carbonic iron?" said John. "You mean steel?"

"Yes."

"Well, the only steel present is in our cars and our firearms."

"It is an insufficient amount."

"No shit. So you can just take the materials and transform them into the superstructure of the ship?"

"Yes."

"So he's got a matter replicator, or transporter, or something like that," said Ray.

Seth blinked. "Yes."

"Still," began John, "the question remains. Where are we going to get those materials?"

"I think I know a place," said Ari.

Thirty minutes later, the group had packed up their things and vacated the cabin. They had loaded their gear into both cars, leaving room in the Expedition for the orb. Once they had managed to place the orb in the vehicle, they would be on their way to Woburn. And, after John finished his CAD drawings, Boston.

Boston, as Ari had pointed out, was full of steel, aluminum, and a lot of other useful items. It was also the home of the USS Portland, a decommissioned Navy dock landing ship. According to Ari, who learned this information from an old boyfriend, the ship was destined to be used for target practice. For now, it remained berthed off of Chelsea near the mouth of the Mystic River, a fact that Christie was able to confirm from memory. The plan was to drive up to it with the orb, take the materials, and stand back while the orb transformed it into the hull. Then they could drive the vehicles into the cargo bay and take off. Seth had assured them that once the hull was complete, that it would be hidden from sight. They hadn't asked for an explanation for that one.

John and Ray approached the orb. It glowed faintly in the evening darkness. A single handprint appeared.

"Are you sure you wouldn't rather let Tycho take a crack at this?" asked Ray.

"We can fool around with Tycho and the orb later. Let's stick with what works for now."

John placed his hand on the orb. He instantly stumbled back. Ray grabbed him and held him upright.

"I got you, buddy."

John regained his balance. "We're okay."

"Good."

John began walking through the woods towards the Expedition. The orb followed behind smoothly. When they arrived at the truck, John guided the orb into the back. Ray threw a blanket over it and closed the hatch. Christie and Ari were waiting by John's car.

"Okay," said Ray. "If there are any problems I'll put on the hazard lights and pull over. Be sure to keep enough distance behind me to stop if this should happen."

"Roger," said Ari.

"I'll drive," said John, heading for the left side of the truck.

"I don't think so," said Ray. "It's too crowded upstairs for that."

"Ray, I'm fine. Seth is holding back his force. It's much more comfortable this way."

"I don't want to risk that changing while we're doing seventy down ninety-three."

"We must insist, Ray."

John's face bore a dire expression. Ray shrugged.

"Okay, fine. There's nothing wrong with an alien possessed driver. I don't mind."

Ray gestured towards the driver's door. John got inside.

"Just please tell me," said Ray, getting in, "that you'll tell me if you sense something is wrong."

"Don't worry, I will."

John turned the key and started up the truck. He looked ahead as if confused.

"Yes, John?"

"Why aren't we moving?"

"Maybe you should try putting it in gear and stepping on the gas."

"Aren't we already in gear?"

"No, we're in park..."

The Ford lurched forward about twelve inches. Some of the stuff piled up in the back seat fell over. The cooler hit Ray in the back of the head.

"What the hell was that?" Ray yelled.

"I don't know," said John. "I was thinking about the truck moving."

"You mean, you thought about it and it happened?"

"I think so. Hold on."

John looked ahead and concentrated. The Ford began to roll forward slowly.

"Holy shit," said Ray.

"There's something... wait..."

John grabbed the shifter and placed the truck in neutral. The truck began to move faster. They arrived at the end of the driveway to the cabin. The access road made a sharp left.

"Uh, John? Are you going to turn?"

"I am turning."

"No, you're not!"

At the last moment, Ray pulled the emergency brake. The truck stopped a few inches from a tree.

"Well, that didn't work."

"No shit. John, why don't you just let me drive?"

"Wait, I just need some practice."

"Fine, but wait a minute. Don't do anything, I'll be right back."

Ray got out of the Ford and walked back to John's car. Ari rolled down her window.

"What the hell is going on up there?" she said.

"John found out that he can control the Expedition using Seth. He's trying to get the hang of it."

"You're kidding."

"No, I'm not. Sit tight, I'm going to try and make sure that he doesn't kill himself."

"Okay."

Ray returned to the Ford. As he got back in, he noticed a very faint blue glow around the undercarriage.

"Ray, Seth is showing me something," said John. "I can see energy flowing around the truck. It looks like a blue flame. It comes from the orb and flows around the whole outside of the truck. I think I can control it."

"Interesting. Why don't you try backing us up and getting us facing the right direction?"

"I'm working on it."

"No way!"

Ray's exclamation was due to the fact that the Ford was now floating about one meter above the road. Ray's adrenaline surged and he turned to John.

"John, put us down."

"It's all right, Ray. I'm in complete control."

The ground shot away. Ray screamed as the Ford rose up above the trees. Ray gave up on this and closed his eyes. A few seconds passed.

"Ray, it's okay. You can open your eyes."

"Are we still flying?"

"We're hovering. We're at a thousand feet."

Ray opened his eyes one at a time and glanced out the window. He saw treetops and a great view of the nearby mountain.

"Eep," he said.

"We can go anywhere, Ray. Seth says it's no problem. We just have to stay below five thousand feet or it'll get a little chilly in here."

Ray locked his door. "Okay, you've convinced me. Can we please go back down now?"

"Sure."

With a barely perceptible sway, the Ford returned to the surface. Christie and Ari were standing outside of John's car, agape. Upon touching down, Ray jumped out.

"That was not funny," said Ari.

"No, it was not funny at all," said Ray.

"Amazing," said Christie, her eyes alight. "It's just amazing."

"All this incredible alien technology, and what do we get?" said Ari. "A flying Ford Expedition."

John got out and walked over. "I hope this doesn't cause your insurance to go up, Ray."

"Wow, you are just frigging hilarious. I can't believe how funny you are."

"Do you have any idea how fast you were moving?" asked Christie.

"We went a thousand feet in one point two seconds," said John. "That's somewhere between five hundred and six hundred miles per hour. And we barely felt a bump."

"You'll have to do a lot better than that for space travel."

"Seth is telling me that speed is the best he can do without ripping the Ford to shreds. It's plenty fast enough for maneuvering in the air."

"At that rate," Ari said, "you'll be in Woburn in less than twenty minutes."

"Looks like we're talking the Ford," said Christie.

"There isn't enough room for all five of us and all of our gear," Ray said.

"It's not like we can't come back later," said John. "We can leave what we don't need behind. Once we get back here with the completed hull, we can pick everything up including my car, and take it back to Woburn."

"Sounds good," said Ray, "there's only one problem."

"What's that?"

"I think I'm going to be sick."

13.

The Ford Expedition, while hopefully not meant to be used as an aircraft, was in fact filling this role quite well thanks to the orb's assistance. For the four occupants, it was the first inkling of how thrilling their futures might be. The flight's most reassuring feature was the same thing, however, that kept the mood relatively sedate: their ride was *too* smooth. At five hundred and fifty miles per hour, there was barely a shimmy or a vibration to be felt. Without looking at the ground it was difficult to sense any movement at all. Only Seth, through John, could provide any useful information. It had taken a full fifteen minutes for the passengers to stop commenting about how insane the entire affair had become, and now a heavy silence hung in the air.

"We're approaching my place," said John.

John had been navigating by dead reckoning, and was simply following the highway south. He was forced to bring the Ford down to five hundred feet to better follow the side roads. John also cut the airspeed down to about a hundred miles an hour. It didn't take long for him to find the correct rooftop.

"I'm going to set down right in my backyard," John said.

"Sounds good," said Ray.

"Won't the neighbors see?" asked Christie.

"No," said John, "the houses here are about fifty yards apart, and the hedges are pretty thick. They won't see us at night."

Without displaying any expenditure of effort, John landed the Ford. Ray, who was a peculiar shade of gray, was more than happy to exit the vehicle. Christie opened her door and Tycho shot past her into the yard.

"Tycho!" Christie yelled, "get back here."

"It's okay," said John. "There's a fence around the backyard. He won't get too far. Come on, let's get the orb inside."

Ray had wandered off to get his balance back, so Ari assisted John with the orb. They kept the blanket draped over the orb, and it followed John into the house like a fleece ghost.

Christie grabbed her things and accompanied the other two inside.

"Christie, this is Friday," said John, pointing to the cat that immediately greeted them.

"Nice cat," said Christie. "How is he going to react to..."

Tycho barked, and Friday became a black streak across the floor as she ran for cover. John shrugged.

"She'll get over it."

"I can keep Tycho outside, it's no problem," said Christie.

"Tycho can use the basement. It's partially finished, but it's warmer than the yard."

"Thanks."

John guided the orb into the living room. He removed the blanket and placed his hand on the orb. Despite his best effort to stay standing, John fell to the floor. Ari rushed to his side.

"John! Damn it, what did you think was going to happen?"

John groaned. "I thought I could handle it this time."

Ari helped John onto the couch. Ray entered the room.

"Is he all right?" Ray asked.

"I'm fine, Ray," said John, shaking off his fatigue. "Let's talk about our plan."

"We're hours ahead of time as far as getting to Woburn," said Ari.

"Yeah, but how useful will this time be?" said Ray. "It's John's job to start the CAD designing. Are you up to starting early, John?"

"I think so," said John. "I might be able to get in some useful programming before bedtime. Normally I rack out around eleven o'clock but today I'd like to turn in early."

"How long will this entire process take?" asked Ari.

"I think I can bang it out in a day. I have existing modules that I can modify for this purpose. That will save us some time as far as creating a secure airframe. Then all I have to do is design the interior space. Since we don't know exactly what kind of interface or equipment we'll need, I'm leaning towards four simple crawlspace access tunnels that run the length of the ship, two between each deck. That will give us the ability to run cable from any part of the ship to the other."

"What do you mean by a secure airframe?" asked Christie. "I thought we were going to have to research the space shuttle in order to make this thing space-worthy."

"I got you covered," said John. "I know how to make a craft space-worthy. Seth can provide the necessary shielding from debris and cosmic radiation. He's been quite helpful in describing what he can contribute to the ship. The only problem is that for every idea he gives me, I feel like he's holding back something. I get the feeling he is either hiding something from me or is genuinely confused about what it is we're trying to accomplish."

"That's hardly reassuring," said Ari.

"Listen," said Christie. "There's something we should talk about."

"Okay," said Ray. "You have the floor."

"I think we need to step back from the project for a moment and ask some critical questions of ourselves."

"You mean like, 'are we nuts?'" said John.

"No, I mean like why are we doing this?"

"We don't know. Seth hasn't told me anything else about the mission. Only that Umber needs our help and we're going to need weapons."

"Wait a minute," began Ray, "when did Seth say anything about weapons?"

"Oh, I guess I forgot to mention it. On the way over here, Seth told me there could be some danger involved, and that we should bring weapons. He wasn't more specific than that."

Ari sighed, and said, "Great, so now we're sure that deep space isn't the only thing out there that can kill us. This is getting better and better."

"The question remains," said Christie. "Or the question really is, what is our reason for building this ship, other than the mission to Umber?"

"It's our duty," said John.

"Duty to whom? Don't tell me that you've already accepted Seth as your lord and master."

"Hardly!" said John, irritated. "I meant to humanity."

"That doesn't make any sense. If we were concerned about how this thing is going to change humanity, we would have turned it over to the government the instant we became aware of the mission. You know what I see, fellas? I see a bunch of willful, selfish amateurs who don't want to share the credit for this find, and damn the consequences to the world, humanity, and the rest of the galaxy for all we know."

"We didn't choose the orb. The orb chose us."

"Is that what you believe?"

"It is a pretty unbelievable coincidence," began Ray, "that this orb came down less than fifty yards from our cabin."

"I don't buy that destiny crap," said Ari. "We were in the right place at the right time, that's all. There was no guiding force that led it to us. And Christie's right about us being amateurs. There are thousands of people that are much more qualified to be working on this thing than us."

"We've already gone through this," said John. "If the government gets involved, who knows what the hell is going to happen to us?"

Christie raised her voice. "I still want to know why you're doing this! Each of you, tell me what your ultimate drive is."

"Discovery," said John.

"Curiosity," said Ray.

Ari shrugged.

"Is that it?" asked Christie. "Science for the sake of science? It's intellectual masturbation! There has to be a goal, and that goal has to be worthwhile."

"I see our motivations as perfectly valid, and our goals as worthwhile," said John. "We're embarking on a mission unlike anything the world has ever seen. Those who choose to go on this mission will go down in history. They'll be more famous than Newton, Einstein, and John Glenn combined."

"And you have no problem waiting until you get back to tell anyone?" asked Christie. "And that's a big if you come back."

"What about you?" John demanded. "So far you've been perfectly happy with being part of our clandestine group."

"Don't think I haven't been considering the alternatives."

"This is ridiculous," began Ari, "this is our ship. This is our opportunity. I am not going to give up the chance for this. I've made up my mind, I'm going all the way."

"We are getting this ship built," said John. "You are either part of this project or you are not. I was happy to see you express interest, Christie. You know we need someone like you to help out."

"Why don't we make a pact?" said Ray.

"What the hell are you talking about?" Ari said.

"A pact, an agreement. Let's agree that if we get stonewalled, or if we believe that we've reached a dead-end that we can't overcome, we'll hand this project over to the government. It seems to me that those who want to stay involved will know way too much about the project to be left behind. By then you'll be the foremost experts on Seth and the ship. They can't kick you out."

"That seems reasonable," said Christie.

"I agree," said Ari. "We give it our best shot and that's that. Anything after that is up to the experts."

"Okay, that sounds good," said John, "but I have no intention of failing Seth. For now, I'm going to start on my designs. I'd like the rest of you to brainstorm about other logistical issues. Do it in the kitchen and see if you can't produce dinner as well."

Two and a half hours later, John saved his work and shut down his computer. So far he had only produced a preliminary bitmap deck plan and a cursory wire frame model of the exterior of the ship, which he continued to call the *Reckless Faith* in his own mind. It was still a significant improvement above his first idea, and the new exterior actually had some style to it. Thinking in terms of weaponry, John had added dorsal and ventral gunner positions, even though he hadn't the slightest of ideas what could be placed there. It seemed quite logical to make sure that if they could be of use, they actually existed. He had also left room for a forward-facing weapon of some sort, to the same usefulness for now.

With unconsciousness becoming less an option and more an imperative, John decided he had to give up. He collapsed on his bed, supine. John was thinking about seeing how the others were doing, and setting them up with sleeping arrangements, but he couldn't seem to move. He was almost asleep when somebody knocked on his door.

"John? It's Ari."

"Come in."

Ari entered. She held a piece of yellow legal pad paper. She sat down on the side of John's bed.

"Are you racking out?"

"I guess so. You guys are going to need to know where to get the spare pillows."

"We'll be fine, John. Ray is sleeping in the living room. Christie's getting the spare bedroom, and I'll be fine on the floor."

"That's ridiculous, why not share the spare bedroom with Christie?"

"We had a coin toss already. I don't think either of us ever considered sharing the bed as an option."

"Suit yourselves. By the way, I wanted to show you my initial deck plans."

John got up, retrieved three pages from his printer, and handed them to Ari.

"Oh, cool. What's the scale on this?"

"Ten by thirty meters. It will also be ten meters in height."

"Anyway, I wanted to let you know what we've been thinking about for the past few hours."

"Shoot."

"Well, we're thinking about several main concerns. One is a computer system that can interface with Seth. You can't be held responsible for being Seth's conduit twenty-four seven, we've seen the result of just a few minutes. We can't expect Tycho to do any better, if that's even really an option. Christie and I both agree that we need a computer interface to interact with manually. It would also be handy if more than one person knew what was going on at a time."

"I agree."

"The only problem is how to integrate an Earth operating system into Seth. We don't know what kind of code he's running. Even if we could look at the raw data, compiling into a form we can use could take years."

"That's no good. And it assumes that Seth is something that can be quantifiable at all."

"True, but so far we haven't been able to come up with another theory. We can cross our fingers and hope that our computers work with Seth 'just because,' but I wouldn't bet on it."

"I hardly thought you would."

"The next thing is supplies. We don't know how long this mission may last. If it's indefinitely, then we have to bring as much food as physically possible. Ray and I estimate that we can pack four, maybe five years of supplies into the cargo areas you've envisioned. That also happens to be the shelf-life of most military rations, which are a natural choice for the ship. I see you included water storage tanks in the design, which addresses my next point. What's their capacity?"

"Each tank will be about one thousand gallons."

"Okay. The next thing to consider is organization. I'm in, I'm guessing you're in, and Ray sure as hell is in. That leaves Christie as the only wild card. If she bows out, we should find a replacement. Either way, we should have some sort of command structure. Ray and I also think that we should have uniforms so that we can more easily identify each other, and show anyone or anything that we encounter out there that we're on the same team. I hate the idea of uniforms but I can see the benefits. I suggested that we have uniforms but only use them when absolutely necessary."

"I agree."

"Then there's weapons and ammunition. Between all of us, we're going to have to make a trip to the gun store for more weapons. We should also invest in some serious tactical training if we expect to utilize them effectively. Ray knows of a school in southern New Hampshire that's supposed to be good."

"I know the one."

"Then there's furniture. We were wondering if you could integrate furniture into your design. That would save us a lot of trouble. Furniture that was part of the ship would be fine except for chairs. Those would need to be mobile. Getting suitable chairs shouldn't be difficult."

"Yup."

"Well, that's it for now. The only real problem is the bottom line. Ray and I estimate that all of this stuff will not only take weeks to realize, but it will run us into the tens of thousands of dollars. I, for one, do not have that kind of loot saved up."

"We'll find a way."

John drifted off completely, leaving Ari's voice an echo in his mind. His last thoughts were of her sitting beside him for the entire night, so that neither of them would be alone.

"We're ready for more information, Page."

Dana spoke into her cell phone. Levi was watching the exterior of the car intently. The two of them had just arrived in Woburn, Massachusetts, and were ready for the next batch of coordinates from ASTRA.

The signal had pointed a clear path to this city, as it had grown in clarity as it moved south towards the listening stations. Page and his colleagues, most of whom had been dragged out of their Sunday night routines for this, were diligently crunching numbers to come up with more precise coordinates for their "field team."

They'd narrowed the area down to a remarkable one hundred square yards, in a neighborhood just off Route 38 on the Wilmington-Woburn town line. That was the extent of their luck, however. No further transmissions were being received. Dana closed her phone in frustration.

"Page had nothing else for us," she said.

Levi nodded. "Without any idea of what we're looking for, this is a wild goose chase."

"I can't believe we didn't bring a remote receiver."

"Well, we can always go to the electronics store tomorrow and build one."

"Do I detect a sudden interest in pursuing this project?"

"I was being sort of sarcastic. We wouldn't have the GPS unit if I hadn't brought it, and you'd be completely S.O.L."

Dana cruised the streets slowly. It was a thoroughly normal residential area. Dana knew they were close. It was driving her crazy that they could be so close but so powerless to pinpoint the transmitter. Levi cleared his throat.

"We can't keep skulking around like this, or somebody's going to call the cops on us."

"Oh, come on."

"Do you see anyone else driving around at this hour?"

"I'm not giving up just yet."

"Fine. Why don't we get a motel room and try again in the morning? Maybe by then Page will have some news for us."

Dana sighed. "All right. Where did Page say the nearest motel was?"

"Lynnfield. Get back on the highway and head north."

Fifteen minutes later, Levi and Dana entered a hotel room. It was a four star hotel, but neither researcher had the energy to find somewhere less expensive. Levi had managed to negotiate for a lower price, but between the two of them they were laying down a hundred bucks. Dana wasn't looking forward to sharing the double with Levi before she realized she had no basis for this sentiment other than simple privacy.

The room was nice enough. Despite the overwhelming feeling of failure, Dana always enjoyed being out on the road. If she could regard the entire affair as an adventure in and of itself, perhaps the experience could be redeemed. The crushing feeling of fatigue was keeping her cynical side quite vocal, however. The transmission source was probably a completely random atmospheric anomaly, and could represent just about any Earth-based device bouncing off the clouds. Logic still pointed to something more distinct, but it was hardly enough to hold onto so late in the day. Dana would have to find something else to think about if she didn't want to stay up for another hour after the lights were out, fatigue or no fatigue.

"Do you have a preference for a bed?" asked Levi.

"No. Wait, I guess I'd like the one closest to the bathroom."

"No problem."

"Damn it, I forgot a toothbrush."

"How could you have brought anything for an overnight stay? We only stopped off at my place before leaving, not yours."

"Yeah, yeah."

"Don't worry, I have a brand new toothbrush that I brought along. You can use it."

"And you'll suffer along quietly with dog breath?"

"No, I also have mouthwash. I was den leader in the Hygiene Scouts."

"You want first dibs, then?"

"Sure."

Levi entered the bathroom and closed the door. Dana spread out the few things she did have on the bed. A hairbrush would have been nice, too. Levi's hair was too short to need one, so Dana figured she was screwed in that regard as well. Maybe it was time for her to invent a universal brush that was good for teeth, hair, and painting. Dana laughed at the chaos that might be caused.

Dana lay across the covers of her bed and tried to clear her mind. She was still surprised that Levi would accompany her on such a fool's crusade, and if she was better up on sleep and food she might have suspected that he was trying to ingratiate himself to her. Such a thing was neither necessary nor possible, at least so Dana believed. She didn't dislike Levi; it was more the fact that he so infrequently offered anything to like or dislike. A day in the car had offered useful insights; in fact, knowing about Levi's military background only improved her respect for the man.

It also reminded her even more strongly how much Levi looked like her father. Dana's dad was a Navy officer, which meant that he was allowed a full beard. Dana didn't know if her dad grew the beard because he could, or because he actually liked the way it looked. Dana's opinion was that while it may have been an old tradition in the Navy, it looked better on him than most.

Dana also thought about the fact that she had almost no interest in her father's career beyond getting to see all the cool ships. His rank of Lieutenant Commander was practically meaningless until Levi had explained it to her. This made Dana feel pretty stupid as her father was evidently a man of some importance. If he hadn't died while Dana was a teenager, she might have grown to appreciate his service. Instead all she had were some increasingly hazy memories and some stubbornly lucid guilt.

Levi emerged. "It's all yours, your majesty."

"Is it really?"

14. October 6, 2003

Christie was staring at the orb. The noontime sun was shining in through the skylights into John's living room, turning the orb a silvery transparent. It was so unlike anything on Earth that Christie found it easy to waste time simply gazing into it. Every so often it would shimmer slightly, as if as a reminder that it was still watching you back.

Everyone had slept in late that morning except for John, who according to Ari had woken up at seven o'clock to resume work on his computer. Ray had gone outside to play with Tycho after investigating a car accident in the nearby neighborhood, and was still doing so. He and Tycho got along quite well, and the dog seemed to appreciate the rougher level of play that Ray offered. Christie thought it might create bad habits later on, seeing as Tycho was a wolf breed and all. She put it out of her mind, figuring that if Tycho mauled Ray to death, she'd have her answer. The two of them were having fun, and it was the first time Christie had seen Ray without a dark cloud hanging over him since she'd met him. John had hinted to her that Ray had been through something rough recently, but so far nobody had volunteered anything more. It was obviously related to the time off he said he had. Christie was sure of one thing, and that was that Ray was the only one who hadn't lied to her, threatened her, or otherwise tried to manipulate her in the last twenty-four hours.

Ari passed by one of the living room windows, smoking a clove cigarette. How she was friends with anybody was a mystery to Christie, but judging by John and Ray's reaction to her more objectionable behavior, she wasn't always quite so much of a load to have around. Either that or the two men liked abuse.

Christie's eyes happened upon a picture on one of the end tables. It was of John and an unidentified young Caucasian female wearing blue hospital scrubs. John hadn't mentioned a girlfriend or sister. She figured he would volunteer the information if he thought it was appropriate.

Friday, who'd made herself scarce since first laying eyes on Tycho, ventured into the living room. Christie tried to get her to join her on the couch, and was surprised when she capitulated.

"John's not being very hospitable right now, is he?" Christie asked him.

"Murph," said Friday.

"Just wait until you're in space, you'll love that."

The cat purred, blissfully unaware of any future star trekking. Christie felt about as useful as the cat. There hadn't been much for her to contribute recently, other than some level-headed thinking and some much needed objectivity. How much use she would be to the crew in space was in doubt. Terran astronomy might not be of much use out there, once perspectives started to change. Her knowledge of astrophysics was rusty, at best, and something relatively simple like calculating Delta-V would be a challenge. Being able to tell the difference between a quasar and a pulsar might be just about the most handy skill she could offer aboard this ship.

As she'd mentioned to the others, Christie was not a big fan of science for the sake of science. Doing experiments just because you could was not a worthy goal in and of itself. Perhaps it was ironic then that her chosen field of expertise was often full of information that was practically useless to the vast majority of humans. Most people learned enough astronomy to know that their sun wouldn't go nova for millions of years, and called it good. Some cared even less than that, content to poke seeds in the ground and eat what they grew into.

Swiping a battleship, or whatever the USS Portland actually was, and making off with the greatest scientific discovery in history was definitely not up there in terms of Nobel prize winning choices. The most distressing thing was the casual attitude of the others. Only John's heart seemed to be in the right place. Christie thought that perhaps the only reason for her to go along was to make sure an ethical scientist was aboard.

Ari and Ray entered the living room. Friday looked at Ray in annoyance and decided to make a break for it.

"Friendly girl," said Ray.

"You smell like dog," said Ari.

"Right."

"Is John still slaving away upstairs?" asked Ari.

"Presumably," replied Christie.

"Well," began Ray, "I don't want to spend all day dicking around. If John's working hard, we should be too."

"What do you want to do, white-wash his fence?"

"No, Ari, we should talk about logistics some more. We still have a lot we need to work out."

"Okay. You talk, we'll listen."

Ray sat in a sofa chair. "I wanted to get a handle on how much money is actually available to us. If we pool our resources we should be able to purchase most of what we need for the mission. Now, I have about three thousand dollars saved up right now. I need some of that to give to my roommate to compensate for taking off early. It's only fair. I should be able to clear twenty-five hundred after that. Ari?"

"I have about fifteen thousand dollars saved up."

"Holy shit."

"Hey, I have a good job. I also happen to have a good deal on rent. I save a lot of money with each paycheck, and I almost never spend it. I bought a modest car and I only keep a credit card for emergencies. Excuse me for being frugal."

"I admire your fiscal restraint," said Ray.

"I'm afraid I won't be of much help," said Christie, "considering that I may not come along. I'm not about to blow my savings on a trip I can't take."

"How much could you contribute if you did come along?"

"What about a tax deductible donation?" asked Ari.

"I could dig up two grand," said Christie.

"Okay," said Ray, "and John tells me that he's got about two grand. Ari, the fund is definitely getting named after you."

"The Ferro Fund for Space Exploration," Ari said. "I like it. Why not publish a web site?"

"So approximately twenty thousand dollars," said Christie. "That sounds like plenty."

"Not for what we have in mind," Ray said.

"Example."

"Okay, we were thinking about bringing ten rifles aboard. Since we wanted to standardize, we agreed upon the

Springfield Armory M1A, the semi-automatic version of the military M-14. These fetch about eleven hundred dollars each. That's eleven thousand dollars right there."

"Why ten rifles?" asked Christie, perplexed. "There are only four of us, and I don't even know how to operate a firearm."

"We're planning on a crew of six. We may yet choose to invite more professionals along. Having a few spare rifles is always a good idea."

"Yeah, but couldn't you choose something less expensive?"

"We feel that the M1A is the perfect compromise of caliber and capacity. There are few other rifles that meet the criteria and they all run at least a grand each. We could buy a gaggle of cheap AKs for three hundred dollars each, but I'm not going to bet my life against aliens with anything less than three-oh-eight."

"What about John's Garand?" Ari interjected. "Don't you have at least one rifle already?"

"Yeah, but the idea here is standardization. When you have a tactical team working together it's a good idea to be able to interchange magazines."

"Fine, if you think it's worth blowing over half of your cash on, go for it," said Christie. "I'd prefer my portion go towards something like food, water, and clothing."

"Nobody's neglecting any one area," said Ray. "If we can't afford the rifles, we can't afford them. We can compromise on five rifles, four even. Nobody even knows how much use they might be. Hopefully they spend the entire mission in the armory collecting dust."

"About that," said Christie, "why is it that we know so little about the mission? Telling us so little is hardly a good way of recruiting people."

"John said he thought Seth was missing some information himself. Seth isn't hiding anything from us, he simply doesn't know. Why whomever sent him would do this is beyond me."

"Maybe," began Ari, "Seth's creators are waiting until we build a ship before sending him the rest of the story. That way they could be sure that even if the current crew said no, they could turn the ship over to somebody else who would be interested. Either way the ship gets built."

"I don't know. I think that the Umberians want us to send a crew that's acting off of faith alone. Telling us too much might result in a large ship filled with soldiers instead of a smaller ship filled with scientists and explorers. I think they want to avoid letting us decide what's appropriate by telling us nothing."

Christie frowned. "Yes, but by telling us nothing they risk the same thing. Not knowing what's out there might just as well result in a warship. As far as I'm concerned I think our response is the most appropriate. A small ship, with a few eager participants who are willing to adapt to the situation."

Ari nodded, and reached up towards the orb. Despite its appearance the orb was still solid to the touch. Ari felt jealous that they couldn't access it without John even though the honor was dubious.

"I still don't know how I'm going to interface a computer system with this thing," she said.

"It seems to me that we need to make something intangible like the mental link into something tangible," said Christie, "like binary code."

"But how?"

"Logic would dictate that there is some sort of signal that connects John and Seth when Seth is sharing his consciousness. If we could figure out how to detect that signal, we could analyze it."

Ray nodded. "That's a good idea, but what kind of detection devices are available to us? Do we have radio frequency receivers? Spectroscopes? Microphones? I don't know what else we might use, but we sure don't have them."

"I think we should just ask Seth," said Ari. "Next time John or all of us are linked to the orb, we'll find out if he can shed some light on the problem."

"Let's see if John wants to take a break and hold a session down here."

"I'll go," said Ari.

Ari turned and walked upstairs. John's door was open a crack so Ari entered his room. John was transfixed on his computer monitor. Ari sat down on his bed as it was the only place left. John glanced at Ari.

"Hello," he said.

"Hi, how's it going?"

"Great. I'm getting some seriously good work done here. I've already finalized the exterior hull. Right now I'm working on a system of doors that are strong enough to resist decompression. Each room has a door that will close if that area loses pressurization. Or if you want some privacy."

"I'm impressed."

"I should be done with the entire thing about eight to ten hours."

"Why not take a lunch break? You've been going full steam for five hours."

"If you could bring me something, I'd appreciate it. I want to keep working."

"Well, the others and I were hoping that we could access Seth. We have some questions about how we might integrate the on-board computers into his data stream."

"If I access the orb I'll become tired. I don't want to have to take a nap."

"You don't have to finish the ship today, John."

"I can't keep taking sick days off of work, either."

"Why not quit your damn job? If we're getting off this planet in a little while what the hell difference does it make?"

John looked at Ari. "Good point. They won't appreciate me leaving so abruptly, though."

"Why do you care what they think?"

"Two weeks notice is simply professional courtesy, that's all."

"Just quit. I'll quit my job, too. We can have a quitter's party."

John stopped working and turned to face Ari.

"Ari, what are we going to tell our families?"

"Tell them that your boss came on to you, what does it matter?"

"No, I mean how are we going to explain the fact that we're disappearing and possibly never coming back?"

"I suppose we could say we joined the military."

"Yeah, but even in boot camp we'd be able to write letters and make occasional phone calls."

"I don't know. Tell them you're becoming a Tibetan Buddhist monk."

"I suppose that's a bit more believable."

"My parents are used to me staying out of contact for long periods. If we get killed out in space they'll never know what happened to me. They'll get over it, people always do."

"That's a pretty cold attitude, even for you."

"Well, if letting your family think that you're dead bothers you, maybe you should reconsider coming along."

"No, it's not that. I'd just like to put them at ease in some way before we take off."

"The monk story works pretty well. It speaks to your spiritual life, so you won't get much objection from your family. It also explains why you'll be out of contact for so long. Aren't there monasteries out in California? That's more believable than Tibet."

"Honestly, I think you've got something there. Maybe a survivalist trek through the wilderness would work, too. People do all sorts of crazy, soul-searching stuff like that."

"Yeah."

The conversation lapsed. Ari smiled at John and looked around the room. John turned back to his work. Ari noticed John's flight joystick sitting on the desk and picked it up.

"I guess I'd better get back to work," John said.

"This is a pretty serious piece of gear. I take it your fascination with airplanes is still strong?"

"Yep. In fact, I'm hoping to integrate this gear into the ship. Flying the ship via the telepathic link is fine but it lacks a certain thrill, if flying an Expedition around is any comparison. I also had to concentrate pretty hard to work with Seth at flying. Having a manual flight control system might make it easier to multi-task. It would also allow somebody other than me to fly the ship."

"So getting conventional computers to work with the orb is more important than ever. All the more reason for us to ask Seth if it can work."

John sighed. "All right, you got my curiosity worked up about it. Let's go find out what Seth has to say. Hopefully if we stick to the illusion world I won't get too tired."

"Good. And while you're up, you can show me where you keep the damn booze."

15.

Ari awoke with a start. She was splayed across the living room couch. Looking over at the wall clock, she confirmed the time of her alcohol-induced nap. She had spent only fifteen minutes passed out, which was fourteen more than she'd planned. Christie and Ray were nowhere to be seen, and all was quiet save for soft noises from upstairs. Nine hours had passed, and John was still banging away on his keyboard.

They had held a conference with Seth inside the vision world of the orb. This time, the orb chose to place them in Christie's classroom at Suffolk, the same classroom they'd all shared as students. After an extremely annoying conversation with Seth, they learned that it was possible to detect and record Seth's data output. Apparently, when Umberians wanted to communicate directly with Seth they used an infrared light modulator. This was her best guess, anyway, since when they'd finally communicated their exact question to Seth a cordless infrared mouse had appeared in Ari's hand, and television remote controls in the hands of the others. She speculated that if she set up an infrared transceiver and hacked the program, they would be able to read Seth in terms of binary code. The question then became how to interpret the data. Ari had some powerful anti-encryption software that she thought might do the trick. Between that and simply asking Seth what kind of data he was transmitting at any given moment could theoretically allow her to write a program to display the data in terms the humans could understand.

After the conference, John had returned to his CAD work and Ray and Christie had gone out for some groceries. Ari was left with the cat and a list of things she wanted Seth to explain to her. The list included relative speed, bearing, yaw, pitch, energy levels, resource management, hull integrity, and all external sensory readings such as temperature, radiation levels, particle density, light levels, and radio transmissions. Given raw data feeds, Ari believed she could create programs to display the information. Any modern computer would do the trick, but Ari planned on requesting a fast machine just for the hell of it. John had a 2.4 gigahertz machine with an opulent

1,024 megabytes of RAM, which was more than enough. Ari wanted additional machines for each room of the ship, networked together, for convenience and collective processing power. Like Ray's rifles, such a plan was probably not possible. Ari was all for stopping by her place of work and stealing what they needed, but John and Ray would almost certainly object.

After Ray and Christie had returned from the store, they'd spent some time in the backyard talking about themselves. Christie seemed like a smart enough addition to the crew, if they could retain her. It would certainly be easier than finding someone new.

Ari had raided the liquor cabinet after that. She and Ray watched the evening news while Christie called her parents. Ari kept one ear on her conversation, but it turned out to be quite routine. After the news, television was pretty boring. Ari was happy to partake of John's selection, which was outstanding. She did not intend to get as buzzed as she did.

Pouring herself a glass of water, Ari noticed Ray standing outside. He was smoking his pipe. From upstairs, John and Christie appeared.

"What have you two been up to?" Ari asked.

"I was looking over John's design," said Christie.

"How's it coming?"

"I'm finished," said John, grinning. "Where's Ray?"

"He's right there."

John went outside and brought Ray back in.

"You guys want to take a look?" asked John.

"Of course," said Ari.

John led the way upstairs, and they gathered around his computer. John began a walk-through of his design. Ari was stunned at the level of detail he'd achieved in such a short time.

"Impressive," said Ray. "I like it."

"Nice windows," said Ari, referring to the hourglass-shaped apertures that complemented the hallways and each of the living quarters.

It was all there, each of the rooms that John had originally conceived of in his first drawing and a few more. Christie grinned despite herself. This was going to be damn cool. John rotated the perspective for a look at the exterior. He then called up a floor plan of each deck, and passed out printed copies of the bitmap image as a visual aid.

Deck three was the lowest deck. It was ten meters shorter than the decks above it to allow room for cargo to clear the ramp. The ramp, which led into the fore cargo bay, was one of two entrances into the ship. The cargo bay took up two decks. When the ramp was closed, a slope was created which led up to the second deck in the fore section. Behind the cargo bay on the third deck was a hallway that led to a space that John had reserved for any external weapons they might install later. It was labeled the Ventral Gun Room. Behind that was the aft cargo hold, accessed by two corridors that flanked the gun room. Last on that deck was the engine compartment, which was also two decks tall.

"Seth specified a minimum space of twenty cubic meters for the stardrive," John said.

Deck two ran the full length of the ship, and began with the fore gun room, accessible from either side of the ramp or the ramp itself when in the closed position. On the port side of the cargo bay there was a slightly-curved staircase which led to the port side hallway on deck one. Next came the armory, which overhung the back of the cargo bay by ten meters, and was accessed from below by a short staircase. Aft of that was the orb room, the geometric center of the ship and the place where the orb would be installed. Next was the galley, which had a staircase to the central corridor on deck one. The orb room and galley were flanked on either side by the ship's water storage tanks. John had placed four windows in the galley through which the tanks could be seen. Furthest aft was the upper area of the engine room, visible through a large picture window at the rear of the galley.

Deck one began with the bridge. A corridor on the port side of the deck started at the door to the bridge and ran back past the entrance to a space reserved for computer servers and storage. On the starboard side of the ship aft of the bridge was the conference room, and beyond that was an area John had designated the Lounge. The dorsal gun room was accessible from there. Next were six identical rooms that comprised the

Living Quarters, split down the middle by the central corridor and the staircase to the galley. Each room was about five meters square save for the bathrooms, which included integrated showers, and a closet. Lastly was a room labeled the Zero-G Room.

"What's that for?" asked Ari.

"The Zero-G Room," John said. "A variable gravity room."

"What's the purpose of that?"

"For fun. Extra living space if we need it, but mostly I just wanted a room I could float around in and relax."

"Oh..."

"It will also function as an airlock. Note the twin hatches on the starboard side."

"That makes much more sense."

John went through the ship one more time.

"Any objections?" said John.

"I like it," said Ray.

"It's almost perfect," said Ari.

"It should do nicely," said Christie.

"Good," began John, "let's get saddled up. We have a date with a Navy girl."

Ten minutes later, the friends had piled themselves and the orb into the Expedition. John was once again acting creepy with Seth inside of his head, and of course insisted on driving.

"You do realize," Ray was saying, "that it doesn't matter whether or not you sit in the driver's seat?"

"Maybe not," replied John. "Is everyone ready?"

In the back seat, Ari and Christie nodded. John stared out of the windshield for a moment and the truck began to move. Ray took a deep breath.

"Here we go again," he said.

The truck rose into the sky. John stopped at about a thousand feet, and tried to get his bearings.

"How long is it going to take us to get to the ship?" asked Christie.

"About two minutes at our top speed," said John.

"How are we going to spot the right one?"

"It's the USS Portland," said Ari. "We just cruise above the water and look for it."

John urged the Ford forward. The landscape began to flit by. Ray directed his gaze upward through the windshield and focused on the stars.

"What if there are people on board?" asked Christie.

"It's a decommissioned ship," Ari replied. "There shouldn't be anyone aboard."

"And if there is?"

Ari shrugged. The possibility hadn't occurred to her.

"What about people nearby?" Ray asked. "Nobody's going to notice a fifteen by forty-five meter section of this ship disappear?"

"We'll take what we need from the top down," said John. "Unless somebody is looking right at the Portland it won't be a problem. Besides, so what if they see something? Good luck explaining what happened."

"That's my attitude," said Ari.

The next couple of minutes passed in silence. John brought the Ford down towards the mouth of the Mystic River. It was obvious which ship was the Portland as there was only one military vessel present.

"There it is," said John. "I can read the name from here."

John's excitement grew as he positioned the Expedition above the ship.

"It's completely dark," observed Ray.

"Seth is telling me there's nobody on board. I don't see anyone on the pier. Looks like we're good to go."

John closed his eyes and spoke to Seth.

"We're ready, Seth. My design is complete."

A rising sound filled the cab of the Ford. It reminded Ray of a shifting glacier. Around them, the night sky began to fade away. In a matter of seconds, their surroundings had been replaced by complete blackness. The others waited in silent awe as John received a message from Seth.

"All set," he said. "Welcome to the Reckless Faith. Seth, lights please?"

A bluish-white light became visible. It appeared as rails of light parallel to the Ford. As the light grew the cargo bay came into view. The lights were set into the wall at floor level. Additional lights set into the ceiling came on. John stepped out of the Ford, blinking in the brightness.

"Come on, it's perfectly safe," he said.

The others stepped out. Their footfalls on the metal echoed slightly. Something was causing a noticeable hum, like the HVAC system of a large building. The cargo bay was exactly as John had designed it. Steel walls and aluminum floors gleamed brightly. The main ramp was closed. The stairway to the armory gleamed.

There were no windows in this section, leading Christie's to ask, "Are we still above the Portland?"

"Yes," said John. "Seth is using his light-bending trick on the entire craft. Nobody can see us."

"That's handy," said Ray.

"Come on, let's go check out the bridge."

John led the others up the port side stairs to the port corridor on deck one.

The corridor had windows. The group looked out at the river.

"Nice view," said Ray.

"That's odd," said Ari, "there doesn't appear to be any mass missing from the Portland."

"Maybe Seth took it from the middle of the ship."

John stepped in front of the door to the bridge, and it opened sideways. The bridge was strikingly beautiful. Large windows swept down from the vertical and became the windshield. Mounting points for five chairs were set into the deck, and a horse-shoe shaped counter swept around the bridge from the front to the sides.

"All of these surfaces are made out of aluminum, so we can drill holes and cut access panels where we need them," said John. "We can set up our computers inside the counters here, and mount the monitors to the top. Once we set up chairs, the people sitting in them will have easy access to the computers. The center chair will also have my flight simulator controls for manual flight operations."

Two more chair mounts were set further back, closer to the walls.

"These chairs will rotate one hundred eighty degrees. They can be used to access the extreme ends of the counter-top or can face each other."

"Let's take a look around the rest of the ship," said Christie.

Five minutes later, the group descended a stairway into the galley on deck two. They'd finished touring the conference room, the dorsal gun room, and all of the living quarters. The zero-g room wasn't particularly interesting, but the airlock hatches worked just fine.

The galley's window into the engine room immediately grabbed everyone's attention because there was something there. Through the window they could see the newly installed stardrive.

"Wow, that is impressive," said Ray.

The stardrive was the length of the room and almost as high. It looked like half of a small passenger car from a 1960s era train had been stuck into the rear wall of the engine room. Smaller horizontal cylinders emerged from each side at floor level, and were reminiscent of a pontoon boat. Pipes and conduits connected various points to other various points. It was the source of the humming.

"How does it work?" asked Christie.

"Seth doesn't know," replied John. "He knows the power source is cold fusion. The amount of hydrogen that will be available from the water tanks will be enough to power the ship for one hundred years."

"Not bad."

Ari walked over to one of the galley's exterior windows.

"Uh, guys? You may want to look at this."

The others joined her at the window. Ari pointed at the Portland.

"It's sagging," said Ray.

"No, it's buckling," said Ari.

Below, the upper decks of the ship were folding in on themselves. The hull bulged outward. Cracks formed on the sides, and with a tremendous bang the entire ship was reduced to dust, which disappeared into the water.

"Oh... shit."

"I think now would be a good time to head home," said John.

Joe's American Bar and Grill in Woburn was not very busy that night. Dana and Levi had spent all day searching the city without luck, and had decided to get some dinner before heading back to Pennsylvania. As exhausted as they were, neither of them much wanted to rent a motel room again. Dana couldn't help but be embarrassed that she'd dragged Levi along on such a worthless trip, and this lead her to be rather quiet as they waited to be served. Levi had ordered a drink and waited impatiently for it to show up.

"When are we going to get some service?" Levi said at last.

"Just as soon as you forget about it," said Dana. "A watched waiter never boils."

"At this rate we'll never be done with dinner."

"Let's stick to appetizers, then."

"Okay."

The waitress had just brought Levi his scotch and soda when his cell phone rang.

"Marks," Levi said into the phone.

"Levi, it's Chris," said Page, on the other end of the line.

"What's up?"

"You're not going to believe this. We just received a huge signal. It's the same type as the others but it is at least a thousand times stronger."

"You're kidding."

"We also got an exact bead on a location this time. The coordinates come back to a pier in Chelsea, the city across the river from Boston."

"I know the area. That's incredible."

"Good, because after this I'm way too curious to let you come back to Bethlehem without checking it out."

"Then next time you can be the so-called field agent, Page."

"Call me back when you get close to the city, and I'll give you directions."

"Will do. Bye."

Levi hung up. Dana looked at him expectantly.

"What does Chris say?"

Levi grinned. "Chris says we gotta get our butts to Boston."

An hour later, with his phone jammed between his head and shoulder, Levi made his way through the streets of Chelsea. Page guided him as best he could, but the information he was getting off of the Internet wasn't entirely accurate. Dana was practically jumping out of her chair with excitement. At this point, discovering a radio transmitting toaster would be satisfying enough for her. Dana was holding onto the GPS receiver.

"We're getting close," she said.

"Page, I'm going to let you go," said Levi, "and go by the GPS unit from here."

"Good luck," said Page, "call me if you find anything."

Levi allowed the phone to drop into his lap, and ended the call.

"Turn right here," Dana said.

Levi rounded a corner, passing a sign that indicated that they had arrived at a pier. Levi guided the truck around a gradual turn until they were facing the Mystic River.

"Holy shit," he said.

Before them, it appeared that every police car in New England had gathered. Levi noticed state and local authorities present.

"What the hell is going on here?" asked Dana.

"I don't know. We're about to find out."

A local cop was flagging them down. Levi pulled up to him and rolled down his window.

"Who are you guys?" the cop asked.

"American Space Transmission Research Association," said Levi. "We're tracking some strange readings and we were lead here."

"You can't be here right now," the cop said. "There's been some sort of terrorist attack, or accident, or something."

"Terrorist attack? What happened?"

"I can't be more specific than that, and even if I did know what was going on I couldn't tell you."

"But we're scientists," said Dana, "this might have something to do with the phenomenon we're tracking."

"Pull over to that area over there and wait," the cop said. "I'll tell the feds you're here when they arrive."

"The feds?" said Levi. "It's that serious?"

"Apparently. Now please, would you get out of the way?"

Levi nodded, and began to pull away. He drove the Bronco to a relatively empty part of the vacuous pier and turned around, pointing the nose of the vehicle towards the activity. He put the truck into park.

"It looks like the area of interest is the pier itself," said Dana.

"It does. They're all gathering around there. I don't see what they're interested in, though."

"Me neither."

Levi's attention was diverted back towards the entrance to the pier. A pair of black Ford sedans had arrived, followed by a camouflage Humvee. The driver of the lead Ford spoke with the officer at the gate, and continued on towards the water. Levi looked astonished.

"The military? That was fast. This must be some serious shit."

"I think we might be in over our heads," said Dana.

16. October 7, 2003

It was midnight, and all was quiet in John Scherer's backyard. The waxing gibbous moon cast a pale light across the lawn. The wind picked up a bit, sending leaves recently freed from their homes swirling lazily about. A horizontal shaft of light appeared thirty feet above the yard, and began to grow. A ramp, jutting out of nowhere, began to lower. The ramp made contact with the ground, and a Ford Expedition appeared. The truck rolled down the ramp silently and into the yard. Three figures followed the truck's path down the ramp. They turned and looked back at the ramp. It began to close. A fourth figure stepped out of the Ford and joined the others. The ramp closed, leaving only the night sky above the yard.

"Remarkable," said Ray. "It's almost completely invisible."

"Aren't birds going to crash into it?" asked Christie.

John closed his eyes. He had a more casual connection to Seth available now that the ship was built, a connection that was easier on him but offered less direct control of the ship.

"Birds won't come anywhere near the Faith," John said, opening his eyes. "They can sense the electromagnetic disturbance."

"Come on," said Ray, "let's get some sleep."

The group headed inside. Friday expressed her displeasure with yet another absence by John, and Tycho added his feelings on the matter from the depths of the basement. Christie went downstairs to tend to the dog while John fed his own animal.

"So, what's our plan for tomorrow?" asked Ray.

"I've got to go to work," John said. "If I'm going to quit, I'm going to do it in person. I feel bad enough not giving them two weeks notice."

"Not me," said Ari.

"We already know how you feel about it. Anyway, Ray, that won't take very long. The first thing we need to tomorrow is sit down and take a really hard look at our finances. After looking over the finished superstructure of the ship I realize just how much furniture we're going to need. I have drills that can cut through aluminum but we need circular saws as well. Those we can probably rent, along with any other tools we might need. There are going to be many more costs involved in this project than we initially thought."

"I can borrow an infrared transceiver from work," said Ari, "but only if they think I still work for them. I'll do a half day tomorrow and come home sick, this time with the transceiver and anything else I think we need. Maybe the day after next I can actually quit."

"Sounds good. Christie says she's still in the clear for Tuesday. She doesn't have class but she will be blowing off some of her office hours."

"Okay," said Ray.

"Well, then, let's get some sleep. We've got an early start tomorrow."

"Speak for yourself," said Ray.

"Yeah," said Christie, emerging from the basement, "we get to sleep in if we want."

John smiled. "True, but once you remember that there's a one hundred foot long spaceship in the backyard, you may not be able to."

Hey, guys," Ari began, "we haven't discussed something I think is rather important."

"What's that?"

"What the hell happened to the battleship after we were done with it?"

The others were silent. John shrugged.

"According to Seth," he said, "we took what we needed and left the rest. I guess we took a little bit from the whole, as opposed to one solid chunk. The process must have left the ship's hull destabilized. Even a small drop in density could have caused the steel to buckle."

"Yeah, but disintegrate?"

"Hey, I'm no expert. I'm just glad we got a ship of our own out of the deal."

"The downside," said Christie, "is that people are going to notice the destroyed ship a lot sooner than a missing chunk of sub-decks."

"What are they going to do, dust for fingerprints?" said Ray.

"I'm just saying that if we were going for a low impact approach we're not off to a great start."

John nodded. "Yeah. The only thing I'm ultimately concerned about is making sure that nobody gets hurt. People can speculate about what happened to the Portland all they want as long as they don't find out about us. For everything else that we do, we have to minimize, if not avoid completely, taking advantage of or victimizing anyone."

"Do you consider theft part of that equation?" asked Ari.

"Yes. We needed the Portland. Anything else we need we should be able to buy. Besides, it's too risky stealing things. We don't need any of the members of the team getting arrested."

"What if it's not so risky after all?" Christie asked.

"What do you mean?"

"Look at what Seth just did. He absorbed all that material from the Portland. He must have some sort of matter transportation and reformation ability."

"Right, so... wait a minute..."

"You're suggesting we might be able to simply 'beam up' anything we need?" asked Ari.

Christie nodded. "That's exactly what I'm suggesting. John?"

John closed his eyes and turned towards the backyard.

"Seth says it can be done," he said slowly.

"Why don't we try it out in the morning?" Ray said, smiling. "We can start with something harmless like the leather captain's chairs you wanted for the bridge."

"Okay. Cool."

"Until then, let's get some sack time. I'm about to pass out where I'm standing."

"Roger that. I'm going to take one last look around the ship and see if we'll need anything else."

"Okay, we have just gone from odd to super freaky," said Levi.

Levi turned off the highway in the Bronco towards the hotel they'd stayed in the previous night. He was becoming more and more agitated with the entire situation, especially with the involvement of the CIA. Levi was flabbergasted that the CIA let them go after what they told them, and he strongly suspected that they'd be back in touch at some point soon. Levi's cell phone rang, and he just about ran the Bronco off the road.

"Hello," he said gruffly.

"Yo, Levi, this is Chris."

"Chris, you would not believe the stuff that is going on over here."

"Really? What's going on?"

"I can't talk about it right now, it's too complicated. When I get to a land line I'll call you back."

"Okay. I have some new information for you, though."

"Shoot."

"We got another signal from the Woburn location."

"Holy shit. Hey Dana, they got another signal from Woburn."

"Awesome," said Dana.

"It gets better," said Page. "I have the location down to the decimeter."

"Outstanding, now we're getting somewhere. Give me those coordinates, we'll head there now."

Fifteen minutes later, Dana and Levi were standing outside of a house in Woburn. The name on the mailbox said "Scherer." Dana was holding the GPS unit out in front of her.

"This is definitely it," she whispered.

"There are some lights on," whispered Levi. "Let's be careful."

"We'd better hurry. If the CIA has found a way to track the signal, they could be on their way already."

Dana and Levi crept towards the house, keeping to the shadows. The neighborhood seemed unusually quiet. Silhouettes of people could be seen at times through the windows, the sight of which caused Dana and Levi to freeze in their tracks. Dana leaned over to whisper to Levi

"If the source is inside," she hissed, "what then?"

"I suppose we go knock on the front door," Levi said, his response more reasonably hushed. "I'm not giving up so easily."

By the side of the house, the pair encountered a four foot high fence. A gate through the fence into the backyard was unlocked. Levi lifted the handle and opened the gate carefully. Dana slipped through and Levi followed her, gently returning the gate to shut. They made their way towards the large, open backyard. Levi was looking to his left and Dana to her right as they cleared the rear edge of the structure. Dana gasped and halted. Levi walked into her.

"What the hell," Levi growled.

Then he saw what had made Dana stop in her tracks. There was a ramp in the backyard. A ramp that led into a dimly lit room which was quite obviously not present in any other dimension but the second. It was like looking into a television screen without being able to see the sides. Levi took a couple of steps to his left to confirm this view. Whatever space the room at the top of the ramp occupied, it was not in this backyard.

"What the hell are we looking at?" Dana squeaked.

"I don't know."

There was a Ford Expedition parked a couple of yards away, and Dana was compelled to go hide behind it. Levi seemed to have more fortitude and began walking toward the ramp.

"Levi, wait."

Levi did not wait. He reached the bottom of the ramp and stepped upon it. He waved Dana on, smiling. Dana huffed and crept up after him.

"This is not smart," she whispered.

"Come on, we have to know what we're dealing with. We've been chasing this thing all over New England."

Dana and Levi reached the top of the ramp, and the full space of the room became apparent. Despite the emptiness of the room, its nature was plain. Dana vocalized it.

"We're on a ship."

What else could it..."

Levi interrupted himself. Somebody was whistling. Levi and Dana did not move, completely uncertain of the source of the sound. Levi realized at last that it was coming from a nearby hallway. There was a stairway leading up to a room above this one, and it was the only place to hide, so Dana and Levi took up shelter behind it. It was lousy cover.

A man emerged from the far hallway and crossed the room to the ramp. He took a look around, his expression one of pride. He walked down the ramp and disappeared into the yard. The ramp began to close. Dana grabbed Levi's arm tightly.

"Levi, let's get out of here," she said.

"Wait. Surely we can open the ramp ourselves. Let's take a look around."

Dana thought this was a baseless assumption, but her curiosity was starting to get the better of her.

"Okay."

The ramp finished closing. Levi's attention was drawn a long staircase on the left side of the room.

"This way," he said.

Levi ascended the stairs with Dana in tow. At the top of the stairway was a long hallway with hourglass-shaped windows running along one side. The closest door was on their left, so Levi opened it. On the other side of the door was a semi-circular room with a long, sloping counter top. Large sweeping windows occupied most of the forward part of the room, offering an unobstructed view of the night sky. Smaller windows flanked the room on either side. Other than the counter space, the room was empty.

"This looks like the command center," said Levi, "but it's obviously still under construction."

"Yeah," said Dana. "It looks like there are meant to be chairs here."

"Wait, look at this."

Levi crossed to a brass plaque set into the wall. There was writing inscribed upon it.

"*Temeraria Fides,*" Dana read aloud, "*2003.*"

"Reckless Faith," said a voice.

Dana and Levi spun around. The man they'd seen earlier was standing at the rear of the room. Three other people, one man and two female, were also there. Three of them were pointing firearms at the visitors.

"Oh, shit," said Levi.

"Who are you?" said the first man.

"My name is Levi Marks. This is my colleague Dana Andrews. We work for the American Space Transmissions Research Association."

"What the hell is that?" said one of the women, the taller of the two.

"Are you familiar with SETI?" asked Dana.

"Yes," said the second man, who stood a couple of inches taller than the other.

"We're a fledgling organization with the same goal."

The first man lowered his weapon a couple of degrees and took a step forward.

"How did you find this ship?" he asked.

Levi motioned with his hands. "Do you mind? We're unarmed."

"I do, actually. Ray, would you please?"

The man named Ray nodded. He handed his shotgun to the woman next to him and stepped forward. He expertly patted down Levi and Dana, sparing no modesty in the process.

"They're clean."

The first man holstered his pistol, as did the taller woman.

"How," said the first man again, "did you find this ship?"

"We've been tracking a signal since last Friday," Dana said. "It piqued our curiosity so we decided to head out and find the source. We finally located it."

"What kind of signal?" asked Ray.

"A low frequency, non-repeating, close pattern cluster waveform," said Levi. "The signal by itself is meaningless and contains no data, at least none that we're aware of."

"How were you able to trace it to this location?" asked the first man.

"We triangulated it with several receivers. Piece of cake. The only problem was waiting until the source stopped moving. I guess you guys have been busy."

"Where have you tracked us?"

"The first signal was detected in low Earth orbit above Pennsylvania, which is where we're based. After that we received the same signal from the ground in Orford, New Hampshire. Then we picked it up again here, in this neighborhood, but we didn't have a precise lock. After that, we followed the signal to a pier in Chelsea. Finally we got a lock on coordinates here. Look, I don't mean to be rude, but what exactly is this ship? Who built it?"

"I don't know if I can give you that information," the first man said.

"Well, you'd better decide soon before the authorities show up."

"What? What do you mean?"

"Whatever you did down in Chelsea," began Dana, "it has the CIA and the military looking for you."

"Son of a bitch!"

"Wait a minute, John," said Ray. "They're investigating the Portland, that's all. They can't track us."

"Unless," said the taller woman, "These two are in fact working for the CIA."

Levi smiled. "I assure you, we're the furthest thing from government agents there are."

"Ray," said John, "search them again, please, this time get their wallets and cell phones."

Ray did so. He and John examined the items.

Levi pointed at his stuff. "As you can see, we are who we say we are. There's no government identification, and no phone numbers listed for any government agencies. Just our ASTRA membership cards."

"They could be undercover," said the taller woman.

"If they are, Ari," said John, "they really suck."

"Look," said Dana, "we can't prove that we do or do not work for the CIA, other than offer our word. If we did, though, why would we give you advanced warning that the CIA is looking for you? But, it doesn't matter one way or the other."

"How do you figure?" said Ari, smirking.

"If we did work for the CIA, you'd boot us off the ship and then figure out what's transmitting the signal we received. Then you'd eliminate the signal and disappear. If we don't work for the CIA, then you'll still boot us off the ship and disappear."

"Or," began Levi, "you could let us in on the truth."

"Will you excuse us for a minute?" said John.

The four crew members whispered among themselves for a moment. Levi and Dana looked at each other. Levi shrugged.

"Okay," said John. "We've agreed to try some quid-pro-quo. You've already answered a ton of questions so you get to go first."

Levi furrowed his brow. "Uh, why are you willing to give us information if you can't be sure of who we are?"

"Because we don't intend to let you go," said John.

"At least not until we're satisfied that you're not a threat to our mission," said Ray.

"Fine," said Dana. "First question. Who do you work for?"

"Nobody," John said. "We work for ourselves."

"Who built this ship?" asked Levi.

"We built it ourselves."

"Oh, come on. Who funded the construction?"

"We did."

"Now I know you're putting me on. This isn't going to work if all you're going to offer us are lies."

"If you don't like our answers we can escort you ashore."

Dana put up her hand. "Okay, okay. What is your mission?"

"We don't know."

Ari started to laugh, and caught herself.

"What's so funny?" asked Levi.

"I'm sorry," said Ari, "but we're honestly not being assholes on purpose. The truth is that we don't know our mission. We only know that there *is* a mission."

The other woman spoke for the first time.

"I'm Christie," she said. "I have a couple of questions."

Levi nodded. "Shoot. Not literally, I mean."

"You said that you received a signal from this ship on Friday night."

"Yes."

"And again periodically over the next few days?"

"Uh huh."

"And it was an intermittent signal, not a constant transmission?"

"That's right," said Dana. "It was non-repeating. Only a few seconds long."

"What sort of equipment were you using?"

"Our main system in Pennsylvania is a cold-war era interferometer array donated by the government. Nothing particularly high-tech."

Christie addressed the crew. "Okay, then. All we have to do is ask Seth where the signal is coming from, and get him to shut it up. The CIA doesn't know anything other than the missing Portland, then, even if these two are working for them they'll never find us. As far as I'm concerned we risk very little by telling them more about what's going on."

"I agree," said Ray.

"I don't know," said Ari.

John was staring off out of the viewscreen. After a couple of seconds he spoke.

"Seth seems to be telling me that the signal they're referring to is a by-product of a certain kind of matter to energy transfer. He can't prevent the signal, but he can create a Doppler wave to cancel it out."

"Who's Seth?" asked Dana.

John stepped forward. "Allow me. My name is John Scherer. My friends and I intercepted signals from space while fooling around with my HAM radio. We were able to translate those signals. They contained blueprints for building this ship. Over the past several years we've been building this ship, which as you now know is called the Reckless Faith. We have only a specific set of coordinates to set off for, and we don't know anything about who sent the blueprints or why. We have to assume that it is another civilization and their attempt at first contact with the human race."

Dana looked dubious. "So, are you all rich? This must have cost millions of dollars."

"We have our ways," said Ari.

John continued. "I've been ripping off the casinos down in Connecticut. Well, not ripping them off really, I'm exceptionally good at counting cards. Ari here has been doing some insider trading on the stock market. Over time we've managed to get the funds we need. We've been assembling the Faith in a remote part of northern New Hampshire. Friday was the first day we got her in the air."

"What's going on in Chelsea?" Levi asked.

"We had to borrow some technology from the US Navy. I guess the CIA is a little pissed about that."

"I'd say so. So let me get this straight. You're building this ship to head out into space, and you were planning on leaving without telling nary a soul about it?"

"Pretty much, yeah."

"Isn't that incredibly selfish?"

"I'd think that you'd be able to understand our motivation quite easily, considering your line of work. Imagine if you had received the plans. Would you be so cavalier about handing them over to NASA? They'd give you a slap on the back and that would be the end of it. You'd be lucky if they let you attend the launch."

"I suppose," said Dana.

"Keeping it a secret was the only way that we could ensure our own participation. Which, by the way, is also the only way you two will be allowed to participate."

"Whoa, wait a minute," said Ari. "You're inviting them?"

"Let's see if they have anything to contribute first," said Ray.

"What kind of technical skills do you have?" asked Christie.

"What sort of technical skills do you need?" Dana asked incredulously. "You seem to have things under control already."

"We could use computer programming skills," said Ari. "I'm not looking forward to writing the code for this entire ship by myself."

"Sorry," said Levi.

"Nothing worth mentioning," said Dana.

"What about engineering skills?" John queried.

"Zip," said Levi.

"Zilch," said Dana.

"Tactical knowledge?" asked Ray.

"There, I might be able to help you," said Levi. "I was an officer in the United States Army, infantry. I served during Gulf War One."

"Okay, so Mister Marks knows his stuff."

John frowned. "That's good, but our priorities lie in the technical aspects of getting this ship space-worthy."

"We're both good at what you'd think we'd be good at working at ASTRA," Dana said, "collecting and analyzing radio transmissions."

"Maybe they could help me figure out how to interpret Seth's code," said Ari.

"Could be," said John.

"Now by saying 'participate,'" began Dana, "do you mean help you finish the ship, or go with you into space?"

"That's up to you."

Dana frowned, and said, "I don't know if I'm ready to make that kind of decision."

Levi nodded. "I agree. That's a pretty heavy choice to have to make."

"You don't have to make it now," said Ray. "If you want to help out for now, that's okay with us. If not, we'll have to ask you to leave. If you leave now you can be sure you'll never see us again."

"I'm in," said Dana.

"Me, too," said Levi.

John cocked his head. "Okay. You can stay. There's just one problem."

"What's that?"

"I'm all out of beds."

The sun was making an appearance above the horizon, and Kyrie Devonai was still awake. The demands of his investigation were many, and questions still outnumbered answers by a large margin.

The divers in the Mystic River had discovered more fragile metal pieces, but nothing that accounted for the mass of the Portland, not even close. Yet, the pieces that they did find were definitely from the Portland. Something had scooped the ship out of the water and left only small bits of the hull behind. Devonai had seen some pretty unbelievable things in his relatively short life, but this was the strangest.

Devonai leaned back in his chair. He was in his boss' office, located on Park Street in Boston, working on his boss' computer, and drinking out of his boss' blue CIA coffee mug. If Hill were there, she might have objected, not to the use of her office (which also contained a conference area), but to the intimacy of Devonai's body to her personal items. He was looking over the file that his subordinates had produced on Levi Marks and Dana Andrews. He'd had the file for three hours now, and had familiarized himself with it. It didn't reveal much, other than the fact that the two researchers were telling the truth at the pier.

The past three hours had been spent trying to track Marks and Andrews down. Devonai had everything he needed, names, social security numbers, driver's licenses, and bank account numbers, except for one. The credit card company used by Marks was taking its sweet time reporting back on usage logs. Since Andrews didn't seem to maintain a credit card, their only hope of tracking them down was Marks' credit card trail. Devonai could have also used Marks' cell phone as a way to track him, but the cell phone was billed through the credit account so they didn't yet know the number.

If they didn't hear back from the credit card company soon, Devonai knew he would have to send agents to Marks' and Andrews' residences down in Bethlehem, Pennsylvania, in hope that they would eventually appear there. Devonai was used to working with his own local team, and he would have preferred to keep any of the other CIA field offices out of it. With such a serious and bizarre event, however, the involvement of the entire organization seemed imminent.

Trying to determine the reasons for the involvement of ASTRA was just one of Devonai's many problems. Not the least of these was that Devonai's team, Omega, was out of practice for this kind of investigation. They were originally created to protect against threats against US government research, but had been employed by the CIA for the last couple of years to chase down various terrorist groups. Devonai, Richter, and other team members had just come back from several months in Afghanistan, and most of them had barely finished a much-needed vacation when the Portland disappeared.

Devonai had come a long way from his meager beginnings as a cop with the Boston Police Department, and it was a time like this that he wondered if he would have been better off staying there. Of course, his direction in life was more complicated than any choices he made in the matter. That was the one thing about the missing ship that didn't surprise him; his involvement in it. That figured.

Richter walked into the office. He seemed to be dealing with the lack of sleep much more easily than Devonai.

"What's up, Richter?"

"I got the metallurgy results from the lab," replied Richter.

"What did Brockway come up with?"

"Delana had to call in a pinch hitter on this one. Doctor Bogenbroom from MIT did most of the work."

"Three cheers for Doctor Bogenbroom. What were the results?"

"The metal that was taken from the river was carbon steel, consistent with the type used to construct the Portland. However, the steel was only five percent the density that it should have been. It was turned into Swiss cheese, or if you will, Styrofoam. If the entire ship lost structural integrity like this then it could have spontaneously disintegrated under its own weight. The rest of the ship may be on the bottom of the river, too. Only as silt, not metal."

"So technically, the Portland isn't missing at all?"

"Apparently not."

Devonai shook his head. "What could have caused something like this?"

"According to the fine doctor, there's no plausible explanation. No man-made or natural force is capable of that kind of structural destabilization."

"Maybe we're dealing with some kind of new weapon. Something like this could be just as devastating as a direct-force weapon like a nuclear device. It sounds like sort of an 'anti-neutron' bomb. It destroys metal, plastic, and glass, but leaves living organisms alive."

"We don't know what kind of effect it might have had on a living organism, since there wasn't anybody on board at the time. At least, I hope to God there wasn't."

"If, by the way, another country has been developing this weapon, and the CIA didn't know about, not the slightest inkling, we're all going to get pink slips from John Q. Public."

"Have you considered the other possibility?"

Devonai looked at Richter ruefully. "What other possibility?"

"Think about it. There were ASTRA researchers there. They said they were tracking a signal that originated from space."

"Yeah, so what? I'm already considering the possibility that a weapon like this could be satellite based."

"Yeah, but what about something from beyond Earth?"

Devonai rolled his eyes. "Come on Richter, after everything that we've been through, all the technological advances that we've witnessed, and the good and evil that it can cause, how can you even entertain the thought of the involvement of extra-terrestrials?"

"You know, Devonai, there is stuff that is classified above even us. I'm surprised that you haven't considered the involvement of ETs in Earth's recent history. Compared to what we do know, little gray men from beyond our planet is hardly a giant leap."

"Oh, I've considered it, Richter. I just tend not to waste my time on trivial matters."

"It seems to me that perhaps it is time to start, Major."

Devonai stared blankly out at the Massachusetts State House. More than ever he wanted to slip into his bed, wrap his arm around his sweetheart Mara, and pass out.

The sound of a fax machine snapped him back to life. Richter collected the paper and announced the message.

"They got a hit on Marks' credit card. It was last used at a motel in Woburn. He's checked in until zero nine hundred this morning."

"No rest for the weary, then. Let's get our hides to Woburn."

17.

The sound of John's bedroom door slamming open woke him out of a fitful, dreamless sleep. Ari stood in the doorway. She would have looked ferociously angry if John could have seen anything.

"This better be good," John said, rubbing his eyes.

"Levi is gone," Ari said through gritted teeth.

"What the hell?"

John threw off his blankets and groped for his bathrobe. He'd forgotten he was only wearing his underwear and Ari grinned at him. She grabbed the bathrobe off of the floor and handed it to him.

"What about Dana?" John groaned.

"She's still here. She's not going anywhere now."

John caught a quick glance at the clock as Ari dragged him downstairs. It was quarter after seven, a scant five hours after he'd gone to sleep. He felt Seth poke at his mind and he refused to let him in. Seth's yen for John's brain was becoming quite tiresome.

Gathered around the kitchen counter were Ray, Christie, and Dana. John noticed a lack of weaponry compared to their previous conversations, and figured that Dana didn't need any extra incentive to stick around this time. John tried to catch his balance.

"What's going on?" he asked.

"Marks took off at some point last night," Ray said. "I noticed his truck was missing a few minutes ago."

"It's not like him," said Dana.

"You mean it's not like him to take off and leave you with a bunch of strangers?" asked Ari.

"Yes, that's what I mean. I don't know where he could have gone. It's possible he just went out to get breakfast."

"Yeah, but without telling anybody?" said Ray. "I think we should assume the worst."

"What do you mean?" asked Christie.

"He's gone to the authorities."

"He wouldn't do that without consulting me first," said Dana.

"Are you sure?" John asked.

"Fairly completely sure."

"That's not very reassuring," said John, crossing his arms. "Okay, here's what we're going to do. I'll consult with Seth and see if I can figure out what's causing the transmission signal. Then we'll clean this place up and leave no trace of the project. We'll relocate to Ray's place so that the CIA can't track us."

Ray shook his head. "I don't have a private yard. Where are we going to board the ship without being seen?"

"Oh, shit, that's right. Well, we can't go to the cabin. Marks already has the coordinates."

"No, he doesn't," said Dana. "I do. He only knows that the signal originated in Orford somewhere."

"Can't he get that information from your ASTRA office, though?" asked Christie.

"Damn it, that's right. Hold on, I have to make a phone call."

Dana withdrew her cell phone and dialed. Page's creaky voice came through on the other end.

"Dana? What's going on?"

"Page, has Levi checked in within the last five hours?"

"No, why?"

"I need you to dump all the files related to signal three one five. Delete everything, all the recordings, coordinates, and locations."

"What? Why? What the hell is going on up there?"

"It's too difficult to explain right now. It has something to do with the military and an experimental satellite. If they find out that we've been listening there's no telling what they might do. They might shut us down, or worse."

"Crap. All right, I'll destroy the files."

"And one more thing. Don't tell Levi anything. He can't be trusted any more."

"Excuse me? Why the heck not?"

"He just can't. If he calls looking for information you can tell him I authorized the deletion. I do have the authority, you know."

"All right, fine. But this is all on your head, Andrews. I'm not taking the fall for this if something happens."

"Okay, blame me, I don't care. Just see to it."

Dana hung up.

"That was a masterful bit of deception," began John, "but they still know about Orford. If they search the entire town they will find the cabin."

Dana nodded. "I thought it would be a good idea to dump the info anyway."

"It certainly gives you bonus points in your favor," said Ray. "I think we should relocate to the cabin. It buys us several hours, anyway. We need to bug out of here immediately. We can think about a more permanent solution once we're on our way."

"Okay. Everybody grab your gear. Be on the Faith and ready to go as soon as possible. If Levi went to the CIA, they could be here any minute."

Dana dialed her phone again, and nodded.

"Okay," said Christie.

"I call downstairs bathroom," said Ari.

"We don't have enough time for everybody to take a shower," said John. "If you insist, Ari, fine. I need one too. The rest of you will have to make do for now."

"Levi's not answering his phone," said Dana.

"That's not a good sign. Let's get moving."

Twenty minutes later, everyone was gathered on the bridge of the Faith. Friday was poking around cautiously. John was concentrating as he communicated with Seth. After a few moments John addressed the others.

"Seth tells me that he can try to mask the energy signature with a Doppler wave by modulating the containment field."

"What containment field?" said Christie.

"Um... Seth says that the containment field is the energy field that secures the ship. It acts as a shield from interstellar debris and radiation. It can also absorb directed energy."

"Directed energy?" asked Ari.

"I'm not sure what he means by that. Apparently neither does he."

"Typical."

"Seth is also telling me that he can try using Tycho or Friday as a medium instead of me. I tried explaining that the animals don't have sophisticated vocal chords like us, but Seth doesn't seem to think this is a problem."

Ray picked up Friday and moved her to the counter top.

"Let's give it a try," Ray said.

Friday looked directly into Ray's eyes. A clear voice filled the bridge. It was the same voice Seth had used inside the orb illusions.

"Hello," the voice said.

"Hello, Seth," said John. "How do you feel?"

Friday looked at John. "There's a lot of room in here."

"It feels good to get you out of my head, no offense."

"How could I be offended by you, squeaky?"

There was a strong emotion of affection evident in the comment. John looked thoroughly embarrassed.

"Squeaky?" Ari said, amused.

"Squeaky is my pet name for Friday... 'cause of her, uh, squeaky little voice. Seth must be sensing Friday's attachment to me."

"That is so sweet," said Christie.

"Yeah, just wait until we try Tycho out up here."

Friday looked at Christie.

"Tycho likes you," Seth said.

Christie smiled in unabashed joy. It was about the most sentimental thing she had ever heard. Christie always suspected that Tycho had only considered her a convenient source of food.

"Seth, get us underway. Our destination is Boston Furniture Supply."

"Understood," Seth replied.

"Boston Furniture Supply?" queried Dana.

"We're going to try Seth's matter transportation technology again. We need furniture for the ship, as you can see."

"What do you mean, 'again?'"

The others became distracted by the view as the ship began to lift off. Dana crossed to the window herself and watched the ground grow distant.

"I think we can trust Dana," said Ray. "Why not tell her the truth?"

"There's more?"

John nodded. "Okay. Dana, we didn't tell you the truth last night. In reality we didn't receive any signals or plans from space. Seth came to us during a trip up to New Hampshire last Saturday. Ray, why don't you show Dana around the ship and tell her the story?"

"Sure," said Ray. "Care to have a look around?"

"Hell yes," said Dana.

"Follow me, then. Through here is an area we plan on using as a conference room..."

Ray and Dana exited through the right rear door.

"Are you sure we can trust her?" Ari asked.

"I think so," said John. "There's still a chance that she's hiding something from us, but I get a sense that she's all right."

"Me, too," said Christie. "We should be more careful, though. Levi could be poised to seriously compromise this mission."

"We have arrived," said Seth. "We are five hundred feet above the specified location."

"That was fast."

"It was only a three mile trip," said John. "Come on, let's go to the cargo bay and try this out."

John led the way off the bridge, down the stairs, and into the cargo bay. Tycho barked at them as they headed down the ramp.

"Christie, could you move Tycho into the armory, please?"

"Sure."

Christie did so. John looked around.

"Seth, are you still here?"

"Of course," said Seth's voice.

"Okay. Can you read the item I described to you before?"

"Yes, that item is present below."

"Transport it into the cargo bay."

A green point of light appeared at the center of the bay. It pulsed and grew in size. Optical distortions similar to waves of heat appeared from the deck to the ceiling. A noise like sand being poured onto a tile floor could be heard. A leather desk chair appeared. It was the executive model, with a high back and large, cushioned arms. John and Ari smiled. Christie came down from the armory.

"Ah, I missed it," she said.

"That was exceedingly cool," said Ari.

John walked up to the chair. "Is it safe to use?"

"Transportation is complete," said Seth.

"Cool."

John hopped into the chair, which immediately crumbed into chunky dust. John hit the deck hard.

"What... the... hell?" John said, shocked.

"I thought you said that transportation was complete," Ari said to Seth.

"Transportation is complete," said Seth.

"Well obviously not!" exclaimed John, standing up.

Christie picked up a piece of the chair. She crushed it effortlessly.

"I think I know what's going on," she said.

"The name is Major Devon, first name Kyle, I told you!"

Levi was getting the royal run-around from the CIA operator. He'd been on hold for almost half an hour now, and the fact that he wasn't sure about the Major's name didn't help matters much.

His cell phone barely got a signal in his concrete bunker of a motel room. Levi wandered from corner to corner, trying to chase down a better connection.

"What is this in regards to?" the operator asked.

"It's private. Look, I told you that the Major was working in the Boston area. Surely you know to whom I'm referring."

"I'm going to transfer you."

"No, wait. Wait! Shit!"

Levi fumed as he was once again put on hold. He paced around the room compulsively.

"This is Lauren Hill, may I help you?"

The new voice was a small measure of progress.

"Yes, I'm looking to speak with a Major Devon."

"What's this regarding, sir?"

"I have important information for him. Look, can you just tell him that Levi Marks is looking for him?"

"I'm afraid that for security reasons you'll have to be more specific."

"This is in regards to the incident at the Chelsea pier last night."

There was a knock at the door. Levi froze.

"Answer the door," Hill said.

"Wh... what?"

"Answer the door, Mister Marks."

Levi approached the door. All was quiet. Opening the door slowly, Levi found himself facing the Major.

"Mister Marks," Devonai said. "I think you can hang up now."

Levi did so. He backed up into the room, confused.

"I had no idea you were capable of that kind of thing," he said.

"What kind of thing? Do you mind if I come in?"

"You triangulated my phone, didn't you?"

Devonai shrugged and let himself in. He crossed to a chair and sat down.

"No, we traced your credit card. The person you were speaking to just happens to be my supervisor."

"Oh."

"Now then," said Devonai, removing a small black tin from his pocket, "what did you want to talk to me about?"

"You traced my credit card? You must have been looking for me before I called."

"Correct."

"Then you tell me why you're here."

"You know why I'm here. I want to know why you called us. Where's your partner, by the way?"

"You wouldn't believe me if I told you."

"The last several hours have been all about believing new things."

"I know this has something to do with a Navy vessel, and technology being stolen. What exactly happened down in Chelsea?"

"How do you know about the involvement of a Navy vessel?"

"What technology was stolen?"

Devonai removed a small cigar from the tin and lit it.

"Mister Marks, countering every question of mine with one of your own is not going to curry my favor. Answer my questions first, and if I like what I hear, I'll tell you more about Chelsea."

"You think that what happened down there is classified? I'm the one with the classified information, as it will surely be once I tell you."

Devonai blinked. "I'm waiting."

"There is a spaceship parked outside of a house not five miles from here."

"Is that so?"

"In fact it is. This ship was created using instructions from an alien civilization, and is being manned by a group of amateurs."

"Didn't Hollywood already take a gander at this one, Levi?"

"This is far from fantasy, Major. All you have to do is come with me and I can prove it. But we have to act fast; once the others know I'm gone, they'll move the ship for sure."

"If there's a spaceship, they'll just take off into space, right? How are we supposed to catch them in a Crown Victoria?"

"The ship isn't complete yet. The crew still has many different things to install before they'll be ready to leave. But if we miss them in Woburn there will be no telling where they'll end up next."

"You seem to have been doing a good job of tracking them so far."

"True. ASTRA is perfectly capable of keeping tabs on the ship's location. By the way, I notice you're humoring my story more than I'd expected. Whatever happened down in Chelsea must have been quite substantial."

"Actually, it was quite insubstantial, and that's the whole point. Did these people tell you how they built their spaceship?"

"They told me they've been building it gradually over the past several years."

"How large is the ship?"

"I don't know, exactly. The exterior is hidden by some sort of light refracting field. It's at least a hundred feet long and three decks high."

"Okay. I'll play along for now. When I see the ship for myself, you can say I told you so. If we miss them in Woburn, I want ASTRA to track them for us. Call your people and tell them that CIA agents will be dispatched to oversee the operation. You're located in Bethlehem, Pennsylvania, right?"

"Tell me what happened in Chelsea first."

Devonai sighed. "Parts of the USS Portland have been stolen."

"What parts?"

"Parts!"

"Isn't the Portland decommissioned?"

"That's correct. Are you familiar with her?"

"She was part of the fleet parked off of Kuwait in 1991."

"Ah, yes. You were part of a military police battalion at the time."

"You've been doing some digging, I see. You also just tipped your hand."

"Is that so?" Devonai asked, smoke swirling around his head.

"If the Portland was anywhere near that pier last night, I would have seen it. Miss Andrews and I got a good look at the activity on that pier before you dismissed us. Either the Portland sank, in which case at least fifty feet of it would still be visible above the water, or it is no longer there. If it is no longer there, then someone or something removed it. You say parts of the Portland were stolen. I say the whole thing has been stolen."

"Very good, Mister Marks, but you haven't figured out everything. And would you care to explain to me what use the crew of the spaceship would have for a vessel of that size?"

"Maybe they're using it to construct a second spaceship."

"That's plausible, given the parameters. Now if you don't mind, call your people at ASTRA and make arrangements for them to receive field agents."

"We should really get back to the ship."

"Make the call first."

Levi shook his head, removing his cell phone from his pocket. He dialed and waited.

"Page, it's Levi."

"Levi?" said Page's voice. "What's been going on up there?"

"It's complicated. Listen, we're going to be getting some serious backup on this project. The CIA has promised us funds and manpower."

"The CIA? Levi, listen to me. Dana called me about ten minutes ago. She told me to delete all of the information about file three-one-five and the search for the signal source."

"What? You didn't do it, did you?"

"Of course not."

"Good, you had me worried for a second. The CIA is sending case officers to the lab to oversee the operation. If the signal moves again we're going to need to track it, as always. From now on, however, it's more than just academic."

"I understand, but why is the CIA getting involved? What did you discover in Massachusetts?"

"It will all become clear in due time. Call me when the operatives arrive."

Levi hung up.

"Excellent work, Marks," said Devonai. "Thanks for your help."

"Hey, you'd still have your thumbs up your butts if it wasn't for me and ASTRA, you know."

"For all I know, we still do, until the evidence proves otherwise. Now what did your colleague say that upset you so much?"

"Dana Andrews is working against us. She tried to get ASTRA to destroy the project data. She's also agreed to join the crew of the spacecraft. That I can confirm personally. That's why I'm here and she's not."

"Okay," said Devonai, standing. "Let's head out, then. Where exactly are we going?"

"To the residence of John Scherer."

18.

Ray and Dana climbed the steps to the bridge, their tour of the Faith complete. John, Ari, Christie, and Friday were there. John had just sent a message to Ray via Seth that he was holding a meeting on the bridge. The timing was perfect, despite the fact that Dana had spent so much time admiring the engine room.

"What's up?" Ray asked.

"Did you notice that pile of dust in the cargo bay?" asked John.

"Yes."

"That's the result of our attempt to transport a chair from the furniture store."

"Oh. Yikes."

"Seth insists that everything went properly."

"I have an idea," said Christie. "I think I might be able to explain what happened."

"Go for it."

"How many of you are familiar with the Heisenberg Uncertainty Principle?"

Christie was answered with silence and blank stares.

"Enlighten us, please," said Ari.

"It comes from quantum mechanics. When physicists began studying the properties of light, they found that they could record either the location of a single photon, or its momentum, but not both. Since the experiment itself changed one or the other, it became evident that it was impossible to know a quantum particle's location *and* its mass plus direction of movement, also known as momentum. The only thing you can do is predict the probability of both factors at any given moment. I think what happened with the chair is that Seth can't determine anything more than the probability of the locations of the subatomic particles that made up the chair. The result was that he only transported up a percentage of the chair, not the whole thing."

"That's an interesting theory," said Dana, "but Seth supposedly used the same technology to create the superstructure of the Faith out of the Portland, right?"

"Yes," said John.

"So why did it work for the hull, walls, decks, and everything else? They seem quite solid to me."

John turned to Friday. "Seth, why did the chair disintegrate?"

"There wasn't enough," replied Seth.

"Enough what?"

Seth was quiet for a few seconds before responding.

"Aluminum, copper, iron, silicon..." Seth said, trailing off.

"Enough material?"

"Yes."

"Why wasn't there enough material, Seth?"

"There was sufficient material at the source."

"Why didn't you use it, then?"

"You directed me to transport only one object."

"Seth," began Christie, "if the chair at the source contained one hundred percent of its own mass, the what percentage did you transport aboard?"

"Thirty-five percent," replied Seth.

"So can you transport one hundred percent aboard next time?"

"Yes."

"Okay, fine," said John. "Transport one hundred percent of one chair from the surface onto the bridge."

"That is not possible. One chair contains only thirty-five percent of the necessary mass for transport."

"This makes sense," said Christie. "In order to compensate for the Heisenberg Principle, Seth has to get extra material from another source."

"That's why the Portland was destroyed!" exclaimed Ari. "In order to create the Faith, Seth used up almost all of the mass of the Portland. What was left behind collapsed and disintegrated."

"That follows," said John. "Okay Seth, using all available materials from the surface, transport one chair to the bridge."

The green dance of light and distortions filled the room, leaving behind another executive office chair.

"That was beautiful," said Christie.

John approached the chair, bent at the waist, and poked the seat. Nothing happened. John grabbed the chair by the arms and shook it. Satisfied, John sat down.

"We have a winner!" said John exuberantly.

"Sweet," said Ray.

"Let's get down to the cargo bay," said John. "We've got a lot of stuff to take before the store opens. But we only take the bare minimum for furnishing the bridge, the conference room, the galley, and the crew quarters. We can't feasibly transport all this furniture on our own so this act of theft is necessary. Let's not get used to it."

Ari shrugged. "I wonder if Robin Hood was this hung up about his job."

Despite John's good intentions, he found himself talked into quite a bit of looting by his fellow crew members. They simply needed too much and had too little money. The logistics of picking up all the things they needed were also quite daunting without the aid of the Faith. The only thing that prevented any transportation was the proximity of people to the desired items, and occasionally, the lack of overall atomic mass. Still, over the last hour the crew had managed to collect chairs, tables, beds, cabinets, wardrobes, and various other items deemed necessary.

This task completed, John was dropped off at his office and Ari at hers. In order to avoid detection, John was dropped onto the roof of his building, while a sufficiently isolated part of the woods near Ari's office was used for her. They would be picked up in four hours, at around one o'clock.

In the meantime, Ray, Christie, and Dana made additional stops with the Faith. They obtained some backup equipment for Seth's basic functions, such as oxygen canisters and industrial-grade dry cell batteries. They also spent a significant time raiding a home improvement store's warehouse for things they would need to secure the furniture to the ship, as well as the plumbing that they suddenly realized they needed to install. Their knowledge of plumbing was limited so they grabbed what they thought they would need initially; any refinements would have to come later (and with further education on the matter). Seth assured them that a fresh water supply would not be a problem, and any waste material would be ejected into space or recycled.

Without Ari's financial backing, they couldn't obtain any computer or network equipment. The only things they knew for sure they would need were twenty-one plasma screen computer monitors, one for each room of the ship and five for the bridge. Ray was perfectly happy to obtain them while John was away as he would most certainly object to the extravagance of the theft.

So far, Seth and Friday were doing a good job of piloting the ship, but Ray got the distinct impression that any complicated maneuvers would have to involve a human. Seth was going off of John's memory of the locations they'd been visiting; however, Seth made it clear that any destination that they weren't aware of by memory would require manual navigation.

Wary of Friday's fear of Tycho, the crew hadn't yet tried using the dog as a medium for Seth. Rather than keep him locked in the armory, Christie had begun to prepare her quarters with what little they had. With a bed, a bare mattress, and a wardrobe, the six identical quarters resembled empty dormitory rooms. Tycho was quite pleased to be in a room with a window, and was transfixed at the view from altitude.

At one o'clock, the Faith returned to a position above John's office building. John was on the roof waiting for them. After a final check to make sure nobody was watching, Seth lowered the ramp and John jumped aboard. He immediately saw a cargo bay full of furniture and supplies. He grinned. Ray and Dana were waiting to greet him.

"I see you've been busy," John said.

"Here's a manifest of everything we've obtained so far," said Ray, handing John a clipboard.

John reviewed the list.

"I would really like to take this thing into orbit," said Dana, "if we have time to do some sightseeing."

"I'd rather not take the Faith out of the atmosphere until we've installed the backup environmental controls."

"Seth says the ship is space-worthy right now."

"I know, but I'd just feel better waiting... you got stainless steel toilets?"

"They seemed more appropriate than porcelain," said Ray. "Where are we going to get replacement toilets in space?"

"Good point... you also got six twenty-one inch and fifteen seventeen inch plasma monitors?"

"Uh huh."

"For God's sake, Ray! We're not Parker and Longbaugh you know."

"I know. We thought plasma was the best choice, and there's no way we could afford so many plasma screen monitors."

"What's wrong with CRT monitors?"

"They're not as cool," said Dana. "Besides, these are touch-sensitive."

John sighed. "All right, then. Where's Christie?"

"Resting," said Ray.

"How goes the installation of the chairs on the bridge?"

"Come and see for yourself."

Ray led the way to the bridge. Upon arrival, Friday approached John.

"Daddy!" exclaimed Seth.

"Man, your cat really likes you," said Dana.

"I treat her right," John said.

The five executive office chairs had been installed on the bridge. They'd been bolted to the deck by removing their swivel bases and replacing them with flat panels, which were then drilled for bolt holes. Various metal working power tools were present, including a drill and a circular saw.

"Not bad, eh?" said Ray. "Aren't you glad I took metal shop in high school?"

"Very glad. I see you got my idea for the pilot's seat to work."

Ray nodded. The center seat had been mounted on rails, allowing it to roll from a more central position to the edge of the control panel. John's idea was to install the manual flight controls at that position, and the pilot would roll forward when he or she wanted to take over. The chair rolled freely, and Ray had even installed a locking lever.

"When did you have the time to do all this?" asked John.

"Dana and Christie concentrated on the transportation of supplies once they were familiar with the task," said Ray. "I came up here. This took about two hours all together."

"Impressive. I'm starting to feel better about this entire project."

"What do we have left to pick up?" asked Dana.

"Ari still needs to put together a list of the computer equipment she needs, which we'll have to buy. We also need rifles, ammunition, and food. There's no reason why we can't buy the ammo and the food, but for convenience sake and to avoid suspicion we'll transport the rifles directly. We need uniforms in case we need to look alike, but so far we haven't decided on what kind."

"Okay."

"Seth, take us to pick up Ari."

"Understood," said Seth.

"When we arrive," began John, "Ari and I will take the Expedition and go shopping for computer equipment. If you and Christie could continue to install furniture, that would be great."

"No problem," said Dana.

"Oh yeah, Dana, did you try calling Levi again?"

"Yes. He's still not answering his phone. I can try calling ASTRA again and see if they've heard from him."

"Please do."

Dana dialed her cell phone and waited.

"I still don't think we have anything to worry about from Levi," said Ray.

"I know," said John, "it's just our only loose end right now."

Page answered Dana's call.

"Hello," said Page's voice.

"Chris, it's Dana."

"Hi, Dana. Are you on your way back yet, or what?"

"I won't be back for a while. Has Levi tried to contact you since we last spoke?"

"Nope. Not a peep."

"Are you sure?"

"I'm quite sure."

"All right. Did you do what I asked you to?"

"Yes, all of that data has been deleted. You pissed off quite a few people today, Dana, and there are many more of us who are upset with you than there are who are worried about what's going on up in New England."

"I understand. All I can say is that I'm doing what needs to be done. I know that's not enough but it's all I have to give you."

"Fine. I guess I'll talk to you later, then."

"Goodbye, Page," said Dana, and closed her phone.

"That's odd that Levi hasn't contacted them," said John.

"I know, it doesn't feel right."

"We should assume that ASTRA has been compromised. It's the safest course of action."

"I agree," said Ray.

"Good. Only one question remains for now."

"What?"

"Did we bring any food aboard? I'm frigging starved."

A soft knock on the door was enough to awaken Devonai. He had crashed for three solid hours on Richter's bed, and despite the way he currently felt he knew it would do him a world of good. Devonai's apartment was a little too far away to warrant a return to his own bed, and as Richter's place was just around the corner from their Beacon Hill offices that's where he decided to go. Richter had given Devonai a sleeping bag to spread over the bed, and Devonai was asleep within two minutes of doing so.

"I'm up," Devonai gurgled.

Richter opened the door. "We've got some new information, major."

"I'll be right out."

Richter returned to the living room while Devonai roused himself from the grips of exhaustion. Their trip to John Scherer's place had proven a waste of time. An empty desk with tell-tale dust borders indicated that a computer had recently been removed, and there was nothing else of interest. Marks was apologetic but blamed the CIA for moving too slowly. Devonai thought that as long as Marks was deceiving his colleague and the crew of the supposed spaceship he could have found a more effective way to let the CIA in on it. Spooking them and giving them a reason to hide wasn't the swiftest move in recent tactical memory.

Fortunately, Marks had given them more with which to work. In addition to Dana Andrews and John Scherer, Marks had identified Raymond Bailey, Ari Ferro, and Christie Tolliver as participants. Before he'd passed out at Richter's place, Devonai had requested a comprehensive dossier on each. Devonai had asked Richter to wake him not only when the files were ready, but when agents were firmly established at the Pennsylvania ASTRA facility. Glancing at his watch, Devonai was surprised to find just how long it had taken. He holstered his pistol, drew on his jacket, and exited the bedroom.

"We got the files back on those people," Richter said. "The office faxed them over for you to review on the way back."

Richter was spreading mayonnaise on two ham sandwiches. He pointed at a pile of papers on the edge of the kitchen table. Devonai procured them.

"John Scherer," Devonai said, reading aloud, "age twenty-seven, occupation, CAD design engineer for one year. Before that he was an avionics technician with the New Hampshire Air National Guard, working out of Pease on the KC-135. Next is Raymond Bailey, age twenty-eight, Manchester, New Hampshire police officer. Arianna Ferro, age twenty-seven, software designer... damn, she is hot."

"And that's just a crappy faxed photo," said Richter, offering Devonai a sandwich.

"Thanks."

"Are you ready to head out? Hill is waiting for us downtown."

"Yeah, let's go."

Devonai and Richter exited the apartment and headed down the street. If it wasn't for the CIA, he knew, there would be no way Richter could afford an apartment in a neighborhood like this. Mount Vernon was just about the nicest street on Beacon Hill and probably the most expensive real estate on the planet, inch for inch.

The walk to the office on Park Street was so short, Devonai had barely finished his sandwich by the time they had stepped into the elevator. Hill's office was on the fourth floor. The door was open. Inside, Lauren Hill and Delana Brockway were waiting.

Lauren Hill had to be pushing forty, as far as Devonai could tell. In the years that he'd known her he never did get her exact age. She was always professional and only the slightest bit friendly on a personal level. It fit her role. Brockway, on the other hand, was as good a friend as Devonai had ever had. They had saved each other's backsides on many occasions. Her skills in the lab belied her efficacy with a rifle. Brockway was much closer to Devonai's own age of 29. Devonai occasionally wondered, if not for Mara, whether or not he could have gotten anywhere with Delana. Last he knew, Brockway was still maintaining a long distance relationship with somebody on the west coast, a fact that Devonai often reminded to Richter, who was unattached and more than a bit obviously interested.

"Good afternoon, gentlemen," said Hill.

"Afternoon," replied Devonai.

"Have a seat. I see you've been reviewing the files."

"Yes."

"What do you think?"

"Well, it's interesting, to say the least. A CAD engineer, a cop, a computer programmer, an astronomy professor, from my alma mater, by the way, and an ASTRA researcher. Besides the cop, I'd say this looks like a pretty good crew to head up a spacecraft such as Mister Marks claims."

"Marks says that they're still in the process of outfitting the ship, correct?"

"Yes."

"Then you'll find this interesting," said Brockway, holding up some papers. "Reports are coming in over the police wires about some very odd thefts. The first report comes from Resin Technologies in Wilmington. They reported eight Type 57 industrial grade batteries stolen from their facility. The odd thing is that these batteries weigh over three hundred pounds each, and the security guard says that there were no vehicles in or out of the facility during the window of time. Even odder than that is that three of the batteries were installed as part of an emergency power system to their power plant, and those batteries were taken out of their mounting brackets without disturbing several large objects blocking them!"

"How can they be sure these objects weren't moved?"

"According to the report, there was dust and detritus gathered around some boxes and barrels. To move them would have left an obvious shape on the ground. There were also no footprints or other marks in the dust, which was thick enough to make them obvious."

"It's strange, but it's not enough to link it to our case."

"There's another report you'll want to hear. This one is of one hundred oxygen cylinders missing from Compressed Air, Incorporated in Stoneham. The man who discovered the missing cylinders claims that there was a large pile of metallic dust in their place... and that one cylinder crumbled into dust when he tried to move it."

Devonai snapped his fingers. "Just like the Portland! Now there's a direct correlation."

"Yes," said Hill, "and oxygen cylinders have obvious use on a spacecraft."

"I suppose batteries would, too."

"Too bad there's no way to predict where they might go next," said Richter.

"That leads us to the next order of business," said Hill.

"ASTRA?" queried Devonai.

"That's right. Our agents arrived an hour ago. According to them, they haven't received a signal like the one they've been tracking since last night. We were only able to confirm Marks' story as well as the coordinates they've been following.

However, if you look at Ray Bailey's file, you'll see that he owns property in Orford, New Hampshire."

"The same town that they received a signal from over the weekend."

"Correct."

Devonai thought for a moment.

"Marks may have screwed us over more than we thought by spooking the crew," he said. "If they knew about the signal that was allowing ASTRA to track them, they could have taken measures to stop transmitting it."

"So should we check out the property in New Hampshire?" asked Richter.

"Of course. I would also like permission to place a two-man team on each of these individuals' home addresses. If the ship was cloaked like Marks said, they could be using any or all of these locations as way points. If they make an appearance, we can have the teams detain them."

"I agree," said Hill. "So that's four Massachusetts addresses and the one in New Hampshire?"

"Actually, that's three in Mass, two in New Hampshire, since Bailey lives in Manchester."

"Okay. I agree to this plan."

"Great."

"And I want you to scout each location yourself, starting with Ferro's apartment on Marlborough Street. Then you and Richter can settle at whichever location you think is most likely to yield results."

"Understood. Richter, get us a comfortable vehicle. We're going to be in it for eternity."

19.

"Your total is six thousand seven hundred thirty-five dollars and twelve cents."

John stared in horror at the LED screen shining in an unwavering fashion from the cash register. The clerk, who had just announced the total, stared at John in a considerably less terrified manner. Ari smirked and pulled a card from her wallet.

"American Express," she said. "Don't leave Earth without it."

John leaned against the shopping cart (which was overflowing) and shook his head.

"You just had to get the three-point-two gigahertz machines, didn't you?"

"This is my money and my computer system, John. Why concern yourself with it? For what we need it for, why skimp out on the funds?"

The clerk waited for the receipt to print out after Ari's card was rapidly accepted.

"It's wasteful. We have a lot left to go."

Ari signed the receipt, and helped John break the inertia of the cart.

"You are so hung up on buying what we can," she said in low tones. "It would be cute if it wasn't so annoying."

John and Ari crossed the parking lot to the Expedition.

"Look, I'll make you a deal. You stop haranguing me about my ethical standards and I'll stop bothering you about your precious computer systems."

"Fine," said Ari, smiling warmly, "I already got my way."

John muttered something under his breath. "Help me load up the truck."

Ari and John moved all of the equipment into the Expedition. John returned the cart to the front of the store before joining Ari inside the Ford.

"Seeing as we're right across the river from my place," said Ari, "can we swing by? I just want to grab a couple of things."

"We already agreed that we were going to wait until we were done with all of our gathering before collecting any personal items."

"John," Ari hissed, "I'm out of clean clothes."

"Fine, just for a few minutes. I feel dumb enough as it is driving around in public. Granted, nobody knows about Ray's involvement, and therefore, this vehicle."

"Didn't Ray introduce himself to Levi?"

"He didn't tell him his last name. It's still too risky right now. Picture what you want from your apartment now so that you don't waste time when we get there."

"Yes, sir."

John pulled out of the parking lot and headed east towards MIT. It was only a few minutes to Massachusetts Avenue, then over the river to Boston.

"How much does one of those infrared transceivers cost?" asked John.

"I don't know. A few hundred dollars I would imagine."

"How long before they notice it's missing?"

"I asked if I could borrow it, remember? They think I'm bringing it back in two days."

"Oh, right."

"How did your company take the announcement?"

"Fine, I guess. They were upset that I couldn't give two weeks notice. It was strange. I hadn't expected myself to enjoy quitting so much."

"You finally realized how much you disliked the job."

"I didn't dislike the job, though. I wasn't thrilled with it, either. I'm glad to be moving on, but if I wasn't moving on to the Faith I probably wouldn't be so happy."

"Are you happy?"

"No, I'm terrified. Well, I mean I'm excited."

"Me, too. I am really going to enjoy quitting my job. I like it all right, but the new freedom is still too much to ignore."

"I wouldn't call this project freedom, Ari. We have a lot of work ahead of us, and even when we finish we don't know what kind of mission this will turn out to be. We're exploring, sure, but the parameters of our exploration have already been set by Umber. I'd prefer not to count our blessings before we get there."

Ari thought for several seconds. "The Faith is a blessing."

Five minutes later, John pulled up in front of Ari's building. As usual there was nowhere to park. This was fine with John since it gave Ari no excuses to dally inside.

"Aren't you coming up?" she asked.

"I have to stay with the truck so that we don't get a ticket."

Ari rolled her eyes. "John, we're leaving the planet soon. Who cares about a parking ticket?"

"It will be Ray's responsibility. If we ever make it back from Umber, he doesn't need to find a metric shitload of late fees on a stupid parking ticket waiting for him."

"Fine, John, I'll pay the damn ticket before we leave if we get one. I need your help carrying some stuff."

John turned on the hazard lights and exited. "Okay, okay."

Ari got out and headed onto the sidewalk. John locked the truck. Ari lead the way into the foyer. John couldn't help but glance back at the Ford as they climbed the stairs to the second floor.

Ari lived on the fourth floor. John wondered why they hadn't taken the elevator, and then he remembered how shapely Ari was.

"*Every little bit helps,*" he thought.

Ari unlocked her front door and admitted John.

"Make yourself at home; I'll be ready in two minutes."

"Okay."

John idled around the spacious apartment, finally settling on a sofa chair for a seat. The apartment was about halfway to total chaos, which in John's opinion wasn't bad at all. Ari opened and closed dresser drawers in the bedroom.

"John," she said, "go make some selections from the liquor cabinet."

John shrugged and got up. He entered the kitchen and began poking around. He located the liquor and perused the selections. Ari had excellent taste.

"Do you have any champagne?" he asked. "We should smack a bottle upside the bow of the Faith."

"No, sorry. I do have a bottle of really nasty apricot brandy I'll probably never finish."

"We want to christen the ship, not curse it."

Ari emerged from the bedroom carrying a duffel bag. She set it by the front door and joined John in the kitchen just as her phone rang.

"Don't answer it," said John.

Ari observed the Caller ID, and said, "It's my father."

"Okay, just be careful what you say."

Ari nodded and waited for John to exit the kitchen. He wandered over to one of the living room windows and watched the street below. Ari pressed the talk key on her cordless handset.

"Hello, dad," she said.

"Arianna, it's your father," said a distant voice.

"How are you? Are you still in England?"

"Yes. How have you been?"

"I'm fine, dad. How long has it been, eight years?"

"I think so. Listen, Ari, I don't have much time to talk right now. There's just something that I've decided you need to know."

"If it's about you remarrying, dad, I already know that. Mom told me that you'd married an English woman."

"I did, and we have a child together. I initially thought you didn't need to know that; I know you had a hard time when your mother and I divorced. Still, she is your half-sister and you deserve to know that she exists."

"Thanks, I guess. You don't want us to have a relationship, do you? I don't need to be friends to a kid just because we're related."

"She's only a baby, Ari, and I don't expect you to fly to England to meet her. However, she may seek you out when she becomes an adult. Whether or not you choose to have any sort of relationship is up to you. Blood runs thickly in our family, although you've always been atypically aloof in such matters."

"Color me cynical, but divorce can do that to a person."

"Please, Ari, I'm just trying to do the right thing."

"I know. What's her name?"

"Miriam."

"That's a beautiful name. Look, I'm kind of busy right now. Can I write you later?"

"Of course. I guess I'll talk to you later."

"Bye, dad."

Ari hung up the phone and joined John in the living room. He continued to gaze out of the window.

"How's your pop?" he asked.

"Fine. Same old stuff. Hey, John..."

John turned around. Ari slipped her arms around his waist.

"Ari, I..."

"Seth interrupted me, you know," Ari said softly. "We never did finish talking that night."

"About us?"

"Yes, about us. You never answered my question."

"What was the question, again?"

"Oh, come off it. You know what it was. This whole situation has only distracted us from the issue. Maybe you consider it an excuse not to get on with the rest of your life, but I haven't forgotten about it."

"Ari, I'm not sure trying a new relationship is such a good idea at this stage. We're all emotionally taxed and worn out. We don't know what we might be in store for."

"Exactly. I want something to be able to hold on to out there. If you and I had something strong... we could be strong together in the face of whatever is out there."

A knock sounded at the door. Ari let go of John, defeated.

"Are you expecting someone?" John asked.

"It's probably my landlady," said Ari, crossing to the door. "She likes to think of herself as my guardian angel... who is it?"

With an ear-splitting crash, the door caved in. Swinging violently off of the hinges, the door smashed to the floor. Two men dressed in dark suits rushed inside. They were holding pistols, and the lead man immediately pointed his weapon at Ari.

"Free..." the man shouted.

Ari did not let him finish the statement. She side-stepped to the left of the weapon, bringing up her hands. She slapped the pistol out of the man's hands and followed up with a backhand to his face. As his momentum carried him forward, Ari swept her right leg underneath his feet and soundly knocked him to the ground.

John overcame his shock and rushed forward. The second man, obviously reluctant to shoot Ari, drew back his pistol and assumed a defensive position. John felt himself drawing his Beretta as he closed the distance to Ari.

Ari reacted to the second man's stance by throwing out a back kick. The blow landed squarely on the man's chest and he stumbled into the hallway. Ari grabbed the duffel bag from the floor and addressed John.

"Get to the truck!"

The first man grabbed John's pant leg. John broke the grip and swung his leg in a tight arc, striking the man on the chin. Ari rushed into the hallway as she drew her Glock, and to John's horror she shot the second man in the chest. The man collapsed onto the floor.

"What the hell are you doing?"

"We've got to get out of here, now!"

With that exclamation, Ari rushed down the stairs. John hesitated momentarily as he tried to assess how badly the second man was hurt. The first man struggled to get up, and John abandoned this idea. Ari had reached the third floor landing before John made it to the top of the stairwell.

Ari glanced back at John. A third man in a trenchcoat rounded the landing and all but collided with Ari. John let out a shout and began to descend the stairs.

The man in the trenchcoat twisted Ari's arm until the muzzle of her Glock pointed almost at her own head. She resisted, but the man swung around with his free hand and landed a blow to her ribs. Ari stepped aside, attempting to swing her weapon arm free. It didn't work, the man stepped with her and strengthened his stance. Ari ejected the magazine from her pistol, and then cleared the muzzle from her body just long enough to fire the round in the chamber. The bullet struck the wall behind the man in the trenchcoat, who released his grip on her. He instantly drew back his right leg and threw a wheel kick to Ari's side, landing on the same point he had hit earlier. She cried out in pain. The man had time to draw his pistol and fire a single shot at John's feet. Ari lunged towards the man and was stopped by a backfist to the face. The man grabbed one of her flailing arms and twisted himself behind her, until he had Ari by the neck with his left arm. He pointed his pistol at John.

"Hold it!" he yelled.

A fourth man in a camouflage jacket appeared on the opposite side of the landing, holding a pistol.

"Major!" he cried, taking a bead on John and firing a shot.

The round passed by John's head and struck the wall. John stumbled back, terrified but confused as to why the man had tried to shoot him. He then remembered that he was still clutching his Beretta. With inhuman speed John reversed course up the stairs in desperate search for cover.

"Richter," the man in the trenchcoat said, "get her out of here!"

Ari struggled against the man's grip only to be rewarded for her efforts with an armlock from Richter. Ari screamed in protest as Richter lead her away. The man in the trenchcoat carefully caught a glimpse up the stairs. John was at the top of the landing, just out of sight.

"John Scherer! This is Major Devonai of the CIA. Throw down your weapon and come out with your hands up!"

John was seized with fear. He knew that if he gave up, the entire mission could be compromised. As he gathered his thoughts John realized that he had to choose between Ari and the Faith and her crew.

"It was Marks, wasn't it?" John yelled. "He sold us out!"

"Nobody sold out anyone. We just want to talk to you. We only want to find out what happened to the Portland."

The man who had first kicked down Ari's door appeared from inside her apartment, pointing his pistol at John. John froze. The man, who was dazed and bleeding, pulled the trigger. Nothing happened. John pointed his Beretta at the man and found himself unable to act.

"Shit!" he hissed.

John lunged at the man, who had just figured out that his pistol's safety was on. John drew back and threw the only martial arts move he knew, a straight front kick to the man's chest. The man was lifted off the ground as his pistol discharged into the ceiling. He collapsed onto the ground and did not move. John, who could barely hear as it was, heard footsteps on stairs. He looked down the stairwell and saw that Devonai was on his way down. John pushed through the haze in his mind and followed.

John didn't see Devonai again until he burst out of the front door of Ari's building. Richter had pushed Ari into the back seat of a Crown Victoria, and he and Devonai turned to face John. They raised their pistols. John sprinted behind the Expedition as the two agents opened fire. John poked his head up around the hood of the Expedition and realized he had a perfect opening on Richter. He raised his Beretta and gained a sight picture. Richter hadn't seen him. John's finger tensed on the trigger but he couldn't drop the hammer. Devonai and Richter jumped into the Crown Vic and slammed it into reverse. They backed up until they got to an intersection and then turned off.

And before John could even realize it, the fight was over. John forced himself to think, and climbed into the Expedition. He clumsily holstered his unfired Beretta and jammed the truck into gear. Traffic was preventing him from pulling the same move as the Crown Vic, so he pulled forward down the street. Gathering his thoughts, John at last vocalized what he was thinking.

"What the hell was that all about?"

John struggled valiantly to remember the layout of Boston's streets. He entertained little hope of finding the

Crown Vic but it was all he could do. John pulled out his cell phone and dialed. He screwed up the first time, hung up, and tried again. At last Ray answered his phone.

"Yo, John," he said.

"Ray, shut up and listen to me! The CIA just grabbed Ari! They tried to grab us and then opened fire on me when we resisted!"

"What? Are you kidding me?"

"No, I am not kidding you! You have got to bring the Faith to pick me up!"

"Okay, right away. Where are you?"

"I'm on Clarendon Street in Boston right now. I need to... I need to think of a place you can come get me."

"Just get on ninety-three northbound and I'll think of a place."

"Okay. Ray, this is a seriously messed up situation. I don't know what we're going to do."

"Take it easy, John. Help is on the way."

"Are you all right, Richter?"

Devonai looked at the bandages on Richter's arms. He had just come from the lab, where Brockway had dressed his wounds.

"Yeah. That wildcat really took a chunk out of me with those claws of hers."

"You got off easy compared to the others."

"How are they?"

Richter was unaware of his colleague's conditions, as they had been transported to Mass General.

"Brackett is pretty soundly screwed up. He's got a broken hand, two broken ribs, and more bruises than they cared to count. Bearden took a nine millimeter round in his chest. His armor stopped the round but he's in observation to ensure there isn't any dangerous bruising around his aorta."

"Hmm. I guess my scratches aren't that bad really."

"I'd say so."

"How is the woman?"

"She's bruised up, nothing worse. I'm about to begin questioning her."

"Okay. I'll be in Hill's office if you need me."

"Thanks."

Devonai turned to face the door to the interrogation room. It was nothing more than an empty office, really, and hadn't been used for this purpose before. Devonai wasn't planning anything special so it would do just fine. Before entering, Devonai removed the magazine from his pistol and cleared the round from the chamber. He reinserted the magazine and secured the weapon in his holster. He kept the round in his left hand. Devonai took a deep breath and entered.

"You sons of bitches have quite a style, you know," said Ari.

Ari sported a cigarette, a cup of tepid coffee, and a weeping shiner on her cheek. Devonai sat down across the table from Ari.

"You'd excuse our tactics if you realize we weren't expecting you to fight back so... effectively."

"I'd say thanks for the compliment, but here I am."

"You should be thankful that my men are going to be all right. I have little sympathy for people who kill my officers."

"Then maybe you should refrain from such idiotic, ham-handed operations in the future."

"Clove cigarettes?"

"Yes."

"May I?"

Ari shrugged. "What do I care?"

Devonai accepted a cigarette from Ari and lit it.

"Enough small talk. My primary concern is to determine what happened to the Portland. I got a pretty wild story from Mister Marks about what happened to it. Perhaps you could enlighten me."

Ari was silent. Devonai puffed the mildly-scented cigarette smoke into the air.

"Okay, then," he continued, "I'll tell you what I already know, Miss Arianna Ferro. You and your friend Scherer assaulted federal agents carrying out a lawful arrest of suspects.

If you hold out on me I'll have no choice but to hand you over to the legal system."

"You can't threaten me," said Ari. "If you handed me over to the locals, you'd have to tell them why your agents were attempting to arrest John and I in the first place. What are you going to tell them?"

"I can tell them anything I wish. Maybe you and Scherer were simply 'persons of interest,' as they like to say these days. We only wished to ask you some questions."

"By kicking down my door?"

"We have direct evidence that you and Scherer were somehow involved in the disappearance of a multi-million dollar Navy vessel. That's enough to detain you for a long time. Even if we did decide to turn you over to the legal system, it wouldn't be for months. So far you've demonstrated that you've got some serious guts, my dear Arianna. But let's not concentrate on what will happen to you if you don't cooperate. Let's talk about what will happen if you do."

"Call me Ari, please. I don't like to be associated with that woman from the news."

"If you want to get out of here anywhere near the sunny side of 2004 you'll start offering me some information. First of all, is Marks' story true?"

"I don't know what you're talking about."

"Your friend John said that he knew Marks had led us to you. What contact did you have with Marks? Why did he decide to come to the CIA?"

"I don't know. Maybe he's an asshole."

"So you're saying that Marks had a valid reason to come see us?"

"I am not."

"Why would Marks come to the CIA with such a wild story if he wasn't telling the truth?"

"What am I, a psychiatrist? I don't know why crazy people do crazy things."

"Okay, then. Let's say that Marks is lying with his crazy story. There is one thing that he said that wasn't a lie. He gave us your name. I send my guys to just ask you some questions and we get into a fuck-for-all. You're already in this way too deep to keep banging the innocent bell, sweetheart. Tell me if Marks' story is true."

"Go to hell."

"Okay, if you don't care about rotting in a holding cell for months, maybe you do care about your friends. John may be hurt and in need of help. If you help us find him you could save his life."

Ari folded her arms across her chest and raised an eyebrow.

"The other thing to consider," continued Devonai, "is the well-being of your other friends, namely Raymond Bailey and Christie Tolliver. We've got case officers waiting for them at their residences, too. It's only a matter of time before my operatives have another confrontation. You can help determine the outcome of those meetings, namely, prevent it from becoming another brawling shootout. Our agents are prepared to defend themselves, as you've seen, and I can't guarantee that your friends won't get hurt. Only you can."

"You'll never find the others now that you let John get away."

"Maybe so. Then again, are they going to just walk away from you? You may be a world-class jerk but I doubt they'll be so willing to leave you to gather dust in our custody."

"They'll probably do just that. There is too much at stake to risk a rescue."

"What's at stake, exactly?"

"Go... to... hell. Remember?"

"I don't expect your friends to stage a rescue, Ari. I'm hoping that we can simply open up a dialog and come to an arrangement that we can all be happy with. As I've said, my mission is to determine what happened to the Portland. Do you know why?"

"What do you mean?"

"Do you know why I've been assigned to the Portland investigation?"

"I don't know. Is it a slow day on the vice squad?"

"My interest in this is national security. I need to know if there's a threat to this country. Navy vessels being reduced to dust sounds like a pretty substantial threat to me. Whether the truth is as simple as a new weapon invented by our enemies or as fanciful as a spacecraft stealing the metal for its own purposes, I need to know how it is going to effect the security and safety of the United States. For such a significant task, my officers and I are authorized and willing to do whatever it takes to succeed."

There was a knock at the door.

"Nice speech," said Ari.

"Enter!"

Richter poked his head into the room. "Major, there's someone here to see you."

"Can't it wait?"

"I don't think so."

"Who is it?"

"I think you'd better come see for yourself."

20.

John could feel Seth's presence as soon as he pulled the Expedition into the cargo bay. John let Seth in long enough to tell him to close the ramp. Ray was waiting nearby. John hopped out of the Ford.

"It was that rat son of a bitch Levi," said John, livid.

"Whoa, slow down," Ray said, "just take it easy and tell me what happened."

John made for the bridge as fast as he could walk. Ray spun on his heels and followed him.

"There were men waiting for us at Ari's place. They identified themselves as the CIA. Things went to hell immediately."

"They just started attacking you?"

"They kicked down the front door, Ray! One of them said they just wanted to talk to us, well shit, that's a pretty lousy way to start a conversation!"

John charged up the stairs to the bridge. Christie and Dana were sitting in the new chairs. Friday leaped down from the counter and scurried into the corner.

"Your buddy Levi sold us out!" John yelled at Dana.

"What happened?" Dana asked, shocked.

"Ray said they took shots at you?" asked Christie.

"The CIA has a funny way of investigating leads," John said. "But we know Levi went to them now. How else did they get Ari's name and address?"

"Whatever Levi's intentions were," said Dana, "I'm sure he never meant for anyone to get hurt."

"John, sit down please," said Ray. "We can't plan our next move until we're all calm."

"I don't want to sit down right now, Ray. I'm sorry if getting shot at leaves me with a little excess energy!"

"Okay, stand then. Just take a deep breath and tell us what happened from the beginning."

John followed Ray's advice. When he had caught his breath he nodded.

"Right. Ari and I had gone over to her place to pick up some stuff. The CIA must have had men waiting outside because we weren't there for more than five minutes before somebody knocked on the door. Then these two guys kicked in the door. Ari took out the first one before he had a chance to act."

"Wait, what do you mean she 'took him out?'"

"You know, she defended herself. The guy had a gun out and Ari used her Aikido to disarm and disable him. She and I fought with the second man until Ari shot him. We made a break for it but there were two more men coming up the stairs. Ari had gotten ahead of me and she ran right into one of them. He disarmed her and then stunned her. Then he took a shot at me as I was coming to try and help Ari."

"Why did he shoot at you?"

"What do you mean, why? We were in combat."

"Did you have your weapon drawn?"

"You bet your ass I did."

"Then that's why he shot at you. What happened next?"

John took a breath. "Okay. I stopped in my tracks when he fired the shot. He told me to drop my weapon. Almost immediately another agent came around the corner and started firing at me. These were not warning shots Ray, he meant to kill me. I ran back upstairs to find some cover. The man who had Ari identified himself as a CIA agent and demanded that I surrender."

"What did you say?"

"I didn't have a chance to say anything. One of the first two men came around and drew his pistol. I lunged at him and managed to kick him before he could fire. As he fell over his weapon went off. It looked like he was knocked out so I glanced back down the stairs. By that time the other agents had given up on talking and were dragging Ari down to the street. I followed them. When I made it to the street they shot at me again. They shoved Ari into the back of their car and took off. I knew there was no way I could follow them so I called you."

John collapsed into a chair.

"This is unbelievable," said Christie.

"What are we going to do now?" Dana asked.

Ray shook his head. "I don't know. This is pretty messed up."

"This is serious, Ray," John said. "The CIA isn't fooling around here."

"It sounds to me like they went in hard and then got hit hard. You guys fought back with lethal force and they had no choice but to retaliate in kind."

"Whoa, hold on there a second. They're the ones that started the fight! They broke down the door and came running in with their weapons drawn. They raised the bar from the get-go. It shouldn't surprise them in the least that we fought back like we did."

"I'm not saying you did wrong, John. It just seems to me that there was a lot of misunderstanding during this whole incident. They may have had a genuine interest in opening up a dialog with you but everything went to hell too quickly. It seems to me that they did intend to arrest you, though. If they were only going to question you why did they do a hostile entry?"

"Exactly."

"A Navy vessel crumbles to dust," said Dana. "I'm not surprised they were so aggressive."

"All right," said Ray, "let's think about this. The CIA has Ari in custody. What are our options? We could contact the CIA and try and talk to them on more even footing."

"And say what?" Christie asked. "We have nothing to bargain with."

"Christie is right," began John, "we can't hand the Faith over to them. The best we could offer them is a tour of the ship. They won't be satisfied with that."

"How else are we going to get Ari back?" Dana said.

"Why don't we ask Seth for help?" said Ray. "With all this alien technology, maybe there's a way for the Faith to help us find Ari."

"Friday, come here," said John.

Friday walked over to John and jumped into his lap. Ray looked at Friday.

"Can you help us find Ari?" he asked.

Seth's voice filled the bridge. "Ari is not here."

"Yes, and we need you to locate her," said John. "Can you do it?"

"Each of you is always with me."

"You mean you can track her?"

"I know where Ari is."

"Great, where?"

"I need John."

"I'm right here, Seth."

"I need your mind. Ari isn't strong. You have her life force in you."

"What the hell is that supposed to mean?"

"Each of you has her life force in you. John has the most. If you allow me to join with your mind I will be able to locate her."

"He's not making a ton of sense," said Ray.

"I'm not sure what he means either," said John, "except that I have to be in contact with the orb in order to find her."

"That is correct," said Seth.

"Wait a minute," Christie said, "I thought that you could be linked with Seth from anywhere in the ship."

John nodded. "I can, but the strongest telepathic connection is when I'm in physical contact with the orb."

"Okay, so let's do it," said Dana.

"There is a problem," Seth said. "I cannot locate Ari without... transmitting a signal. To create a Doppler signal as you required for *gephentrefol* operations would prevent the signal from detecting her."

"Gephenter... what?" asked Ray.

"That's the word Seth used to describe matter-energy conversions," said John. "I didn't understand it myself until Seth showed me what he meant in my mind. Seth, from now on use the term 'matter-energy transfer.'"

"I understand," said Seth.

"Seth used a lot of words that I didn't understand when the two of us were linked. Often I tried to translate them before I passed along the message."

"Oh. So if we find Ari, then ASTRA will be able to detect the signal?" asked Dana.

"Presumably," said Christie.

"So what?" said Dana. "They'll get a pinpoint signal location. Then we move and they can't find us again."

"Good point," said Ray.

John sighed. "All right. Let's take the Faith to a random location as a red herring. Then I'll use the orb to find Ari."

"Okay. Seth, put us a thousand feet above Little Haystack."

Devonai had never seen the man seated across from Lauren Hill. Both he and Hill regarded Devonai with what looked like unforgiving ire as he entered Hill's office. Devonai was quite used to that look from Hill but so far, to his knowledge, he hadn't screwed up yet. The man was obviously military, as he sported an appropriate haircut and the familiar Navy peacoat.

"Major, sit down please," Hill said, gesturing. "This is Lieutenant Commander Guilfoyle of the Defense Intelligence Agency."

"Major Kyrie Devonai. Nice to meet you."

Commander Guilfoyle accepted Devonai's handshake. "Likewise," he said.

"I wish we had something for you, commander, but our investigation is still in the preliminary stages."

"I'm sure your people are doing a fine job, major. It has been the determination of the Department of Defense to turn this investigation over to the DIA."

"Indeed? Interesting how you guys show up some fourteen hours late and demand control. Where were you when the Portland disappeared?"

"Washington. We didn't have any personnel in the area at the time."

"Exactly. If you guys want more involvement in things like this, maybe you should have more field offices."

"Major Devonai," Hill snapped, "you are out of line."

"It's all right," said Guilfoyle. "I read your file, major. You're kind of young to be heading up an investigation like this. Never mind the fact that your rank doesn't reflect any military training."

"Rank earned is rank earned. I proved myself as an asset to the agency and was granted officer rank to facilitate an operation. Since that operation was successful, it was determined to keep that rank as part of my official title."

"Either way, this kind of case is way above your expertise and ability."

"I beg to differ. Besides, let's quit this idiotic banter and get to the point. Hill, does the DIA have the authority to take this investigation away from us?"

"Pretty much," said Hill.

"Then why are we even discussing it?"

"Before you came in here and made an ass of yourself," began Guilfoyle, "we were hoping to keep you in the loop. Hill seems to have a lot of faith in your abilities. If you're not interested in acting like part of the team, however..."

"Look, I'm sorry if I'm being defensive, but this is a fascinating case. I'm more than a little curious to find out just what the hell is going on. I apologize for my remarks, commander."

"That's fine. Please understand that while the DIA does in fact have full jurisdiction in this case, in the interest of future cooperation we would like the CIA to participate. Hill has offered the conference room on the third floor as a command center. Meet me there in two hours ready to present your findings. Is that acceptable?"

"Yes, sir," said Devonai.

"Very well, then. If you'll excuse me..."

Guilfoyle smiled half-heartedly and exited the office.

"You didn't mention Ferro," said Hill.

"Neither did you," Devonai replied. "So what gives?"

"She hasn't given us anything useful yet. Therefore, I don't see any point in informing the DIA of her presence."

"Why are you interested in keeping her a secret for now?"

"Leverage. In case the DIA takes the investigation in a direction I don't like."

Devonai smiled. "Lauren, I'm impressed. You've got more ambition than I gave you credit for."

"Ambition is like a charge card, major. It is best used infrequently and only when absolutely necessary. Didn't they teach you that on the farm?"

"I didn't spend all that much time there. Not like a normal recruit. What do you want to do about Miss Ferro's recalcitrance?"

"So far she doesn't seem to care about anything. We need to find something that she does care about, and exploit it."

"She's playing the hard-ass card right now. She doesn't place much value on herself in whatever is going on here. She says her friends won't contact us or attempt a rescue mission. I'm more inclined to believe that they would."

"Have we leaned on Marks as much as we can?"

"I think Marks has already told us everything he knows. The others hate his guts by this point, without a doubt. I think the only one we can appeal to is Dana Andrews, but we have just as little chance to contact her as we do the others. In my opinion, all we can do is continue surveillance on the other residences and keep ASTRA looking for more signals. If we're lucky, the others will contact us themselves."

Hill nodded. "Okay, until we can think of something else, proceed with that plan. I want you and Richter to scout out each of the residences like you were doing when you ran into trouble. If anything it will let our field operatives know that we're serious about this surveillance. I have visions of them napping soundly out on location."

"What about the DIA briefing in two hours?"

"I'll handle it. I want you out in the field. If the commander doesn't like it he can take it up with me."

"Roger that. I have one more idea."

"Oh?"

"Why not put Marks and Ferro in the same room? We can record their conversation. Maybe, if we're lucky, one of them will slip up and reveal some useful information."

"That's a good idea. I'll see to it. Let's just hope they don't decide to kill each other in the process."

Richter was the kind of man who solved problems. Marks could see that plainly. As a military man he could spot a squared away soldier easily, and Richter could be the poster child. Marks was tempted to engage him in idle conversation about his service, but squared away soldiers don't engage in idle conversation. At least not with prisoners. Marks was beginning to feel more like a captive, despite his complete cooperation with the CIA so far. Richter, who was escorting Marks somewhere, didn't seem like the sympathetic type. Asking him about what was going on would be a waste of time.

When they'd reached a room on the fourth floor, Richter stopped.

"In here, Mister Marks," he said.

"What's going on?"

"We're moving you to a more convenient location while we conduct our investigation."

"Where's Major Devonai?"

"Busy."

In fact, Devonai was waiting downstairs for Richter so that they could be on their way. Richter didn't like Marks, but he couldn't pin down the reason. Something about the way Marks had approached them didn't feel right.

"Sir, please step inside the room. If you need anything just dial zero on the phone."

"Okay."

Levi passed through the door. Before he could realize who was with him in the room, Richter had closed and locked the door. Ari sat in the back of the small room, hidden in shadow and swirling cigarette smoke. Levi felt a twinge of adrenaline despite the obvious disparity of force.

"Well, well, well..." she said. "Levi Marks. They say loose lips sink ships. In this case, the ship was already sunk."

"Did you... did you decide to leave the Faith?"

Ari sat up and moved slowly into the light. Marks noticed her injuries.

"Not exactly."

"What happened to you?"

"Adversity."

Ari drew closer to Levi until she was face to face with him. Levi found his back to the wall.

"Did the CIA do this to you?"

Ari traced her finger down Levi's chest. Levi's expression changed from concern to pure confusion.

"I just want to know one thing, Marks," she said, making eye contact and refusing to break it. "Why? Why did you betray us?"

"This ship is the greatest discovery of the history of mankind. Manning it with a bunch of amateurs is irresponsible and does a disservice to all of us. I saw what was going on. I made the decision to get the authorities involved. Whatever mission you're going on could be seriously compromised by your lack of expertise and..."

Ari interrupted Levi by grabbing his crotch and slamming her elbow into his throat. Levi gurgled.

"Am I displaying," she said through gritted teeth, "a lack of expertise now?"

"You're... fucking crazy," Levi gasped.

"We should have shot you the moment you set foot on the Faith. Dana has proven useful but you're nothing but a traitorous son of a bitch."

Levi began to turn blue. Richter burst into the room and separated the two. He moved Ari to the other side of the room. Levi struggled to catch his breath. Ari calmed down immediately, and smirked.

"Please tell me," Richter said to Ari, "that you're single."

Byron had always found it odd that the main office for the Suffolk University Police was in a basement area. It seemed vaguely inefficient to him that the officers should have to run up a flight of stairs to get outside. At least, he mused, they could weed out the truly out of shape from the fold that way.

Byron had only been down there once before, to get a new ID card. It hadn't changed much in four years. A female student was manning the dispatcher position, and looked up expectantly at Byron.

"Hi, I'd like to see the director, please."

"Do you have an appointment?" asked the dispatcher.

"No, but it's urgent."

"Whom may I say is waiting?"

"Byron Sterling. I'm a senior."

Byron sat down across from the dispatch desk as he waited. The dispatcher spoke with the director briefly over the phone.

"Go ahead in," she said.

Byron got up and opened the nearby door to the director's office. Inside, a severe-looking middle aged man in uniform was working on a computer. The office was sparsely decorated and lacked any personalization that Byron could see. The nameplate on the desk said "Chief Cohen."

"What can I do for you?" he asked.

"Hi. I wanted to talk to you about Professor Christie Tolliver."

The chief stopped typing and looked at Byron.

"Yeah? What about her?"

"Well, the Professor and I are friends, and she hasn't been around for a couple of days. She didn't show up to class yesterday, and today she canceled all of her office hours."

"I haven't heard anything about it. She's probably not feeling well, that's all."

"That's not all, though."

"What do you mean?"

"I happened to be walking down Cambridge Street on Sunday. I saw Professor Tolliver get into a SUV with two other people. I'd swear she was being coerced."

The chief raised an eyebrow. "What makes you think that?"

"There was something odd about their body language. It just didn't sit right with me."

"Well, did you get a plate off of the truck?"

"Yeah, in fact I wrote it down."

Byron passed a small piece of paper to the chief.

"Okay. Here's what I'm going to do. It's probably nothing, but I'll give the professor a call at home and see if she's all right. If I can't get a hold of her I'll look into this vehicle tag, just to make sure the SUV wasn't stolen or anything else blatantly obvious like that. Otherwise, I think you're overreacting."

"Fine with me. I appreciate you looking into it."

The chief nodded. "Not a problem, Mister Sterling."

21.

Blue Line Police Supply was a small store, tucked away in an unassuming corner of Manchester, New Hampshire. Ray had recommended it for what they needed. It was easy enough to find a secluded spot to drop off the Expedition, and John and Ray had left to do some shopping.

Their plan for rescuing Ari had been drafted on a preliminary level. When John contacted the orb to find her, and the resulting signal was sent, hopefully the CIA would send agents to check it out. If they were fortunate, this would leave Ari's location more lightly guarded. Using the Faith to get as close as possible, John and Ray would enter the location, disable whomever might be present, and rescue Ari. Christie had reservations about such a plan but offered no alternatives.

Since the last thing that John and Ray wanted at that point was another shootout, a trip to the police supply store was necessary. Ray's department had a close relationship with the shop, ensuring the best prices and the least hassle.

Ray pulled the Expedition into the parking lot at just past four in the afternoon. John was fighting fatigue again, and struggled to stay awake. Ray put the Ford in park and nudged John's arm.

"Yo John, we're here," he said.

John blinked and rubbed his head. Ray turned off the truck and the two exited. The storefront was remarkably bare. It was the kind of store that neither wanted nor needed random customers to come in off the street. Inside the shop, which looked to John like a very boring version of an Army-Navy store, two old men lounged behind the counter. They immediately greeted Ray.

"Hi, guys," Ray said.

"We heard about what happened," one of the men said.

"We're real sorry about that," the other one said. "If there's anything we can do to help..."

"I'm still recovering, but life must go on," replied Ray.

"The chief sent your Smith by for a cleaning," said the first man. "It's all set if you want to take it with you."

"Really? Sure, why not?"

One of the men went into the back of the shop to retrieve the pistol.

"So, what can we do for you?"

"We need some stuff. We're having a training session for the latest batch of newbies out of Concord. We need four canisters of ten percent OC/CS and two one hundred thousand watt stun guns."

"Sure thing. Do you want me to bill it to Manchester?"

"No, I'll be picking it up. I haven't filled out the requisition forms yet, so I'll just buy them and send the forms in later."

The first man gathered the requested items while the other returned with Ray's pistol, holster, and duty belt. Ray slung the belt over his shoulder.

"That will be four hundred eighty dollars," said the first man, clacking away at the register.

Ray handed him a credit card. John reviewed the purchase.

"These aren't the kind that fire electric leads?" John asked.

"Those are way too expensive," said Ray, "and they're special order items. These contact guns will work just fine for what we have in mind."

"I hope so."

The first man handed Ray his receipt.

"Stay safe, Bailey," he said.

"Thanks."

Fifteen minutes later, Ray pulled the Expedition into the cargo bay. Dana was waiting for them. John and Ray jumped out of the truck.

"Seth, take us to a thousand feet," John said.

"Understood," Seth said, his voice quiet in the open space.

"Are you sure you won't let me help you?" asked Dana.

John and Ray headed up the stairs to the armory.

"It's dangerous enough as it is," said John.

"It's nothing personal, Dana," said Ray. "You simply don't have any training."

Dana trailed the two men through the empty armory and into the orb room.

"You guys are hardly SWAT, to hear Christie tell it," she said.

"I think the plan will work better with two infiltrators, that's all," said John. "Now you two get to the bridge. I'll join you once I'm done here."

"Okay," said Ray.

Ray and Dana exited the orb room. John turned to face the orb. A single handprint appeared on the surface. John placed his hand upon the orb.

John found himself standing in Ari's apartment. It looked the same as it did earlier that day. John could hear someone in the bedroom.

"John, go make some selections from the liquor cabinet."

Ari's voice came from the bedroom. John could feel something strange about the illusion. It was too real. Perhaps it was due to the memory being so recent.

"Seth, are you here?"

Nothing happened. Ari emerged from the bedroom.

"Aren't you out of range for Seth?" she asked.

"I need to find Ari," John said.

"What are you talking about? I'm right here."

"I think I see what's going on. You're going to give me a chance to follow her. Am I supposed to do the same thing I did when the agents came in?"

"John you're being really weird. Are you in contact with Seth or not?"

"I'm beginning to wonder if I am."

"Well, you can stand there and talk to yourself. I'm going to get some booze."

Ari walked into the kitchen and opened the cabinet. John drew his Beretta.

"If this is an interactive illusion, maybe I can indulge my desire to actually shoot those agents this time."

"I'm sorry I don't have any champagne," Ari said, "it would hardly be appropriate to christen the Faith with apricot brandy."

"Hey Ari, do you want to help me take out the CIA agents who are about to kick down the door?"

"John, quit fooling around."

John crept forward towards the front door. He couldn't hear anything from the hallway.

"That's funny, they should have been in here by now."

Ari walked over to John with two glasses of bourbon.

"Let's take a break for a second and have a drink. I think we've both earned it."

"I don't get it," said John, "what am I supposed to do?"

"Did you lecture me about waving a firearm around recklessly? I think you're wound too tight today."

Ari sat down on her couch. John shrugged, placed his pistol on the coffee table, and joined her. He accepted the offered bourbon.

"If I can find you by drinking bourbon, fine by me."

"John, seriously, are you all right?"

"Yeah, I'm fine."

John sipped from the glass. It was the best bourbon he'd ever tasted. Ari drained her glass in one gulp.

"You know John, there was something we never finished talking about."

"You're right, there is."

"I've been waiting for an opportunity to talk to you about it. This is the first chance we've had. I was beginning to think I would have to pay the others to give us a couple of hours alone."

"Ari, I don't think this is something we should discuss right now."

"Why not? I've already made my feelings clear on the matter, haven't I?"

"Yes."

"Then tell me how you feel."

John turned around. "Will this have any effect on finding her, or should I change the subject?"

"Stop stalling."

"Okay, fine. Ari, I want to jump your bones. Let's get wasted and do the mattress mambo."

"Hey, I'm being serious here. I'd appreciate a serious response."

"Sorry. I do want a relationship. I most sincerely do. Let's become John and Ari, space pirates, terror of the Tarantula Nebula."

"Good. Because I've been looking forward to this for a long time."

Ari straddled John and drew him close. She leaned in and gave him a long kiss. Like the bourbon, the effect was fantastic.

"Good Lord," said John, "I think I'm getting a little too excited..."

Everything around him melted away. John found himself suspended in mid-air above a city. John screamed in shock. It took him a moment to realize he was not falling. He looked down. It was obviously downtown Boston, as evident from the unmistakable dome of the state house. One building in particular seemed to gleam in the light. It was the one on the corner of Beacon and Park Street.

"Gotcha."

The illusion ended and John was back in the orb room.

"Ray, this is John. We're headed back to Boston."

"Roger that," said Ray's voice, "how did it go?"

"Great. If we ever get bored, Seth can produce some outstanding entertainment."

"Why, what happened?"

"Ha! I'll tell you what almost happened. Then again, I'd better wait until we're alone."

Devonai and Richter stepped out of their Crown Victoria and onto the street. The Somerville neighborhood was quiet, but densely packed. The two men approached a Ford Expedition that was parked a few feet away. The driver's window on the large SUV lowered. Two men were inside.

"Officer Dowling, Officer Sinclair, hello," said Devonai.

"Major," said Dowling.

"Still nothing, eh?"

"Not in the three minutes since you called, sir."

"Okay. Richter and I are going to have a look in the lobby. I've set my phone to vibrate, so call me immediately if anybody shows up."

"Understood."

Devonai motioned to Richter and they headed across the street. Tolliver's place was three houses down from the Expedition. It was a featureless three story brick apartment building. Devonai scanned the names on the mailboxes once they'd arrived.

"This is definitely her place," he said. "And it doesn't look like she's taken her mail in for a few days."

"Yup," said Richter.

Devonai carefully pulled on the front door. It was locked. Devonai took another look at the mailboxes. He picked a name he liked and rang the buzzer for that apartment. A moment later the lock clicked, and Devonai pulled the door open.

"How did you figure that would work?" Richter asked.

"Just lucky, I guess."

Devonai led the way up to Christie's apartment.

"Now this is going to be a bit trickier," he said.

"Allow me," said Richter.

Richter removed a lock pick set from his jacket. Devonai took up a strategic position in the hallway while Richter went to work. Less then fifteen seconds went by before Richter opened the door.

"The lock is as old as the building," he said. "No challenge at all."

"Good work, Richter."

The two men slipped inside the apartment and closed the door. Christie's place was sparsely furnished, and immaculately maintained.

"Do take it easy," Devonai said. "There's no reason to trash the place."

"What do you take me for?" Richter said, smiling.

"I take you for a crazy ex-Marine, that's what."

"When the game is soft, I play it soft. When the game is hard, I play it hard..."

Richter's voice faded as he walked down a hallway. Devonai began poking around the living room. Tolliver had an extensive collection of movies. One of the few spots of color in the room was a house plant. Devonai thought about watering it.

"Shit!"

"What?" Richter hissed, hurrying back.

"My phone is ringing."

Devonai fished his cell phone out of his pocket. The number displayed was not Dowling.

"It's Hill," Devonai said. "Hello, Hill, what's up?"

"Where are you guys?" asked Hill, her voice rife with urgency.

"We're still checking out Tolliver's apartment."

"Well you'd better get mobile again. ASTRA just reported receiving another signal."

"Really? Where from?"

"They've triangulated a position that comes back to a wooded area outside of Manchester, New Hampshire."

"Is it near Bailey's residence?"

"No, it's on the other side of town. You and Richter check it out right away."

"Roger that. Listen, Dowling's vehicle has a GPS navigation system in it. Our Crown Vic doesn't. I'll swap vehicles with Dowling and Sinclair then call you back with the vehicle identification number. Then you can feed me the coordinates directly."

"Agreed."

Devonai hung up.

"Another signal?" asked Richter.

"Yup. We'd better haul ass."

Lauren Hill exited her office and headed towards the kitchenette down the hall. Her briefing to the DIA was in less than an hour, and so far she had little to present to them. Despite her role as mediator, she was just as upset about the situation as Devonai. Hill didn't have the luxury of expressing her opinions in the same manner. If he wasn't so damn good, she'd consider a verbal warning for his conduct. She gave him a modicum of leeway as a favor for his loyalty. He was well aware of this and never took advantage of it, at least as far as she knew.

At the kitchenette, Hill started brewing a pot of coffee. The last fresh batch had been consumed by a rattled Levi Marks, who was currently being held downstairs. Their plan to extricate information from Ferro had worked well, just with more violence then they'd anticipated.

Hill heard the elevator door open, and turned around. Out in the hallway, Devonai walked by. Hill ran after him.

"Hey, I thought I told you to get your ass to Manchester!"

"I'm on my way," Devonai said without stopping. "I decided I wanted Miss Ferro along for the ride."

"Why? You're wasting time."

"Ferro is our only bargaining chip. If we run into the others up there, I want her along for leverage."

The two stopped in front of the door to Ari's ad hoc prison.

"And you might give them a chance to rescue her, too."

"I think it would be preferable if they could see her in person. It shows our good faith, and we need as much as we can get after that Marlborough Street melee."

Hill sighed heavily. "All right. Take her. But if that bundle of razor wire causes more trouble it's on your shoulders."

"If I can handle Fledgling I can handle this one."

Hill smirked. She and Devonai entered the room. Ari was sitting at the table looking terminally bored.

"Your friends are on the move again, Miss Ferro," Devonai said.

"Wonderful."

"We've got a fix on their location. I'd like you to accompany us on the way."

"Like I have a choice?"

"I was just being polite."

Hill spoke. "Your little encounter with Mister Marks was quite helpful. You confirmed that what he was telling us was true."

"I did no such thing," Ari replied. "I was talking about a pleasure yacht out of Bermuda called the Faith. We had a little illegal gambling going on, and Marks ratted on it. What a stupid jerk."

Devonai produced a pair of handcuffs from his pocket.

"Stand up and turn around, please," he said.

Ari held up her hands. "As you wish, your majesty."

Devonai cuffed Ari's hands behind her back, and led her out into the hallway.

"Richer is waiting downstairs, I presume?" asked Hill.

Devonai nodded.

"We're not bringing Marks along?" Ari asked. "That's too bad, I'm sure the others would like a word or two with him."

Devonai and Ari entered the elevator. After the doors had closed, Devonai turned to Ari.

"There's no reason to hold back anymore, Miss Ferro," he said. "If you tell us the truth about what's going on we can avoid any more misunderstandings. Like I said before, there's no reason to let another confrontation go bad."

"I'll keep that in mind."

"Look, I'm going to tell you something. I'm just a normal guy who's been through some extraordinary circumstances. I've always done what I thought was right. Fortunately, so far, that's been in line with my orders and the wishes of the CIA. Well, not counting some initial unpleasantness. If what Marks said is true, who is to say that you and your friends aren't the right ones to pilot this spaceship?"

The elevator arrived on the first floor, and Devonai led Ari outside to the waiting Expedition. Richter was in the driver's seat. Devonai got into the back seat with Ari.

"Somehow I doubt that decision is yours to make," Ari said.

"Let's go, corporal," Devonai said. "No, it's not. But I know how to keep an open mind. I'll report back on what I find and interject my opinion into the report."

Richter pulled the Ford out into traffic and headed for the highway. Ari stared out the window for a minute or two before responding.

"Who cares what you think if you're not the head honcho?" she said.

"I have some pull with the organization."

"Not enough for something like this."

"All I'm asking is that you at least consider trusting my judgment. If not for the sake of the ship, then for the safety of your friends."

Ari shook her head. "I can't do that."

"Then who among us isn't keeping an open mind?"

"You'd better cooperate," began Richter, "or we'll set you up the bomb. Then all your base are belong to us."

"Richter, shut the hell up!"

22.

The outdoor café was on a busy street in a middle-eastern city. Dana sat at a table shaded by an umbrella, the item necessary to ward off the noonday sun. She was wearing a sleeveless sun dress and a pith helmet. Across from her sat the phantom Seth, as he had appeared in the virtual world of the orb. The androgynous person offered her an odd smile, and gestured toward the meal set before them. Dana had been served a pastrami on rye with a pickle spear, and Seth had a large Belgian waffle with whipped cream and strawberries. Dana picked up a mug next to her plate, and found it to contain Lady Grey tea. It was delicious, and she moved on to the sandwich. It was equally wonderful, but even as the spicy mustard hit her tongue she knew something was wrong. Seth nodded knowingly and pointed into the sky. Dana followed his arm and noticed that the sky offered not just a bright sun, but also several stars, a view familiar to space-borne individuals free of an illuminated atmosphere. As she gazed at the sight, she noticed that they were in fact underneath a very high ceiling, and the entire city was indoors somewhere.

"Beware of the Kira'To," said Seth.

Dana awoke with a start. She was alone on the bridge of the Faith, save for Friday who was asleep in her lap. The others had been there, last she knew, planning for Ari's rescue. Dana roused Friday and apologetically placed her on the floor. Standing up, Dana looked out the window. They were about a thousand feet above Boston Common.

"Seth, where are John and Ray?"

"We are in the conference room," said Seth.

Dana crossed the bridge and entered the conference room. John, Ray, and Christie were standing over the table. John had a yellow legal pad and was drawing on it for Christie and Ray's benefit. Dana noticed that the drawings were floor plans.

"What's going on?" she asked.

"We're still planning the rescue," said Ray. "John's hosting Seth so that we can get a look at the floor plan of this building."

"This is why we need Ari to get that infrared transceiver working," John said. "So we can hook our computers up to Seth and avoid this kind of laborious interaction."

"This is the fourth floor, where they're holding Ari," said Ray, pointing to the pad.

"Okay, this is the layout," John began, "and this room is where they've got... what? Say that again so that everyone can hear it!"

"Ari is no longer in this place," said Seth.

"Why didn't you tell me sooner?" yelled John.

"You did not ask me sooner."

John smacked the table with his hand. "Damn it! Well, can you tell us where the hell she is now?"

"Yes."

John stared off at the opposite wall for a few seconds as Seth relayed the information to him. John began to speak slowly.

"She's in a car, no a truck... being transported... north, on Route 93. She's with two other men."

"They must be headed to the last transmission point," said Ray. "They're taking her with them."

"Shit, that ruins our plan, doesn't it?" asked Dana.

"No, it just means we need a new plan," said John, running for the bridge.

The others followed him. John sat in the pilot's chair.

"What do you have in mind?" asked Christie.

"We're going to snatch that truck right off the highway," said John with intensity.

"How are we going to do that?" Ray demanded.

"Yeah, we can't transport them aboard," said Christie.

"It's easy," began John. "All we have to do is get in front of them and drop the ramp. We hit the brakes, and before they know what the hell is going on they'll drive right into the cargo bay."

Ray gestured towards the rear of the bridge. "What's to stop them from smashing right into the opposite wall?"

"If Seth and I can time it right, their momentum will be canceled out as soon as they hit the ramp. That, and the driver will probably be slamming on the brakes."

"Why not just wait until they get to the transmission site and grab them there?" Dana asked.

"Seth doesn't know if there are any other vehicles present. There could be more agents than we can handle if we wait. If we grab this one truck off the highway we can surround them and take control before they have a chance to react. Even if they resist, where are they going to go? If Ray gets the drop on them with his pistol they'd be suicidal to fight back."

"I guess it might work," Ray said. "How fast can Seth drop the ramp?"

"As fast as gravity can pull it down."

"Okay, let's give it a shot."

"We're already on our way to their location. We'll be there in thirty seconds. Better clear out some room in the cargo bay."

"Got it. Dana and Christie, you're with me."

"I'll stay here," said John. "It's easier for me to concentrate while seated."

"Okay."

Ray led the way downstairs with Christie and Dana following. They arrived in the cargo bay. The most obvious obstacle was the Expedition.

"You two get those boxes out of the way," began Ray, "I'll move the Ford to the left side of the bay. John, can you hear me?"

"Loud and clear," said John's voice.

"Okay, listen up. You're going to need to position the ship so that the CIA's truck comes in on the right side. There will be barely enough room so don't take any chances."

"You forget to whom you're talking."

Ray smiled and ran over to the Ford. He jumped in and started the engine. When Dana and Christie were finished moving the boxes, he maneuvered the SUV as far to the left as he could. He turned off the truck and jumped out.

"I wish we had more time to clear some more space," said Christie.

"This should be enough," said Ray. "Come on, let's watch from the top of the armory stairs."

Christie and Dana nodded and the three of them climbed the stairway. They had a perfect view of the ramp.

"How's it going, John?" yelled Ray.

"I'm waiting for a long stretch on 93 that's free of overpasses. Fortunately the driver of that Ford is keeping a safe distance behind the lead car. Ten seconds, get ready."

Ray drew his pistol and handed the women an OC spray canister each.

"I almost forgot," he said, "you might need these when we rush the truck."

Suddenly the ramp flew open, assaulting the three crewmembers with the impossibly loud sound of the exterior. The Faith lost just enough speed to send the truck and its horrified occupants careening into the cargo bay. The Faith lurched forward with an almost imperceptible bump, but the burst in speed wasn't enough. The Ford struck the rear wall of the cargo bay at about thirty miles per hour.

"Shit!" yelled Ray. "Close the ramp, John!"

Ray ran down the stairs, leveling his weapon at the truck. The driver was unconscious, having been struck by the airbag. The closer passenger in the back seat was Ari, who was trying to shake off the brunt of the impact. A second man was next to her, and he looked at Ray with wide eyes. Ray opened the passenger door and yanked Ari out onto the deck. He pointed his pistol at the man in the back seat.

"Don't move!" Ray cried.

The man put his hands up.

"I surrender, for God's sake," he said.

Christie and Dana helped up Ari. With one hand, Ray handed Dana his keys.

"The little one is a handcuff key," he said. "Come on out of there, nice and slow."

"Okay," said the agent.

"Christie, search him for weapons."

Christie approached the man while Dana freed Ari from the handcuffs. Christie patted down the man and removed two pistols.

"Let me see if my partner is all right," the man said.

"We'll look after him," Ray replied. "Okay, Dana, now put the cuffs on him."

Dana did so.

"You must be Raymond Bailey. I'm Major Kyrie Devonai of the CIA. Sorry I can't shake your hand."

"Me, too."

Ray moved to the driver's door to look at the other man. He was out cold, but looked uninjured otherwise.

"Dana, could you please look after that guy?" asked Ray. "Christie, help Ari to the bridge. I think it's time we all had a nice chat."

Dana dragged the other man out of the truck while the others headed to the bridge.

"Wait, what do I do if this guy comes to?" she said.

"Get his weapon, and if he wakes up, point it at him."

"Oh. Okay."

Ray holstered his pistol. He put his hand on Devonai's shoulder and led him up the port-side stairs. Christie followed, supporting Ari.

A moment later, they arrived on the bridge. John was facing in the other direction in the pilot chair.

"John?" Ray queried.

John spun in his chair slowly. He had his hands pressed together in a V shape. Friday sat on his lap, purring.

"Thank you for coming, Mister Bond," he said.

"Devonai, actually. You must be John Scherer."

"Ah yes, I almost didn't recognize you without a pistol pointed at my chest."

"Hey, pal, you came running down the stairs with a weapon in your hand. You're lucky nobody got killed."

"What about the guy Ari shot?"

"Kevlar."

"Well, that's fortunate. For what it's worth, I apologize for the misunderstanding. I still think you could have waited before kicking the door down."

"That was a bad call. We only wanted to talk to you."

"I'd say so. Anyway, sorry to interrupt your trip to Manchester, but I had to get Ari back. She owes me five bucks."

"I do not, you liar," Ari said, groaning.

"So I see that Marks was telling the truth," said Devonai. "You guys look like you're doing a pretty damn good job so far."

"Thank you," said John. "Sorry about the Portland, by the way. That didn't go exactly as we planned."

"You don't say?"

"Mister Devonai..."

"Major."

"Major Devonai, what are your orders?"

"To determine the cause of the disintegration of the USS Portland."

"And?"

"And... what?"

"Surely your superiors are interested in this ship as well, if they believe what Marks has told them."

"All my superiors really know is that we've been chasing some unknown signal around New England, a signal that probably has something to do with the Portland. The existence of this ship is no less plausible than any other explanation, considering that the Portland is a pile of chunky dust at the bottom of the Mystic River."

"How do we know you're telling the truth?" asked Ray.

"Because I have no reason to lie to you."

"You seem awfully blasé about the circumstances," said Christie.

"You should meet a couple of friends of mine. There are some pretty strange things that the CIA keeps secret, believe me."

"You mean like aliens?"

"No, not that I'm aware of. This would be the first."

"Except we're all human," said John. "It's the ship that's alien."

"What do you intend to do with me?"

"Nothing. We'll find a nice quiet place to drop you and your friend off. You see, major, we know how you've been tracking us. The last signal was a diversion. Once we drop you off, you'll never see us again. So there's no reason to keep you prisoner, or to try to lie about our ship."

"I don't suppose you'll at least tell me what your mission is."

"Truthfully, we don't know. Our information is rather poor in that particular area."

"You don't know? Are you kidding?"

"Nope. We're leaving Earth and we don't even know why."

"For a chance like this, I can't say I don't understand. I just hope that you don't screw up and get yourselves killed. Marks seemed to think that you were out of your league."

"Marks may ultimately be right. It's not his decision to make, however. Neither is it yours."

"Some would say that you're doing a disservice to humanity by keeping this discovery to yourself. Marks believed that, so much so that he betrayed your trust."

"He's still a sneaky bastard," said Ari.

"We believed," began Christie, "that if we told the authorities about our discovery that we would never be allowed to participate in the project. We have every intention of telling everybody about what happened when we get back from the mission. If we get back, that is."

Devonai nodded. "Far be it from me to admonish your thinking. I would probably have done the same thing. The difference now is that I have the security of the United States to think about. Unless there's some insidious part of this mission that you're withholding from me, I don't see a security breach here. You simply owe the US government millions of dollars for what you stole, and that's not really my problem."

"So are you going to stop pursuing us?" asked John.

"I'm still accountable to my superiors. If they tell me to keep looking, I'll keep looking. I want to keep my job. If you're as stealthy as you claim then you have nothing to worry about."

Dana's voice filled the bridge. "John, this is Dana. The driver is coming round, and I'm not really sure where the safety is on this gun."

"I think that's my cue," said Ray.

"We'll all go," said John, standing. "We should give our guests a proper send-off."

Twenty minutes later, after having dropped off Devonai, Richter, and the wrecked Expedition in the woods outside of Manchester, John joined Ari in her future quarters with a first aid kit. Ari was lying down on the bare mattress, holding her hand to her head. A bruise was forming on her forehead from hitting the driver's seat. John pulled up a chair and sat down next to the bed. He began to sort out the items he wanted.

"Guess what?" he said. "We found your Glock in the glove compartment of their Expedition."

"Hey, that's great," said Ari unenthusiastically.

"Hold still," John said, daubing antiseptic on Ari's cheek.

"That was a hell of a rescue plan."

"Thanks. It was my first."

"Marks really screwed us over by going to the CIA. And the sanctimonious prick, if you can believe it, actually told me to my face that the Faith would be better off without us."

"If we accidentally fly into the sun because we don't know what we're doing, then he'll be right."

"Somehow I doubt Seth will let us do anything that stupid."

"Seth's memory is shot. That's becoming more and more obvious the longer we work together. I'm convinced that he would tell us what the mission is if he could remember it."

"He's a computer, right? If the data is gone, it's gone. Don't ask me to crack that thing open and recover the data."

John placed a bandage over the cut on Ari's cheek. He activated a cold compress and placed it on her head.

"How did the CIA treat you?"

"Oh, they were perfect gentlemen. Polite, but forceful. I can't say I hold any ire towards them; they were just doing their job. It's Marks that I'd like to ventilate."

"So, they didn't coerce anything out of you, did they?"

"No, nothing. I mentioned the Faith to Marks in passing but I didn't admit to anything. Unfortunately, it didn't take much for my behavior to reinforce Marks' story."

"What do you mean?"

"I mean offering no alternative explanation was just about as bad as if I'd spilled the beans."

"Oh."

"At least now I know I can drop the hammer on the bad guys."

"None of us had any doubt about that, Ari."

"I was impressed with Major Devonai. He made me look like a five legged man at an ass-kicking contest."

"I suppose you'll have to admit that there may actually be some superior martial artists out there."

"Well, we know of at least one. Then again, he could have simply been lucky."

"I wouldn't classify anything that happened today as 'lucky.'"

Ari sighed. "This is turning out to be the longest day of my life."

"Tell me about it."

"I think we should suggest to the others that we find a quiet place to hide out for the rest of the day and start fresh in the morning."

"Ari, there's something you should know."

"Yeah?"

"I think I could have prevented the CIA from grabbing you."

"And if wishes were horses, then we'd all... well, I can't remember how it goes."

"I hesitated. I wanted to protect you, but I couldn't get myself to make the final leap."

Ari patted John on the knee. "You did the best you could."

John ignored the gesture. He stared at the wall with a grim expression.

"Next time, I won't hesitate."

"You had Arianna Ferro?"

Hill squirmed uncomfortably in her chair. Across her desk was Commander Guilfoyle, and he was pissed. Hill had just called him in to tell him what had happened to Major Devonai and Corporal Richter. Unfortunately, she couldn't tell him the story without revealing the involvement of Ferro.

"We ran into her and John Scherer in Boston earlier today. There was a scuffle, and we were able to detain Ferro. Scherer got away. Devonai brought her along to investigate the last signal. That's when they were grabbed."

"I thought we had an agreement, Hill. The CIA was supposed to cooperate fully with us."

"I thought it best to wait until we knew more before briefing you again."

"But you had Ferro during the first briefing."

"If this arrangement is going to work, Commander, you've got to trust us a little bit more. We were planning on telling you about Ferro when we had a better picture of the situation."

"Let's cut the bullshit, Hill. I know you're not comfortable with this relationship. If you want to play games with the DIA you'll find yourself in a world of trouble. You and your pet organization Omega will be bagging groceries within the month."

Hill leaned forward, shocked. "How do you know about Omega?"

"Are you serious? Do you think that you can run operations in Pakistan and Afghanistan completely under the radar of the Department of Defense? You may think that you have autonomy, but take my word for it, there are a lot of powerful people who have their eye on Omega Group, going back as far as the Merciel affair. So far, based on what I've seen, you have a good reputation. Your actions today reflect poorly on that."

There was a knock on the door.

"Come in," said Hill.

Devonai and Richter walked in and were distressed to find Commander Guilfoyle sitting across the desk from Hill. Somehow they'd managed to forget about the DIA.

"Have a seat, gentlemen," said Hill.

"Corporal Richter," said Richter, offering his hand to the Commander.

Guilfoyle accepted the shake. "Lieutenant Commander Guilfoyle, DIA."

"Are you prepared to debrief us?" asked Hill.

"Yes, Ma'am," Devonai said, settling into his seat.

"How are you, Corporal?"

"I'll be all right, Ma'am," said Richter. "I just got a little banged up."

"Good. Major, I've briefed the Commander about our telephone conversation. Please fill in the details."

"Okay," said Devonai. "It seems that Marks is correct. A small group of friends and colleagues have constructed a ship based on instructions received from space. The USS Portland was used as a source of material. It is possible, by the way, that there is more than one ship based on the sheer amount of material taken from the Portland. Anyway, at approximately sixteen hundred hours today the crew of the ship executed a rescue plan to recover their crewmate, Miss Ferro. Richter and I were detained briefly by the crew before being released. I called you as soon as I could."

"Please describe the ship."

"The ship was definitely still under construction. There were all sorts of materials scattered about waiting to be installed, including furniture and plumbing fixtures. I also noticed a large amount of computer equipment in the back of Mister Bailey's Ford Expedition, which was parked in the cargo bay. The ship's design was very utilitarian; just about the only interesting architecture was the windows. Richter was unconscious after our accident so I alone was brought to the bridge. I spoke mainly with John Scherer, who appears to be the leader of the crew. The bridge was designed for five crewmembers, but the only thing present there were chairs. I have no idea how they were controlling the ship unless there were controls elsewhere on the ship. Mister Scherer did not reveal any details about the origin of the project, but he did tell me that they don't know what their mission is."

"They don't know what they're doing?"

"They don't know why an alien race has told them how to build a ship or why they should return with it, no. As a group of amateurs, they seem motivated entirely by curiosity."

"There's something that doesn't make any sense," said Hill. "These people managed to build the superstructure of the ship using materials taken from the Portland, but they need to provide their own furniture, plumbing, and computers? Why would technology capable of creating the superstructure of the ship not be able to provide everything else that they need?"

"I don't know. They also have incredible cloaking technology but there was no explanation for that either."

"Why did they let you go?"

"They told me that they know how we've been tracking them, and they've taken measures to prevent it. Based on the events of the last couple days, I have no reason to doubt them. They let Richter and I go because they don't believe that we pose any threat to them, a very confident conclusion considering that we were shooting at each other no more than two hours earlier."

"What's your recommendation, major?" asked Guilfoyle.

"If you'll pardon my candor, commander, I think we're screwed. We destroyed any chance of a meaningful dialog by going in too hard, too fast. I doubt we'll hear from them again until they get back from their mission, and who knows when that might be."

"I'm hardly willing to close the case based on that, major. Do you have any ideas on how to proceed regardless of any cynical conclusions?"

Devonai shrugged. "The only thing we can really do is continue to keep their residences under surveillance, despite the fact that they know we're there. I suppose they might try something incredibly stupid anyway, but I wouldn't hold my breath."

"What about the residence in New Hampshire?" asked Hill.

"What about it?"

"Do you think they'll show up there?"

"They know that we know who they are, and that ASTRA got a bead on the ship while it was in Orford. If I was them I wouldn't go anywhere near that location any more than I would the others. We lost Ferro, so we don't have anything on them now."

"I want you and Richter to check out that location, anyway. There might be something useful that they left behind. At this point, any new information is better than nothing."

"If you want us to go, we'll go."

"What are you going to do with Marks?" asked Richter.

"We're sending him down to Bethlehem," Hill replied. "There's no reason to hold him here, as he's outlived his usefulness, so he might as well help out at ASTRA. He's promised us to see if they can come up with a new way of tracking the ship."

"Major," began Guilfoyle, "you don't seem as enthusiastic as you did earlier."

"That would be an accurate assessment, sir."

"Would you like to be relieved from this mission?"

"No, I would not. I'm simply trying to express my realization that this mission has probably failed. It failed the moment they got Ferro back on board that ship."

"Just go to Orford," said Hill. "Enthusiastic or not, we need to hold on to whatever last shred of hope this case may have left."

"Yes, Ma'am."

Devonai and Richter got up and moved toward the door.

"Oh, and major," said Guilfoyle. "Try not to screw things up any more than you already have."

"Thanks a lot."

23.

John's quarters were completely dark. Through the hourglass shape of his window, John could see a deep starfield. It was a wonderful way to wake up.

John had slept solidly despite having only a bare mattress. A quick check of his self-luminous watch confirmed that it was ten minutes to midnight. The stillness of the room was complete; John could hear only himself breathing. This confirmed that the ship was still at rest, as a low hum filled every corner of the ship while they were underway. Though he had only been asleep for five hours, John found himself wide awake. He decided to see if anyone else was up. When he moved, he found Friday sleeping beside him. John paused to pet the cat, and then stood up.

"Medium lights," he said.

Seth had been informed what such a phrase meant, and soft bluish-white light filled the room. Like the rest of the ship, the sources of the light were recesses in the wall by the floor. John smiled, the effect pleased him greatly.

Another look through the window confirmed that the ship was still where they'd left it last night; invisible against the side of a nearby mountain. They hovered a few feet above the nearest trees, safe from prying eyes and wayward aircraft. Unfortunately, the terrain offered no creature comforts, some of which the crew was beginning to desire desperately. That would have to be addressed sooner than later.

Entering the hallway, John headed towards the conference room. He blinked at the light upon entering the room, which was brighter than the hallway. Ray was inside, down on his hands and knees, attaching a chair to the deck.

"Hi, John," Ray said. "Awake already?"

"Yeah. Friday is in my room. Did you decide to go completely offline for awhile?"

"No, Tycho is pulling a shift on the bridge. You should talk to him, he's got a really interesting perspective, what with being a dog and all."

"I will. What else is going on?"

"Ari slept for a few hours, then she took the infrared transceiver to the orb room. She's got it hooked up to her laptop computer. I suppose it's wishful thinking to hope that she'll decode the signals anytime soon."

"The way she obsesses over things, I imagine it won't be quite such a long time."

Ray tightened a bolt and stood up.

"That's it, all the chairs in this room are done."

"Nice. Are Dana and Christie still asleep?"

"Dana's been up for a while, I think. She's down in the orb room watching Ari. I don't know where Christie is."

"Okay."

Ray grabbed his tool bag. "I'm going to start installing the furniture down in the galley."

"Don't you ever sleep?"

"I had a catnap. I've just got so much energy for this work. It's so rewarding I can't stop."

"Good, with that attitude we'll be done in no time."

"Well, have fun."

Ray exited the conference room via the main hallway. John looked around the room. It was starting to look rather professional. John smiled and headed onto the bridge.

"Hello, John," said Seth.

Tycho was sitting in the pilot's chair. He was looking at John. Past him, Christie was working on one of the plasma screen monitors.

"Hello," said John.

Christie turned around. "Hi! Up already?"

"Yeah. You, too?"

"I've had plenty of sleep today, unlike some of us."

"I see you're working on the monitors."

"Yeah. It's not like there's anything to plug them into yet, but I didn't feel like sitting around. And since we can't take this thing into space yet, I have to amuse myself somehow."

"I don't blame you. Since everyone is up, I'd like to call a meeting."

"Okay."

"Hey, buddy," said Seth.

"What?" John queried. "You mean me?"

Tycho was looking at John again.

"Hey buddy," Seth said enthusiastically, "how fast can you run?"

"I don't know. Fairly fast, I guess."

"I can run really fast!"

John grinned at Tycho. "That's because you've got twice as many legs as me!"

"That's a terrible excuse. You should be able to run fast. We should go running sometime."

"Sure, Tycho, I'd like that."

"I bet I can take a pheasant faster than you, too."

"That depends. Can I borrow Ray's shotgun before we hunt?"

Tycho cocked his head. "Shotgun?"

"I don't think he knows what you're talking about," said Christie.

"That's okay," said John. "He certainly has more of an effect on Seth than Friday does."

"Friday won't play with me," said Seth.

"Friday is scared of you, Tycho."

"I don't see why. I'm a great dog!"

"I agree, kid."

John scratched Tycho behind the ears. The light level on the bridge fluctuated slightly.

"It does that when he's happy," said Christie.

"Cool. Well, if you're ready I'll call the others to the conference room."

"Okay by me."

"Crew of the Faith, this is John. Meet me in the conference room for a meeting."

"Keep an eye on things for us, Tych," said Christie.

"You can count on me," Seth said.

John and Christie moved into the conference room. John took one of the end seats.

"I feel like the captain," he said.

"Do you want the job?" Christie asked.

"I've been leaning away from such a strict command structure. I think that certain people should be in charge of certain areas, but I don't think one person should have command over everyone else. Everyone has equal say in what we do."

Ray arrived in the conference room.

"I just got started," he said.

"I didn't know that everyone was awake," said John. "I think we should discuss some things."

"That's fine with me."

Ray chose a seat. A moment later, Dana and Ari arrived.

"Good evening," said John.

"Hello," said Ari.

"How's it going with the orb?"

"I have good news and bad news."

"What's the good news?" Ray asked.

"The good news is that I can read a binary stream from the orb quite easily."

"And the bad?" asked John.

"The bad news is that it's going to take a lot of programming to interpret the data stream."

"Time we have in excess. I only wish that some of us were more knowledgeable in that area so that we could help you out."

Dana cleared her throat.

"Hello? I have some experience in computer programming, remember?"

"Oh. Right. Sorry."

"Ari's still the expert."

Ari grinned. "And don't you forget it."

Dana and Ari sat down at the table.

"So, what's on your mind?" asked Ray.

John grabbed the pad of paper and pen that he'd left on the conference table.

"I thought we should plan out our activities from here on out," he said, removing the pen cap.

"Not a big fan of flying by the seat of your pants, eh?" said Christie.

"No. Now the first thing I had on my mind is the exit strategy for Christie and Dana. Christie, how are you planning on getting your life in order before you leave?"

"Well, my family and the university are getting the missionary story we talked about. I won't make a lot of friends back at Suffolk, but my parents should understand. They've always been supportive of my endeavors, even when I applied to NASA straight out of college. I should head over to Suffolk at some point tomorrow. I don't want to string them along longer than necessary."

"Okay. Dana, what are your thoughts on this?"

Dana leaned back in her chair. "Well, I don't really have any friends, and my parents aren't an issue. My mother and I don't talk except on holidays and my father died when I was fourteen."

"Good. We'll all have to budget time to put our affairs in order. That being said, I'd like some estimates on completion times for the remaining projects. First is the computer code. Assuming you can get a translation program running, Ari, how long will it take to set up the network?"

Ari sighed. "I don't know. No more than four days I'd imagine. I think I'll need four days to decode the orb's language and six to eight days to write the control programs for all of the functions we talked about, so I'm looking at… at least two weeks total."

"Okay. Next is plumbing. I'm thinking three days if Ray and I work on it together."

"I think that's reasonable," said Ray.

"And that leaves the one thing we haven't discussed barely at all," said John. "External weaponry. Seth and I have been talking and I think that the most powerful Earth weapons we can use are slug throwers."

"Slug throwers?" asked Dana.

"It's a term for firearms, to distinguish them from missiles, lasers, or anything else."

"Oh."

"As far as I know the most powerful weapon out there that will be practical for our use is the GAU 8 'Avenger' thirty millimeter weapon system used on the A-10 Thunderbolt. Seth and I think that two of these weapons would be good for the forward and rearward mounted armaments, despite the fact that Seth still can't say whether or not we'll need them or whether or not they'll even be effective. Still, if that's the best we can do, that's the best we can do. The trick here is that Seth doesn't know what kind of molecular redundancy will be necessary until we can scan one of these. So until we can take a trip down to Bradley Air National Guard Base, we won't know for sure. If it's three-to-one like the chairs, batteries, and oxygen canisters were, there may simply not be sufficient aircraft present."

"Can't we take a trip to the factory that makes them?" Ray asked.

"I don't know where that is. We could research it. But if we take units right out of the chassis of the A-10s, we'll know that they'll be all ready to go. I hate to pull a trick like that on my compatriots in the Air Guard, but so be it. The problem will be getting them to work with Seth's power system. Seth assures me that he can assist us in installing them, insofar as getting the muzzles sticking out of the hull."

"Don't you want them for the dorsal and ventral guns as well?"

"No, I was thinking of something smaller. These guns need to be mounted in such a way so that they're fully articulated. GAU 19 fifty-caliber machine guns will work well in that role, and we can just copy the top and ball turret designs from the good old B-29 Superfortress. Then we should be able to steal right out of the factory with as much ammunition as we need, or barring that, from a National Guard armory. Then, if we need to, we can get fully intact turrets from the B-29 display at the New England Air Museum."

"It's going to be a challenge."

"What fun would it be if it wasn't? I estimate seven days for Ray and I to get those weapons installed."

"How are you going to fire those weapons in the vacuum of space?" asked Christie.

"Seth tells me that the forward facing cannons will be inside the energy shield. The bullets can exit through it just fine. In the case of the fifty caliber guns, the turrets will be outside the hull proper but they'll still have enough oxygen surrounding them to fire the ammunition. So, that's a minimum of three weeks time. It wouldn't surprise me if it took twice that long with complications, delays, and good old fashioned ignorance."

"What's on the agenda for tomorrow?" asked Ari.

"We can recon the Air Guard base and continue to gather other supplies. I'd like to pick up my car from Orford so that we have another vehicle for running errands."

"I'd like to resign from the force in person," said Ray. "I'd rather not delay that any more."

"Okay."

"We need to come up with a better solution to our sanitation problem than the bucket," Ari said.

"Indeed. Until we get the plumbing installed the way Seth described we'll have to either rent a motel room somewhere out of the way or perhaps swipe a portable toilet from somewhere. Since we could all use a shower, too, I vote for the motel room."

"I concur," began Ray, "in fact, there's a motel nearby to the cabin that we could use. If we pay in cash the CIA won't be able to track us."

"Won't that put us unnecessarily close to any agents looking for us up there?" asked Christie.

"It's on a route north of the cabin. There's no reason for them to look for us up there. We have to pick up John's car anyway, and we might as well use an area that's isolated and that at least one of us, namely me, is intimately familiar with."

"Okay, fine," said John. "We'll scout it out first thing in the morning. As for everything else, we'll discuss the particulars after that. I'm starting to become drowsy again. It must be the overwhelming realization of what's ahead of us. Anybody who wants to keep working tonight, keep in mind that a full night's sleep is a good idea. Don't stay up too late."

"You're forgetting the most important thing we have to do tomorrow," said Ari.

"What?"

"Get some damn sheets for the beds!"

October 8, 2003

Mara Fledgling was making noise. A lot of noise, in fact. A Colt M4 carbine on fully automatic was not quiet by any comparison except maybe a thermonuclear explosion. Alone at the range, Mara was not afraid to rattle off an entire thirty round magazine at once. She was adept with the weapon, placing all of her rounds into a human silhouette target at twenty-five yards. It was one of those skills that Kyrie Devonai happened to find rather endearing, and was one of many reasons why they maintained a romantic relationship.

Mara dropped the empty magazine out of her rifle and replaced it with one that was full. She changed her mind about her goals and flipped the selector switch to semi-automatic. There was an orange-colored shard of a clay pigeon on the berm at thirty-five yards that required her attention. Mara tucked her cheek into the stock and began to fire slowly. Becoming as accurate as possible one round at a time was the closest thing to Zen philosophy that Mara ever tried, requiring a significant lack of conscious thought for success.

Mara and Devonai had met during college, but they hadn't decided to form a relationship until years later, after they were both already working for the CIA. Mara was a member of Omega Group under Devonai's command. It wasn't always that way. Mara had started out in the FBI, and while Devonai was cutting his teeth in the Boston Police Department (and sealing his fate with the CIA) Mara was floundering in a frustrating manner with white collar investigations. It was Devonai who had changed all that, with an intensity that eventually carried over into their relationship.

Mara had the day off, and had decided not to waste it lounging around her apartment. While she had access to better firing ranges, her current choice offered more privacy and dynamics. Some of what she had in mind would get her kicked off of a monitored range in short order. When she was sufficiently satisfied that her basic skills were solid, she could proceed to the fun stuff.

Mara had fired about half of the magazine when she became aware of a ringing sound. Her hearing protection was in place, so it wasn't the rifle. Mara realized her cell phone was demanding her. She placed the rifle on safe and peeled off her headset.

"Hello, Kyrie," she said, responding to the caller ID.

"Hi, Mara. How's it going?"

"Good. I'm just giving my Colt some love. How about you?"

"You'd hardly believe it if I told you."

"You mean you're not going to tell me?"

"It's way too difficult to explain right now. If I ever see the inside of our apartment again, you can be sure you'll hear about it. Your assistance may yet be needed on this case anyway."

"I see."

"I'm on my way up to New Hampshire to investigate a lead. I thought I'd call and say hello."

"Always appreciated, of course."

"I'm having a hard time with this one, Mara. I find myself forced with a difficult ethical decision, well potentially anyway."

"You're notorious for always making the right ethical choice, Kyr."

"Yeah, but this time it may go against the wishes of the CIA."

"Oh. Shit."

"Indeed. Well, here's the gist of it. There's a group of people working on a project that the CIA became aware of two days ago. The worry was that the project may have been a threat to national security. We checked it out and it is my assessment that it poses no such threat."

"I take it that your word isn't enough this time?"

"Yup. The problem is that the DIA is breathing down our necks on this one, and they're not going to close the case based on my recommendation."

"The DIA? This is serious."

"No joke. Not only is the DIA demanding that we continue investigating this group, but they've ordered the arrest and interrogation of any of its members. That's the problem. If it was up to me I would just leave them alone and let them do their research. If I find where they're hiding, I'll be forced to go against what I believe is right."

Mara sighed. "Kyr, it sounds to me like it might be time to remove yourself from the case."

"I'd like to, but I'm too worried about how Brockway might handle it without me. So far, she's been a second-stringer on this one, so I haven't spoken to her about the ethical issue so far. I trust her completely, but somehow I don't think she'd reach the same conclusions as me."

"I trust her, too. I think she would in fact reach the same conclusions. It sounds to me like Omega shouldn't be involved in this case at all. The DIA has different goals. I think you have a tough choice here, Kyrie. You've got to decide either to stay on the investigation and compromise your ideals, or you've got to remove yourself from it and accept that this research group may not receive justice. I don't envy you."

"Thanks a lot. I think there's a third choice, by the way."

"You can't take out all of them," Mara said, laughing.

"That's not what I meant. I could stay on the investigation and conduct it as I see fit, regardless of what the DIA wanted."

"I don't think even you could avoid getting fired for pulling that kind of shit, my dear."

"I know."

"Who's backing you up on this one?"

"Richter, of course. Smith and Ragulin are following us in another vehicle."

"Is Richter listening to this conversation?" asked Mara incredulously.

"He ain't whistling Dixie."

"I'm surprised his loyalty is to Omega and not the CIA as a whole."

"Good people are hard to find, but when you do, you hold onto them."

"Are you talking about me?" Richter asked, his voice faint in the background.

"Yes we are," said Devonai.

"You know, Kyrie," began Mara, "if you're going to go against orders I'd really rather be there to back you up. I don't want to be elsewhere and have to make that decision alone."

"You should stay out of this, Mara."

"I can't stay out of it, Kyr! Even if I wasn't a member of Omega, I'm still your girlfriend."

"I know."

"I'm going to render my decision now, Kyr. I think you should remove yourself from the case, you and Richter and anyone else who would rather get fired than see this mysterious group of yours get arrested."

"I hate to sound so trite, but the only thing I can say right now is that I'll have to think about it."

"I'm sure you'll reach the right decision. Please don't rush into anything. Just know that whatever you decide to do, you've got my support."

"That's why I love you, Mara."

One hour later, Devonai and Richter pulled up to a small red cabin in the woods. Orford, New Hampshire was pretty much the same no matter where you went, but at the end of this dirt road it looked especially isolated. The morning was gray and the skies threatened rain. The wind whipped up the recently fallen leaves as Devonai and Richter stepped out. Smith and Ragulin exited their vehicle as well.

"This has got to be it," Devonai said. "Smith, Ragulin, you check the perimeter. Richter and I will investigate the structure."

"Yes, sir," said Smith.

The other men headed out while Devonai approached the front door. The formidable portal was locked.

"What do you think, corporal?"

Richter looked at the lock. "It's a newer deadbolt. It may take some time."

"Time we have. Let's check around back."

The men circled the building. The cabin had a back door, which a much less imposing padlock presenting the only obstacle. Upon closer inspection they noticed the lock had been compromised.

"Somebody smashed it," said Richter.

"It looks recent," said Devonai, drawing his pistol. "I'll take the lead."

Richter drew his weapon and nodded. Devonai cautiously pushed the door open. The first room was sparse. There was a portable mattress folded up against the wall, and a charcoal grill next to it. There were some cleaning supplies as well. Another door lay before them. Devonai slowly turned the doorknob, listening for any stirring. He opened the door a crack and peeked inside.

The main room of the cabin was empty. There was a central table with chairs, a rocking chair, and a sofa recliner. An open door led to another room. Devonai crept forward for a look. That room, which contained two bunk beds, was also empty.

"Clear," said Devonai.

"Clear," echoed Richter.

"The table is free of dust," said Devonai. "Somebody's been here recently."

"Major, look at this," said Richter in hushed tones.

Richter pointed at the gas stove. A mug with a teabag stuck in it was there. The water inside was steaming.

"Shit," whispered Devonai, grabbing his radio. "Smith, this is Devonai. Subjects are in the area. Use caution, over."

"Roger, out," replied Smith quietly.

"They can't have gone too far," Richter said.

"I agree. Go help out the others, I'm going to start poking around."

Richter nodded in the affirmative and exited. Devonai began looking around more closely. There wasn't much in the way of interesting material. The cabin was well stocked with survival rations and emergency water, enough for a couple weeks anyway. There were a few board games, a deck of cards, and a couple paperback books. Devonai rifled through the cabinets. Plates, glasses, blankets, sleeping bags, coats...

"Hello, there," Devonai said.

On one of the bunk beds there were two sheets of yellow paper from a legal pad. Devonai picked them up. There were pencil diagrams of what appeared to be a ship, with each section of the ship labeled. Devonai recognized it as the ship he and Richter had been on, even though he had only seen the cargo bay and the bridge. On one of the pages the words "Reckless Faith" had been inscribed.

"No argument there," Devonai said softly.

"Smith to Devonai," the radio crackled.

"Go ahead, over."

"We've secured the perimeter, sir. There's nobody in the immediate area. Do you want us to continue looking?"

"Sure, why not? Send Richter back inside and take Ragulin with you, over."

"Roger, out."

Devonai folded up the drawings and pocketed them. A few moments later Richter re-entered the cabin.

"Yo," he said.

"This is definitely the right place, and somebody was here recently. But judging by the lack of a vehicle this far off the main road, and the broken lock, I'd bet it we have a squatter. He heard us coming, no doubt, and took off. I doubt the others will find him if that's the case."

"That would seem to make sense. What do you want to do now?"

"I'll station Smith and Ragulin here for the time being, just in case I'm wrong. I'd like to spend some time here myself, but I don't think that Hill would go for it."

"Do you think there's any chance that the crew of the ship would be dumb enough to come back here?"

"I don't know, there's nothing of value really. They know we know who they are so they must figure we'll be watching. Then again, it's possible that whoever made that tea is a member of the crew. If so, they'll be back for him. Maybe this isn't such a waste of time after all."

Richter smiled. "No, boss, I'm sure it is a waste of time. Why ruin the curve?"

24.

John stepped out of the shower feeling like a king. It was five minutes after seven o'clock in the morning, and the Tenney Mountain Motor Lodge had just become the Faith's new home base. After another five and a half blissful hours of sleep, John and the rest of the crew had departed their mountainside hiding place to check out the motel. Ray was right on the money; the motel was right next to a nice quiet section of woodland that provided a discreet point of debarkation. The motel clerk never noticed that the group hadn't arrived in a vehicle, which was just as well since there was no path for the Ford to take through the woods.

John opened the bathroom window a crack to let in some cool air. There were no complementary toiletries save for a bar of soap, but it was enough. John and Ray had reserved one room while the ladies had obtained another. The running water and proper facilities were welcome enough, and John had no doubt that the women were equally glad to make use of them. Ray had finished his use of the bathroom before John, and was channel-surfing in the main room. John opened the door to the bathroom so that he could speak with Ray.

"Hey Ray, I'm thinking that we can turn our private bathrooms aboard into their own shower stalls."

"What?" Ray asked.

"You know how we were worried there wasn't enough room in the bathrooms for a shower stall?"

"Yes."

"Well, why not simply make the entire room the shower? We can drill a drain in the center of the floor and mount the shower spigot to the wall. The entire room is already steel and aluminum, it's not like the paint is going to peel."

"That's actually a really good idea. Don't they do that in Japan?"

"I think they might, yeah."

John finished drying himself off and entered the bedroom.

"How much longer do you want to give the girls?"

John shrugged. "They have three showers to take. I imagine they'll be longer than us. I'd say we wait another forty-five minutes."

"You know, by the time we get down to the Air Guard base they'll probably be working on the A-10s. Should we steal the weapons right out from under their noses?"

"I don't know. Seth said it wouldn't harm anyone nearby to transport them. Why pussyfoot around now? The government already knows we're out there."

"I guess it seems a bit rude, that's all."

"I agree."

John watched television with Ray while he got dressed. The news wasn't reporting anything about the Portland. John wasn't surprised by this, despite the fact that the ship was in plain few of at least half a dozen residences across the river. Perhaps before too long, the feds would release a cover story. It seemed easy enough to claim that the Portland had been moved to another location during the wee hours of the morning.

"It's really starting to piss me off that I can't get some of my stuff out of my apartment," said Ray.

"Yeah, I got lucky in that regard," said John. "There's still a lot more I would like to grab. It would almost be worth negotiating some kind of agreement with the CIA to get it."

"We're through with the CIA."

"I know. Anyway, it's not like we can't buy whatever we want. Ari's contribution makes up for all the trouble she's caused."

"Barely. You know John, I've been thinking about something I wanted to talk to you about. This is sort of the first chance I've had."

"Oh?"

"Do you really want to bring Dana with us?"

"Why wouldn't we want Dana along?"

"I don't see her contributing anything to the crew, except to be another resource-consuming human."

"The crew is a skeleton as it is. Dana is obviously very intelligent and even if she has no specific skills, she'll no doubt adapt to become valuable. If she can help Ari learn the orb's program she's already paid her fare as far as I'm concerned.

Besides, I really think that we should have six people on board. Recruiting people willing to drop their entire lives and come with us wouldn't be easy, so we shouldn't count out Dana so quickly."

"All right. Then whom do you propose for the sixth?"

"I don't know, I was just thinking out loud. I wouldn't even know where to start. We could approach another college professor, but Christie is obviously more adventurous than most. I don't think we'd easily find another like her. Not without taking out a classified ad."

"We could always get a CIA agent to come with us."

"Ha! Ray, don't you watch movies? The agent always betrays everybody else three-quarters of the way through the story."

"I'm not serious. I think we should stick with five and call it good, unless one of the others knows a particularly good candidate."

"Yeah. Join the crew of the Faith, meet new and interesting aliens, and kill them."

One hour later the bridge of the Faith was full. The ship was about to arrive at the Air Guard base, and the mood was tense. John could sense how his friends were feeling. Theoretically there was nothing to worry about, but the fact that one wrong move might get them into a dogfight with F-16s was hard to ignore. John hadn't tested out the maneuverability of the Faith yet and so far it was not unlike flying a one hundred and fifty ton brick. John hoped that with practice he would become more adept.

John was giving the animals a break and was linked with Seth himself. As they approached the base, John began to picture the A-10s in his mind. Seth would find them.

"Anything?" asked Ray.

"Just a moment," replied John. "I'm getting an image in my head. There should be some of them over by that hangar."

John pointed out of the viewscreen. Sure enough, several A-10 Thunderbolts sat on the flight line. Various Air Force supernumeraries milled about. John half expected them to look upward and start screaming. As it was they were able to hover right over the planes without detection. None of the technicians appeared to be actively working on the planes.

"Go to the gun room," said John. "Seth is figuring out how much matter dispersal there will be for the cannons."

"You got it," said Ray. "You guys coming?"

"I'll stay here," said Dana.

Ari and Christie stood up to follow Ray. He led them downstairs and into the forward gun room. Part of the hull in front of them disappeared quite unexpectedly, and bright sunlight streamed into the room.

"What the hell?" Ray said. "John, what's going on?"

John's voice filled the room. "We're preparing the room for transport. Stay near the door."

A humming sound began to emanate from the center of the room. Green spheres of light danced in graceful patterns, and a massive thirty millimeter cannon took shape. The green light faded, leaving behind a perfect cannon. The muzzles of the barrels protruded out of the newly formed hole in the wall, and the receiver and drum-shaped ammunition magazine filled the rest of the space.

"We got it, John," Ray said.

"Is it solid?" John replied.

Ray tapped the hydraulic drive motor. The power cables had been cut neatly.

"It looks like it. The rounds are staggered, John. There's one high explosive four every four armor piercing."

"Good. The transportation ratio this time was two-to-one, so we got two weapons out of the deal. Unfortunately, the ammunition was four-to-one, so we only got two hundred seventy five rounds each of ammo. Get back up here, please."

Ari led the way back up to the bridge. John and Dana were standing next to the left side window.

"The crew just noticed the missing weapons," said John. "They're shocked."

The others joined them by the window. Down on the tarmac, the A-10 crews were clearly flabbergasted. They shrugged their shoulders and spoke into portable radios.

"Sorry, fellas," said Ray. "Business is business."

John returned to the pilot's chair. "Seth tells me we can pick up ten thousand more rounds of ammunition at a nearby location."

"Excellent."

The ship began to move again. John guided it to a small building next to the hangar. The activity on the ground had grown to a frantic pace, and blue Security Forces pickup trucks were heading towards the A-10s. The main gate was also closing. The base was being locked down.

"I'm going to put all of this ammo in the rear cargo bay," John said. "It's going to be a tight fit."

"So far we're doing pretty well on storage," Christie said.

"I think we can afford to take up the space," said Ari. "I'd rather have too much ammo than not enough."

"Agreed," said John. "I'm transporting the ammunition now."

Ray had a flash of insight. "What about cleaning kits for these things?"

John nodded. "I'm grabbing one of those, too."

"They are going to be pissed at us," said Dana, grinning.

A slight bump reverberated through the ship.

"Transport is complete," said John. "Friday to the bridge, please."

The door to the conference room opened and Friday entered. John stood up, holding his hands out towards Friday like a magician.

"Zzzap!" he said.

Friday jumped into the pilot's chair. Seth's voice filled the bridge.

"John, I was sleeping," he said.

"You're always sleeping, Friday. Do me a favor and fill in while we prepare for our next stop."

"I'd be glad to, cutie."

"What's next on the agenda?" asked Dana.

Ray smiled broadly. "More guns."

It was a beautiful morning on Boston Common. Lieutenant Commander Peter Guilfoyle was too distracted to notice. He had departed the CIA's building to get some space, having spent another uncomfortable night on a couch therein. Guilfoyle had resigned himself to renting out a hotel room for the upcoming night, despite the fact that he was holding onto a shred of hope that the entire affair might progress before then.

He had also hoped that Norfolk would send him some more personnel. As the only representative for the DIA, Guilfoyle was beginning to feel like a guest in the CIA's home. It wasn't supposed to be like that and he sure wasn't used to it that way. Guilfoyle had left a message for his commanding officer and was anticipating a response. He fantasized about what he would say to the Admiral if he could really speak his mind.

The wind was whipping across the Common fairly well. A college student attempting to squeeze one last day of studying outdoors finally gave up. Elsewhere, businessmen make rapid bee-lines across the many paved paths. Many of them were drastically under-dressed for the weather. Guilfoyle's peacoat was a veritable mockery to their condition. After ten years in the DIA and five in the Navy before that, the coat was still the best piece of gear he was ever issued. His Colt 1911A1 may have been the second best, if it had been issued and not a personal purchase. He'd never needed it before now, and he hoped he wouldn't in the future. From what the CIA agents were able to learn, it wouldn't do him much good anyway.

Guilfoyle thought about his training, and the fact that he had washed out of the SEALs. It was hardly the end of his Navy career, and it didn't stop the DIA from recruiting him. It was, however, one of the most inescapable failures of his life. Ringing the bell to show one and all that he had given up was a haunting memory, and his desire to make up for it provided all the ambition he needed. It meant nothing to him, though, if he couldn't take back that moment of weakness.

Leaves swirled around Guilfoyle's legs as his cell phone rang. The caller ID confirmed his hope, and he answered.

"Commander Guilfoyle," he said.

"Commander, this is Admiral Phair."

"Good morning, sir."

"How are things progressing in Boston?"

"They're not, sir. Like I told you yesterday, Case Officer Devonai compromised our only means of finding the ship. As long as we're letting the CIA cover so much of this case we won't accomplish anything."

"What do you propose to do better?"

"We can work more efficiently with the CIA out of the picture entirely."

"You didn't answer my question, commander."

"Sir, honestly, I don't know what we should do next. I am certain, however, that this clumsy cooperation with the CIA is getting us nowhere. If we're going to spin our wheels we might as well do it alone."

"You were never much for politics, Guilfoyle. It's not as simple as that. The CIA beat us to the case. All the jurisdiction in the world doesn't mean squat if we hurt our working relationship with them. This goes much further than you, Omega Group, and I."

"Agreed, sir, but considering the magnitude of this case, we should be employing every resource we can muster. I would like to request more manpower, for..."

"Commander, there's been another incident, this time at Bradley Air National Guard Base in Connecticut."

"You're kidding. What sort of incident?"

"Several thirty millimeter cannons and over thirty thousand rounds of ammunition have been stolen."

"Holy shit."

"It gets better. The weapons were stolen right out of the fuselages of the A-10s of the 103rd Fighter Wing, and the rounds from the well-secured munitions building. There was nothing left but a little bit of metallic debris."

"The ship is stealing weapons now? Damn it, who do these people think they are?"

"Right now they're the masters of their domain, which is wherever they damn well please. Commander, you have got to find out a way to track this ship before half the military's armaments end up in a dustpan."

"We've got agents at ASTRA working on the problem. Any other suggestions would be appreciated, sir."

"Get a team over to Bradley and run some tests. See if there's anything about that debris that can give us any help."

"With all due respect, sir, the debris from the Portland wasn't particularly useful."

"At this point, testing the material from Bradley is still a viable course of action. I'll tell you what, Guilfoyle. I'll dispatch a team for you. That way, you can at least be a little more autonomous from the CIA. But you can't go off on your own. Our agencies still need to work together on this one."

"Aye, sir."

"I'll be in contact with you. Goodbye."

Guilfoyle hung up the phone. A dog ran over with a stick in its mouth and requested the commander's assistance. The owner, some eighty yards distant, bid the dog to return. Guilfoyle took the stick and threw it in the appropriate direction. The dog took off running.

"Go fetch, Guilfoyle."

25. October 15, 2003

It had been a full week since the crew of the Faith had obtained their weaponry, and Ray was only marginally closer to getting them installed properly. Christie and Dana had managed to explain voltage to Seth, who then modified a standard power port to suit the devices. Heavy-duty power cords had been run through the central conduits, and every room now had power available, including the weapons rooms.

The thirty-millimeter cannons had been relatively easy to install, since they were already pointing in the right direction. The fifty-caliber machine guns, however, would have to be fully articulated. This necessitated integrating the turrets from the B-29. Fortunately, two fully intact turrets and several spare parts for such rigs were discovered and stolen from the New England Air Museum located only a mile from Bradley. Since the parts were unique, John and Ray had to engage in a midnight burglary, an act facilitated by the lack of any physical security at the museum. They simply circumvented the alarm system and brought the parts out on palettes. Installing them was proving to be more difficult, and Ray and John had already spent many hours sweating and swearing at the turrets as they struggled to get them working correctly.

The only weapons that were immediately available were the Springfield M1A rifles they'd stolen out of an Illinois factory. It had required three rifles for every one transported, so the company had discovered thirty weapons missing from the warehouse the next day. They'd been stowed in the armory, along with extra ammunition and magazines. The others had promised Christie and Dana some practice with the weapons, but as of yet they hadn't visited a range.

The most important breakthrough so far, however, had been three days ago when Ari cracked the orb's computer code. A powerful algorithm-detection program had been running constantly and had finally hit on a pattern. Ari jumped in with both feet to begin translating the transmitted information into a format they could use. This involved a lot of trial and error, with each ship function being specifically mentioned as the code program was transmitted. Ari had brought a coffee machine into the orb room, and had only emerged for bathroom breaks and meals. Dana helped her when she could, but her priorities were helping John and Christie install the plumbing system.

The only expertise on the plumbing was coming out of a series of do-it-yourself tomes purchased from a home repair store. John and Christie had become quick experts on the subject, or so they hoped. After all the hard work, they were beginning to rue the day they'd ever learned of the material polyvinyl chloride.

That morning, the object of attention for the entire crew was Ray's toilet. The crew had crowded into his personal bathroom to watch the inaugural flushing.

"Ready?" asked Ray.

"Flush, flush, flush," the others chanted.

Ray tipped the lever. The water in the bowl disappeared so quickly that it caused a popping sound. The bowl began to refill a moment later.

"Success!" Ray declared.

"I guess the suction pressure is adequate," said Dana.

"Adequate?" Ari asked, smiling. "Don't forget to stand up first or you'll be the one sucking pressure."

"Well, I'm aroused," said Ray. "Who wants to try it again?"

The others objected loudly and made their way out of the chamber.

"I have a hated five-gallon bucket to toss overboard," said Ari, exiting Ray's quarters. Dana and Christie followed her out.

"What, nobody?"

"Let's get back to work, Ray," said John. "No rest for the weary. We can celebrate our indoor water closets after dinner tonight."

"You and Christie deserve a break, don't you think?"

"We've still got a lot to do. We've only begun to start installing the individual computer stations. Ari hopes to start up the network by tomorrow."

"Okay."

"How's the dorsal turret going?"

"Better. I'm still getting too much friction swinging through the five o'clock position. The plasma screen is working fine. There's just nothing to hook it up to yet."

"Okay. Give me a call if you need more help."

"Sure. I think I'm all set for the dorsal gun. The ventral one is the one I'm worried about."

"Don't remind me."

John exited Ray's quarters and headed towards the bridge. Ray departed for the lower deck. John gazed out of the hallway windows as he approached the bridge. It was a rainy day out in the woods behind the motel. John saw movement in the trees. He stopped walking, scanning the terrain. Nothing happened.

"Probably a deer," John said to himself.

John entered the bridge. Tycho was sitting in the pilot seat. Christie was drilling holes under the counter to mount one of the computers.

"Hi, John," said Seth's voice.

"Hi, Tycho," John replied.

"What took you so long?" Christie said.

"You're not interested in taking a break? We just got done with the plumbing."

"No, thanks. You go ahead."

John grabbed a pair of safety goggles off of the counter. Putting them on, he knelt beside Christie.

"You're getting good at that," he said.

"Thanks. Ray showed me how to do it."

"Ray likes you, you know."

Christie stopped drilling. "What?"

"Well, I don't know if he likes you. But he should."

"Are you trying to play intergalactic match-maker? What the hell?"

"Sorry, I'm being ridiculous. Ray does look at you a certain way."

"I know."

"Not interested?"

"I would've had to think about it for a microsecond to be interested. I've been a bit distracted since meeting him."

"But you're not repulsed by him."

"I'm not repulsed by much. I mean, I like him just fine. I'm more interested in knowing what the heck is going on between you and Ari."

John sighed. "I wish I knew."

"You two used to go out?"

"No, we never did. Ari and I were oil and water most of the time we've known each other. These days, though... who knows?"

"Probes from outer space make for strange bedfellows."

"That sounds really bad."

Christie laughed. "You know what I mean."

"I do. It wasn't Seth that complicated our friendship. Time did."

Ari's voice filled the room.

"Hey John, it's Ari."

"Go ahead," John said.

"I'm ready to move my operation to the server room. It's time to start laying the network cables through the conduit tunnels."

"Did you drill the holes already?"

"Yes. I need somebody to help Dana roll the cable spools from the orb room to the server room."

"Okay, I'll be down in a minute."

"Have fun," said Christie.

"Thanks."

John stood up and headed for the cargo bay. Ari and Dana were waiting for him. They had begun unpacking two large spools of CAT-5 cable. The spools were way too large for the conduits.

"You know we'll have to unroll the spools from the orb room," John said.

"We just realized that," Ari said.

"Okay. Let's start with this one."

John grabbed one end of the dowel that was stuck through the center of the spool. Dana placed herself at the other end. Together they lifted the spool off the deck and began shuffling towards the orb room. Ari led the way.

"Oof! How much cable is this?" Dana asked.

"Two hundred and fifty meters," replied John. "We won't use it all in one pass."

"No duh."

It seemed to take half an hour to get the spool up the stairs to the armory, but in fact it was only a few minutes. Ari was content to watch John and Dana break a sweat doing so. Once through the armory, they were in the orb room.

"Piece of cake," John said, panting.

"We need to use the upper starboard conduit," Ari said.

"I know. Somebody want to give me a boost?"

Dana offered her knee and hands. John carefully climbed up to access the hatch to the proper conduit, which was placed on the bulkhead up by the ceiling. He had designed it as a manually-operated door, and it occurred to him there was no reason he couldn't have made it automatic. He was forced to keep the swinging hatch open with one arm while he pulled himself into the conduit with the other. He at last made it inside, and turned around to face the hatch.

"Geez," he said, "I should have entered from the upper hatch."

"There's an upper hatch?" Dana asked.

"Yeah, each conduit is accessible from at least four points. This one can be accessed from the bridge, the dorsal gun room, here, and the third starboard quarters."

"Ah."

"Pass me the end of the cable."

Ari picked up the cable and unrolled a few feet. She reached up and handed it to John.

"Enjoy, it ain't fun," said Ari.

"Dana, meet me in the server room," John said.

Dana nodded. "You bet."

Dana exited the orb room. John waved goodbye to Ari.

John quickly realized that the best place for the cable was between his teeth. He needed his palms to be flat to traverse the low conduit. John began crawling forward.

"Dis is fum," he mumbled around the cable.

After a few painful minutes John looked up and saw a pair of fingers poking through a hole in the conduit. John took the cable out of his mouth and pressed it into Dana's fingers. Dana grabbed the cable and pulled it through the hole.

"I'm going to the bridge," John shouted.

"Okay," came Dana's muffled response.

John continued crawling until he reached the hatch to the bridge. He pushed it open roughly and it clattered open. John popped his head up and was met with an epithet.

"Holy shit!" Christie yelled. "For God's sake, don't do that without warning!"

Corporal Richter thrust his arms into the air and yawned. He was alone in Hill's office, awaiting her arrival. Major Devonai was also expected for this meeting, which like the ones preceding it promised to be a waste of time.

Over the past week, the investigation of the ship known as the Reckless Faith had gone nowhere. Logging an unbelievable number of surveillance hours had yielded nothing, save for the daily schedules of a few unrelated neighbors. Richter felt especially bad for Smith and Ragulin, who were stuck back up in New Hampshire at Bailey's cabin. Whoever brewed the tea (and ate some of the food, they'd discovered) hadn't returned. Considering the broken lock they had to assume it was a squatter they had scared off.

The crew of the Faith hadn't surprised anyone by staying away from their respective domiciles. Meanwhile, more bizarre thefts had been streaming in. Both military and civilian sources had reported missing weapons and weapons systems, compounding their quarry's expensive tastes. It was obvious that the crew was expecting some serious trouble wherever they were going, but so far they were sticking to conventional arms. They hadn't messed with the experimental weaponry that the Department of Defense kept a tight secret, proving, according to Devonai, that their gear was only as good as their intel. There were limits to their abilities. Unfortunately, they were not limited in staying hidden from the CIA.

Richter and Devonai were good friends, and the latter confided in the former with regards to his doubts. Devonai had made it clear to Richter that he no longer supported the mission, and only continued to participate because he honestly believed they would fail. Richter agreed that things looked hopeless, but wished that Devonai would let go of his prideful need to stay involved. Richter wanted some time off already.

Richter had always been a man of action. The kind of work they were currently doing was boring him to tears. He was a victim of his own success; he had performed so well on previous missions that eventually the CIA began to ask more of him. Refusing a promotion to sergeant was just about the only thing Richter could do to show them that he didn't want the extra responsibility. He still ended up being assigned to Devonai's investigative arm of Omega Group. Devonai, for his part, made it entirely Richter's choice. Richter conceded to the assignment after realizing that if not for the offer, he could be placed somewhere much less desirable. The CIA was also looking for someone to become the assistant firearms instructor for the Boston division, a role that Richter could have filled easily but did not appeal to him. He may have been a crack shot with a rifle but he hadn't the patience to relay that skill to others.

Devonai entered Hill's office and nodded a greeting towards Richter.

"Morning, major," Richter said.

Devonai found a seat and flopped down. He made no effort to hide his emotional state, which was doubtlessly identical to Richter's own.

"Don't you wish we could phone in our reports?" Devonai said.

"It's not like we have anything new to reveal," replied Richter.

In reality, Richter was quite glad to be actively working again. During his time off the CIA provided him a stipend, and it was just enough to live off of. The full-time pay of late would allow him to indulge some of his more expensive luxuries, if he ever got the chance. Since the case was going nowhere, however, Richter would have been glad to cut his losses and take what was already earned. Richter had long since learned that there were only two states in which he was truly happy; those were spending money or boondocking somewhere exotic with his M40 rifle. His recent adventures in Afghanistan had been very satisfying, even if the majority of his activities revolved around spotting for mortar crews. Richter loved being in the field and enjoyed being completely self-sufficient. Carrying everything that mattered in his rucksack, and relying on his weapons and skills for survival was visceral and thrilling. It was also profoundly peaceful to him, interrupted only occasionally by combat, which he found unobjectionable. After all, he couldn't enjoy the rest of the experience without the periodic fire fight. Richter was at peace with himself, and he was ready to die at any moment. He wasn't fatalistic, just pragmatic. To survive boot camp, he had to let go of his worries. Richter happened to be so good at this that certain worries never bothered him again, and that included the possibility of dying young.

It was Richter's unflappable demeanor that drew his teammates to him. Devonai's own experience did not involve as much combat conditioning (though certainly as much actual combat) and it was always a source of great strength to him to look over and see Richter. The picture of calm, Richter raised morale for those around him.

Devonai sipped his coffee. Richter hadn't bothered to brew any on his way past the kitchenette, but Devonai obviously had. Richter decided to go get some of his own when Hill entered.

"Good morning, gentlemen," she said.

The men offered a less than enthusiastic greeting. Hill sat behind her desk and shuffled some papers around.

"Where's Guilfoyle?" Devonai asked.

"The DIA no longer deems it necessary to attend our daily briefings," Hill said.

"That figures. Why do we get dragged in here?"

"It's nice to see you too, Devonai."

"That's not what I meant. I say go ahead and let the DIA take over. At this point, the sooner we all give up and go back to our normal mission, the better. Who really cares if a few million dollars worth of gear disappears into space? The defense industry needs an excuse for increased output anyway."

Hill rolled her eyes, and said, "Just say the word, Devonai, and this mission will be out of your hands."

"I don't really have a good enough reason to hold onto it except out of spite. I do, however, have a personal interest in seeing whether or not those guys actually get that ship into space."

"You think they're going to give you a send-off?"

"In this case, no news is good news."

26. October 21, 2003

"Okay, tell me what you've got for read-outs."

Ari's voice floated through the bridge. She was in the server room, controlling the feeds to the computer stations on the bridge. Christie and Dana sat at the right and left forward stations, regarding the plasma screens. Ari's environmental sensor program, barely two days old, presented dozens of possible variables. Christie read from the screen.

"Internal temperature sixty-two degrees. External temperature fifty degrees. Internal radiation zero point two five rads. External radiation zero rads. Internal relative humidity five percent. External relative humidity zero percent. Internal oxygen percentage, no reading. External oxygen percentage, no reading."

"Damn it," said Ari. "Okay, skip the inert gases. Try the hazardous gases."

"Internal chlorine zero percent. External chlorine zero percent. Internal ammonia zero point zero three percent. External ammonia zero percent. Internal methane zero point zero five percent. External methane zero point five percent. Internal phosphorus no reading. Same on the external phosphorus."

"Shit. Okay, try the particulates next."

John's voice came onto the bridge. "Bridge, this is John."

"Go ahead, John," said Dana.

"Ray and I are ready to test the armaments. How are things going on your end?"

Dana typed on her keyboard. "I'm showing all weapons armed and ready. Controls are locked at local for the fifties."

In the background, Christie continued to read off statistics to Ari. Dana lowered her voice to prevent confusion.

"Roger that, Ray and I have the fifties set on local. I'll reset them to remote control. Ray and I are on our way to the bridge."

"Understood."

"We're all set for the neutrino sensor array," said Christie.

"Okay," said Ari, "get John to the bridge, I'm ready to connect the manual flight controls to the system."

"He's on his way."

Moments later, John and Ray arrived on the bridge.

"Ari says she's ready to test the manual flight controls," Dana said.

"Excellent," replied John.

"Bridge to Ari," began Ray, "what's the status of the main forward cannon and the flight controls?"

"It's all set. Find a target and I'll keep you apprised of the feedback."

"Now you're talking," said John.

John sat in the pilot chair. He slid the chair forward in the rails until he was snug against the counter. Doing so changed the plasma screen from standby mode to a read-out of flight controls. Below the counter, John's favorite joystick, throttle lever, and rudder pedals had been mounted.

"Switching to manual flight control," John announced.

John reached forward and pressed a key on the keyboard. The ship bumped slightly.

"Everything looks good from here," said Ari.

John gingerly grasped the joystick. He pushed forward on the thrust control and the ship began to move. Relative speed on the display changed from zero to thirty miles per hour.

"I'm taking her to ten thousand feet," John said.

"Roger that," replied Ari.

John pulled back on the stick and pushed the thrust forward. With glassy smooth motion, the ship began to climb. Even though it wasn't necessary, Ray chose to join the others and sit down. His station displayed information on the fifty caliber guns. A joystick of his own was mounted next to the keyboard.

"I'm testing remote control of the ventral guns," Ray said.

"Understood," said Ari.

Ray chose the ventral guns on the display and moved the joystick. According to the read-outs, the gun swiveled and elevated properly.

"Ten thousand feet," said John, "speed is constant at five hundred miles per hour."

"No problems here," said Ari. "I'm switching systems control to bridge station five."

"Okay."

The far right monitor switched from standby to read-out mode. A few seconds later Ari appeared on the bridge and took her seat. Tycho barked at her.

"I'm getting a constant signal degradation of twelve percent," said Seth.

"All right," Ari said, "I'm not seeing any packet loss on my end. Let me know if the degradation increases."

"I will."

"Increasing elevation to thirty thousand feet," said John. "Increasing speed to Mach One."

The ship vibrated slightly. Bright sunlight streamed onto the bridge.

"All systems in the green," Ari said.

"External temperature fifteen degrees," said Christie. "Internal pressure holding at one bar."

"I'm satisfied," said John. "Let's see what she can do. Ray, find us some targets."

Ray smiled. "Well, there's the aircraft graveyard in Arizona. We should have plenty of safe targets there."

"Do you know exactly where it is?"

"No."

"Seth, set a course for the geographical center of Arizona."

"Understood," said Seth.

The information appeared on John's screen. He pressed a few keys and the ship fell into a new course.

"Increasing speed to Mach Two," John said.

The ship vibrated momentarily and then smoothed out.

"How's our energy output?" said Dana.

"Holding steady at zero point zero zero zero one five percent," said Christie.

"She's barely awake," said John. "Seth, what is our maximum sub-atmospheric speed?"

"Maximum speed to maintain stealth mode is forty-two hundred miles per hour. Above this speed stealth will be compromised."

"Why's that?"

"Friction will become too high. I will become a visible ball of fire."

"Cool, but not what we're looking for. I'm increasing speed to Mach Five."

It was a matter of a few minutes travel time and a quick search by Seth before the crew found the aircraft graveyard. It was so massive that they easily located several targets that were almost a full two miles away from the nearest human on the ground.

"The Reckless Faith declares war on Arizona!" John cried.

John began a near vertical dive from thirty thousand feet, which was almost imperceptible by motion but dizzyingly obvious by sight. The crew offered various expressions of shock and discomfort as John added a tight port spin to the dive.

"Is that really necessary?" Ray said through gritted teeth.

"Of course not. *Banzai!*"

John pulled back on the throttle and pulled up before planting the ship into the desert. It was too much for even Seth to compensate for and the crew experienced triple the normal gravity. Everybody but John groaned. Ray struggled to keep his breakfast down.

"First target locked!" John said, grinning like a madman.

A low hum came up from below the deck as the main forward cannon spun up. John opened fire. A hellish cacophony of pounding thunder filled the ship, just barely muffled by the single deck that separated the bridge from the cannon. The remains of a DC-10 on the ground looked as if it had been hit by a bomb. The pre-programmed twenty round burst was over in a split second. The Faith swooped over the target. Dana locked in an external view on her screen.

"Holy cow, I'd say you got it," she said.

"I have a lock," said Ray. "Ventral turret is ready to fire."

"Go for it," said John.

John adjusted his course to circle the target. Ray pressed the trigger and the ventral guns fired. With a rate of fire one fourth that of the main cannon, the staccato signature of the fifties was much more comprehensible. Sustained fire was also more reasonable. Dana gave Ray a thumbs-up as she observed the resulting damage to the DC-10.

"Automatic leading is working properly," Ray said.

"Excellent," said John. "Try the dorsal guns."

Ray switched his control to the other fifties. John banked the ship sharply to give the weapons proper bearing on the target. An alarm sounded at Ray's station. Ray swore quietly.

"The dorsal turret is jammed in the track. Articulation has failed."

"Okay," said John. "Try the rear cannon."

Ray worked his keyboard for several seconds.

"Rear cannon is off-line."

"What?" said Ari, checking her screen.

"I'm not getting any response from the rear cannon."

"What the hell?"

Ari furiously typed for about a minute, then stood up quickly.

"We're lucky the other two weapons worked properly the first time out," said John.

"I'll be in the server room," said Ari.

"I'm setting us down," announced John. "Ray, you want to take a look at the dorsal gun?"

"Naturally."

"Wait a minute," Christie said. "I'm getting a lot of positive read-outs on my station. I think we should try taking the Faith into low orbit."

John shook his head. "We're all excited about our progress, but I think we should get everything working absolutely perfectly before we leave orbit."

"I agree with Christie," Dana said. "We're ready to give space a try."

John brought the ship about and hovered above the desert. He looked at Ray.

"Why not?" said Ray.

"Take a chance," said Ari, her eyes twinkling.

Tycho barked.

"Home is calling us," said Seth.

John shrugged. "Hell, why not indeed? Better to die now than later when we're even more overconfident."

"Sweet!" exclaimed Dana.

"Prepare the ship for space flight!" John said.

"What do you mean, prepare her?" said Ari, frowning.

"It just sounded good. Take a seat everybody; I'm not going to hold back."

"Great," Ray said.

John pulled back on the stick and shoved the throttle forward. The ship jumped into action. The crew found themselves pressed up against their chairs as John again pushed the limit of Seth's momentum compensation abilities. Seth had told them he would make sure to keep gravitational variance within human tolerances, but stuff like this was beginning to make the others doubt. After a minute or so, their bodies caught up with the rest of the ship and they were able to regain their balance. John was flying straight up at full speed, heedless of Seth's warning about their stealth abilities. Bright orange flames began to streak from the bow and past the windows. It was terrifyingly quiet save for the rhythmic throbbing of the engine. Christie remembered to start paying attention to her screen again.

"Exterior temperature four thousand degrees Fahrenheit!" she exclaimed.

"We're leaving the atmosphere now," said John.

The bright blue of the Arizona sky faded into black. Gradually the flames disappeared, and inky darkness replaced them. The exterior temperature read-out on Christie's screen began to drop rapidly, as did oxygen, nitrogen, and just about everything else.

"Calculate an orbital path," John said, apparently to Seth.

Dana's screen unexpectedly displayed the information requested.

"Uh, piece of cake," Dana said.

Dana transferred the information to John's station. John plugged the data into his flight controls and settled the ship into orbit. He rolled the ship over 180 degrees so that they could look up and see the Earth. Ray groaned in protest.

"My God," said Christie. "It's beautiful."

The Earth at 350 miles filled almost the entire viewscreen. North America was the most obvious feature, with only a few areas obscured by clouds. The crew stared out of the windows in awe. With the engines quiet, it was the most peaceful scene any of them had ever experienced. A gentle alarm sounded from Christie's panel, distracting her.

"I've got subtle variations in the artificial gravity field. It looks like Seth isn't used to it quite yet."

"Keep an eye on it," said John. "Seth, lights at ten percent."

The bridge grew dark. John rolled the ship back over. This time, they were met with the unhindered and perfectly clear starfield of the Milky Way.

"It's so... deep," said Ari. "You never get this sense of depth from the surface."

"Whatever happens on this journey, I doubt boredom is going to be a problem."

October 22, 2003

Devonai and Richter were fed up with being bored. Another daily meeting with Hill had gone by, uneventful as usual. Their lack of activity had reached a critical point, and Devonai and Richter had but one recourse: a trip to the range.

The two men had loaded up their Expedition with handguns, rifles, shotguns, machine guns, and grenades. It was catharsis, CIA style.

The only appropriate range for this kind of firepower was over at Devens Reserve Training Area, formerly known as Fort Devens. Arrangements had been made twenty-four hours in advance, and Devonai and Richter were good to go. Stuff needed to get blown to hell.

Devonai put the Expedition in gear and began to pull out of the parking garage. Omega Group shared a State Police armory buried underneath a government building on Beacon Hill, much to the bemusement of the troopers stationed there. Today's choices only elicited jealousy from the troopers. This kind of fun went across agency lines easily.

Richter played with the radio as Devonai pulled onto the surface streets. It was a forty-five minute drive to Devens, and since they had already talked about everything they could think of over the past two weeks, he was content to let Richter find something on the airwaves. Devonai's favorite radio program didn't come on until three that afternoon, but he still hoped that Richter would choose the same station.

Devonai headed south on Route 93 and thought about his path. He would pick up Route 90 and take that west until 495. A quick switch to Route 2 would put them right at Devens. In the middle of the day they shouldn't have to contend much with traffic, so he was...

"Wait a second," said Devonai, as three Ford Expeditions had just passed him going the other direction on 93.

"I saw them," said Richter.

"Those looked like our guys, didn't it?"

"Yes, it did."

Devonai fumbled for his cell phone, and called the office.

"What is it, major?" answered Hill.

"Hill, we just saw three Expeditions with government plates heading north on 93. I could have sworn I saw CO Dowling driving one of them."

"The DIA is investigating a lead, major. It's probably nothing. Are you at Devens yet?"

"Wait a minute! Why wasn't I informed of this?"

"It's just a minor lead, Devonai. It wasn't worth pulling you and Richter back from Devens."

"But it was worth sending our guys? Why couldn't the DIA check it out on their own?"

"You know what the deal is. We're supposed to be helping each other out."

"What's the lead?"

"It's just a possible source of information. It's probably nothing."

Devonai took a deep breath. He looked at Richter. Richter shrugged. Devonai chose his next words carefully.

"Lauren, we've known each other for too long for this. Don't you dare hold back from me here. What the hell is going on?"

"Major, I'm sorry, but you'll be better off not knowing."

Devonai yanked over on the steering wheel, suicidally crossing two lanes of traffic to make the South Station exit. Richter raised an eyebrow.

"If you won't tell me, I'll find out for myself."

"Devonai, you're not authorized to participate in this investigation. I'm sorry to have to tell you like this, but you have been removed from the mission."

"What are friends for?"

"Screw you, Kyrie. I didn't want it like this. Guilfoyle heard you talking in a sympathetic matter about the crew of the ship. You're too emotionally involved."

"Emotion has nothing to do with it, for fuck's sake!"

Richter hit the blue lights hidden in the grill of the Expedition as Devonai broke several traffic rules. After a few near collisions they were on 93 northbound.

Hill continued, "Their mission is to stop the ship from leaving Earth at all costs. This comes from upon high, Devonai. Do not mess with them on this one."

"I can't do that. I'm the one who spoke with the crew. I have a responsibility to do what's right."

"I can't protect you if you follow them, Kyrie. You're on your own from this moment onward."

"Fine. How did they get a bead on the ship's location?"

"An anonymous tip."

"Fine, don't tell me then."

"That's the truth. We got an anonymous call. I'm sorry, Devonai. I can't continue to speak to you on this matter. I hope you understand."

"I probably will before too long. And don't worry, Lauren. I'm just going to discourage Guilfoyle and his team."

"That's what I'm worried about."

27.

"To reckless faith, and the ship that bears the name."

John held high his glass of champagne. For the five crewmembers gathered at the small New Hampshire restaurant, it was a solemn reminder that night could be their last on Earth. The others around the table, Ray, Ari, Christie, and Dana, each lifted their glasses in response.

The few other patrons of the restaurant looked on with curiosity. This sort of spectacle was all but unheard of in an establishment that rarely saw outsiders past Labor Day. The bottle of champagne came out of the owner's personal stock for a not inconsequential sum, as did the unopened twin already secreted away in John's backpack. As the glasses were drained the eyes of the other customers returned to their own meals.

The feast that had been consumed was of epic proportions, at least to the currently gathered group. No expense had been spared, although the restaurant wasn't the sort to provide anything too prohibitive anyway. Ari had just enough left in her checking account to cover the visit, still surprising to her even after the long list of expenses incurred during preparations. Throwing enough cash onto the table to make the waitress very happy, Ari refilled her glass.

"Don't hog the grog," said Ray.

"Fine, here you go," Ari said, filling Ray's glass.

"Take it easy, you two," said John. "You don't want to start off tomorrow morning with a hangover."

"You should relax a little bit more," began Christie, "there will be enough time for panic later, I'm sure."

"Somebody has to drive us back to the Faith."

"You should have brought Seth with you," said Dana. "Then we could get the Faith to come to us."

"I'm quite glad to be able to keep Seth out of my mind. He tends to be an untidy guest."

"Come on, let's head out," said Ray. "It is getting late."

Slowly, the group gathered their things. Saying goodbye to the waitress and host, they exited the restaurant. The evening was cold and clear. They crossed to Ray's Expedition. It was the only vehicle left, since John had sold his earlier in the week. It was coming with them, to what benefit nobody knew. Only a meager 55 gallons of gasoline had been brought aboard in reserve, but Seth claimed to be able to synthesize more if the appropriate ingredients could be found.

"You know," began Dana, jumping into the Ford, "I might get cold feet as we're passing Pluto. Just swing back by the Bahamas and leave me behind if so."

"If only it were that easy," said John, climbing into the front passenger seat.

"Why not? How long could it possibly take?"

Ray got into the driver's seat. John looked at him.

"You never told them," Ray said.

John shook his head. "No."

"What didn't you tell us?" asked Christie from the seat behind Ray.

"Are you talking about the stardrive system?" Ari asked.

"Yes," said John. "We forgot to tell you and Dana about the limitations of the stardrive."

"Oh?" Dana said.

"Yeah. The stardrive is very versatile. The pilot has a lot of control over the ship even at relatively high speeds. We can go from zero to six point seven million miles per hour in a few seconds. But to travel faster than light, the Faith has to use superluminal travel."

"Is that like ludicrous speed?"

"Heh, I don't know. It's a special setting that will get us to Umber in six weeks, as opposed to over a thousand years at our top subluminal speed. The problem is that once superluminal operations have commenced, they can't be shut down. Not without draining the fuel reserves so far that it would take another six weeks to recharge them."

Christie frowned. "I thought Seth said that he could run the ship for years off of the hydrogen atoms in the water storage tanks, or some kind of high rhetoric like that."

"He did. I'm not sure why it would take so long to recharge the system. The short version of the story is still that once we depart for Umber, we can't turn back. Not without wasting another six weeks on Earth. So if you're having second thoughts, now is the time to hash them out. We depart first thing in the morning."

"I was mostly joking about Pluto," said Dana, "but I'll take your words to heart."

Ray turned the ignition key and fired up the Ford. He pulled the truck onto Route 25. They were only a couple of minutes away from the motel. The conversation lapsed as the dark countryside rolled by. Ray felt the need to say something.

"You never did get your six," he said to John.

"Oh, well. Five will have to do."

"Huh?" said Dana.

"John thought the crew might be better of with six people," Ray said. "John must have been disappointed with you worthless dogs."

"Arr, ye be worthless curs," John snarled.

Ray steered the Expedition into the parking lot of the motel. As they drew close to the structure, Tycho came running up to greet them.

"What the hell?" Christie said.

"Didn't we leave Tycho aboard the Faith?" said Ari.

"We certainly did."

Everyone hopped out of the Ford. Tycho licked Christie's hands.

"Maybe he asked Seth to be let out," said Dana.

"Maybe," replied John, "but I doubt it. Something isn't right."

Ray walked towards the nearest corner of the motel.

"Perhaps Tycho and Friday had a spat," began Ray, "and Tycho decided he needed some space."

"Yeah, but come to think of it I specifically forbade Seth from allowing the animals to have control of command functions."

"Maybe he sneaked down the ramp after we..."

Ray stopped talking. He had reached the corner of the building and had noticed something that he obviously didn't like.

"What?"

Turning swiftly, Ray headed back to the vehicle. He opened the back gate.

"What is it?" Ari asked.

"There are three black Ford Expeditions parked back there. They have government plates."

"Holy shit," Dana whispered.

John and Ray threw open the rear compartment of the Ford. Below the panel were John's Garand and one of their recently acquired M1A rifles. John grabbed his rifle and handed the M1A to Ray. There was one magazine in the M1A and one spare attached to a buttstock pouch. John's Garand had a bandoleer of clips next to it.

"What are you planning on doing?" asked Christie, mortified.

"We're getting back aboard the Faith, that's all," said Ray.

John nodded, taking the bandoleer. "I'm not letting anything stop us now."

Ari drew her Glock, the illegality of which had long ceased to be a concern for the others.

"Good," Ari said. "Now you've got the right idea."

"Now are you glad we took the time to practice with small arms?" John asked of Christie.

"Glad?" said Christie. "Are you insane?"

"Ask yourself the same thing," John said, offering Christie his Beretta.

Christie took the pistol. Dana looked near panic.

"We only have one more weapon, and that's my Smith," said Ray. "Are you comfortable using it, Dana?"

Dana shrugged. "I suppose I have no choice."

Ray passed his sidearm to Dana, along with two spare moon-clip reloads. John motioned for the group to head towards the opposite end of the motel. As they moved, John addressed them quietly.

"Okay, listen up. We just want to get back to the Faith, and we want to do it as peacefully as possible. Do not engage anyone you see unless they fire first. If we have to talk, then we talk. Do not be intimidated if they have weapons drawn. It doesn't mean they want a fight any more than we do. If we're lucky we can sneak aboard and be gone."

The others nodded in approval.

"You wanna take point, Ray?" John asked.

"No, but I will."

Ray cradled his rifle in his shoulder and headed for the south side of the motel, the opposite end from the government vehicles. The others fell in line behind him, single file. John took up the rear. It was a quiet night around the motel and there was little chance of them being seen before they could get to the cover of the woods. As they crept into the tree line, Ray paused to let his eyes adjust to the low light. In the peace of the evening he could almost hear something ahead. He turned toward Ari, who was next in line, and pressed his index finger against his lips. Ari nodded and passed the gesture to Christie.

Ray began moving forward again. His steps were careful, and his pace maddeningly slow. Ari knew it was necessary but found it annoying. Dana was too frightened to care either way. John kept a watchful eye on the parking lot until it was out of view, and then directed his attention to woods behind them. Tycho seemed to understand the proper decorum and sidled along next to Christie.

After a few minutes, Ray held up his hand and stopped. An erratic pattern of white light was coming from the direction of the Faith. Ray recognized it as several flashlights. Someone was speaking, but so far Ray couldn't see any figures. Ray held his index finger up to his ear, and pointed forward. Ari nodded and passed the message down the line.

Beginning to move at an even slower pace, Ray led the crew closer. Soon, he could see the silhouettes of people. Abruptly, the flashlights were all switched off. Ray hit the deck. He heard John follow his lead, and the ladies as well a moment later. When the leaves underneath him had settled, Ray realized he could understand the voices.

"If it is here, we can't reach it," someone said.

"You could always try shooting at it," a second voice said. "You brought enough hardware."

"Then you realize how seriously we're taking this. If it's just out of reach, as you say, then yes, we could fire towards it. How do you know this 'cloaking device' won't be able to compensate anyway?"

"I don't. But I'm fresh out of ideas."

Ari leaned over until her face was directly next to Ray's ear.

"Who are they?" she whispered.

Ray turned his head slightly to reply.

"I don't know," he breathed.

"All right, we'll set up a perimeter," the first voice said. "Team A will take the woods. Team B and you agency guys will take up overwatch positions on the road and the motel. If they return, we'll have them."

"Where do you want me?" asked the second voice.

"Never more than a few feet away from me, kid."

"Who the hell is that?" thought Ray.

"It's not Levi," whispered Ari, as if reading Ray's mind.

Ray nodded his head in agreement. The shuffle of footsteps could be heard, and Ray realized that at least two people were heading right for him. It was too late to withdraw without being heard. Ray motioned for the others to remain silent and prone.

His only hope was to disable the men as silently as possible, a prospect Ray regarded with significant angst. He'd subdued unruly suspects before, but not without them raising the dead with their objections. If the men stopped before reaching them, there was a chance that they could overpower them and make it aboard the Faith before the others could react, no matter how much noise they made. Then again, they could all be shot in the attempt. Ray longed for John's counsel on the matter but such an exchange was impossible. It was up to Ray to make their move.

The two figures drew closer. Ray checked to make sure the safety on his rifle was off. The easiest option was to simply kill the men and run for the Faith under cover fire, a fact that did not escape Ray. Considering the alternative, it didn't sound too bad.

The men approached and then stopped, not two meters from Ray and Ari. At this distance Ray could easily identify their weaponry and gear. They were outfitted with MP5 submachine guns and black tactical gear. Ray drew a bead on the closer of the two. He was startled by a shadow moving to his left, and realized a second later that it was Ari.

Ray couldn't call her back; Ari had seized the initiative. Ray watched breathlessly as Ari walked silently towards the first man. Amazingly, she slipped behind him undetected. Ari drew to within arm's reach of the man. The man slipped his weapon onto his shoulder by way of the attached sling, and withdrew what Ray recognized to be a pair of night vision goggles. As he did this Ari grabbed the MP5 right off his shoulder. In a blur, she slipped the sling over the man's neck, twisted the weapon around 180 degrees, spun on her heels, and flipped the man over her back. Ugly sounds emanated from the man's neck before he landed in an angular heap. Ari dropped to the ground and lay flat.

The noise of the first man hitting the ground was far too obvious to be ignored. The second man froze in place, scanning the darkened woods.

"Palmer!" he hissed. "Palmer! Where are you?"

"Over here," whispered John.

The remaining man took a few steps towards John's voice.

"Where?"

Ari rose up from the gloom and slipped her left hand over the man's mouth. Her right hand went between his legs. Ray cringed.

The man let loose a hideous scream, muffled for the most part by Ari's hand. Ray jumped up to help her. The man's right index finger twitched, and an ear-shattering three round burst from his MP5 tore through the trees. Ray batted the submachine gun aside and slammed the butt of his rifle into the man's stomach. The man gurgled and crumpled to the ground.

"Palmer! Budak!" someone shouted.

"Shit!" grumbled Ray.

A beam of white light hit Ray and Ari like a cannon. Ray flung himself to the prone but Ari hesitated, the second man's MP5 in her hands.

"Enemy contact, southeast!" the man behind the flashlight shouted.

John's rifle barked twice in response. The man dropped his flashlight and fell over.

"So much for the stealthy approach!" Ray said.

"Seth, open the ramp!" John yelled.

The Faith made herself known as the ramp lowered, spilling soft blue light into the clearing. At least four more men were nearby, surprised by the sudden appearance of the gangway but not distracted enough to ignore the group. Two men nearest to the ramp began firing their weapons towards the crew. Ari threw herself down and rounds whistled overhead.

"Damn it," she said.

John crawled over to Ray.

"It's too late for diplomacy," he said. "If we want aboard the Faith, we're going to have to engage those men."

"This is a departure from your normal attitude," Ray said.

"I'm through screwing around, Ray. This is our ship!"

"Cease fire! Cease fire!"

Ray recognized the voice as belonging to the first man he heard upon arrival at the ship. The men near the ramp concealed themselves in the underbrush and followed the order.

"Get on line, everyone," Ray whispered hoarsely.

Ari moved into position next to John. Christie and Dana looked at Ray, terrified and confused. Ray motioned for them to move forward. Christie began to crawl ahead but Dana didn't budge.

In the clearing, a lone figure appeared. He didn't seem to be carrying any weapons. He faced the direction of the group.

"This is Commander Guilfoyle of the Defense Intelligence Agency," he shouted. "There is no need for further violence. Drop your weapons and come out with your hands up, and you will not be harmed."

"You want the honors?" Ray whispered to John.

"Naturally," he replied.

John tried to conceal himself in behind the nearest tree, and spoke.

"I'm afraid we can't comply with that demand, commander. We have a rather pressing engagement aboard our ship."

"John Scherer, I presume?"

Ray shook his head at John. John shrugged at him.

"That's correct," John said. "I have to say I'm impressed you found us. Your resources are outstanding."

"Why not come out where we can talk on even footing?" Guilfoyle said.

"I don't think that's possible, no offense."

"I'm standing out here. The least you could do is the same, so that we can establish trust."

"I can't afford to do that, sorry."

"All right then, let's look at it another way. You, Mister Bailey, Miss Ferro, Miss Tolliver and Miss Andrews are surrounded and outnumbered. You've already fired on my men, which proves your resolve. This standoff has only two outcomes. Your surrender or your demise."

"Well, Ray," John whispered. "What do you think?"

"I think we're screwed either way," Ray said.

"While you're making up your minds," Guilfoyle began, "mind if I take a tour of your ship?"

Guilfoyle took a couple of steps up the ramp. John rose up onto his elbows.

"Don't take another step!" John yelled.

"This ship is ours, Scherer! It's time you accepted that. It's also time for you to negotiate your place aboard. If you don't surrender you'll make certain you never see it again."

Guilfoyle took another step. John squeezed off a shot from his Garand. The round bounced off of the ramp directly in front of Guilfoyle and caromed into the woods beyond. Guilfoyle ran off the other side of the ramp and dove behind the nearest tree.

The crew began receiving fire from several different positions at once. If Guilfoyle had anything else to say, it was lost in the thunderous staccato of fully automatic weapons fire. John drew a bead on one of the men near the ramp and fired his weapon dry. The clip ejected with the distinctive ping unique to the rifle. Ray tracked muzzle flashes and returned fire while John reloaded.

"Head towards the ship on the right flank!" Ray screamed at the top of his lungs.

Ari was too busy firing her newly acquired MP5 to notice the suggestion. Christie and Dana remained motionless, horrified at the prospect of rising up into the path of the incoming rounds. John slapped a new clip into his rifle and patted Ari on the shoulder.

"Get the others around on the right flank!" he shouted.

Ari ceased fire. "Okay!"

"Covering fire!" John yelled.

John and Ray fired quickly in the direction of the enemy. From the report of the weapons belonging to the opposition, John correctly guessed that they were trying to flank them on the left. That was fortunate. Ari got up and sprinted behind him and Ray, speaking to Christie and Dana as she did so.

"Let's go!" she said.

Christie got up and sprinted towards the right side of the clearing. Ari waited for Dana to do the same, but Dana didn't move. A split second later Ari was about to ask why when Dana got up and ran. In the opposite direction.

"To hell with this!" Dana screamed, utterly terrified.

"Last mag!" said Ray, reloading.

"Dana!" Ari shouted, aghast. "What the hell?"

John emptied his rifle again and fumbled in his bandoleer for another clip. For the moment, all fire on their side ceased. Ari fought everything that her conscious was telling her and ran after Dana.

"Where the hell are you going?" John demanded.

From a few meters away on the right side, Christie began firing the Beretta.

"We've got to move, now!" shouted Ray.

"Go!" yelled John, reloading his rifle.

John resumed fire as Ray sprinted towards Christie's position. Ari ran after Dana, who was making a bee-line back towards the motel. Ari reached out for her, but fell short by a scant few inches.

"Damn it, Dana, stop..."

A figure appeared out of the darkness and grabbed Dana. She screamed and dropped her pistol. Ari tried to stop short and got a rifle butt in her left shoulder. Another man stepped forward as Ari fell to the ground in agony.

"Hold it right there, sweetie," the man said.

Dana continued to scream and struggled against the first man. Ari struggled to regain her balance against the pain. She looked up at the man and recognized him as one of the CIA agents she saw wandering around the facility in Boston. Ari reached for her Glock and the man stepped forward, stepping on Ari's right arm. She screeched in pain.

"That's enough!" he said.

A third figure approached.

"What are you doing here?" the first man said.

At first Dana thought that the man's head had popped off. Then she realized his helmet had been knocked off of his head. The third figure drew his rifle back and hit him again, this time in the face. The man dropped like a sack of bricks.

The man restraining Ari turned around just in time for a fourth man to kick him in the face. He was out before he hit the ground. Ari recognized the fourth man.

"Richter?" she said, astonished.

"I thought I was the only one who was ever glad to see Richter," the third man said.

"Devonai?" Ari said, agape.

"Who are these guys?" Dana squeaked.

"The good guys, apparently."

Random bullets zipped through the woods. Devonai and Richter crouched down. Richter picked up Ray's pistol and offered it back to Dana. She accepted it as if it was a three-day-old dead fish.

"Why?" Ari asked.

"That's why," said Devonai, pointing towards the action.

"Ari!" yelled John through the trees. "Ari, come on!"

Ari picked her MP5 up off the ground. "Well, if you're with us let's get going!"

Richter took Dana by the arm and led her forward. She seemed comatose.

"Allow me," said Devonai, taking the lead.

Ari gestured willingly. Devonai shouldered his rifle, which Ari recognized as some sort of M16 variation, and led the way back towards the clearing.

"Incoming friendlies!" Ari yelled, and then added, "We've got some new friends on our side!"

Devonai sensed some people to the left. He aimed high and fired off a volley. He reached the point where John and Ray used to be, and hit the prone. He could see two men on the opposite side of the ramp. He aimed for their feet.

"Go, go!" he yelled, and fired.

Behind him, Richter, Ari, and Dana ran to the right. John, Ray, and Christie came into view. Ray had run out of ammunition for his rifle, which was now strapped across his back, and had taken control of the Beretta from Christie. He stopped firing and looked over at Richter.

"Who the hell are you?" he said.

"Call me the cavalry," Richter replied, grinning.

Ray said something in response but the report of John's rifle drowned him out. John's rifle ran dry once again and he reached for another clip. Christie looked at Dana and carefully took the pistol out of her shaking hands. Christie and Richter simultaneously noticed that the two men across from the ramp were attempting to flank to their left. Richter raised his weapon every bit as smoothly as Christie raised hers clumsily. They fired together, but only Richter's shots found their mark. The two men fell and did not move. John and Ray looked over in surprise.

From the east side of the clearing, opposite their position, fire renewed in earnest. The crew and Richter pressed themselves against the ground as shots passed by. Devonai shifted his attention to the muzzle blasts and began returning fire.

"Devonai's in a good position," Richter said, "but I need to be forward of that ramp."

"There isn't any cover out there!" shouted John.

"The ramp is good enough cover. When I'm in position I'll cover you."

Without another word, Richter sprinted forward. He passed underneath the ramp and came up on the other side firing. He immediately shifted to the other side of the ramp and fired again. Shots smacked into the ramp and ricocheted into the fuselage of the ship.

The bullet impacts created a wave effect on the hull of the ship as the force of the hits dispersed the stealth field.

Richter reloaded his rifle with inhuman speed and dropped to the ground. He waved the others forward and resumed firing. John joined him for a quick eight shots of his own.

"Run for it!" John yelled.

Devonai and Richter laid down a hellish slew of fire as the crew ran up the right side of the ramp. Tycho was the first one up the ramp, with Ray right behind him. When Ray got to the top he ducked behind the nearest piece of cover, a 55-gallon drum. Shots raced by in a big hurry. Ari ran up the ramp next. Ray looked for a target, found one on the right side of the clearing, and fired. The Beretta ran dry and Ray fished in his pockets for another magazine. He realized that Christie still had them. Fortunately, Christie was the next one up the ramp. Ray grabbed her and pulled her behind the drum.

"Give me the spare mags!" he cried.

Christie did so, and then looked at the drum.

"Are you crazy?" she said, scrambling away from Ray. Ray reloaded the Beretta and resumed firing. Dana made it into the cargo bay and immediately ran for the bridge. Ari took cover behind some wooden crates and began firing her pistol down the ramp.

"Come on, John!" screamed Ray. John loaded his last clip into his rifle as he ran up the ramp, several shots following him inside. John dove behind the same crates as Ari.

"That's everybody!" Christie yelled.

"Richter, get out of here, we're closing the ramp!"

Richter nodded without looking, and broke cover. He ran forward a step, firing his rifle, and began to run for the northern tree line. A round impacted his chest and he fell backwards onto the ramp.

"Shit!" Ray yelled.

John had a shot on the man who had hit Richter. He fired his rifle slowly and his third shot found flesh.

"Close the ramp, Seth!" John shouted.

The ramp began to close. Ray ran forward and dragged Richter's limp body into the cargo bay. The ramp shut solidly.

"Seth, get us out of here," said John.

"Please state the desired destination," said Seth.

"Anywhere but here! But drop the light refracting shield first. I want to force those bastards to see us leave."

"Understood."

Suddenly everything was deathly quiet. Each member of the crew struggled to catch their breath. Ray noticed the source of Christie's reaction. He had been hiding behind the gasoline drum.

"And you call yourself a Doom fan," he said to himself.

"What about Devonai?" Ari said.

"He made his choice," John said. "He's on his own now."

Fifteen minutes later, the Faith was safely in low Earth orbit. Richter, whose Kevlar vest had stopped the 9mm round that hit him, was regaining consciousness in one of the spare crew quarters. Christie gingerly removed Richter's shirt. Ray sat beside him on the bed, looking through a first aid kit. He found a cold compress and activated it. Richter groaned as Ray carefully applied the compress to the bruise on Richter's chest.

"How are you feeling?" Christie asked.

"Like I got shot," Richter said. "Am I aboard the ship?"

"Yes."

"Where are we?"

"About three hundred miles above the planet."

"Oh, cool."

Richter sat up and looked out the window. All he could see were stars.

"John, this is Ray. Roll to starboard so our guest can get a look at the Earth."

"Roger," said John's voice.

Imperceptibly the ship began to move. A moment later the Earth came into view.

"It's beautiful," said Richter, and flopped back down on the bed.

"You should rest," said Christie. "We'll drop you off when you have a little more strength."

"Drop me off where?"

Ray shrugged. "Where would you like?"

"I don't know. You aren't accepting applications, are you?"

"What, do you mean... do you mean for the ship?"

"Yeah, that's what I meant. From what I've seen it looks like fun. And since you don't know what your mission is, I've always wanted to see a group of people crazier than myself."

"That can be arranged, but I don't think that you want to come with us."

"I've been thinking about it since you rescued Ferro. I didn't see much of the ship, but Devonai told me about what he saw. I listened in on his conversations with Ferro. I can't say the thought of your mission wasn't intriguing. Speaking of Devonai, do you know if he's all right?"

"Sorry," said Christie, "the last we saw of him he was still on the ground fighting."

"He'll be okay, as long as he didn't kill any of Guilfoyle's men. I did. Major Devonai might have enough standing to talk his way out of prison, but I'm screwed. That's why I'd like to stay, if you'll have me."

"What about your family and friends?"

"None, and well, Devonai excepted, none. The Marine Corps was my family. My rifle was my friend."

"We'll consult with the others," said Ray. "Your combat skills are an obvious bonus, and it just so happens that we have enough supplies to support another crewmember. You proved your allegiance to the cause. We'll vote on it and let you know."

"But be warned," said Christie, "we may all die a horrible and agonizing death in deep space."

Richter sat up again, and groped for his shirt. "Nobody lives forever."

"You shouldn't be walking around quite yet," said Ray.

"I request an audience with the captain of this vessel."

"Captain? We don't have a captain."

"We're all equals aboard this ship," Christie said.

"Then I'd like to speak with the crew."

As soon as Richter got to his feet all signs of his discomfort disappeared.

Ray gestured towards the door. "All right then, follow me. Just keep that compress on your bruise."

"Yes, doctor."

Ray led the way out of the bedroom, down the corridor, and towards the bridge. Richter walked slowly but surely, with Christie behind him ready to aid him if need be. Richter stopped to look out of the hallway windows, which offered a larger vista of the exterior. Satisfied, and grinning widely, he continued on his way.

John was sitting in the pilot chair on the bridge, and Ari sat at the systems control console. Dana was standing in the left corner, holding Friday.

"Good, everyone's here," said Ray.

"Mister Richter, welcome back to the Faith," John said sincerely.

"Have you got a first name?" asked Ari.

"Chance, wildcat," said Richter.

"That seems appropriate for a man like you," said Christie.

"Perhaps, but I don't believe in luck."

Ray approached John. "Chance wishes to join the crew."

"Did you bump your head, too?" asked Dana.

"Well, like I told Christie and Ray," Richter began, "the most I have to look forward to back home is prison time. Right or wrong, I don't really feel like becoming the next Oliver North. And he made out much better than I certainly would."

"We could drop you wherever you pleased," said John.

"I'm an action junkie. I suppose I could find a new life and hide, but where's the fun in that? I can see what's going on here, and I want in. I don't see how any self-respecting adventurer could resist."

"All right, so we'll vote on it. All in favor of letting Chance stay, raise your hand."

Everyone but Dana raised their hand.

"All opposed?" asked Ari.

Dana's hand remained down.

"Dana?" said John.

"I don't really care one way or the other," Dana said. "Besides, I've got a cat."

"Fine, you're in," said Ray. "Now please sit down before you kill yourself."

Richter grabbed the nearest chair and sat down. "When do we leave?"

"Immediately," said John. "So you have exactly ten seconds to change your mind."

"I don't need ten seconds."

"Suit yourself. Seth, begin final preparations for superluminal travel."

"All systems ready," said Seth. "Awaiting your command."

"Here we go. Any last requests, folks?"

Christie choked back tears. There were no objections.

"I'm sorry," said Christie, "I always get emotional about goodbyes."

"Goodbye to Earth?"

"Yeah."

"We'll be back, God willing."

"Go ahead," said Ray.

"Engage stardrive, Seth. Next stop, Umber."

Epilogue

"For God's sake, commander, take the handcuffs off."

Lauren Hill regarded Guilfoyle with ire. Bringing Devonai into her office in shackles was rather offensive. Devonai, for his part, simply looked bored.

"With all due respect, Hill, I don't think you understand the seriousness of this situation."

"I understand that you've placed my best case officer under arrest," said Hill, rounding her desk and approaching Devonai. She produced a handcuff key from her pocket and unlocked the restraints.

"You can try to override my arrest now," began Guilfoyle, "but once my report is filed Devonai won't be able to hide behind the auspices of the CIA."

"I'll let the facts speak for themselves. Until then, Devonai will be placed on leave status and confined to this facility."

"Your case officer," Guilfoyle said through gritted teeth, "shot at my men. Shot at his own men! Five men are dead, at the hands of Richter and the crew of that ship."

"This wouldn't have happened if you would have let me approach the situation," said Devonai. "You got greedy and you paid the price. Richter and I did what we thought was right. That's all that matters to us. I feel bad for the men that were killed but they all understood the situation. They could have chosen not to fire on us."

"Your arrogance is unprecedented."

"Enough arguing," said Hill. "There will be plenty of time for that during the formal investigation. For now, I get to try to explain this whole mess to the director."

"You're right. There is a time and place for this. Don't be too surprised if Omega ceases to exist after this. You're like a pit bull that's too aggressive for its own good. Somctimes your only choice is to put it down."

Guilfoyle waved goodbye at Devonai and exited. Devonai sank into a chair.

"I acted on my own, Hill," he said. "This had nothing to do with Omega Group."

"Do you think that matters? Damn you for putting me in this position, Devonai."

"I know. I'm sorry."

Hill returned to her desk and sat down. She folded her arms across her chest and sighed.

"It makes you wish for simpler times, doesn't it?" she said quietly.

"Or for a nice change of venue."

"Do you think we'll ever see Richter again?"

"Somehow, I think we'll definitely see him again. Someday. Whatever mission that ship is on, I feel as if the Earth is inextricably bound to it. We may think we've weathered a storm, but the worst is yet to come. There are black clouds on the horizon, Lauren. And we're fresh out of plywood."

Traveling faster than light through space did not look like what the crew of the Reckless Faith expected at all. Rather than the streaking stars flying past the ship that their television experience had ingrained into them as natural, the starfield was instead nearly motionless to their perception. Only a sharp eye could detect movement over time, sort of like watching for the movement of sunlight on a featureless floor. The one point of reference, their own star, had rapidly receded from their view and had become indistinguishable from the others within the matter of an hour. The only way they could tell they were still in motion most of the time was that the stars in front of them were bluish, and the stars behind reddish. As Christie said, that was to be expected. The crew had voted on whether or not to sight-see some of the other planets in the solar system. The vote was negative, mostly due to Seth's admonition that Umber was waiting. And so it would remain for the next six weeks, barring an unexpected interruption.

Richter had returned to his quarters to convalesce. He seemed remarkably at peace with his new fate. The others wondered if he had all his marbles, but the CIA must have trusted his sanity. Then again, perhaps that's precisely why they kept him around.

Dana was shaken by their violent departure from Earth and had decided to try out the zero-g room to relax. Ray, John, and Christie were compelled to go find out how she was doing, as she had quickly adopted a veneer of hard-boiled resolve that was obviously not natural. For now they would let her float in peace.

Ari had commandeered the armory to clean the firearms used in the escape. It was a task that could wait, and they certainly had plenty of time coming up, but Ari said she wanted to be alone for a little while so why not do something productive in the meantime. Ray didn't know if she had the technical skills to disassemble the various weapons used. He realized he didn't feel like going to find out. Ari would have to muddle through on her own.

For John, Ray, and Christie, their greatest interest was simply being on the bridge. As usual, the bridge lights were low to maximize the outside scenery. Christie was leisurely familiarizing herself with the different control stations, taking ample time between tasks to stare out the windows. John sat in the pilot chair, but he was not in control. Friday, acting as Seth's intermediary, sat in his lap. Ray was also staring out of the main viewscreen, a half-smile on his face. The insanity of their mission was beginning to become more apparent.

"Ari thinks Dana is a liability," said Ray.

John turned his head slightly. "Why, because she froze up in combat?"

"Yeah."

"We shouldn't blame her for that," said Christie. "We were all scared. Nobody knows what they'll do the first time they're faced with that kind of situation. Ari is just being arrogant because she thinks she's an expert now."

"Ari is growing up fast," said John. "I don't think she's going to be quite so self-assured from now on."

"After six weeks together on the ship, we should certainly become well acquainted," said Christie. "At least, those of us who aren't yet lifelong friends. I can see the humanity in Ari, underneath her put-upon stoicism. We should become a good team."

"Richter should have some good stories," said Ray. "He's got quite a past, you know."

"I'm sure," said John. "I still wish we had brought more games with us than a deck of cards."

"Are you kidding?" said Christie, laughing. "Do you have any idea how many computer games Ari installed on the servers?"

"No, I had no idea she would even bother."

"Well, let me put it this way: You are all in for a serious ass-kicking, for I am the deathmatch master."

"You're on," said Ray. "John, maybe there's a flight sim on there."

"What would I need that for?" said John detachedly.

The hallway door opened and Ari entered.

"I need a break," she said. "Cleaning all of those guns by myself would take forever."

Ray smiled. "And taking a break will help how? Back to work, knave!"

"Anybody check on Richter lately?"

"I'm sure he's fine," said John.

"You got your six crewmembers after all," said Ray.

"For the mission to be truly blessed, seven is much more divine."

Those present on the bridge spun around in shock, for the man speaking was a stranger. Before them stood a man in his early twenties. He had long hair tied into a ponytail, glasses, and was smiling wryly despite a rather nasty bruise on his forehead. Ray thought about drawing his weapon when Christie spoke.

"Byron?" she gasped.

"Good to see you too, professor."

"What the hell are you doing here?"

"Do you know this guy?" Ray said, astonished.

"Byron is, or was, a student of mine."

"Indeed. But that is not how I came to be here. Providence, it seems, is not without a sense of humor."

"What the hell are you talking about, kid?" asked Ari.

"Perhaps I may tell my story over drinks in the galley."

"Perhaps I should kick your ass out of the airlock."

"Ari, take it easy," said John, standing. "No need for ceremony, Mister...?"

"Sterling, Byron Sterling. If you prefer it, John. It is a bit long, though."

"Time we have."

"All right," said Byron, sitting at the systems station. "Remember a certain Sunday morning earlier this month, Christie?"

"Um. What?"

"Seventeen days ago. When you were first approached by John and Ari."

"What about it?"

"Well, I saw that meeting. From my perspective, it looked like you had been kidnapped."

"That was sort of true," said Ari.

"I went with them willingly," said Christie.

"I know that now," said Byron, "but at the time I suspected foul play. After you missed your classes over the next couple of days, I approached campus police. They were of no help, so I decided to swing by your place and check see if you were home. When I got there, the CIA was camped out in front. When I saw my chance, I sneaked into the back of one of their vehicles. As it turns out, this vehicle was the very same one that was used to transport Ari later that day, and the same one that you swooped down and grabbed off the highway. During the confusion I sneaked out of the SUV and gave myself a nice self-guided tour of your ship. I even had a nice conversation with Seth while you guys slept that night. The next morning, when you went to pick up John's car, I decided to disembark. I broke into the cabin that was right there and stayed there for a little while, but the CIA showed up and I had to skedaddle out of there. I found my way to the motel, and was quite surprised that you ended up choosing the same one as a base of operations."

"Why the hell didn't you make yourself known the whole damn time? Why all the sneaking around?"

"To be frank, I didn't think you'd let me come with you."

"So you figured stowing away was the better choice?" said John. "What if we do decide to boot you out the airlock?"

"I knew that once we were underway that there was no turning back. I just figured I'd remove any doubt from the process by staying hidden until then."

"That was all quite unnecessary," said Ray. "You shouldn't have assumed that we would reject you as a member of the crew. In fact, we couldn't have said no, we had no right to refuse anyone who wanted to come with us, up until we ran out of quarters. Right, Christie?"

Christie remained silent.

"Well you succeeded," said John. "You might as well tell us what kind of special skills you think you bring to the ship."

"I'm just that good," Byron said.

Ari walked over to Byron and crossed behind him.

"You know what I find interesting?" she said. "The CIA couldn't track us anymore after we figured out about the signals Seth was inadvertently transmitting. We never went back to any of our homes after I got grabbed. The only phone calls we made were on pre-paid cells purchased with cash. And yet, here we come back to the motel and find two dozen jack-booted thugs waiting for us. You wouldn't know anything about how that happened, would you Byron?"

"Sure. I called them."

The others expressed various forms of pejorative surprise.

"Why the fuck did you do that?" asked John, livid.

"Whoa, take it easy. I can explain."

"Good," said Ari, "because the airlock is starting to look too good for you."

"Come on, you guys. I saw what was being forged here. I'm an amateur like you when it comes to this, but I could tell you weren't hard enough for what might come. You were too naive and too innocent. I knew what you needed was a baptism by fire. So I arranged a little meeting. I wanted to see how far you were willing to go."

"Holy shit," said Ray.

"You are seriously messed up in the head, Byron," said Christie.

"You'll thank me later," Byron said, "you can bet on it."

"There won't be any later," began Ari calmly, "because I'm going to take you down to the waste reclamation bin and cave your skull in with the side of my boot."

"And you think I'm crazy? You're the one with Lizzie Borden as a crewmate."

"Don't give me any ideas, kid."

John approached Byron. "Byron, you are responsible for the lives that were lost tonight. You caused that fight, and you have to live with knowing that those men died because of you. We can't kick you off the ship, but you're no member of this crew. You're going to spend the next six weeks confined to quarters. Perhaps dropping you off on the first habitable planet is in order after that."

Byron shrugged. "You'll change your mind before too long. You can't keep me away from this mission forever."

"John," began Christie, "we don't have any more crew quarters available. Richter took our only spare."

John nodded. "We'll set up one of the spare mattresses in cargo hold. The less comfortable the better as far as I'm concerned. Ray, would you mind bringing our new guest downstairs?"

"No problem," said Ray, grasping Byron's arm.

"No need for that, I'll go with you," Byron said.

"Seth," began John, "lock Byron out of all command functions other than light and temperature controls for the cargo hold."

"Understood," said Seth.

Ray and Byron exited the bridge. John sank down into his chair.

"I can't believe this kid," he said.

"Byron worried me a little bit, but I didn't think he was downright insane," Christie said, shaking her head.

"He's delusional," said Ari. "He expects us to appreciate his attempts at *deus ex machina*. The firefight as a crucible? None of us wanted that kind of experience."

"We'll see if a couple of weeks in the cargo hold changes his mind," said John.

Christie looked at Friday. "Seth, why didn't you tell us there was somebody sneaking around the ship?"

"You didn't ask," Seth replied.

John rolled his eyes. "Fine, from now on I want you to warn us if there's anyone or anything aboard other than who is currently here."

"Understood."

"We've sort of been ignoring Seth's development as an artificial intelligence," said Christie. "Does this kind of behavior really surprise you?"

"Ever since we started trying to integrate our technology aboard, it's been all about what Seth can do for us," said Ari. "I think we've become complacent with his role in all of this. He's still the only reason any of us are here right now."

"As long as his memory is fragged, we'll have to do our best," said John. "Like I've mentioned before, I don't think Seth is supposed to be so... slow on the uptake. Let's just hope that Umber didn't actually go nova and all that's waiting for us is a dust cloud."

"Indeed."

Christie stood up. "I'm going to go see how Dana's doing, and tell her about our new visitor."

"Okay."

Christie exited the bridge. Ari walked over to John. They stared out of the viewscreen for a while in silence.

"One more surprise in a string of unbelievable circumstances," Ari said.

"It makes you wish for something stable," John said. "Something you can rely on."

"We can rely on each other."

John looked at Ari. "We need to decide where we stand."

"Let's just say we stand together. Let's leave anything else up to chance."

"I can live with that."

Ari rested her hand on John's shoulder.

"What do you think will happen at Umber?" she asked.

"I don't know, but I sure as hell can't wait to find out."

The adventure continues in The Tarantula Nebula, available now! Bonus content follows:

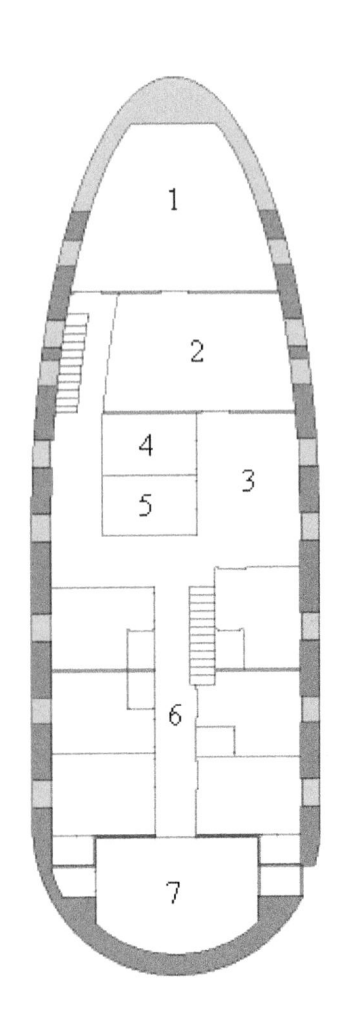

FACILITIES: DECK ONE

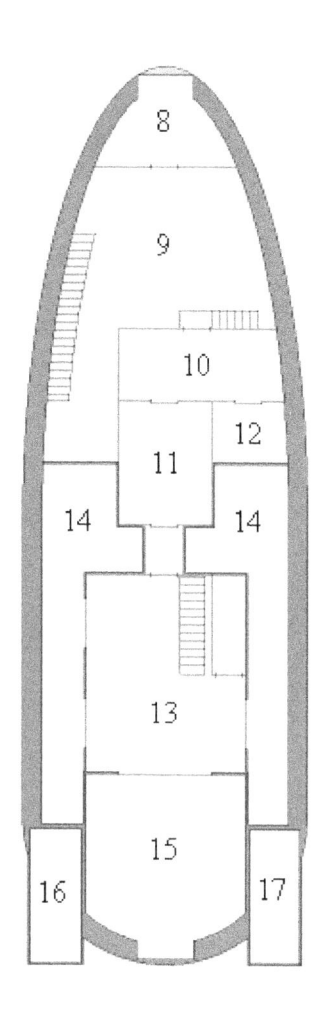

FACILITIES: DECK TWO

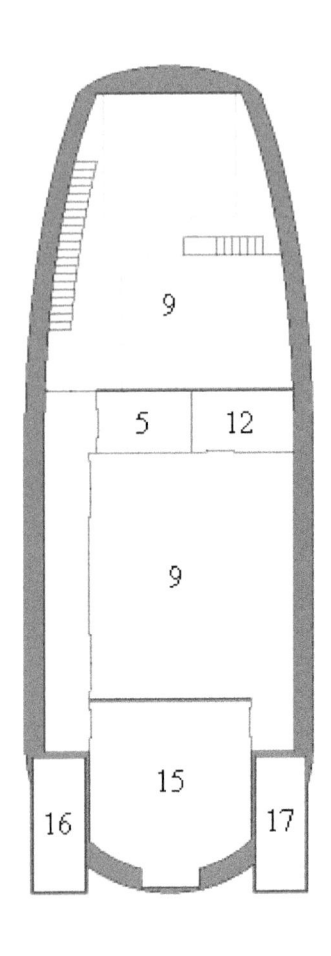

FACILITIES: DECK THREE

1. Bridge: The nerve center of the ship, the bridge consists of five computer consoles, one of which is also a dedicated piloting station. Each station can be used for any purpose, but they are usually configured, counter-clockwise from right to left: navigation, communications, pilot's station, remote weapons operation, and systems monitoring. The forward-facing window is also capable of projecting a wide-angle Heads-Up Display (HUD).

2. Conference Room: A room with eight chairs around an oval table, with a large wall-mounted monitor for demonstrations.

3. Lounge Area: An open area with several couches.

4. Secondary Server Room: This room contains two of the twelve computer servers, and is also used for spare storage.

5. Dorsal and Ventral Gun Rooms: These rooms provide gunner stations for and access to the dorsal and ventral GAU 19/A turrets. A limited amount of spare ammunition can also be stored here.

6. Living Quarters: Six nearly identical quarters, each with a private lavatory. The lavatory can also be used as a shower stall.

7. Zero-G Room/Airlock: A variable gravity area, this room can be used for Extra-Vehicular Activities (EVA) and for docking with other vessels while in space. It is also used for spare storage and occasionally for recreational purposes.

8. Forward Gun Room: This area houses the GAU 8/A weapon system and magazine.

9. Cargo Bay and Cargo Hold: These areas are used for storage. The cargo hold has also occasionally served as a brig or spare quarters. The cargo bay has a ramp (outlined in gray) for accessing the exterior of the ship and loading large pieces

of cargo. The cargo bay is double height, with the armory overhanging the rear portion of the bay.

10. Armory: All small arms used by the crew are stored here, along with ammunition, spare parts, and cleaning supplies.

11. Orb Room/Primary Computer Server Room: The Quasi-Actualized Intraspace Quantum Grid is stored here, along with ten of the twelve computer servers.

12: Storage Room

13: Galley: The galley contains a full kitchen, dining area, and a cold storage room.

14: H2O Storage Tanks: These tanks store 1000 gallons each of water for fuel, drinking, and sanitary purposes.

15. Engine Room: This area is home to the fusion drive and most of the secondary components. It also houses the rear-facing GAU 8/A. Located on decks two and three (double height).

16 & 17. Port & Starboard Engines

ACKNOWLEDGMENTS

Special thanks to Marc Housley and John Wheaton for brainstorming sessions, and to Matthew and Sarah Campbell for editing assistance.

Cover art by Alejandro "Alex Knight" Quiñones

Instagram: alexknightarts

Twitter: alexknight_

Note from the author:

Thank you for reading Reckless Faith, I hope you enjoyed it. Feedback is always appreciated, please take a minute or two and submit an honest review on Amazon. I always hope to improve my writing. Also, please visit my blog for updates and new fiction.

devonai.wordpress.com

Also available on Amazon:

The Tarantula Nebula (The Reckless Faith Series Book Two)

Bitter Arrow (The Reckless Faith Series Book Three)

The Fox and the Eagle (The Reckless Faith Series Book Four)

The Heart of the Swan (The Reckless Faith Series Book Five)

Dun Ringill (a stand-alone novel, sci-fi adventure)

Printed in Great Britain
by Amazon